Dear Reader,

The *Scarlet* romances I've found for you this month offer very different backgrounds around the world and heroines with a range of intriguing and unusual jobs. I do hope you'll find these brand new stories as interesting to read as I have!

Kathryn Bellamy's *Summer of Secrets* gives us a heroine who's an interior designer mixing with jet-setters in the enthralling world of tennis (including some old friends from Kathryn's first two very popular *Scarlet* titles!). *Return to Opal Reach* by Clarissa Garland features an equally glamorous background – the international modelling circuit. But it's an artificial world which Clarissa's heroine rejects in an attempt to find happiness in the Australian Outback. Julie Garratt's heroine in *The Name of the Game* certainly isn't afraid to get her hands dirty: she's a car mechanic! And last but not least we have *Hidden Embers* by Angie Gaynor. Angie's heroine combines two challenging careers (accountancy and running a lodging house) with motherhood!

As always, I've tried to find something to suit everyone this month. Let me know if I've succeeded!

Till next month,

Sally Cooper

SALLY COOPER,
Editor-in-Chief – *Scarlet*

ANGIE GAYNOR

HIDDEN EMBERS

SCARLET

Enquiries to:
Robinson Publishing Ltd
7 Kensington Church Court
London W8 4SP

First published in the UK by Scarlet, 1998

Copyright © Angie Gaynor 1998
Cover photography by Colin Thomas

A copy of the British Library Cataloguing in
Publication data is available from the British Library

ISBN 1–85487–886–7

Printed and bound in the EC

10 9 8 7 6 5 4 3 2 1

This book is dedicated to my young, distant cousin, Sarah Nicholl in Geelong, Australia, because she loves books; to another young, distant cousin, Lee Ann Vidamour in Liverpool, England, in the hope that she will continue to develop her interest in writing; to my second cousin, Julie Haycock of North Delta, BC, who hopes to make romance writing her career; and especially to my first cousin, Mary Seward in Port Orchard, Washington, name-sake of the wandering Mary Elizabeth Gaynor, our grandmother.

PART ONE

CHAPTER 1

He didn't like her. One look told Lynne Castle that her hope for this company's sponsorship during her articling year was about to be shot right out of the sky because Cliff Foreman, the junior partner, had taken an instant dislike to her.

He stood there, tall, with an olive complexion, dark curly hair, and eyes a shade of brown verging on black, and glared at her from behind his affable partner, Grant Simpkins. Mr Simpkins, somewhere in his fifties, with a round, cherubic face and a few strands of ginger hair combed carefully across his bald spot, smiled warmly at her.

'Take a seat, Miss Castle,' he said, waving her to a chair then sinking back into his own, which creaked. His partner remained standing, leaning against the wall, arms folded, one ankle crossed over the other, body language saying, *Keep away from me.* 'Cliff here and I have both read your résumé, and are impressed with the grades you've maintained. We did notice, though, that it took you nearly six years to attain your university

3

degree. Would you comment on that?'

Lynne squared her shoulders in the jacket of her neat navy suit and tilted her chin up half an inch, trying to look as confident and professional as she suddenly did not feel. She just *knew* that no matter what she said, she was not going to impress the tall younger partner. Still, it never hurt to be polite, and this interview would be good practice for subsequent ones.

'Shortly after I graduated from high school, my mother was diagnosed with cancer and needed me at home. She was ill for a long time and died four months ago.' To her dismay, her voice wobbled just slightly on the last few words. She firmed it and added, 'I took most of my courses at night-school, because my brother could be with her then.'

'I see.' Mr Simpkins looked sympathetic. 'I'm very sorry for your loss. Any other family?'

Lynne couldn't contain her smile. 'My brother has a wife and an infant daughter.'

Mr Simpkins scanned the papers before him on his desk, turning them over with deliberate slowness that set her nerves on edge. Why hadn't she just said a polite no to his question about family? Maybe she'd come across as immature and gushy, overly involved with her family, an involvement that might reflect adversely on her ability to focus on her studies.

No one had told her that selection interviews would be so harrowing – or that she would walk into her first one and know within seconds that she wasn't going to be accepted.

'Would your relocating to Vancouver Island be a problem?'

'In what way, Mr Simpkins?'

'If you and your brother are close, you might find it difficult to be away from him. We're looking for someone who's in for the long haul. You do understand, don't you, that if we agree to sponsor you for your articling year, and you leave for any reason, you'll have to start over again from scratch with another firm?'

'Yes, sir, I do understand that. I don't intend to quit before I'm fully qualified. It's important to me to be self-sufficient, to make a full life for myself.'

'Why is that?' Cliff Foreman asked, with no change in his stance. His voice, deep, rich and somehow compelling, drew her gaze to his face, which remained impassive.

She hesitated, cleared her throat, then replied, 'I saw my mother devastated and unable to cope when my father died. She had no career, no saleable skills. I don't want to be that way, to have to be dependent on anyone the way she was on my brother. Taylor's a good man, and was a dutiful son, but he has a right to his own life now.'

'How noble of you, not to want to depend on him.' His tone and manner conveyed doubts as to either her nobility or her veracity. His next words cleared up the matter quite well. 'Or is it that he told you to get out and fend for yourself?'

She forced herself to meet his gaze. 'Not at all. The decision was mine. He wanted me to stay with them during my articling year. He and his wife have recently bought an old house out in the Fraser Valley – Ladner – and are busy renovating it. And Victoria's certainly not too far away from my family for frequent visits.'

Cliff Foreman shifted, standing away from the wall. 'Of course, and living here offers you the added benefit of getting out from under the eagle eye of an interfering big brother.'

His attitude provoked her as much as his insulting words. 'I'm twenty-four years old, Mr Foreman. My brother does not interfere. He treats me with respect and fully understands my need to have a life of my own.'

'I suppose you're aware there are five young men working in this office . . . and no other single women.'

Lynne's temper, never far below the surface, simmered. 'No, I wasn't aware of that.'

'Really.' His tone was flat, yet somehow mocking. 'Then you didn't do your homework before applying?'

'I believe I did what was required of me, Mr Foreman. I ascertained that this was a good and reputable accounting firm that had trained a number of articling students, and had hired several on a permanent basis once they qualified.'

'But nowhere in your investigations did you learn that there were no other women here who might, shall we say, provide competition for your not inconsiderable charms?'

As his partner swiveled his chair around to stare at Cliff Foreman, Lynne yelped, '*What?*'

She didn't come equipped with red hair for nothing. Before she could stop herself, she snapped to her feet. 'If you're suggesting, Mr Foreman, that I applied to this office because I'm on some kind of man-hunt, you're wrong.'

He almost smiled. 'You wouldn't be the first young woman to use a job to find a husband.'

'If that were my intention, I could have approached any number of offices in the Greater Vancouver area, offices where the ratio of men to women is far greater than five to one. I applied here, and to two other smaller firms in Victoria, because I believed I'd learn more working in a less stressful environment than I would in a high-powered, big-city situation where juniors do little more than count chickens during restaurant inventories for a couple of years before they're given any real work to do.'

'Just so long as you're not counting your chickens before they're hatched,' Foreman said smoothly, with a note of triumph, she thought. 'Of our five male employees, only one is single and I believe he's in a relationship. Does that disappoint you, Miss Castle, or change your mind?'

'Cliff, I think you've taken this line of questioning far enough,' Mr Simpkins said. 'Please, Miss Castle, sit down again. I'm sure you have questions of us, just as my partner and I have of you.'

'Your partner wasn't asking questions,' Lynne said, remaining on her feet. 'He was making a judgment. Well, fine. Everyone's entitled to his own opinion, and clearly Mr Foreman formed a

7

negative one of me the minute I walked through the door. Perhaps even before that.'

'I – '

She didn't let him continue. 'I'm not denying I enjoy the company of men. I'm female. It would be surprising if I didn't. I also work well with them. A good sixty per cent of my classmates were men. Over the six years of my studies, I never let the fact that I was surrounded by the opposite sex interfere with my work. Nor would I have here, if I were to continue considering pursuing the opportunity to article here – which I am not.'

Foreman opened his mouth again as if to say something, but Lynne was on a roll now and not to be shut up, regardless of how intimidating the man might try to be, standing there with his shoulders hunched up and his head thrust forward belligerently. Lord, what a vulture! Since she wasn't getting this job, she might as well say what she wanted to say and go out in a blaze of glory.

'I applied to Simpkins, Foreman and Associates for sponsorship because I was assured I could learn a lot here.' She paused momentarily, pinning him with a glare. 'From *you*, Mr Foreman. One of my instructors was also one of yours. He suggested I try to get in here because he admires your skills and depth of knowledge and believed you'd be capable of passing them on to me.'

She gestured at the file on Mr Simpkins' desk, a file she now doubted Foreman had done more than skim, if that. He'd probably decided against her the moment he saw by her name she was female. Surely it wasn't by accident that all the accountants in this office were male? Would she have been offered so much as an interview if Simpkins hadn't insisted?

'He wrote one of my letters of recommendation,' she continued. 'When he suggested I come here, though, he was obviously unaware that the man he once considered his "star pupil" had since turned into a misogynistic anachronism from whom no woman would learn anything of value, nor with whom she'd be able to further her career.'

With a quick nod at Mr Simpkins, she said, 'Good morning, gentlemen. Thank you for your time.'

With that, she pulled open the door the receptionist had left ajar and strode across the outer office, through the heavy glass doors and into the corridor. Angrily, she jabbed at the button for the elevator, then jabbed again when it didn't arrive immediately.

Once more, she poked her finger against it, holding it there this time, watching her hand and wrist tremble with the intensity of her anger. She was about to abandon the elevator and head for the stairs when a large brown hand wrapped itself around her wrist and took her finger off the button.

'That won't do any good,' Cliff Foreman said. 'Elevators come when elevators come. You push the button once, and wait. Demanding their immediate presence is of little value.'

She glared up at him. 'You, Mr Foreman, sound like a Vulcan straight off the *Star Trek* set.'

She thought for a moment his eyes might have

9

held a hint of a smile. 'My apologies to Mr Spock.' He hesitated briefly. 'And to you.' This time, there was no doubt a smile lurked in his eyes. It spread slowly to his mouth, which curved up at both corners until a dimple flashed in each cheek and Lynne's mouth went suddenly dry. Dammit, she'd always been a sucker for dimples.

But not on this guy! No way, no how. Not a chance.

'To me?' she asked. 'I can't imagine why.'

He relaxed the gentle grip he'd kept on her wrist, and let her go as the elevator finally arrived with a faint "ping" to announce its presence. 'For my attitude back in the office,' he said, stepping in with her. 'I have orders to take you out for lunch to make up for it, and to ensure that you don't have time to attend those other two interviews.'

Lynne stared at him wordlessly until the doors swished open in the lobby of the building. 'I have to attend those interviews.'

'Why?'

'Because I need a job.'

'You have one. With Simpkins, Foreman and Associates.'

With a light laugh that in no way conveyed her true emotions, Lynne stepped out of the elevator. 'No, thanks.'

'Listen,' he said, taking her elbow as she went outside into the bright June sunshine. 'I'm going to be in deep doo-doo here if I don't convince you I was being a jerk for personal and not very valid reasons, and that we really do want you to do your articling with us.'

'Whatever your reasons, Mr Foreman, you were most definitely being a jerk. Since you're a partner, I seriously doubt Mr Simpkins can fire you if you fail, so your saying you have "orders", and complaining that you'll be in deep trouble if you fail, carry very little weight. Even if I did think my non-compliance with your wishes would cost you your job, frankly, it couldn't matter less to me.'

'It wasn't Grant Simpkins who sent me out to drag you back – by the hair if need be – but his wife, Nita, our secretary-receptionist and seldom-silent partner. Nobody disobeys Nita when she's on the warpath, not even me. She says she likes your spirit and wants you in the office. What Nita wants, Nita gets. Trust me on this. You're hired.'

She twisted her elbow free. 'Obviously, if she suggested you drag me back "by the hair if necessary", she's aware of some cave-man tendencies of yours I only half-suspected. Knowing that makes me no more disposed to work in the same office as you, Mr Foreman, than I was before. Now, if you'll excuse me, I need some time alone, a cup of strong coffee, and a bite to eat so I can prepare myself for my next interview, which is in –' she consulted her watch '– less than two hours.'

Something like admiration sparkled in his eyes, having an odd, breath-stealing effect on her. 'Miss Castle, I insist – '

She cut him off with a wave of her hand. 'Insist all you want. It'll do you no good. If you're in trouble

11

with the senior partner's wife, that, my friend, is your problem, not mine.'

Lynne spun and strode away, intensely proud of herself for maintaining her stand. She needed work, yes, but she did not need it badly enough to take a job where she'd have to end up kow-towing to a man like Cliff Foreman. And that, she suspected, was what everyone else in that office did – except possibly Nita Simpkins – otherwise he wouldn't be so arrogant.

Still, as she slammed the door of her car and pulled out into traffic, she couldn't help wondering about those "personal, and not very valid" reasons that had contributed to his bad attitude towards women, or maybe just her in particular.

Nor could she stop seeing, in retrospect, those damn dimples of his.

The next two interviews went moderately well, but both ended with that "don't call us, we'll call you" kind of feeling. One firm, clearly expecting all applicants to be youngsters still living at home, was offering the kind of slave-wages that wouldn't permit her to rent much of an apartment if she took the job. She would have taken it anyway, and roomed in a boarding house if necessary. However, it wasn't offered.

Lynne caught the ferry back to the mainland, disheartened and weary. Had she been too hasty in rejecting Foreman's apology and offer of employment? She shrugged and pulled a rueful face as she set the hand brake on her car. Probably, but if "hasty" were not her middle name, it should be.

She arrived back at the Vancouver YWCA where she'd had a room for the past two months while finishing her courses, to find a stack of phone messages and several faxes waiting for her.

One message simply asked her to call her brother and sister-in-law. They worried about her, she knew, and called them at once to tell them about the interviews.

'Well, if you didn't have any success, forget it,' Ann said. 'You know we both want you with us, and this house is as much yours as it is ours. I'm sure you can find lots of work out here in the Valley. You could even set up your own book-keeping office right here in the house. Lord knows there's plenty of room.'

Along with noise and confusion, too, with renovations going on, Lynne could have said, but didn't. Besides, she didn't want to be just a book-keeper. She'd studied long and hard and needed this year's articling to achieve her goal of becoming a chartered accountant. 'It's early days yet,' she said. 'I've just started looking.'

Nor did she want to live in Tay and Ann's pocket. They had a right – a need – for a life of their own. She'd thrown in her share of the sale of their mother's house toward buying the old place in Ladner, knowing they couldn't swing the deal without her help. She looked upon it as in investment in the future. If, at some time, they wanted to, and could afford it, the agreement was that they'd buy her out. In the meantime, she considered it their home, not hers, though she knew she was welcome there any time.

The next couple of messages were from friends, one with an invitation to dinner which she accepted happily, another an unflatteringly fast response from one of the Victoria accounting firms saying that the position had been filled. But what interested her most were three faxes on Simpkins, Foreman and Associates letterhead.

One, predictably, from Foreman, simply read, 'I'm sorry we couldn't do business. If you change your mind, please call me at home.' He gave his number.

'Hah!' she said, flinging it on her dresser. 'Not likely.'

The second one made her laugh aloud before she was halfway through it. 'You've done it, my girl! You're the first woman to get under Cliff Foreman's skin and answer back to him in much too long. You owe it to yourself, and to all women worthy of the name, to put on your stompin' boots, get over here, and kick butt. I truly hope you'll reconsider taking a position with our company. I was personally delighted with the way you took Cliff to task then sailed out of here with your nose in the air. I want to shake your hand.

I'd also like to know exactly what you said to him when he chased after you. Whatever it was, he stormed back in here with a face like a used broom, slamming doors hard enough to buckle hinges. Clearly you've rattled his cage. Come on back and do it again.

14

Dearly as my husband and I love the man, it's high time someone beat down that stone wall he's surrounded himself with.'

It was signed by Nita Simpkins.

The third, from her husband, said much the same, only in a less forthright manner. He closed with a challenge she found it difficult to ignore: 'You didn't strike me as the kind of young woman to be scared off so easily. Please don't prove me wrong.'

Lynne dropped the last two faxes on top of Foreman's and stood looking out the narrow window at a sign advertising tacos. He hadn't "scared her off". What he'd done was *tick* her off. Royally.

But . . . did that mean she had to deprive herself of a job she wanted? Was she cutting off her nose to spite her face?

She pulled down the window blind and started stripping. She'd shower, change, meet Janice for dinner at a local pizza place they both liked, then get an early night before she started making a list of other companies where she could send her résumé. There were plenty of smaller cities where she could apply, or she could even bite the bullet and stay right where she was, though that would not be her preference. As her mother had always said, sleeping on a problem often provided an answer.

Actually, it was her friend Janice who provided the answer the minute they'd been served their mugs of beer. 'What kind of luck did you have with your interviews in Victoria today?'

Lynne shrugged. 'I did get one offer. I'm . . . considering it.'

Janice beamed. 'If it'll make your decision any easier, I have a piece of great news for you. My aunt wants to rent out the basement suite in a house close to downtown Victoria. I've seen it and it would be perfect for you. It has two bedrooms, a small but very compact kitchen, good-sized living room, and five appliances. It's nice and bright, and squeaky-clean. It was recarpeted only six months ago. She called me when her tenant left and asked if I wanted it.'

Janice had been talking of moving to Victoria, but had since met a new boyfriend and changed her mind. 'I said I didn't, but knew someone who might, and she said she'd rent it to you cheap if you'd keep the grass mown and the flower-beds weeded. An elderly man rents the main floor, and doesn't like yard-work. I told her you love it.'

Lynne did. Gardening was one of her favorite ways to unwind.

Was it fate? Was it serendipity, having an apartment, exactly what she'd have been looking for anyway, dumped into her lap out of the blue? Was it a sign that maybe she should take the job at Simpkins, Foreman and Associates?

Her head spun. Her heart raced. 'When will your aunt's place be vacant?'

The waiter came and set a large pepperoni pizza with black olives and pineapple in front of them. 'You could move in tomorrow,' Janice said around her first hungry bite. 'The last tenant skipped out in the middle of the night owing three months' rent, so she's really eager to get someone nice in it.' She half rose. 'What do you say? Shall I call her and tell her she has a deal?'

Lynne laughed. 'Sit down and eat, for Pete's sake. She's not likely to find a tenant in the next fifteen minutes. Besides, as I said, I'm only considering the job. There might be . . . complications.'

'What kind?'

'Of the male variety.'

Janice leaned forward eagerly. 'Yeah? This I definitely want to hear.'

When Lynne had finished telling her friend about her first encounter with Cliff Foreman, Janice sipped her beer for a minute or two then said with clear disbelief, 'Tall, broad-shouldered, with dark curly hair and dimples, and you consider him a *complication*?'

'Dark curly hair, dimples and an attitude,' Lynne reminded her, nibbling at the crust of her last slice of pizza. 'I'm not sure I'd be happy if I found myself having to walk on eggshells around him.'

Janice hooted derisively. 'You? Walk on eggshells? That'll be the day. Don't you worry. You can hold your own. Go on. Take the job. Do as the partner's wife said, "kick butt".' She grinned. 'I almost wish I hadn't met Rollie. I'd like to come to Victoria with you, share that apartment and watch what happens between you two.'

'*Nothing*'s going to happen between us! If I go to work for the company, he'll probably have as little to do with me as possible, and I know that's what I'll aim for myself.'

'Uh-uh.' Janice shook her head. 'In all the best

romance books, when the man and the woman strike sparks off each other at first meeting, they end up in bed together within the next few chapters.'

Lynne laughed. 'This,' she said, 'is not a story. This is real life.'

'Yes,' Janice agreed. 'And real life is exactly what stories are patterned after. Besides, you wouldn't have given me such a full physical description of the guy if you hadn't noticed, and if you hadn't been attracted, you wouldn't have noticed.'

'That's not fair. All I said was that he was an arrogant, misogynistic jerk. You were the one who demanded that full description.'

'Right, because your eyes looked like blue fire when you talked about him, and honey, it wasn't all anger, not by any means. You're attracted all right, and I bet he is too, which is why he acted the way he did. Don't you see it? He immediately saw you as a threat to his freedom. He was fighting back any way he could. And that's why you're still waffling about taking the job we both know you really want. You're running scared, too. I tell you, that's the way it works.'

'In your pop-psychology terms, maybe, but not in my life. Arrogant jerks get pretty short shrift. And,' Lynne added darkly, 'nowadays, they also get lawsuits if they step over the line between appropriate and inappropriate office behavior.'

Janice grinned. 'Don't tell me. Tell him.'

Lynne sighed. There was just no talking to Janice sometimes. She was a born romantic who spent a large portion of her life with her nose in a book –

when she wasn't falling in and out of love as often as most sixteen-year-olds.

Well, that was not Lynne's way, which was the only thing that made her feel reasonably safe and secure when, the following morning, she called Grant Simpkins and accepted the position.

She hadn't fallen in love even once, and had no intention of doing so any time soon. She might be twenty-four, but, attracted to the man or not, she could protect her heart if she had to.

It was her heart, and she controlled it just as she controlled her life.

Let Janice dream her impossible dreams and build cloud castles in the air. Reality was what kept Lynne heading in the direction she wanted to go. That, and hard work, and no distractions, were what would get her there.

Cliff Foreman's dimples notwithstanding.

CHAPTER 2

On Monday morning, Cliff heard her laughter before he saw her and his head snapped back with enough force to jar him.

The joyful sound of that laughter sliced into him, and, though he'd never heard her laugh before, he knew exactly who was in the corridor. Even his second of advance warning wasn't enough to prepare him adequately.

Grant, entering after a brief knock, ushered her in, beaming as if he'd personally followed the rainbow and located the pot of gold.

'Look who's joining us after all,' he said to Cliff.

Cliff rose to his feet. 'Miss Castle,' he said, wishing his voice had sounded stronger, hoping its ragged edge hadn't given away the strength of the jolt the sight of her had produced. How could merely looking at her make him dizzy? Dammit, it hadn't. His immediate and potent response to this woman . . . *woman*? – hell, she was scarcely deserving of the term – this *girl*, could be put down to his having stood too abruptly, or having overslept and

20

missed breakfast. It had nothing to do with the whiff of delicate perfume that wafted toward him.

As she had the last time he'd seen her, she wore a tailored suit, this one pearl gray, with a pale blue blouse and a small gold locket, but his mind, playing tricks on him, immediately re-dressed her in something gauzy and soft and pastel. He could see her with a breeze toying with her hair and clothing, sunlight gilding her lashes, tinging her cheeks with pink. He could see her in a field of wildflowers and grass, almost smell them, almost hear gentle windchimes as the echo of her laughter slowly faded from his mind. *Sylvia* . . . that was the main trouble. She reminded him of Sylvia, whom he hadn't so much as thought about for years. Sylvia, his high school sweetheart, the girl who'd laughed and turned her back on him when she found out what he was . . .

He blinked, bringing Lynne Castle back into proper focus and perspective. Her blue eyes were still alight with amusement at something Grant had said. Grant, at fifty-seven, overweight, balding, happily married, the grandfather of six and counting, had never lost his charm. Cliff, on the other hand, had never developed any.

Well, now was not the time to wish he had. Now was the time to call on every bit of strength within himself and meet this challenge face to face. Lynne Castle was not going to get to him.

But even as he made the silent vow, he could almost laugh at himself.

This was one woman whom it would be impossible to ignore. His gaze, try as he might to keep it off her, returned repeatedly until he felt she must think he was a dolt who could do nothing but stare. What was it about her that could so easily punch such a hole in his defenses? The red-gold hair, the curls lying softly against her cheeks and forehead? Was it the freckles sprinkled across her small nose? Or had her blue eyes cast a spell over him? Was it the hint of vulnerability she appeared to be trying to hide as she met his gaze squarely, bravely, her lips just slightly atremble, suggesting the nervousness she clearly fought to control?

'Lynne,' Grant said, waving her to a chair, 'as your former instructor said, Cliff is just the man to show you the ropes. He was right. You'll learn a lot from Cliff. I know you won't let him intimidate you. He's a pussycat underneath all that gloom and glower. He'll be taking you under his wing, getting you set up, and keeping me up to speed on your progress.' He grinned. 'To begin with, Cliff, take her out for that lunch she refused on Friday. I think you two need to get to know each other.'

Cliff watched Lynne as, looking worried, she perched uncomfortably on the edge of the chair as if she might flee at any moment. Grant, in his customary manner, swept on like a small but well-armed tank. 'You look after this girl personally, Cliff, especially while Nita and I are away.'

It was not something Cliff had to be told. The other men in the office, married or not, were going to be kept at a long distance from Lynne Castle if he had anything to say about it. And with Grant away for a month, he planned to have plenty to say about it. He'd be in charge of assignments, deciding who worked with whom, and Lynne, since she was here to learn from him, would be working with him. Closely, very closely.

'I leave you in good hands, my dear,' Grant said, patting her shoulder. Her gaze flew upwards, suddenly filled with apprehension, like a small child, Cliff thought, about to be abandoned by her mother to an unknown kindergarten teacher. 'I'll see you both in a month.'

'A month?' she echoed.

'Yes. Now that we have a full staff again, Nita and I are taking a much-needed vacation.'

Cliff watched those blue eyes widen, watched Lynne's shiny white teeth bite into her lower lip, and watched her pull her shoulders back.

'How nice for you both. I hope you have a wonderful time.'

'We plan on it.' He gave her a quick wink, stuck his thumb up in a 'good-show' gesture at Cliff, said, 'Toodle-oo, kiddies,' turned on his heel and waddled out, shutting the door behind him, leaving Cliff alone with Lynne Castle.

He tried to breathe, but his lungs felt paralyzed. He tried to speak, but his voice was caught somewhere deep in his throat. He tried to move, but his knees suddenly buckled and he sat down hard on his chair.

His instinctive consternation when she'd appeared last week came rushing back. She didn't belong here. It was nuts, the whole idea of putting her into this office full of men. Surely she couldn't really be an articling student for an accounting firm. Instead, she was some dainty fairy of a girl right out of any man's fantasy. Regardless of what he'd read in her résumé and the transcript of her credits, if she could add two and two and come up anywhere close to four, he'd eat his desk. She just didn't look the part.

He was tempted, for a moment, to say so, if only to watch her now wary eyes snap with temper as they had the day of her interview.

That wariness disturbed him, striking at his core. He hadn't missed the almost pleading glance she'd sent toward Grant as he made his departure, as if she were silently begging him not to leave her unprotected in the lion's den.

'You're regretting your decision, aren't you?' he said. 'If you let Grant and Nita bulldoze you into this . . .' He left it hanging, offering her an out if she wanted it. There was that kid he and Grant had discussed, Rodney something, whose grades hadn't been as high as Lynne Castle's, and who had a somber, plodding manner and a red and white polka-dot bow-tie that had grated on both of them. Still, he'd do.

'I still have some reservations,' she admitted, 'but your partner and his wife were both quite eloquent in their desire that I take the position. That had some bearing on my changing my mind.'

'But my message had none.' He didn't make it a question, because he already knew the answer. He didn't even know why he bothered tossing it in as a statement.

She met his gaze squarely. 'None at all.'

Good. At least she wasn't a liar. 'What reservations do you have?'

'If you don't want me here, then it won't work, will it? Your training me, that is.'

Her chin wobbled the tiniest amount as she finished speaking, but it was enough to bring forth every protective instinct Cliff had ever laid claim to and a whole truckload he'd never known he had. He wanted, suddenly, to reassure her, tell her there was nothing to worry about, that with him around, nothing bad would ever happen to her and –

Insanity!

With him around, bad things *always* happened. How many lives had he already screwed up? He didn't want to think about it. Anyway, this was business, and he made it a solid practice never to mix it with his personal life. In fact, he didn't even have a personal life any more. Not that kind, anyway.

'It's not that I don't want you here,' he said – not quite truthfully, but how could he tell her she made him afraid? Afraid for himself, afraid for her. Afraid because of his response to her. He knew it could lead nowhere. This was the kind of girl who needed a husband and a houseful of babies, a picket fence, rose bushes and the PTA, things a man like him could never provide. *Wanted* never to provide. Yet, looking into her wide blue eyes, he found himself hurting from a futile, foolish wish that life could be different, patterns changed, the past expunged, reality eradicated . . .

'I'm just not sure you'll fit in. You seem so . . . young.'

Lynne smiled, struggling to maintain her cool, pressed her knees together, hands folded neatly in her lap, ankles crossed, legs slightly to one side. 'I imagine you were twenty-four yourself once, Mr Foreman.'

'Yeah. About a hundred years ago, it sometimes seems. And call me Cliff.'

Lynne wondered how old he was. Surely not more than mid-thirties. What had so jaded him? Again, she wondered about those personal and so-called unimportant things that had caused his initial dislike of her.

He cleared his throat. 'What, other than my friends' eloquence, changed your mind? You seemed quite certain last week that you couldn't work with a misogynistic, arrogant jerk.'

Tilting her chin up, she replied, 'I'm strong. I can work with anyone, regardless of his attitude. It's my attitude I have to concern myself with, not yours.' She had the pleasure of seeing a faint tinge of color darken his high cheekbones.

'In other words,' he said, 'the problem is mine.'

'Mr Foreman, I hope we don't have to *have* a problem. If I did or said something last week to give you a poor first impression, then I hope for a chance to change that.' What she could have done or said, she had no idea. He'd taken one look at her and made up his mind against her before she'd so much as opened her mouth.

After a long moment, he nodded. 'Nothing you

did or said caused my attitude. You simply reminded me of a part of my life I'd like to forget. We won't have a problem, Lynne. I'll see to that.'

The warm baritone of his voice slid right under her skin and skittered pleasurably along her nerves until it reverberated in her bones, deep and rich and somehow fulfilling. He stood, came around his desk and held out his hand – a peace offering. As she rose and accepted his hand, she decided she liked the firmness of his grip. He wasn't one of those men who thought women's hands should be scarcely touched, lest their tender flesh or sensibilities be bruised. She snatched her hand free the instant she realized how much she enjoyed the feel of his fingers around hers.

Seconds later, she realized exactly how little he cared for her sensibilities. 'Come on,' he said, reaching for a suit jacket hanging on a coat tree near the door, and shrugging into it. 'I'll show you around and introduce you to the others, then I suppose we should go out for lunch, since that suggestion came down from on high.'

Lynne swallowed. He didn't have to sound so put-upon, did he? 'I'm not very hungry,' she lied.

His gaze swept over her. 'Are you ever?' he asked as he straightened his tie. 'You look as if you live on fog and feathers.'

She couldn't help laughing. 'Feathers? Sounds disgusting. I like fog; it feels nice on my skin, though I haven't tried it as sustenance.'

Actually, since she'd moved into the Y, which provided only minimal cooking facilities, she'd lived basically on canned tomato soup and peanut butter sandwiches, with the odd bit of fruit and raw vegetables thrown in for vitamins. Right now, though, she thought she could wolf down a ten-ounce sirloin plus all the trimmings, then look around for seconds before dessert. She'd been too nervous to eat breakfast on the ferry.

'Nevertheless,' he said, 'we'll have lunch.'

Lynne suppressed a strong desire to salute and snap out a brisk, 'Yessir.' Instead, she walked at a swift clip to keep up with his long strides. As she paced beside him, she wished the corridor wasn't so narrow, and that the subtle scent of his aftershave didn't have such an effect on her senses.

She was able to get herself under firm control as she met three of the other accountants who worked in small offices lining the hallway. Kim Wong, a short, sturdy-looking man in his late twenties, had twinkling brown eyes and a shy, self-effacing manner. She liked him at once, as she did Donald Frayne, who didn't stand, but stayed behind his desk, looked her over carefully, then offered her a totally charming grin and a firm handshake.

Ralph Cummins, around Cliff's age, had dark, professionally styled hair, broad shoulders, blue eyes, a mustache . . . and dimples. He flashed them at every opportunity. Oddly, they had utterly no effect on her, and that had nothing to do with his wide gold wedding band, either.

The other two men were both out of their offices and Cliff said she'd meet them later.

He showed her the small cubicle that would be

hers, directly across the corridor from his much larger office, and told her to ask for anything she couldn't find. 'Ask me,' he said, with that almost-smile that hinted at his dimples. 'The woman from the temp agency who's filling in for Nita has only been here a week. She's still finding her way around, too.'

Lynne had already met Carolyn Wilkes, a bewildered-looking woman in her late fifties who kept patting her hair looking for the pencil which she stuck either behind her ear or in the bun at the back of her head.

'And now, that lunch we're supposed to have.'

'Lunch isn't necessary. I'd rather get right to work, Mr Foreman.'

'Cliff,' he said. 'We're all on first-name terms in this office.'

'So Grant and Nita said.'

He cocked a brow. 'Another decree from on high. I suggest you heed it.'

Lynne wished he weren't so tall. It was mildly annoying having to look up at him whenever he spoke. It was more than mildly disturbing that he walked so close to her side, placing a hand lightly on the small of her back as he guided her out of her little office. She bit back the impulse to tell him she was quite capable of aiming herself through a doorway without bashing into the walls.

But no. If they were to get along, she was going to have to curb her tongue . . . as well as her reactions to this man.

As they walked outside, she fished her sunglasses

from her purse and put them on in the dazzling brilliance of the June sunshine.

Around the curve of the Harbour, the Empress Hotel stood in antique splendor, ivy softening the appearance of its stone walls. Closer, tourists watched as a cameraman filmed a TV news reporter interviewing an affable politician on the steps of Provincial Parliament building.

She felt like a tourist herself as a double-decker bus swept past, and she promised herself a tour of the city on one of those just as soon as she could afford it.

Her companion glanced at her shoes and said, 'It's only a block or two, if you don't mind walking to my favorite place for lunch.' He hesitated for a moment then added, 'You like seafood?'

'Yes,' Lynne said, then, after the first hundred feet, tossed breathlessly into his silence, 'and I like walking, too. But not running in high heels. Maybe if you tell me where you're going, I can catch up when you get there.'

He glanced down, looking startled, slowed his pace and took her elbow. Then to her amazement, a slow, warm smile curved his hard mouth. 'Darn. You have such a big personality, I forget you're only half my size physically. I'm sorry, Lynne.'

His voice seemed to linger on her name, as his gaze lingered on her face. *Lynne* . . . He'd said it slowly, carefully, as if tasting it, adjusting to the feel of it on his tongue. He smiled again, his gaze resting on her face. Quickly, she pulled her elbow from his grasp and tucked it in close to her side as a shiver, half pleasure, half apprehension, trickled through her.

Part of her wanted to skip lunch and flee to the ferry, cross over to the mainland and the safety of her brother's home, but another, even stronger part of her wanted to meet the challenge this man presented.

'Here we are.'

Cliff's voice interrupted her thoughts as he steered her toward a restaurant with several empty outdoor tables on a patio overlooking the harbour. Lynne gazed in delight at the startling white of the circling gulls, the twinkle of the water, the boats moving, some sedately, others frenetically, and dragged in a great draught of the salty air. He opened the door to head inside.

'Oh, couldn't we sit outside, please?' she asked, but he gave her a long, assessing look, then shook his head.

'Not a good idea,' he said firmly. 'Not with that red hair of yours, and your fair skin. You'd be burned to a crisp inside of fifteen minutes.'

Lynne closed her eyes in sheer exasperation behind her sunglasses.

'You,' she said, 'sound exactly like my brother.'

'Good,' he retorted. 'Get used to it. Because that's exactly the way I mean to deal with you.'

'Deal with me?' Lynne took off her sunglasses as they entered the restaurant and stood waiting to be seated. '*Deal* with me?'

Cliff drew in a deep breath as he looked into those indignant blue eyes. When the hostess approached, he said quickly, 'We'd like a table outside, please, with an umbrella.'

Outside, at least Lynne would keep her sunglasses on. If he didn't have to look into her eyes, maybe he could make it through lunch without disgracing himself irreparably.

Oh, Lord, what a package she was!

To his dismay, under the shade of the umbrella she took her sunglasses off again, leaving him exposed to the power of her expressive gaze.

Cliff watched in awe as Lynne, who was "not hungry", ate one heck of a lot more than "fog and feathers" for lunch. She devoured – relished – a huge plateful of steamed prawns, an action that no man should have been forced to witness. Still he could hardly take his eyes off her plump, pink lips as she lifted each prawn by its crisp tail and nibbled at its body in an unconsciously erotic manner that had him shifting uncomfortably in his chair.

He glared at a man at an adjacent table who was leaning around a large potted palm in order to enjoy the sight of Lynne enjoying her prawns. The man glanced away, but moments later Cliff caught him staring again. It had been a long time since he'd felt the need to do physical violence to another human being, but he came close in that moment. As if sensing it, the man tossed some cash on the table and left.

To Cliff's further relief, Lynne dug into her salad periodically, leaving the prawns alone, offering him momentary respite during which he could eat his own meal.

'Tell me a bit about Lynne Castle,' he said when he thought the worst of her hunger had been assuaged, and he'd regained some control of his voice. He'd even managed to choke down a few spoonfuls of his thick clam chowder. 'You mentioned a brother.'

She lifted another prawn and slid it between her lips, smiling around it. He came too damned close to groaning aloud. After she'd taken a bite and swallowed, she said, 'Oh, yes, that decree from on high that we get to know each other. Well, let's see. Taylor is ten years older than I am. He and his wife Ann, and their baby Amanda, are all very dear to me.'

'Who else are you close to?'

She shrugged. 'They're the only family I have left.'

Frustrated, because that wasn't at all what he'd wanted to know, he could only say, 'Tell me about them.'

Her smile widened and he saw genuine affection flood her face. 'Actually, Taylor's my half-brother but we tend to forget that. His father died when he was only a little boy of four or five. When he was eight, our mother married again and she and Dad had me.'

'That must have been hard on your brother.'

She looked startled. 'Why?'

'To be supplanted.'

'Tay didn't seem to feel that way. He was my champion from my very first memory. Our parents gave the two of us a wonderful childhood. Perfect, I'd say, and I'm pretty sure he'd agree.'

He laughed, wondering if she heard the bitterness he tried to hide. 'There's no such thing as a perfect childhood.'

'Of course there is.' She sounded offended by his statement. 'We had it. We lived it. Loving parents who cared about us as much as they cared about each other, and showed it every day.'

She leaned toward him, white teeth crunching into another prawn, blue eyes darkening in compassion. 'Didn't you have that kind of childhood?'

Cliff shrugged. He never discussed his childhood, such as it had been. 'So your brother's married now. Does that make you feel left out?'

Her eyes widened. 'Of course not. He'd never let that happen, nor would his wife. I love Ann, too. We're all very close.'

'You recently lost your mother,' he said. 'What about your father?'

For a moment, her upbeat mood faltered. Cliff wished he hadn't asked. 'Dad died in a car accident when I was fifteen, and Taylor just sort of took over, looking after both Mom and me until Mom was on her feet again, emotionally.'

She stared down at her plate for a moment, her hand clenched into a fist on the table. Cliff couldn't help himself. He reached out and covered it with his own hand, stroking the silky back of hers. 'Lynne, I'm sorry. I shouldn't have asked.'

After another second or two, she looked up and slid her hand out from under his. 'It's okay.'

'I don't think so. Because then you lost your mother, too.'

'Yes, we did, but for every loss there seems to be a gain. Shortly after Dad was killed, Tay found Ann and added her to our family circle. Then, when Mom was ill, Ann got pregnant. Mom was so proud to know she was going to be a grandmother I thought she'd burst. She held on just long enough to see Mandy, and hold her. I think that's all she was waiting for.'

She told him more about Taylor, Ann and Mandy, about the 'wonderful' old house they had bought in Ladner, that to Cliff's mind sounded terrible. He'd spent enough years in the construction industry not to see romance in a leaky roof and dry-rot.

'They're renovating it, both working at outside jobs, raising the baby, and spending their weekends tearing things out, rebuilding, replacing, refinishing. They're having a ball, and I figured it was time for me to move on and make my own life.

'They worried about me too much, though, because I was living right downtown in Vancouver, rather than in the suburbs. They felt they had to keep checking up on me. I know they didn't have time to be running into the city to do that, so I decided to do my articling somewhere a bit farther afield.'

'Ah,' he said. 'Hence Victoria.'

'That's right.' She looked at him hopefully. 'I'm confident I can do the job you and Grant need me to do. I really want to make it work, Cliff, and I promise to try hard to please.'

'Yeah.' He shoved aside his half-finished chowder in favor of his seafood club sandwich when the waiter brought it. She wouldn't have to try. All she had to do was sit there, finishing her prawns, her salad and two dinner rolls, talking, laughing now and then, reminiscing about her childhood, about different aspects of her classes, about some of the renovation bungles her brother and sister-in-law were making along the way.

To his amazement, he found himself giving bits of advice he remembered from his days on a construction crew. He discovered he'd like to go and see what Taylor Castle – no, his name wouldn't be Castle, would it? – was doing with the old place. Maybe Lynne would invite him to accompany her one weekend soon and . . .

Whoa! He reined in that line of thought so quickly he nearly got whiplash.

She pleased him in ways he didn't want to be pleased, simply by her very presence, and tempted him in ways he refused to be tempted. The only way to overcome that was to make every effort to replace the big brother who had spent the last nine years looking after her. Even if she didn't want another big brother, by heaven, she had one.

When he caught her hungrily eyeing the French fries he had shoved to the side of his plate, he couldn't help smiling and sliding them toward her.

'Go ahead,' he said. 'I've had enough.'

It both amused and delighted him that she didn't try to deny her appetite. Most women of his acquaintance nibbled at lettuce leaves and low-fat dressing in order to maintain their anorexic figures. Lynne might eat like a stevedore, and, while nowhere near anorexic, was girlishly slim. He thought his hands would fit around her waist.

He clenched them into fists. He was never going to find out. He'd see this girl through her articling year, help prepare her for her final exams, and then most likely watch her get gobbled up by some huge conglomerate that would pay her a lot more than he and Grant with their low-key firm could pay. Then, she'd meet some high-profile lawyer or accountant or businessman, get married, raise a pack of red-headed babies and try to give them the kind of warm, secure childhood she alleged she'd had.

He doubted she'd succeed. He even doubted her own memories were anything but rose-tinted. She'd lost her mother not long ago. She was probably still seeing things through a haze of grief that tended to blur sharp edges, blunt in retrospect the faults and failings no parents could avoid in rearing their children. No one could have been that happy, no lives as perfect as she had painted. He'd seen too many of the other kind to believe in what she claimed.

But if she believed she could have it, he'd wish her well, and maybe, just maybe, she could. If so, that was the way it should be. She had her whole life ahead of her. He, at eleven years her senior, felt as if he had his all behind him.

CHAPTER 3

'It's going to be great, guys!' Lynne flopped back on her motel room bed following her first day at work. Her brother and sister-in-law, each of whom was on an extension phone in their home, tried to speak at once, but Lynne cut them off. 'After I accepted the job, I had lunch with the junior partner, then spent the rest of the day getting my office organized.'

She laughed. 'Though "office" is something of an exaggeration, I have to admit. There's room for a small desk, a computer, a visitor's chair, and me and not much else. But at least it has a window.'

'With a view?' Ann asked. In the background Lynne heard baby Mandy fussing.

'A view of a perfectly gorgeous gray concrete wall,' Lynne said. 'I'm hoping some enterprising artist will paint a beautiful scene on it, but I'm not holding my breath.' She laughed. 'Even some graffiti would be an improvement, but unless it was so innocuous as to be totally uninteresting, I'm sure Cliff Foreman would personally paint over it. He's as bad as you are, Tay, in thinking I need to be "looked after".'

'Glad to hear it.' Taylor's voice came jerkily and Lynne could picture him bouncing the baby against his shoulder. It made her homesick.

'After work,' she went on, 'I checked out the suite I'm going to be living in. It's great! I paid the first and last months' rent, plus a damage deposit, and signed the lease, so it's all mine. I'll move in tomorrow. It's close enough to the office that I can bike to work as soon as I get my bike over here.'

'What about getting your things over there?' Ann asked. 'You need furniture, linens, everything. We'll have to figure out a way.'

Lynne, knowing the other two didn't have time to spend getting her settled, said quickly, 'I have nearly everything I need, Ann, and Janice is going to bring a few things for me tomorrow. The place belongs to her aunt, who's a real sweetie, so don't you worry about me.'

'Is your apartment in a secure building, a good neighborhood?' Tay demanded.

'It's in a great neighborhood full of old houses you'd love, Taylor. It's a basement suite, but since the lot slopes, the back of my unit is at ground level and leads right out into a beautiful, walled yard with a patio that has a table, four chair, and a barbecue the last tenant left. There are fruit trees, berry bushes, and an overgrown vegetable garden. No one has cared for it in years, and I can't wait to get my hands on it.'

'I don't care about the garden. Is it safe? Ground-floor apartments aren't a good idea for a girl on her own.'

'Taylor, I'm a woman, not a girl, and I know about locks on doors and windows. How about if I promise to take the fireplace poker to bed with me every night?'

Ann squealed in delight. 'It has a fireplace? A real one, or gas?'

'A real one, though it has a stove insert and glass doors to minimize heat-loss, but I'll still be able to see the flames and hear the crackle of burning wood.'

'To say nothing of having something to cook on and warm yourself in the event of power failures,' her practical big brother said.

'I hadn't thought of that, but you're right, Tay. There's a shed full of dry wood that will last me for at least two winters. The landlady says no one else uses it, so I might as well. Of course, there's also electric heat, and it seems really snug. I'll be fine, ground floor or not.'

Taylor might have argued further, but Ann cut in with questions about color schemes, floor plans and view, and said he'd leave them to girl-talk while he put his daughter to bed.

After hanging up, Lynne crossed a leg over her bent knee and lay watching her pink-painted toe-nails as her foot bounced with impatience. She wished she'd moved in today, but she'd already paid for the motel room and she needed to shop for basic groceries before she could so much as make herself a sandwich. Besides, she'd have nothing to sleep on until Janice came over from the mainland with the air mattress and sleeping bag she was lending her.

Janice was there when Lynne arrived at her new home from work the following day, laden with grocery bags. She and her aunt had cleaned up the patio table and chairs and brought them inside, and added a comfortable canvas deck chair, a small side table and a lamp. Janice's aunt Steph, a round, warm-natured woman, had also provided basic kitchen utensils.

To Lynne's joy, Janice had managed to fit her bike into the station wagon she'd borrowed, so now she'd be really mobile. She had only two more days on her car insurance before it ran out – and no money to buy more.

Alone at last, she looked around her first real home-of-her-own, proud of it, proud of herself, and delighted with her surroundings, regardless of how spartan they were.

Today, her new life had truly begun.

Dammit, she was laughing again! In the nearly two weeks since Lynne's arrival, he should be used to it, Cliff told himself. Inured to its effect on him. But he wasn't. He'd taken to keeping his office door firmly closed each day after assigning Lynne a task that should have kept her fully occupied.

Today, this was the second time in ten minutes that merry sound had floated across the hall, as teasing whiffs of her scent had done all morning.

Though *that*, he told himself impatiently for the tenth time, was purely his imagination – unless it clung to his own clothing from when he'd leaned close to her to show her what he wanted done.

A rowdy male voice joined Lynne's laughter and, with a grumbling mutter, Cliff shoved his chair back and strode out. Her door stood open.

Her head was tilted back, bands of sunlight flooding through the half-closed blinds casting sharp blades of light, streaking fire across her hair and gold over her face. She held a bottle of orange juice in one hand, its straw sticking up at an angle, a half-eaten sandwich in the other, and was clearly enjoying the attentions of one of the younger men who worked for the firm. The only single man other than himself.

'Barnes.' Cliff made no attempt to hide his irritation. 'Don't you have work to do? If not, I'm sure I can find you something. And I know Lynne does.'

Joe Barnes unfolded his powerful, stocky body from the corner of Lynne's desk. His raised brows evinced his surprise at Cliff's brusque tone. 'Afternoon, Cliff,' he said. 'In case you haven't noticed, it's lunchtime.'

Cliff glanced at his watch. 'Oh. Yeah. Lunchtime.'

'Sorry if we disturbed you,' Barnes continued. 'Lynne's air mattress sprung a leak last night. It whistled and woke her up. She went flying into the kitchen, sure she'd been sleepwalking and had somehow put the kettle on and . . .'

Barnes' voice trailed off and he shrugged uncomfortably under Cliff's steady gaze. 'Guess maybe you had to be there – '

'Were you?' Cliff barked.

'Me? No! Of course not. I was saying, I guess maybe you had to be there or hear Lynne tell the story herself. She's a very funny lady. Did you notice?'

'No.'

'Oh.' With that, Barnes sidled out, leaving Cliff and Lynne alone. He stepped inside and shut the door.

'Air mattress?' he demanded. 'Don't you even have a bed?'

'It's only temporary,' she said. 'Just until I can afford to get some of my mother's furniture shipped over.'

'You rented an unfurnished suite?'

'It was such a lucky find,' she said with a glowing smile that spoke of genuine delight. Everything seemed to please this girl! 'I couldn't turn it down,' she went on. 'I'm getting the place at a reduced rent in return for taking care of the gardens, which I love doing anyway.'

'And in the meantime, you're sleeping on a leaky air mattress.'

'I'll buy a patch-kit on my way home tonight.' She took a swig of her orange juice. Cliff looked at her sandwich. His nose told him it was peanut butter. He'd noticed she always brought a meager lunch from home. Frowning, he recalled the huge one she'd put away when he'd taken her out.

He hated the thought of her pinching pennies, skimping lunches, sleeping on an air mattress and doing gardening to reduce her rent. Hell, she'd been living in the YWCA before moving here. Did she even have bedding? What was the matter with her brother, letting her do something like this? Unless, of course, the brother didn't know.

Well, he, Cliff, knew, and wasn't about to let it go on.

'Didn't Grant tell you about the moving allowance?' he asked.

She looked mystified, and her head tilted questioningly to one side, sending a slash of sunlight across the bridge of her nose, highlighting her freckles. 'No,' she said.

Cliff drew a deep breath and improvised as fast as he could. 'I guess he forget, in the rush to get away on vacation. Whenever we hire someone from out of town, we pay to have their belongings shipped. Just tell me where they're stored and I'll take care of it.' He'd have to pay for it out of his own pocket, but Lynne would never know that.

'They're not exactly stored,' she said. 'They're in my brother's house. All I need to do is go there and choose the pieces I want, then rent a truck and bring them over.'

'Right,' he said, 'and unload them yourself. I can see how easy that will be, your being such a big, strapping girl.'

She laughed. 'Oh, I'm certain I can find help. Joe, for instance, said he'd lend a hand, and bring along Kim and Ralph Cummins.'

Cliff bristled. Over his dead body would Ralph Cummins ever learn Lynne's address. Married he might be, but that never stopped a dedicated womanizer.

'It won't be necessary for Barnes or anyone else to help you,' he said. 'If you go over next weekend, choose the items you want, then arrange to have them shipped, the firm will take care of the costs.'

'That's very generous. Thank you. But I won't be able to do it next weekend.'

Cliff leaned on the wall, folded his arms across his chest and made a supreme effort to keep his tone level, almost uninterested. 'Big date?' he asked as a picture, too graphic, formed in his mind of Lynne, dainty, tiny, innocent, accompanying the burly Barnes somewhere. She could do better. A lot better.

'No.' She laughed as if the idea of a date was comical. 'I have to wait until I get paid before I can renew my car insurance. Paying the first and last months' rent, plus damage deposit, nearly cleaned out my bank account.' She didn't seem at all concerned. She smiled. 'It's a bit of a trip from here to Ladner on my bike.'

'I'll drive you,' he said, and if his offer surprised her, it nearly floored him. Where in hell had it come from? Dammit, he knew. It had come from the same place as that outrageous lie about the company's paying moving expenses for employees. If Grant ever found out, he'd never let him live it down. Cripes, he was acting like the CEO of a huge corporation trying to recruit a high-level employee, instead of the junior partner in a struggling, mid-sized accounting firm who'd just taken on a new articling student.

Still, he'd said he'd see to her moving expenses and he wasn't about to back down. He had no one, and nothing, really, to spend his money on.

Her blue eyes shone as she smiled at him. 'Thank you, Cliff. That's more than generous, but I wouldn't want to put you to all that trouble. Really, I don't mind camping out for a few more weeks. It's sort of fun. And you know, this is the first place I've ever lived that I can really call my own? There's something special about that. So special it makes waiting to get it all properly furnished worthwhile.'

'It's no trouble. I have to go to the Lower Mainland anyway. I'll take you out to Ladner Friday after work, drop you at your brother's place, give you the weekend to decide what you want brought over, and then pick you up Sunday afternoon.'

He didn't wait for her to argue, but gave her a quick nod and left her office.

Out of his mind, that was what he was. Out of his freaking mind! He nearly tripped over Donald Frayne, another accountant with the firm, who came wheeling around the corner in his chair, lunch tray on his lap, obviously headed for Lynne's cubicle.

God! She attracted them like a magnet did metal filings, didn't she? He glanced pointedly at his watch, caught Donald's grin out of the corner of his eye and slammed into his own office. At least

Donald's chair wouldn't fit in Lynne's space with the door shut. Nevertheless, in fifteen minutes, when his watch read one o'clock, he'd be out there to make sure everyone was back at work.

In Grant's absence it was his duty.

Lynne stuffed a tote-bag with the things she'd need for the weekend, fixed it to the carrier rack on her bike and set out for work Friday morning. The light drizzle misting the air did nothing to dampen her spirits. She was going home. She'd get to cuddle baby Mandy, feel warm and secure in her family circle, and see all the latest changes her brother and sister-in-law had made to their house.

The fact that she'd be traveling with Cliff Foreman had nothing at all to do with the bubbly, disorganized sensation inside her, she told herself as she dismounted and rolled her bike inside the office building. She bumped it down the stairs to the basement where it would remain safely locked up in the janitor's storage room over the weekend. Leaving it there meant, of course, she'd need to walk, or get a bus to work Monday, but that would be no problem.

The day, to her surprise, didn't drag. She, along with Donald, went out to oversee an inventory at a hardware store going into receivership. The mood among the staff there was low, and she found herself worrying over what would happen to them.

Would they all get jobs? she wondered aloud as she and Don left. What about the couple who'd put all their life's work into the business, only to have it fail? Would they recover from the financial as well as the emotional blow?

Though the sun now shone bright and warm following the early-morning rain, she felt even more disheartened by the time she and Donald arrived back at the office shortly after four o'clock. Rolling to a stop outside the entrance, he took her hand and held it. 'Hey,' he said, looking up at her, 'you can't spend your life worrying about other people. It isn't your fault their business went belly-up. They aren't your concern.'

Knowing it must get tiresome for a chair-bound person always to be looking up at people standing, Lynne sat on the edge of a low, octagonal cedar planter filled with red and cream tea-roses and multi-colored miniature snapdragons. 'I know it's not my fault, but I still feel concerned,' she said. 'Two of those women are single mothers. One of the men who works – worked – there has three kids. And that nice old couple who built the business from the ground up are shattered, seeing it fail after all those years. They tried so hard. It wasn't lack of expertise that killed it, but the economy. It just seems so unfair.'

'Maybe it is unfair, Lynne, but life is like that.' He sandwiched her hand between his own bony ones. 'The employees will find other jobs and the owners are close to retirement age. They'll be getting their pensions soon, so don't waste your tears on them.'

Lynne had to smile. She hadn't been aware of the tears flooding her eyes until he mentioned them.

She blinked, and one rolled down her cheek. He wiped it away with the back of his hand.

Don had also told her not to waste her tears on him. Sure, he'd suffered irreparable spinal-cord injury in a skiing accident and he and his wife were separated as a result, but he still had a good mind, two great kids he loved, and a lot of friends, he'd assured her. She liked his positive attitude toward life. She liked him. Leaning over, she kissed his cheek. 'Thanks, Don. You're a nice man.'

'We have a ferry to catch,' Cliff said behind her, his voice taut and angry. 'If you're finished making your tender goodbyes, maybe we could be on our way.'

'You said after work,' Lynne retorted, popping to her feet. His tone, and her own embarrassment at having been caught kissing Don's cheek, whipped her temper. 'You didn't say you'd be leaving work early.'

Donald sat staring from one of them to the other. Lynne could almost read the unspoken questions on his face. 'Cliff is heading for the mainland and offered me a ride to my brother's place for the weekend,' she said.

Donald grinned. 'Have fun,' he said, 'and remember what I said. Don't take things personally. You aren't responsible for other people's problems. You just look out for Lynne.'

Because she felt like it, and because Cliff was watching, Lynne bent down and kissed Don on the other cheek. 'Thanks, friend. I'll keep it in mind.'

With a quick wave, he wheeled away through the

automatic doors, which whooshed shut behind him leaving Lynne not knowing quite where to look. It was one thing to be brave when she wasn't alone with Cliff, but quite another when she knew the minute she knew his stare would impale like an icicle.

'Shall we go?' Cliff sounded as if he was speaking through clenched teeth. She glanced up. He had been. A muscle bunched in his jaw, bespeaking his displeasure. Impatiently, he swung open the passenger door of his dark blue Buick.

'Sure,' she said, 'but there's plenty of time, isn't there? It doesn't take that long to get to the ferry terminal from here.'

'It does, considering we need to go to your house and pick up whatever you want to take with you. If you're like any other woman I know, packing will take you twice as long as you estimate, and checking for dripping taps, overflowing toilets, unplugged appliances and whatever other time-wasters you can think of will make us late.'

She glared at him, at the clear contempt she saw on his face. If he held women in such low esteem, why was he bothering with her? She could get through life quite nicely without his assistance. It was all she could do not to kick him in the shins, tell him to take his offer of a ride and cram it, but in the circumstances she chose not to. He was her means of getting home this weekend, and of getting some furniture for her apartment, both of which she wanted badly enough to put up with him and his attitude.

Still, she couldn't speak through the surge of

anger that rose up in her throat. She whirled, marched inside and all but flew down the stairs to the janitor's room. There, she grabbed her tote-bag, raced back up and out the door, to where Cliff still stood, exactly where she'd left him. This time, his expression was not of contempt but of utter perplexity, as if he hadn't had time to decide whether to wait or leave without her.

Since he'd waited, she held the small bag out toward him. Automatically, he took it.

'All packed, sir,' she said. 'Taps turned off. Iron unplugged. Toilet checked. Windows and doors securely locked. Bird-feeder filled. Crumbs left out for the mice. Sir.'

She gave him a smart salute she'd learned years ago in Sea Cadets and ducked under his arm, planting herself securely in the passenger seat and fastening her seatbelt. He continued to stand there holding the door open, holding her bag, holding, she thought, his breath, or his temper, or both, with great difficulty.

'Well?' she said, raising her eyebrows. 'Shall we go?'

To her amazement, he threw back his head and laughed.

Moments later, with her bag in the trunk of his car, and him behind the wheel, he still hadn't started the engine.

Half turned to look at her, he said, 'What does it take to intimidate you, Lynne Castle?'

'Thunderstorms,' she responded smartly, 'but that's all I can think of. Though,' she added thoughtfully, 'I've never met a grizzly bear up close and personal.' She grinned. 'Until recently, that is.'

He puffed out a long breath, turned the key in the ignition and pulled out into traffic.

Several blocks later, once they were on the highway heading for the ferry terminal, he said, 'I'm sorry if I've been acting like a grizzly.'

'I'm sure you have your reasons,' she replied. 'I've simply decided not to take it personally.'

'So that's what Frayne was talking about.' His tone was clipped. 'Been complaining to him about my treatment?'

Lynne twisted around and stared at his set profile. 'Of course not! That's not my style, Cliff. If I have a complaint about you, I'll make it directly to you, not to my co-workers.'

'*If* you have a complaint?'

'So far, I have none to speak of.'

'Then what was he on about?'

Lynne would have preferred not to talk about it, but with the car stopped at a red light, and Cliff turned to face her, she felt compelled to respond truthfully. He listened, looking away from her eyes only when a car horn behind him forced his attention back to the traffic and the changed light.

'Don gave you good advice,' he said eventually. 'Our firm does a lot of contract work for the Receiver's office. You're going to be meeting up with a lot of gloomy people in sad situations. If you let it start eating at you, you won't be able to do your job effectively.'

'I know that,' she said. 'And I believe I did my

job well today. But it bothers me that a Mom and Pop operation like that works on such a small margin that it can be so easily put out of business simply because a megastore moves in two blocks away. I can't blame consumers for wanting a larger selection and cheaper prices, but that couple worked long and hard to create something, only to see it snatched away by a huge conglomerate.'

'You're going to be seeing a lot more of it, Lynne,' he said, 'so toughen up.'

To Cliff's surprise, she let the subject go then, and remained mostly silent for the rest of the drive. He missed the sound of her voice, and cast around in his mind for a subject he thought might interest her, but everything he could think of would surely sound banal to her. He'd lost the art of small-talk, assuming he'd ever had it. He was out of touch with how men and women related now. Socially, that was. Publicly. The other way, at least with Lynne Castle, he had to keep from so much as considering, though it was there within him, a visceral need, a growing desire that made him ache. Still, he'd have to suppress it.

CHAPTER 4

Little boats scurried out of the way as even the behemoth car ferry responded to the forces of tide racing through Active Pass, being forced this way, that way, its path twisting and turning between the close shores of the two islands flanking the pass. The warm, gold and green slopes of Galiano Island to the left and Mayne Island to the right rose in rocky humps, their broken reflections dancing sunlit in the sea.

Lynne's coppery hair flew around her face until she turned into the wind, which then molded her soft silk blouse to her shape, forcing Cliff to avert his eyes.

'What would you do if a big, international accounting firm moved in next door and started undercutting your rates, taking your clients away from you and you had to start laying off employees?' she asked, surprising him by bringing up the subject again.

'I wouldn't like it, but I'd have to learn to live with it.' He shrugged. 'Then, on the other hand, maybe I would like it.' Putting his hands on her shoulders, aware of the delicacy of her bones, he turned her to face the rail again. 'See that red roof right there, high on that bluff on Galiano Island?'

Her hair tickled her face as she turned her head in the direction he pointed. 'The one with the two arbutus trees, one on either side of it?' she asked.

'That's right. That's mine. My hideaway. If our firm went bust, I'd probably go live there. It wouldn't cost me much. I'm a good carpenter, so any upkeep I could-and can-do myself. I could do income tax returns and keep the books of a few small businesses to earn spending money, and the rest of the time, I'd fish. That, at least, would keep me fed.'

Lynne's light laughter filled his ears as her scent filled his nostrils. The feel of her under his hands told him he should take them off her, but they remained wrapped over her shoulders as if glued there.

'You'd probably get pretty tired of fish after a few weeks,' she said.

'Then there'd be oysters and clams, crabs, prawns, scallops.'

Her laughter gained strength. She tilted her head back until it almost rested on his shoulder. Her brilliant eyes met his gaze. 'And you could even learn to grow your own vegetables,' she said, expanding on the fantasy. 'Keep a few goats, maybe some chickens or pigs. Become a gentleman farmer.'

'On an eighty-by-two-hundred-foot lot?' he asked. 'Much of which is taken up by the house and the swimming pool.'

'Oh, a swimming pool?' Her eyes grew big and round, though anything but serious. 'Then you could raise ducks.'

'Thanks,' he said, chuckling. 'I'd rather not share my pool with ducks. They have some-shall we say-uncivilized habits.'

'Tsk. No pioneer spirit at all. When you get tired of fish, though, you might be forced to develop one. Live on roots and berries. Forage for edible plants on the forest floor. I'm told dandelions make good salad, and you can always find wild onions and parsnips. And then there's seaweed,' she added as they rounded a point of land glistening with wet brown bladder-wrack.

'Maybe if Simpkins, Foreman and Associates were to go under, you'd be out of work, too, and have to come and teach me where to find all these edible things,' he said.

She laughed and slipped out of his clasp. 'Not a chance! I like my creature comforts too much ever to become a pioneer.'

'Yet you were willing to camp out on an air mattress until you could afford to transport your furniture.' He moved two paces back from her and sat on a large locker whose label said it contained life jackets. 'Why didn't you ask your brother for financial help?'

In order to face him, she turned to hook her elbows on the rail behind her, the motion lifting and outlining her breasts, emphasizing the narrowness of her waist. Cliff swallowed.

'I'm a big girl, Cliff. I don't need to run to my

brother for help. He has other responsibilities now. And as I said, I was willing to wait for the furniture because I'm quite comfortable the way I am. I have a roof over my head, a job I enjoy, and I'm making new friends every day.'

'Where?'

'In my neighborhood. There was a block party – a barbecue – last weekend. I met most of the neighbors. I chat with the clerks in the supermarket and drugstore, and the two little boys from down the block come to visit me nearly every evening.' She grinned. 'Though I'm not sure if it's me or my strawberry patch that attracts them.

'And then there's the people in the office. Carolyn's a real sweetheart.'

'Carolyn?'

'The receptionist. I can't believe you don't know her name, Cliff.'

'I call her Mrs Wilkes.'

She lifted her brows. 'Whatever happened to the "first-name-basis office policy"?' Cliff shrugged, and she went on, 'Well, anyway, she gave me half a dozen hand-made tea-towels as a housewarming gift when she dropped in one evening to see my new home. I was so surprised and touched I nearly cried. We've had coffee together a few times since I've been with the company. She sort of reminds me of my mom.'

'And, of course, you've made friends with all your other co-workers,' he said. 'You've been with us two weeks and you seem to have everyone wrapped around your little finger. How do you manage it?

I figure we're going to have to move you into Grant's office so you'll have more room for your luncheon parties.' He sounded sour, knew it, but couldn't hide the way he felt.

'I'm just a novelty, Cliff. It'll wear off. No one's coming on to me, and I'm not coming on to any of them. You don't have to worry about the business suffering because of an office romance.'

He studied her. Her open face, her clear eyes, her half-smiling mouth told him she believed what she said. He, on the other hand, did not. He could see trouble brewing. From several different directions. 'You know Donald's wife left him after he became crippled.'

She nodded, but began to look wary.

'He's vulnerable. He might misunderstand your . . . friendship.'

'I doubt that. And he and his wife are working on their difficulties. They're taking joint counseling.'

Cliff pulled one leg up and wrapped his arms around his knee. That was news to him.

He might have commented further, but Lynne shivered and wrapped her arms around herself as the wind shifted.

'Let's go inside for coffee,' he said, standing. He took her arm, wishing he had the right to slide his around her and draw her into his warmth, shield her from the wind. But of course he didn't. And of course he wouldn't. Ever.

That kind of life was outside the realm of possibilities. For him.

* * *

Their mother, Cliff realized the moment he set eyes on Lynne's brother, must have had powerful red-head genes to produce two offspring with such vivid coloring. Taylor's hair was a lighter shade, and cut so short it curled crisply all over his head, but the resemblance between the two was startling, considering they were only half-brother and sister. Taylor stood an inch or two taller than Cliff, had the shoulders of a manual laborer and the hands of a welder, covered with small burns in varying stages of healing.

He swept his little sister into a bear-hug, which she returned with obvious enthusiasm before turning to hold out her hand to Cliff.

'Come and meet my brother,' she said.

With a reluctance he didn't quite understand, he did so, stepping forward slowly. 'Taylor Morrison, Cliff Foreman.' As the two men shook hands, taking each other's measure, a tall, rounded brunette flung herself down the steps to the front yard and embraced Lynne with the same kind of glee her brother had evinced.

When introductions were complete, Ann took Cliff's arm as if they were old friends. 'The wine is chilled, the salad's made, the barbecue's heating, and the steaks are about ready to fling on,' she said, towing him toward the house, past a pile of lumber loosely covered with an orange tarp.

'But I'm not staying,' he protested, futilely, he soon realized.

'Of course you are. You're not driving all the way out here to bring our little sister home to us then going away without being fed, especially when it's all ready. Besides, aren't you even the least bit interested in the renovations we're doing? If you aren't you'll be the first man I've met who's not.'

'He'll love it,' Lynne said. 'He told me on the ferry that he's a carpenter.'

'Really?' Taylor asked, his face eager. 'Great! Then I can pick your brain over dinner.'

'I'm not a professional carpenter. I worked in construction for a while many years ago,' Cliff said dismissively. He had no intention of discussing his past. That was a closed book.

Showing his interest was unavoidable, though. While Taylor stood ready to cook the steaks the minute the barbecue reached optimum temperature, the two women dragged Cliff on a tour of the big, old house. Lynne wanted to see all that had been accomplished since she'd last been there, and Cliff didn't want to get far from Lynne. Especially if it meant going one-on-one with Lynne's big brother. He knew that men knew exactly what other men were thinking about.

He found himself running his hands over the smoothness of reclaimed wood paneling that Ann said had been hidden by coats of hideous paint. Someone had done a fine job of refinishing it. He admired the sweep of a banister on a circular staircase that had for some inexplicable reason, been boarded over, only rediscovered when they'd torn out a wall to make the kitchen bigger and created an adjacent, sunken family room. In single file, they ascended the stairs.

'This is our room,' Ann said presently, lowering her voice as she opened a door and ushered them through into a room large enough it could easily have been divided into two bedrooms. As it was, in addition to the bedroom furnishings, it had a love-seat, and armchair and a coffee table at one end, with a television and CD player on a stand nearby. Large sliding glass doors led to a balcony. 'We finished it first, along with the nursery, which is through there.'

'Can I –?' Lynne began.

'No.' Ann's tone was firm and she took her sister-in-law by the hand and led her out of the room. Cliff followed in their wake.

'And this is Lynne's room,' Ann said, gesturing at a door along the corridor where it turned at right angles.

Cliff waited, scarcely breathing, for her to open it. He found within himself a burning need to see the room where Lynne slept, to discover if it smelled like her, if it looked like the kind of place he would have envisioned her in if he'd ever let himself do such a thing. To his disappointment, Lynne simply dumped her tote outside the door and they went on.

'This is a big house,' he said to distract himself. 'Bigger than it looks from the outside.'

'We need all the room we can get. We plan a large family,' Ann said with a grin. 'I was an only child and Tay was lonely as a child until Lynne came along and –' She broke off and reached out to snag Lynne, who'd been sidling away, heading for the nursery again, no doubt.

61

'Don't you dare!' she hissed. 'She'll be awake in no time, and I'd like, for once, to eat my dinner in peace.'

'But Ann, I thought I heard – '

'You heard nothing. I'm the mother. I'm the one whose ears are attuned to the least little sound and Mandy didn't make so much as a peep. You have all weekend to hold her and play with her and be the adoring auntie, but dinner time is mine.'

Cliff laughed at Lynne's pout, but he could see that in her sister-in-law she'd met her match.

'All right,' Lynne said. 'I won't even take a peek at her. But I am going to change into something more comfortable than this,' she said, plucking at the neat skirt she'd worn to work. Her blazer, Cliff realized, must still be in the back seat of his car. He watched her return along the corridor, missing her presence already.

'For some reason, the upstairs was built in two sections,' Ann went on, leading the way through a doorway at the end of the hall. 'The house has been patched together over the years, added on to, and the upstairs on this side was never finished, though this is where the main staircase leads.'

She reached overhead and pulled a string, turning on a set of bare light bulbs to illuminate the area. 'This is our latest bone of contention,' she said cheerfully. 'Tay wants to get rid of the wall entirely and make five more rooms up here, and one more bathroom in addition to the ones in Lynne's room and ours. I want to leave it so we have a modicum of privacy on our side, and put in three larger bedrooms, each one with a bath, over here.'

Cliff ran a glance at the wall in question. It was easier to judge from this side. 'Looks like a bearing wall to me,' he said.

'What's that?' Ann asked.

'A wall that goes from the foundation up and supports the roof, as opposed to simply a partition. The architect's drawings would tell you for certain.'

'Hah! Assuming we had such a thing,' Taylor said, coming up behind them. 'So you figure it's a bearing wall. I was afraid of that.'

'Sorry,' Cliff said, waving his arm to indicate the big, open space around them. 'If, as your wife says, this part was built on after the original, that was likely one of the outside walls.'

'Sounds to me as if you've done more than "a bit of construction".'

Cliff shrugged. 'Maybe, but I'm no architect. Even without the drawings, though, any good builder should be able to make an educated guess. Have you had the place checked out?'

'Before we bought it, sure, to make certain the foundations were sound and that it was fit to renovate.' Taylor slipped his arm around his wife's back. 'I came up to tell you dinner's ready. Let's go before the boss wakes up. Where's Lynnie?'

'Right here, and starving.'

'So what else is new?' Taylor gave his sister a quick hug and let her go. Cliff could only stare at her.

She matched the fantasy he'd had during the first moments of their meeting, wearing something soft

63

and pastel and floaty, a skirt that moved with her, swung as she swung, a blouse that left her collarbones showing and just a hint of the top curves of her breasts. She'd run a brush through her hair, and put on some lipstick. Her lashes looked darker, as did her eyebrows.

Cliff would have liked to stand and stare at her, hold her back as the others left, on the pretext of doing some more exploring, but that was impossible, of course, because he'd be unable to keep his hands from exploring her. He followed her down the spiral staircase, leaving the sawdust-scented upper floor to find a table set on the wrap-around veranda overlooking the back yard. The aroma of barbecued beef filled the air and suddenly he realized how hungry he was. But not just for food. For good company, for conversation, for . . . fellowship.

He found himself listening closely to Taylor's thoughts and ideas, involved despite himself. Periodically, he couldn't resist pointing out a minor issue that might, if done the way Taylor had planned it, cause trouble down the line.

'Wish we'd met you sooner,' Taylor said. 'Especially when we realized the inside dimensions of the kitchen didn't match the outside dimensions of the house, even given that there was a storage cupboard inset on the porch. Our intention was to close that cupboard off on the outside and open it from the inside to turn it into a pantry.'

'There's a discrepancy in area?' Cliff asked, leaning forward. 'Have you found out what accounts for it?'

'There was a discrepancy – there isn't anymore

since we opened it up. We found not only those spiral stairs, but a secret room,' Taylor said.

He reached for the bottle and refilled the glasses with the rich, red wine, except for Ann's. She put her hand over the top of hers and shook her head. 'Mandy doesn't like more than half a glass of wine.'

Taylor went on. 'When we tore out that wall we discovered the stairs and a twelve by fifteen room behind it, two-thirds the size of the cupboard on the porch.'

'With no access?'

Taylor grinned. 'Oh, there was access, all right, a trap door with pull-down stairs neatly concealed in a dark corner of the cellar. The grow lamps and hydroponics system were still in place. We cleared that out in a hurry.'

'Someone trying to pay the rent with a pot-plantation?'

'I guess so. They must have had to bolt in the night and left all their stuff behind. Maybe the law was on their tail. At any rate, we wanted no part of it. This is going to be a family home.' He and his wife shared a smile.

'But we're just getting around to planning the top floor, and creating bedrooms for that future family. Any tips you want to pass on are welcome.'

'It's a good space,' Cliff said as non-committally as possible. 'You should be able to make plenty of use of it.' But before he knew quite how it had happened, he and Lynne's brother had shoved their empty plates aside and spread floor-plans across the table between them.

'If you run the partition this way –' Cliff said. With a pencil he drew a faint line on the plan '– you'll end up with a short corridor here that will give you access to both those rooms with no real loss of space because the back-to-back closets, one in this room, and one in this one, will fill the end of it.'

'Yeah, right. I see it. Sure, that'll work.'

Ann leaned over her husband's shoulder. 'So, I guess this means we can go with my idea of three bedrooms and three baths on that side.' If she meant not to sound or look triumphant, she failed.

'I guess,' Taylor said.

'It's for the best,' she assured him, kissing the tip of one sunburned ear. 'At least according to everything I remember from listening to friends in school who hated sharing bathrooms with siblings.'

'How could that be worse than sharing a bedroom, which your way they might end up doing?'

'There's a difference,' she said. 'Believe me. There's a big difference. Two girls might manage to share one bath without too much wrangling, but more than that, and we'd have constant battles.'

'What if the next eight or ten are boys?' Taylor asked with a grin that reminded Cliff of Lynne's.

'They won't be,' Ann assured him, laughing. 'I want an even mix so neither one of us is outnumbered.'

She glanced over her shoulder at the sound of footsteps. 'And here's number one daughter, whom I didn't hear make a sound. I guess Auntie Lynne's ears must be better than mine after all.'

Cliff couldn't speak as Lynne, cradling her niece,

sat on the chair next to his. She pulled back a thin blanket and he looked into a pair of huge, solemn blue eyes set wide in a tiny, pointed face. 'This is Mandy,' she said, smiling at Cliff. The expression on her face created such a deep and painful ache in him he had to bite back a groan.

He knew he had to say something, anything. 'Uh, how old is she?'

'Four and a half months,' Lynne, Ann and Taylor said in unison, each one equally proud, he could see. He swallowed hard again. Of course. He knew how old the baby was. She'd been born just before Lynne's mother died.

He should have kept his big mouth shut.

'She's all clean and changed, Mommy,' Lynne said, glancing at her sister-in-law. 'And she really was awake. I heard her when I went in to put the coffee on.'

'Right,' Ann said, disbelief in her tone, but her expression held nothing but loving indulgence.

Lynne continued to rock the baby, stroking a finger tenderly along the Mandy's cheek. In response to that touch, a small, pursed mouth made sucking motions as the infant turned her head toward Lynne's breast.

'Wrong fountain, angel-face,' she said with a laugh, dropping a kiss on the soft, downy, pale red hair before passing the baby over to Ann. 'Better go see your mom.'

Ann, quite unselfconsciously, discreetly lifted her T-shirt, snuggled the baby close and let her nurse.

Cliff looked at Lynne, and the heavy, dragging

pain grew to unmanageable proportions. 'I have to go,' he said, abruptly shoving back his chair. 'Thanks for dinner.'

'Oh, dear, I've embarrassed you,' Ann said. 'I'm sorry. Come on, Lynnie, let's us girls go inside and build castles in the air, while these two sit out here and build houses on paper. We'll be having coffee and dessert as soon as Mandy's done, Cliff, so don't run off.'

'No, no, you didn't embarrass me,' Cliff said. 'It's just that I have a ways to go.' Determinedly he headed for the door.

'All right, if you're sure. But we'd love to have your company longer.'

'Another time,' Cliff lied, and knew it. This was one place he'd have to avoid. It did bad things to his equilibrium, seeing the happy couple, their baby, the house, the life they were building together, and seeing the unconscious longing for the same in Lynne's face. 'Thanks again.'

'I'll come out and get my blazer,' Lynne said, and her brother followed, determined to continue the conversation about the renovations.

'Taylor, honey, could you give me a hand here, please?' Ann said, interrupting a question he was asking Cliff. Taylor stopped in his tracks, turned to look at his wife.

'Oh!' he said. His tone told Cliff quite clearly that he knew why he'd been called back. He wanted to assure the other man things weren't the way Ann thought, that he and Lynne didn't need time alone together to make their goodbyes.

But still, he appreciated Ann's sensitivity.

'I'll arrange to have a moving van here by noon on Sunday,' he said, taking Lynne's elbow as they walked down the new front steps. They had a good, solid feel to them. He might not have much experience, but Lynne's brother was building something to last.

'I could do that,' Lynne said.

'No.' It came out more curt than he'd intended. 'You'll have enough to do tomorrow, getting your stuff all sorted out.' He smiled. 'And playing with your niece.'

'Yes. Isn't she beautiful?' Lynne's eyes glowed luminous as she gazed up at Cliff in the dusk.

'Very beautiful.' He wanted to touch her. Some kind of flowers perfumed the air, competing with the scent of fresh-cut lumber. Lynne's blouse slipped down one shoulder, exposing the thin white strap of an undergarment. Was it a bra? Was it a camisole? He wanted to kiss her shoulder. He wanted to learn what she wore under her blouse.

He strode toward his car because he wanted so badly to stay. It was the first time in a long while he'd really *wanted* to be in any particular place, with any particular people. Or person. It was, he thought, an odd sensation.

'Thanks for bringing me home,' said Lynne. 'And thanks for staying awhile. I know Taylor feels better about my living in Victoria now he's met you.'

He cleared his throat. 'I – uh – like your family.'

He cast around for something else to say, but his mind was blank of everything but the desire to bend and kiss her, hold her, make love to her. He swallowed, hearing a grating sound from his too-tense throat.

'How far do you have to drive tonight?' Lynne's voice was soft, maybe even wistful, as if she were no more eager than he for the evening to end.

'Not all that far,' he said. He'd spotted a motel only a few miles away. Maybe he'd spend the weekend there, explore the area a bit, then show up back at this house around noon on Sunday to pick up Lynne. The one thing he didn't want her to know was that he had nowhere to go, no one to see, and that she had been his sole reason for this trip to the Fraser Valley. 'But your sister-in-law looks like she needs rest more than company.'

'Yes. She works much too hard. She's a nurse with a full-time job at the local hospital, and now a mother, as well as a home-renovator. I guess you noticed the dark circles under her eyes.'

Cliff nodded. But he'd also noticed the glow of happiness that surrounded Ann. She might work too hard, but everything she did was a labor of love. Her little daughter was destined to grow up lucky, and maybe enjoy the same kind of idyllic childhood Lynne claimed. Having met her family, he found it easier to believe what she'd said.

'Goodnight,' he said, and because he couldn't resist, he stroked her cheek with the backs of his fingers, much as she had the baby's. He didn't recall ever touching an infant, but he thought its skin couldn't be any more velvety than Lynne's. A stray breeze teased a curl forward and it wrapped around his finger. He slid it back behind her ear, his hand cupping the side of her head.

Then, without thought, driven purely by need, he bent and brushed his mouth over hers. Her lips trembled, parted slightly, and it took him a mighty effort to lift his head and leave it at that.

If only she had let him! But she didn't. She curved one hand around the back of his head and drew him to her again. This time, the kiss was deeper, sweeter, and her giving nature called out to something lost within him. He clasped his arms around her, held her, tilted her head back and parted her lips fully. She trembled. Her tongue fluttered against his, shy, inexperienced, but willing, oh, so willing to learn.

He ached all over, the heaviness in his groin spreading out to smolder deep inside him, heating his blood. He shifted his stance, his legs apart, and pressed a hand to her firm buttocks, holding her tightly against him. A groan he couldn't suppress growled out of his throat.

She made a sound, soft, pleading, and he realized what he was doing. Clamping her shoulders in his hands, he set her away from him.

'Lynne . . .' He ran one hand through his hair. 'I'm sorry. That shouldn't have happened. It was a mistake. It – '

He broke off, knowing there was nothing else to say, no words that would mitigate his actions.

'It was . . . beautiful,' she said, her voice tremulous. 'No one's ever kissed me like that before.'

'*Lynne!*'

Quickly, he got into the car before he gave in to the temptation to kiss her like that again, to say something he knew he'd regret. 'Sunday,' he said. 'Around noon.'

She nodded, and as he backed out of the driveway, stood watching him. She was the last thing he saw in his rear-view mirror as he turned and headed away. That image was one he carried with him for the rest of the weekend, Lynne, her arms wrapped around herself as it to ward off a chill – or as if she wished his were the arms around her again . . .

No. It could not be.

'Nice man,' Ann said, eyeing Lynne. 'Where's your jacket?'

Lynne felt her face heating and was glad her brother, with his eagle-eye and swift perceptions of her every mood, was upstairs settling the baby for the night. 'I – uh – forgot it.'

'No doubt for a good reason.'

Lynne refused to meet Ann's gaze. 'It was kind of him to drive me here. I'm glad you invited him for dinner.'

'Taylor wanted to check him out, as I'm sure you realized. So did I, of course.'

'He's just my boss,' Lynne said. 'One of them. The junior partner. Nothing to check out.'

'Uh-huh.' Ann took the last bite of her apple pie and scooped up the empty plates. 'Why am I having such trouble believing that?'

'For goodness' sake, sit down. Let me do that,' Lynne said, snatching the plates from Ann. 'Even Cliff, as misogynistic as he is, noticed how tired you look.'

Ann relinquished the job of clearing the table of dessert dishes, but her eyes twinkled.

'Misogynistic?' she asked, following Lynne into the kitchen and shutting the door. The evening had grown suddenly cooler.

'Totally.'

'Uh-uh. That man is smitten. With you, my love. At least that's the way it looked to me.'

Lynne did not like the speculative gleam in her sister-in-law's eyes. 'Then you weren't seeing straight.' Deliberately changing the subject, she said, 'What's the plan for tomorrow? I hope you saved lots of good jobs for me.'

Ann sat at the kitchen table and rested her chin on her fists. 'Why so evasive, little sister?'

Lynne slid the plates into the dishwasher, sent a handful of cutlery clattering into its basket, and added detergent. 'I'm not being evasive. I don't know what you're talking about, is all. He's no more smitten than I am.'

'Well, there is that, of course . . .'

'Ann!' She turned the name into two syllable of warning and slammed the dishwasher shut. 'As I said, the man is my boss. He doesn't even like me very much. He didn't want the company to hire me. He's afraid I'm on a man-hunt because I elected to work in all-male accounting office.'

Warming to her subject, Lynne outlined her first

few encounters with Cliff, and his continued attitude towards her. 'He's on my case constantly, and watches to make sure I don't try to seduce any of the male employees.'

Ann laughed. 'Garbage. He likes you all right. He can't keep his eyes off you. If he's worried about anything, it's his response to you, not that of any of the other guys in the office.'

'If you believe that, you're a nutcase.' Lynne turned on the dishwasher. 'He's a woman-hater, Annie.'

'Yup. Sure. A woman-hater who drove his newest employee all the way out here so she could gather up her belongings to make her own apartment comfortable. Sounds like a real rat, to me, to say nothing of a scoundrel, a rotter and a cad.'

Lynne laughed at Ann's tone. 'I didn't say he was any of those things!' She squirted cleaner on the sleek new forest-green counter-tops and wiped them down. 'But the truth is, he offered me a ride out here this afternoon only because he was coming this way himself. It's company policy to help relocating employees make their move.'

'Generous company,' Ann murmured.

Lynne polished both shiny stainless steel sinks, rinsed out the sponge and set it to dry on the side of the right-hand one. 'He'll be back Sunday around noon with a moving van. After that, I'm sure he'll feel his duty is done and we'll have no more contact than necessary – and that all in the office.'

Ann's eyebrows disappeared into the lock of hair that had fallen over her forehead. 'Do tell. Since when have moving companies started working Sundays?'

Lynne blinked at the question, and frowned as she sat across from her sister-in-law. 'Well . . . I guess they must. I hope they do. Cliff seemed to think so. He told me to collect up everything I wanted moved and he'd see to the truck. But if they won't come Sunday, I don't know what I'll do. You and Taylor will both be at work Monday, and there'll be no one here to let them in. Darn, I wish I'd thought to ask where he's staying.'

Ann yawned as she stood. 'Nothing to be done about it now, sweetie. I'm going to bed. Tomorrow, after you pick out whatever you want to take, I'm going to put you to work and simply stand over you with a whip. When good-looking men start commenting on how tired I look, I figure it's time to start taking better care of myself.'

'What? I don't count?' said Taylor, entering the kitchen. 'I've been telling you that since six months before Mandy was born.'

'Yes, but you're my husband. You're supposed to want to look after me. It's when your little sister's boyfriends start doing it, I have to sit up and take notice.'

'He's not my – '

Lynne broke off and cupped her chin in her hands, knowing neither Ann nor Taylor was listening. Arms around each other, they mounted the stairs to their private quarters.

CHAPTER 5

Lynne spent the next hour wandering through the main floor and basement, making notes of pieces of furniture she thought would fit in her apartment. There was so much here! All her mother's things, all Taylor had bought when he had his own apartment, and all of Ann's things as well. In the basement were boxes and boxes of dishes, cutlery, knick-knacks and linens. There'd be no difficulty finding enough. The difficulty would be in trying to choose.

Tomorrow, she reminded herself. She'd worry about it tomorrow. Now, she'd go to bed, sleep like a log, and be ready for a hard day's work.

But, as she lay there breathing in the perfumed breeze, picking out the individual aromas of night-scented stocks, nasturtiums and freshly cut grass, sleep was far away. She wandered to the balcony and watched the moon reflect on the water of the river, silvering a rippled path that seemed to arrow right into her heart the way Cliff's kiss had.

No. He was too old. He really didn't like her. He was all she'd said, and more. If he showed glimpses of a compassionate and caring nature, that was all they were, merely glimpses, flickers of something that likely didn't exist outside her own – and Ann's – imagination.

But then Ann was as big a romantic as Lynne's friend Janice.

She, on the other hand, was not a romantic. Not that she didn't believe in romance. She did. She expected to find it some day, but she did not expect to find it in a man like Cliff Foreman.

So why, she wondered, was her first thought upon waking Saturday morning a graphic memory of the sensation of Cliff's arms cradling her, the pressure of his mouth on hers, the exciting and scary knowledge that he'd been instantly and fully aroused and that she was responsible? Why couldn't she shake the memory of Cliff's eyes, deep and dark and mysterious, giving her messages she didn't understand, but wanted desperately to interpret?

And why, despite being frantically busy all day, working with her brother and Ann, playing with her darling little niece, sorting, too often tearfully, through her mother's things, was Saturday so long?

Then when noon Sunday arrived, and Cliff did not, Lynne had to force herself to stay in the back yard, carefully weeding the small vegetable garden she had planted there some months ago.

When he did come, and Ann brought him out to where Lynne crouched, and she looked up at him in a spangle of sunlight dappling through the leaves of a tree, her heart raced. Her mouth went dry, and the soil on her hands turned to instant mud.

Ann murmured something about not wanting to leave her half-papered bathroom wall and dashed back inside, leaving Lynne all alone. With Cliff. Who had touched her face in the night. Who had kissed her. Who had stayed front and center in her mind in all the hours they'd been apart.

He smiled, reaching down a hand to help her to her feet. Mud and all, because she knew her knees would never support her, she let him pull her erect.

His smile died. 'Don't look at me like that,' he said softly.

Lynne swallowed hard. 'Like . . . what?'

'Like . . . I can't describe it, Lynne.' Suddenly, his tone was harsh and his lips thinned. 'Just . . . don't.'

Stung, she jerked her hand free. 'I can't help my looks,' she said. 'They were caused by the imprinting of a certain genetic code at my conception and were none of my doing. I'm sorry if they bother you. I take it you're ready to go? I'll wash my hands and meet you inside.'

She whirled away to the tap at the edge of the garden, fully aware, though her back was to him, of Cliff's long-legged stride as he put as much distance between them as possible, in as little time as possible.

Well, fine. That suited her, too.

Though how, she wondered as she wiped her hands dry on the seat of her shorts, was she going to survive the long drive back with him in the confines of his car?

A moot point, she discovered as soon as she'd showered and changed and packed her tote-bag, ready to leave.

Cliff, along with Taylor and a neighbor, had just finished loading her things into a U-Haul van. His Buick stood off to one side.

'Throw your bag in there,' he said, tossing her the keys. 'You'll drive the car. I'll drive the van. Follow me. That way I can be sure you don't speed.'

'Well, ex-*cuse* me!' she said. 'I'll have you know I do not speed. My brother taught me to drive and he did it right. Right, Taylor?'

Taylor cocked one eyebrow. 'I taught you to drive when you were sixteen, half-pint. Who knows what bad habits you've picked up in the past eight years?' He reached out to give her a hug and she had to fight tears. It was always so hard leaving him.

'You could have backed me up,' she muttered. 'I thought families stuck together.'

He chuckled. 'So do guys, honey, so do guys. Before he even considered letting you drive his car, Cliff grilled me about what kind of driver you are. I told him your talents were minimal, but if he kept close watch over you you should get home safely.'

'Oh!' All thought of tears fled as she socked him in the arm. Laughing, he kissed her cheek.

'Bye, baby-doll. See you soon?'

'Yes,' she was happy to be able to tell him. Now her moving costs were taken care of, she could buy insurance for her car next month, and as soon as she did, she'd be back for a visit.

Saying goodbye to Ann and the baby was no

easier – until Ann said, 'Smitten, I tell you. Head over heels. Do you know how long it was before your brother let me behind the wheel of his car? *Two years*!'

'Get off that tack,' Lynne hissed. 'There is nothing, and I mean *nothing*, along the lines of what you're thinking.'

'We'll see,' Ann said with a complacent smile. 'We'll see. Now you'd better scram. I think your shepherd is getting impatient.'

Her shepherd.

Right.

As if she needed one.

As soon as they hit the freeway, Lynn zipped out and around the U-Haul truck and led the way back to the ferry – at a sedate, legal speed. But she still led.

No man was going to dictate to her. At least, not outside the office.

'Thanks, fellas,' Lynne said, standing back to admire her newly placed furniture. Kim Wong ducked his head shyly, his straight black hair falling over his almond-shaped eyes. Despite his small stature, he'd shown as much strength as stocky Joe Barnes and tall, muscular Cliff. How Cliff had arranged to have the other two accountants there waiting for him and Lynne to arrive, she had no idea. Maybe he'd organized it all before they left.

'Now, sit down,' she went on, gesturing at the sofa and chairs positioned around the room. 'I'll bring you something cold to drink, and then put dinner on the table.' She'd thrown a huge salad together while they unloaded, and broiled a bunch of chicken breasts. That, along with a loaf of French bread, would have to do.

'Sorry.' Kim shook his head. 'My wife's expecting me. We're going to her folks' for dinner.'

'Sounds good,' Joe said, but, after a swift glance at Cliff that included a silent exchange Lynne couldn't possibly have missed, or misunderstood, added that he'd take a rain-check.

'But . . .' She protested, following the two younger men toward the door. 'You worked so hard, the least I can do is – '

'The least you can do is let them get on with whatever plans they have,' Cliff said, wrapping his hand around her arm. His skin felt warm and dry against hers as he turned her to face him and shoved the door shut with the two men on the other side.

'Joe, in case you haven't noticed, is single. Footloose, fancy-free. Probably has a date.'

'He didn't act like a man who had a date. I think he wanted to stay.' It both scared her and thrilled her to know that, even if Joe had wanted to, Cliff had *not* wanted him to. She shivered deep inside, remembering what Ann had said. *Head over heels* . . .

Cliff ignored her protest as, still holding her arm in a firm clasp, he steered her back toward the kitchen. 'Now, I, on the other hand,' he went on, 'am none of those things.'

Lynne blinked, remembering his harsh tone as he'd told her not to look at him 'like that.' *Just . . . don't*, he'd said. 'Not single?' she blurted, tilting her head back slightly to look up at him.

His laugh held little humor. 'Oh, I'm that, all right, and intend to remain that way.' He let her arm go, leaving a band around it that felt cold. She rubbed it.

At once, he was alert. 'Did I hurt you?'

'No, of course not. You're a very . . . gentle man, Cliff. My brother and sister-in-law both said how much they liked and admired you.'

He met her gaze for a flashing second. 'I'm not a gentleman,' he said flatly. 'Don't make the mistake of thinking I can ever be one. I'm a hard man, a harsh man. I . . . hurt people, Lynne.'

'I said a gentle . . . man, not a gentleman, though I suspect you're that as well. And now, since you sent your assistants away, you're going to have to stay and help me eat the dinner I fixed.'

'I was going to take you out for dinner,' he said.

'Tsk. I guess you can't have everything all your own way all the time, Cliff.' Lynne slipped past him and around a stack of half-emptied boxes.

'So I discovered when you passed me on the freeway,' he said, his tone dry.

She flicked a glance at him. To her amazement, he'd said nothing about it on the ferry. She been almost disappointed, half looking forward to a rousing argument with him over the issue.

'He warned me,' Cliff said, taking the bottle of Chablis she pulled from the refrigerator and picking up the corkscrew she'd left on the cluttered counter.

'Who?'

'Your brother. He said I'd made the mistake of

giving you an order, and that having done so, all I could do was sit back and watch you gleefully break it. He only gives you orders when he wants you to do the opposite of what he says.'

Lynne planted her hands on her hips. 'Well, darn! And here I thought he'd stopped giving me orders because he figured I was all grown up and he didn't have the right to do it any more.' Then she laughed. 'I hope he never figures out I've known about his silly reverse psychology since I was about ten years old. He's such a sweetie, and I adore him, but he can be a pain in the neck at times.'

It delighted her to see Cliff smile and lower himself into one of her mother's oak captain's chairs. He looked good there. He looked right. When he lifted his glass in a toast to her new home, Lynne clicked hers against his.

'And to new friendships,' she said, then turned quickly from the burning expression in his eyes. She didn't know if it scared her or thrilled her. But she did know it affected her more strongly than she'd ever been affected before.

Cliff Foreman was a very dangerous man.

Lynne Castle was an extreme hazard to his peace of mind and Cliff didn't like it. All Sunday night, as he had both Friday and Saturday, he tossed, dozing periodically, only to dream of her. His stomach churned. He wondered, briefly, if he was heading for another episode of the colitis that had plagued him periodically for years. It had been at its worst during his marriage. Maybe it was a female-induced illness, instead of, as the medical community wanted him to believe, stress-induced.

Of course, women meant stress. That was a given. He laughed silently at himself for the thought. There was absolutely no comparison between innocent little Lynne Castle and Julia, his ex-wife.

Julia had been a hard woman – even harder than he was, though he hadn't seen it in the beginning. What he'd seen was a woman of singular physical beauty who wanted, as he did, another human being with whom to share the triumphs as well as setbacks of life. He'd enjoyed her company, liked her humor, even appreciated her dark side, her moods, because he knew he had his own and that she accepted them in him. He had loved her.

He had promised 'in sickness and in health' and heard the promise given back to him, yet, when it had come right down to it, she had seen a lack over which he had no control not as a sickness but as a betrayal. She'd had their marriage annulled because of it.

A divorce from Julia he might have handled better; he'd suspected for some time that whatever had brought them together in the first place was gone. Despite that, the annulment had been a slap in the face, a public statement that what he once had perceived as very real, though perhaps far from perfect, had never existed at all. It also branded, him, not their marriage, a failure.

Over the scars, calluses had grown, leaving him hardened and not at all the kind of man Lynne Castle needed. Nor did he need a soft little girl like her, a delicate, gentle person who would never be able to understand the demons that drove him – nor withstand them when they came out of hiding.

Mindful that Lynne had left her bicycle in the office building over the weekend, Cliff arrived at her house Monday morning in what he thought would be plenty of time to offer her a ride to work. Once he learned from the old man upstairs she had set out walking half an hour before, he slammed his car door so hard, it likely did internal damage to its workings.

Why couldn't she have waited for him? Didn't it occur to her that he'd come by to get her?

When he arrived at the office, she was safely ensconced behind her desk, peering at the top sheet of a sheaf of papers as Joe tapped a pencil on it and explained something to her.

Unseen, Cliff watched as Lynne slanted a smile up at Joe and thanked him for his help. Before they could notice him, he slipped into his own office and shut the door.

All the rest of the day, he forced himself to keep his office door closed, to ignore the sound of Lynne's voice, her laughter, both of which he heard during the lunch break. He knew half the men would be clustered around her desk, the rest crowded into the doorway just to be near her.

He wanted to go and clear them all out but it was lunch hour and they had every right to eat wherever they wanted.

He kept his head bent over his work, his hands

busy on his computer keyboard, tried to keep his mind filled with the crisp cleanliness and logic of numbers. Yet she was there, just across the hall, and he knew it, was aware of it on some elemental level that couldn't be ignored.

He remained in place, even hearing all the others exchange their goodbyes for the night. Then, when all was quiet, he allowed himself to lean back in his chair and let his shoulders slump.

They ached with tension. Knotted ropes of muscles shot pain into his head. His stomach hurt.

Tuesday was no better. He kept himself locked away in his office, emerging only when, during the lunch hour, he realized everyone else must have gone out in the warm June sunshine to eat. He envisioned Lynne surrounded by every other man in the office, possibly on a patio at a nearby restaurant, or maybe sitting on a park bench eating take-out or home-made sandwiches. He hoped they'd make sure she was protected from the sun.

After writing a page of instructions, he took a folder out to the receptionist's desk, asking her to give it to Lynne on her return with the instructions that it was her next day's assignment. The plump, matronly Mrs Wilkes smiled angelically at him and promised to see to it. Was he, she asked, planning to be out of the office this afternoon and the following day?

In other words, he assumed, she was asking why he didn't give Lynne the assignment himself.

He didn't explain, merely said he'd be busy and preferred not to be disturbed.

He could only hope that if Lynne had any questions about the account she'd ask someone else, and leave him alone. The less time he spent in her company, the better.

What the hell had he been thinking of, agreeing with Grant's proposal that he make himself Lynne's mentor? She didn't need him. There were other qualified accountants in the firm, any and all of whom appeared more than willing to take her under their wings. Especially that damned Joe Barnes. Had Joe broken up with his flavor of the month, and did he see Lynne as the prime replacement?

The thought made his stomach churn.

If Lynne did have questions about the Peterson account on Wednesday, she didn't bring them to Cliff and he told himself he was glad. After listening to everyone leave for the night, he slammed his chair back, rose, and grabbed his jacket. With it draped over his shoulder, he shut and locked his office door, turned and saw Lynne still sitting at her desk, head bent over a ledger.

'What are you doing here?' he said, and realized, as she jumped, that he'd startled her, maybe even frightened her with his harsh bark.

She didn't look frightened. She looked, well, glad to see him. Her blue eyes shone as she smiled at him. 'Cliff! I didn't know you were still in the office. I haven't seen you for days. I'm not quite finished the Peterson account. Did I do okay on the project you gave me yesterday?'

He hadn't seen it. 'You did fine.'

She smiled again and turned back to her work.

He stepped inside her office. 'Leave it,' he said. 'We aren't slave-drivers here and you won't get paid extra for overtime. Your hours are from eight to five with an hour off for lunch. You need all your extra time for studying. In case no one's thought to mention it, your final exams are going to be tough. You'll need to be prepared.'

Her smile had gone when she glanced back up at him. 'I will be, and wasn't looking for overtime pay. I ran into a few problems, though, and it took me longer than I anticipated to get them sorted out.'

He leaned in the door-frame. 'What kind of problems?' Perversely, now, he was annoyed that she hadn't asked him for help. 'You're supposed to bring them to me so I can help you.'

She shrugged. 'The guys said when your door was shut it meant you were either very busy or in a –' She broke off and closed the ledger on her desk, made a few strokes on her keyboard and shut down her computer.

'Or in a foul mood,' he finished for her as she dragged a plastic cover over her monitor.

Head tilted on one side, she looked at him speculatively. 'Which was it?'

His own laughter surprised Cliff.

'Come on,' he said, without elaborating on the mood he'd been in the past several days. As usual, in her company, he found his ill-humor evaporating however hard he tried to maintain it. 'It's time you went home.'

'Okay.' She stood and tugged a small green

canvas knapsack from behind her door. 'I have to change, though, but don't worry, I'll lock up. Good night, Cliff.'

He didn't move out of her doorway. 'Change?'

She ran her hand over her pale gold jacket and beige linen skirt. 'Into my bike shorts and shoes. I can't ride home like this.'

He gestured at the window where rain sheeted down. 'You can't ride home *in* this.'

She laughed. 'Of course I can. It was raining when I came to work this morning and I survived.'

'It wasn't raining this hard then and you are not getting on a bike tonight, Lynne.' He plucked her bag away and took her elbow with his free hand. 'Let's go.'

Lynne gave serious consideration to digging in her heels, but the rain beating against her office window did look vicious and she knew how it would sting her skin as she rode. The streets would be slick and visibility poor. It would be downright stupid not to accept a ride home. It would also, she realized as she and Cliff stepped into the elevator together, be futile. The grip on her elbow never eased off even after the door had slid shut, as if he were afraid she might somehow escape.

'This isn't the way to my house,' she said five minutes into the drive.'

'I know.' His tone was curt. 'We're going out to eat.'

'But I have chicken-barley soup in my slow-cooker,' she protested. 'It'll be ready just about now.'

'So save it for tomorrow.'

'Tomorrow it might be eighty degrees and I won't want to eat soup.'

He pulled to a stop in the drenched parking lot of a chain fast food restaurant. 'Well, I need dinner, and since I always eat out except when I'm at my cabin, you're just going to have to join me.'

Now Lynne did dig in her heels. 'If you want to go and ruin your constitution on a greasy hamburger and greasier fries, feel free. I can either wait here for you, or take a bus home, or walk. Or,' she added, 'since your prime concern seems to be not having to cook for yourself, you could come and help me eat that big pot of homemade soup and the salmon sandwiches I plan to make to go with it.'

He stared at her as if he didn't quite believe what he was hearing. 'You'll come inside with me, and you'll eat.'

She folded her arms across her chest. 'I'm staying here, thank you very much.'

His already square jaw seemed to grow sharper corners. 'You are not. You'll come in if I have to carry you.'

Excitement fluttered through her at the notion. She remembered the strength of his arms around her. He could pick her up easily and carry her. 'Would you really go to those lengths?'

He hesitated. 'Probably not, but don't tempt me, Lynne.'

'Even if you force me to go into that restaurant with you, I won't eat. I'll sit there patiently and quietly and watch while you do.'

His eyes narrowed as he studied her. 'You'd do that, wouldn't you? Just to spite me.'

'Not to spite you. To save my own digestion. I cooked soup and intend to eat it.' She smiled. 'As I said, you're welcome to join me.'

'No.'

She shrugged. 'Suit yourself. Would you rather I wait here, or inside?'

She watched the battle he fought with himself and bit back a smile when he caved in. 'All right, dammit, I'll drive you home so you can have your soup.'

'And you'll join me?'

He glowered as he backed the car out of the lot. 'No.'

If it hadn't been for the fire truck, police car and ambulance in her driveway, Cliff would have simply dropped her off and run. But there they were, lights flashing in the rain, and Lynne's gasp of dismay, her white face and huge eyes kept him from fleeing.

She was out of the car before he could stop her. He followed, ears assaulted by the ululating wail of a smoke-detector. He'd nearly caught her when she grabbed the arm of a fireman who stood, axe poised to batter down her door. 'No! Don't! I have a key!'

Lynne's soup was, in a word, toast. Disgusted, she flung the slow-cooker into the garbage can, burned soup and all. Clearly, her mother had had good reason to have tucked it into in its box and left it unused for years. The darn thing didn't work! She should have remembered her mother's propensity

91

for not throwing things away, but storing them against the day when she 'might' get them repaired.

The old man upstairs, hearing her smoke-detector start screaming, had come hammering on her door. Receiving no answer, he'd dialed 9–1–1 and, not knowing if she was in her suite or not, the dispatcher had sent an ambulance as well as the fire department. The police, thinking something big was going on, had also attended. And all because her mother's old crock-pot had a wonky thermostat.

'That,' she said, glaring at the small white disk in the ceiling, 'is one hair-triggered smoke alarm.'

'Good.' Cliff propped his elbows on the table. 'It'll keep you a whole lot safer than one that's slow to react. Now,' he said, 'since all the emergency vehicles have departed and you've done away with your miscreant pot, are you ready to go out for dinner?' He lifted a hand to forestall her refusal. 'I promise you, no greasy burgers or fries. You can even have soup and a sandwich if that's what you want.'

What could she say? What could she do? Lynne hesitated only briefly before nodding. To her amazement, when they returned to the outdoors, it was to find the rain had stopped, the sun shone brightly again, and great puffy white clouds drifted slowly up the sides of the mainland mountains on the far side of Georgia Strait.

The restaurant Cliff took her to was quiet, intimate, and dim inside. Soft music soothed her rather frazzled nerves and the menu, as he'd promised, did offer minestrone soup and several varieties of sandwiches. But before she could order that, he recommended the lasagne, making her laugh by kissing his fingertips like an Italian chef and tossing the kiss toward the dark-beamed ceiling. 'And a bottle of Chianti,' he said to the aproned man who stood patiently waiting.

Over the delicious meal, Lynne found herself relating more and more details of her childhood, the great times she and her family had enjoyed.

He laughed when she told him of one camping trip when she was six. Her parents had gone out for drinks with friends, leaving her with her big brother in the tent. A violent electric storm had erupted and, terrified, she'd cowered in her sleeping bag until she was nothing but a small ball of quivering humanity down in its bottom. 'Like,' Taylor had said, 'an orange in the toe of a Christmas stocking.' It had taken all his persuasive powers to talk her out of there before she smothered.

The next year, her parents had bought a trailer so Lynne wouldn't feel so exposed to the weather.

That had been lucky, she said, not just for her family, but for a bunch of other campers the next summer in the Rockies where a nocturnal visitor from the forest had sent a whole series of tenters shrieking in terror. That night, the Castle family's trailer had been refuge for eight frightened campers who refused to return to their frail tents with a bear on the loose.

Daylight though, had proven the visitor to have been not a grizzly, but a family of curious and hungry raccoons.

'Did you always go camping on vacation?' Cliff asked. Was he just making conversation, or did she detect a wistful softness in his eyes. In the dim restaurant, it was difficult to tell. Still, something in his voice reached out to her and she had to clasp her hands together so as not to take one of his and give it a comforting squeeze.

'No,' she said. 'A couple of times we went to Hawaii, once to Disneyland, and once we took the train from coast to coast. That was great! We met so many interesting people. Taylor and I spent almost every waking moment in the observation car.'

'Did you and your brother never fight?'

'No. The age difference may account for that, though I think it's simply because Taylor is such a fantastic person. He's so . . . *good*, Cliff. I adore him and admire him. I've never met another man like him, not even my dad, who was a great man in his own right.'

'That'll make it difficult for any man who wants to marry you. He'll have to compete with your big brother for your affections.'

She laughed at his sour tone. 'Don't be silly! Taylor is my brother. If I ever marry, it will be because I love the man in question in an entirely different way.'

Abruptly, he changed the subject, and soon after, paid the bill and they left.

'Thanks for dinner, Cliff,' Lynne said as they stood outside her door. 'I owe you one. How about Friday?' She grinned. 'I promise not to burn it. I **really** am a good cook.'

'I believe you,' he said. 'You don't have to prove anything to me.'

'So you'll come?'

She watched the hesitation in his eyes, saw his mouth harden into a taut line. He shook his head. 'No. Thanks all the same but I have . . . plans.'

Disappointment clogged her throat, but she swallowed it. 'Of course,' she said. 'I understand.'

'Do you, Lynne?' he asked. 'I wonder.' He took her chin in his hand, tilted her face up and kissed her gently. She shivered as pleasure trickled through her, and slipped her arms up to his shoulders.

'No,' he said.

'Yes.' She slid her hands into the thickness of his hair and then his mouth was on hers again, hard, demanding, seeking a response she had no hesitation in offering. He pulled her so close she felt the strength of his desire, and for the first time, knew the deep, primordial need that draws a woman to a man. She shuddered, arching her back, pressing herself to him.

Gasping, he jerked his mouth from hers, put his hands around her upper arms and set her away. His breath rasped in and out harshly. 'Now,' he said. 'Now do you understand? I want you, Lynne. But it's not going to happen. Ever.'

'Why, when I want you, too?' she asked, but doubted if he'd heard her, though. He'd turned to stride back to his car.

Once there, standing behind the open door as if it could somehow protect him from her, he turned. 'I'll pick you up in the morning.'

'You don't have – '

He cut her off. 'Eight-fifteen. Be on time.' He ducked into the car, slammed the door and reversed out of the driveway, leaving strips of rubber as he turned on to the street.

What a strange, contradictory man he was. How he confused her. And how he fascinated her . . .

CHAPTER 6

Stay away from her. Cliff clenched his teeth and repeated the sentence over and over silently every time he found himself drawn to Lynne's office during the next week. He checked once per day to make sure she wasn't having any difficulty with the tasks he assigned her, but beyond that, he kept to himself.

It did him no good at all and it was his own fault. He'd kissed her that evening upon leaving her brother's home. And he'd kissed her again outside her apartment. What a fool! If he hadn't done that, he wouldn't remember the soft trembling of her lips, the way they'd parted shyly for him, the feel of her in his arms. Her scent somehow lingered in his car, even days after she'd last been in it.

She invaded his dreams at night to the point where he wondered if he should even bother trying to sleep. When it became impossible to escape thoughts of her, he'd put on jogging clothes and run until he was physically exhausted. Sometimes after that he could get a few hours' rest.

When, one Saturday night in early July, he was jogging and heard the low rumble of thunder in the distance, he turned and headed for home. Half a block later, as lightning flashed and forked in the sky, and black clouds billowed up to blot out the stars, he made a quick left and headed toward Lynne's house. He wanted not to, but his feet kept running that way, his stride lengthening as the storm worsened.

She's all right, he told himself.

No, she's not. She's afraid.

A particularly loud crash of thunder sped him onward, even when the rain began to pelt down in hard, stinging drops. Wind rose, whipping his sodden shorts against his legs, plastering his T-shirt to his chest and back. The sky lit up again and almost simultaneously, the crack of thunder shattered the night.

The vision of Lynne, cowering and terrified, curled in her bed with her head under the covers propelled him onward. She was young and single and female and alone. She was an employee of his company. He had a duty to see to her well-being. He had promised himself he'd act as her big brother would and this – going to make sure she was all right – was exactly what Taylor would do.

His plan to knock lightly, not to terrify her more than she must already be, deserted him. He pounded on her door as he called her name.

As if she'd been waiting for him, she jerked the door open and gaped at him. Her eyes were wide, her face pale, her hair a circle of glowing color all around as if she'd been dragging her hands through its curls – or hiding her head in her arms. She wore a thin, cotton robe, white with tiny flowers on it. Her feet were bare. Her toenails were painted the same pale pink as her fingernails. Her mouth parted as she stared at him.

She took two steps back and he followed her in as the wind slammed the door behind him. 'What in the world are you doing out on a night like this?' she demanded.

Water streamed from his hair down his face. He wiped it off with a bent arm. It did no good. 'I came to see if you were all right.'

'Of course I am,' she said, but her trembling voice belied her words. 'You're not, though,' she went on, her voice steadying as if having someone with her gave her courage. 'You're soaked! Look at you.' She plucked his T-shirt away from his stomach. It sucked back tight when she released it. 'Right to the skin.'

She grabbed his arm and dragged him with her. Cliff didn't quite know how he let it happen, but before he realized he should resist, she'd pulled him into the bathroom and tossed a towel over his head. 'You must be out of your mind, jogging on a night like this!' she scolded, shoving him down on to the edge of the bathtub. Stepping in between his knees, she scrubbed vigorously at his hair with the towel, pulling his face against her front to hold his head still.

The scent of her skin was like a blow to his heart. The warmth of her body, the feel of her breasts, the sound of her voice nearly made him pass out. He tried not to breathe, but that only increased his light-headedness. He wanted to shove her away, but his hands, once locked around her narrow waist, wouldn't move.

He tried speak, but could not. He wanted to warn her of the danger she was in, wanted to beg her to step away from him, but his voice remained locked in his throat even as his heart threatened to explode from his chest.

Just when he thought he could stand not one more second of this, mercifully, she stepped back and he was able to draw a shaken breath. Before he could muster the strength to stand, she crowded in on him again and to his shock, dragged his soggy T-shirt off him and dropped it into the tub with a splat.

'What idiots men are!' she grumbled. 'This is exactly like something Tay would have done.'

'I know. That's why I – '

She shut him up by the simple expedient of flinging a larger towel across his back and tugging on the ends as she seesawed it over his skin. It smelled clean and fresh, and felt slightly rough, as if it had been dried outdoors.

Then, to his shock, she crouched before him and tugged off his soaked shoes and socks, lifted one of his feet and began to rub it dry.

Finally finding some strength of will, he put a stop to that and snatched the towel from her. His shorts still dripped down his legs as he stood. His wet face had made a damp spot on the front of her robe. Her skin glowed pale pink through it. He nearly groaned aloud. Dammit, was she wearing nothing at all under that frail garment?

Of course not. She hadn't been expecting anyone to come pounding on her door. She'd called him an idiot plus a few other choice terms while drying his hair.

'I'll get you a blanket,' she said. 'Take those off.' She gestured at his shorts.

He caught her arm and glared at her. 'No.' To his surprise, she glared right back. He tried to stare her down. 'I'm fine.'

She refused to be intimidated. 'You are not fine. You're shivering. Your skin is covered with goosebumps.' She touched his arm, running the tips of her fingers from wrist to elbow. He had to squeeze his eyes shut for an instant as he brought himself under tight control. 'Look,' she said. 'Your hairs are all standing on end.'

From the cold drenching or from her touch, he couldn't have said, and didn't really want to know. In self-defense, he clasped his hands over her shoulders, meaning to shove her aside so he could squeeze out the bathroom door, but she slipped away from him and shut the door on her way out.

Seconds later, it opened a crack and she shoved a folded sheet at him. 'Take off those wet shorts and wrap yourself in this. Throw them and your other stuff out here so I can put them in the dryer.' Her voice rose on the last word, the result of another clap of thunder. Even in the windowless bathroom he saw the flash.

'Lynne, dammit, don't try to mother me. I just came to see if you were all right. Now I know you are, I'll be on my way.'

The last couple of words were all but drowned out by a crash of thunder so close it rattled the windows.

He heard Lynne squeal in fright.

Quickly, he stripped off his dripping shorts, wrapped the sheet around him sarong style, tucking it in tightly, and stepped out to where she waited.

Then another blast shook the house and the lights went out, plunging them into an inky black so deep it was almost palpable. Suddenly, Lynne was plastered against his bare chest as tightly as his T-shirt had been, her warm cheek pressed to him, her arms around his waist as she clung to him, trembling.

For a long, aching moment he tried not to hold her, but it was a futile attempt. When he locked his arms around her, rocking her gently from side to side, murmuring comforting nonsense, she burrowed closer, tightening her grip.

He groaned. The need to touch her skin overcame him and he stroked his thumb down the curve of her cheek, then pushed her hair back on one side, exposing the most beautiful, perfect little ear he'd ever touched. Before he could stop himself, he kissed it, outlining its shape with his lips, feeling her quiver in his arms. Curved like a shell, her ear lay flat against her head and had no lobe to speak of. Her skin below it was as soft as rose petals, as fragrant as any garden he'd ever been in, and as tempting as if Satan himself had conjured it up just to entrap him.

The next flash of lightning left him with an after-image of the short hallway leading to her living room and he scooped her up, carrying her from the bathroom.

Somehow, in the heavy darkness, he blundered his way to an overstuffed sofa and lowered himself into it, still holding her. Her arms slid around his neck and she hid her face in the bend of his shoulder.

'Don't be afraid,' he said. 'I won't let it hurt you.'

'I'm not afraid,' she said. 'I'm not. I'm just . . . a little nervous. I know thunderstorms are nothing more than noise and light. I know it, but . . .'

He lowered his cheek to her hair. 'But inside, you're still a six-year-old curled up in the bottom of your sleeping bag.'

'Y-yes.'

'And that's why I came.'

She nestled closer, her lips warm against his skin as she spoke. 'I'm glad.'

Two simple words. A soft tone of voice. An admission of need. Cliff knew, in that moment, he was a goner.

He didn't realize, though, just how far gone he was until she slid her lips up his throat, cupped one hand around the back of his head and pulled him down to her.

'Cliff, kiss me. Please.'

Lynne didn't know where it had come from, that boldness of hers, she knew only that if Cliff didn't kiss her something in her was going to tear apart into small, shattered bits.

She felt him shudder, felt the heat now emanating from his body, heard his soft groan, then his mouth was on hers, his hand thrusting through the tangles of her curls, cradling the back of her head as he tilted her to a more accessible position.

The hot, hard thrust of his tongue parted her lips fully, and she tasted him, loving it. He smelled of rain and fresh air and something else she imagined was uniquely him. His biceps bunched as she slid one hand down his shoulder and arm. Something, she didn't know what, instinct, maybe, told her to rake his flesh gently with her nails.

His groan told her he liked it and she did it again. His arms convulsed around her as he deepened the kiss. His day-old beard prickled her skin, adding to the heady sensations. She wanted more, aching in deep, secret places as she had never ached before. In all her encounters with boys and men, nothing had ever felt like this. He filled her every sense. The sound of his breathing, the taste of his mouth, the scent of his skin, the feel of his hands on her, all enhanced by the total darkness surrounding them.

When his hand slid inside her robe and cupped her breast, she gasped with the mingled pleasure and pain that shafted through her on golden threads, uniting all her erogenous zones until she felt she might go up in flames.

'Cliff . . .'

'Baby, baby,' he murmured against her throat, thumb and finger tugging gently at her nipple. 'So sweet, Lynne, so soft. I want to kiss you everywhere.'

'*Yes!*'

She arched her back and his head dropped lower as his hand slid to the underside of her breast, then his mouth was upon her, drawing her nipple into his heated wetness, his tongue flicking it, teasing it, making her squirm and cry out his name again.

Something . . . something unknown, something only hinted at before in her body's responses, but something she sensed would be stupendous, flowered outward from her core. It grew, filling her with a need that could surely never be met however hard she strained to reach it. It had to do with the gentle, rhythmic tugging of his mouth at her breast, that set up an echoing pulse deep in her lower belly. She wanted . . . She needed . . . There were no words to describe the indescribable, only a sure knowledge that whatever it was she sought, Cliff could give her.

'Please, please,' she moaned as she shifted against the hardness of him under her buttocks and thrilled to it. He wanted her just as much as she wanted him. His need was as great. 'Cliff, I need you!'

His breath rushed in and out. Under her hand, she felt the rapid tattoo of his heart slamming against his ribs. It echoed the racing of her own. He tilted her back on to the cushions of the sofa, kneeling over her, his mouth hot on her breasts, one, then the other, teasing, suckling, making her strain closer, want more.

'Cliff . . .' She knew she was on the verge of an incredible discovery. It was something she had wondered about, dreamt about, read about, and with him she'd found it, surely she had. Another flash showed his eyes, all but closed, as he traced her shape with both his hands. Slowly, sensuously, he slid his palms over her breasts, down her waist, around her hips and along her thighs.

She quivered and slid one leg out and around him, hearing his swiftly in drawn breath. 'Lynne . . .' It was a hoarse, almost pained whisper, filled with need and a strong protesting of that need. It made her want to soothe him, ease him, show him how right this was.

'Make love to me,' she said, drawing his hand to that hot, aching part of her, yearning for his touch. She shuddered as he parted her folds, stroking her slickness, probing gently, first with one finger, then two, opening her.

She writhed against his hand, shifted her other leg until it, too, slid along his flank, dragging his sheet with it. She raked her hands down his chest again, reveling in his heated skin, the quiver that her touch elicited. She felt at once weak and powerful, wanting to take, and wanting to give. Confusion made her head spin. She'd never done anything like this, never felt such a need. Did he think she was a wanton? She'd drawn his hand to her, begging for his intimate touch, and now even that wasn't enough.

Shyly, tentatively, she touched his erection, felt him jerk away from her. 'No!' he hissed.

'Yes,' she cried. 'Oh, please . . .' Need overcame doubts, allowing her to plead, to touch him again and then, with a groan, he cupped his hands around her bottom and lifted her to him.

Cliff shook so hard with wanting her he didn't know if he could control himself long enough to pleasure her. The sensation of her hot, slippery wetness against his tip nearly put him over the edge. He clenched his teeth, easing into her. His exploration with his fingers had told him how small she was, how tight, and her kisses, though heartfelt, suggested lack of experience.

But it wasn't until he felt a slight resistance as he entered her, felt her flinch, that he knew exactly how inexperienced she was. With a cry, she surged up against him, locked her legs around him and held him tightly. He squeezed his eyes shut as thunder rolled through the air with almost as much force as the blood that pulsed through him. His heart set up a steady, hard rhythm as he loved her for the very first time.

Her first time!

Oh, God, he felt like a giant, he felt like a louse, he felt like a hero and a villain all rolled into one, but nothing could have made him stop as her muscles begin to spasm around him and he heard her sharp, startled cry. Then she sobbed and writhed against him, pressing closer, tighter, her hips moving in a series of surges he could scarcely follow as they tumbled him into ecstasy.

He tasted her tears, felt her soft weeping, and hated himself for what he'd done to her. 'Hush, little Lynne,' he murmured. 'I'm sorry, baby. I'm so sorry I hurt you. I didn't know. Oh, God, Lynnie, why didn't you tell me?'

She slid her hands into his hair, pulled his head

down for a salty kiss. 'Cliff . . .' Her whisper was soft, filled with awe, he thought. 'I didn't know either.'

He jerked halfway up. 'Didn't know you were a virgin?'

'Oh, that,' she said dismissively. 'Of course I knew that. But the rest of it . . . I didn't know it would be like that.'

'The pain. If you'd told me I could have – '

'Pain?' she said as the lights came on. She blinked at him in the sudden glow of the lamp across the room and two more tears fell from her eyes. 'There was no pain. I'm talking about the . . . the glory of it. It was so . . . magnificent.'

'Then why were you crying?'

'I wasn't.'

'You were.' He caught a drop of moisture that hung just under the edge of her chin, held it up on the tip of his finger for her to see.

'Well, I'll be darned,' she said. Then, with a devastating smile and another little wiggle of her hips, she asked, 'Do you think we could do it again?'

'No . . .' His voice grated softly through his ragged breathing. 'I've done enough damage, Lynne.'

'Damage?' she asked, sliding her palms down his chest. His nipples responded, too swiftly, too intensely, as her fingertips brushed over them sending jolts of sensation straight to his groin. 'I don't feel damaged, Cliff. I feel . . . wonderful.' He watched her throat work as she swallowed. Her eyes shone. 'And I want, very much, to feel all that magic again.'

Her eagerness made him laugh. It also made him rock-hard again. 'Lynne, you'll be sore, honey. Enough now. Please.'

But it wasn't enough, Lynne knew. Not for her. She didn't think there could ever be enough for her. Enough of Cliff Foreman. She trailed her fingers over his face, hearing the midnight rasp of his whiskers. They had scraped her cheek and chin and breast, sensitizing her skin so that his kisses felt like warm honey wherever his lips touched her. How much she wanted those indescribable sensations again!

He tried to jerk his head away but she knew he wanted her again, felt the hard press of his penis against her belly. She moved subtly, and he froze. 'Lynne! No. No more. God, girl, do you have any idea what you're doing to me?'

What *she* was doing to *him*? 'Nothing more than what you're doing to me, Cliff,' she said, her voice unsteady. 'And I am not a girl. I am a woman.'

In that moment, she knew she was, finally, a real woman. Never had she felt more like one, or been more certain of her destiny. Maybe it wasn't supposed to happen this fast, but it had. Maybe it wasn't supposed to go this deep, this soon, but there was no denying it had. He had changed her, and there was no going back. She could never be what she had been before.

'A woman, Cliff,' she said again, wanting him to understand. *A woman who had found her man.* How she wished she dared to say it.

'You only think you are,' he said, his voice as low

as the fading rumble of thunder as it moved off into the distance. 'But I can see what you are. You're an innocent girl, Lynne, a soft, gentle child a man like me would crush.'

'No way! I'm tougher than I look. And I –' She broke off, swallowing the words she really wanted to say. 'I . . . need you,' she substituted.

He laughed, the sound without mirth in the darkness of the room. 'I'm not what you need.'

'How can you possibly know that?'

'I have eyes in my head, Lynne. I saw you with your niece. You need some nice, tame boy who will marry you and give you lots of babies and a good, clean life with no upsets, no turmoil, no pain.'

'No life is without pain.'

'Yours should be. If you don't believe me, ask Taylor. He'll agree.'

She had to laugh. 'This is something I think I'd prefer not to discuss with Taylor.'

Guilt flooded his face. 'Oh, God. Me too.'

'Then we won't,' she said, stroking his shoulders. 'But you and I, Cliff, we'll discuss it. And we'll do more than that. Won't we?'

He closed his eyes again, but not before she saw the yearning in them, the struggle for control that quivered in every taut muscle in his body. Reaching down, she clasped him gently, moving her hand. 'Is this how you like me to touch you? I want to make you feel as good as you made me feel. Am I doing it right?' she asked. 'Show me how, Cliff. Teach me.'

CHAPTER 7

'Yesss . . .' His breath whistled in and out and then, as she made the same motion again with her hand, he capitulated. He covered her hand with his and moved it just the way he wanted, then, only moments later, he tore it from him and entered her in one strong thrust that filled her with his power, sent need spiraling again deep inside her.

This time, he moved slower, holding her so she couldn't increase the pace, taking it slowly, kissing her eyelids, her face, her mouth, all the while stroking in and out of her with a deliberate rhythm. The sensations grew stronger, rippling through her, sending her head tossing from side to side, making her squeeze her eyes tightly shut.

'Look at me,' he said raggedly, and she opened her eyes to see the darkness of his turned even blacker, lines of strain in his face, his mouth a hard, taut slash. She managed to lift one trembling hand and cup his cheek with her palm. He pressed his lips into it, thrusting with his tongue as he thrust with his body and great waves of color washed over

111

her vision, along with spasms so intense she thought she might die. Then she was shattering, flying apart into thousands of points of dancing light, and only dimly heard Cliff's shout of triumph.

When she woke, she was in her bed, alone, and, from the silence in her apartment, suspected Cliff had gone. A quick search proved her right, and she cringed inwardly, remembering how she had flung herself into his arms when that huge clap of thunder had shaken the walls. She remembered, too, his tortured expression when he'd said, 'I'm not what you need.'

He'd said no. He'd tried to stop what was happening, but she had made it impossible for him to call a halt. And so he'd left, likely ashamed, or angry, or both.

She covered her face with her hands, reliving the moments of the night before. Oh, she had been shameless! She *had* been the one to instigate their lovemaking, even after he'd made it clear it wasn't what he wanted.

Restlessly, she paced through the back door to the sun-warmed patio. The damp garden steamed. Fresh strawberries gleamed wet and red within their nests of dark green leaves. Brown-eyed susans glowed bright yellow against the brick wall and bachelor buttons bobbed their blue heads. The peaceful scene did nothing to soothe her ragged emotions.

A quick search of the papers in her desk produced the fax he'd sent her after their disastrous first interview, giving her his home phone number.

She punched it into her portable phone and curled on a garden seat, breathing in the scent of grass and flowers and newly washed earth, listening to his phone ring and ring at the other end. Maybe he just wasn't home yet.

She brewed a pot of coffee, drank a cup, and tried again. Still no answer. An hour later, following repeated unanswered calls, she slipped her bike out of its storage locker and mounted it, riding it fast all the way to the Harbour where gulls called, water sparkled, and sun gleamed on clean, white sails. What would she do if Cliff were so angry with her and himself he told Grant he couldn't work with her any more? What if they sent her away for being a bad influence on office morale? Where she'd find another firm to sponsor her during this crucial year, she didn't know, and the thought terrified her, but not as much as the thought of never seeing Cliff again.

The salty breeze finally calmed her, and she rode home in better spirits. On Monday, the two of them would discuss what had happened, and, like the rational adults they were, would reach a reasoned decision as to what was to be done about it. She knew what she wanted. About Cliff, she was much less certain.

To her dismay, he wasn't at work either Monday or Tuesday. Grant and Nita had returned, well-pleased with their ship's cruise to Alaska and the long drive home along back-roads through mountainous country. It wasn't until Wednesday that she learned Cliff was on vacation.

On vacation? Without so much as a phone call to say goodbye? On vacation, after what had transpired between them, as if it had meant nothing to him? Which was, she slowly began to realize as the days passed and she heard nothing from him, exactly the case. What, to her, had been a magical awakening had been, to Cliff, a momentary loss of self-control. She'd been making love; he'd been having sex with a willing, if inexperienced partner.

He'd probably given it no more thought than he would a stroll in the park – pleasant, maybe, but entirely forgettable.

Late one Friday afternoon, Lynne looked up from her computer when Grant tapped on the open door of her office. She smiled. She'd begun to relax since Grant and Nita had returned. Cliff's absence helped, but in only two more weeks he'd be back from his vacation.

'Lynne,' Grant said, 'I have a special job for you.' An unaccustomed frown creased his brow. 'Kim was slated for it, but his mother's just been taken into the hospital with chest pains.'

'Of course,' she said. 'Whatever I can do to help.'

Grant smiled. 'That's the spirit of co-operation I like to see. By the way, have I told you how impressed we all are with the quality of your work?'

Lynne laughed. 'Only about a dozen times since you've been back, but I love to hear it.' What she would have loved more was to think that 'we' of Grant's included Cliff. He was constantly on her mind. She dreamed of him every night and all too

114

often during the day, as well.

Even going out with Joe Barnes to watch beach volleyball and have a swim one evening, a movie another, and a drive last Sunday afternoon to Englishman River Falls, where they'd hiked for hours, hadn't helped her to stop missing Cliff. She'd dated a couple of the men she'd met at the block party shortly after she moved in, but didn't expect to see either of them again except in passing. Neither had interested her much and she thought the feeling mutual. The bar-scene didn't appeal to her.

'This'll be good for you,' Grant said, breaking into her thoughts. 'It'll get you outdoors for a while, maybe put some color in your cheeks.'

'What? I'm outdoors most days. I ride to and from work, I spend what free hours I can gardening.'

'Nevertheless, you're pale. Nita was saying just last night how peaked you've been looking. You're not sick, are you?'

Only at heart, she could have said. 'No, of course not. You're just used to seeing everyone else with nice summer tans, which I never get because I use thirty-power sunblock. I only look pale in comparison.'

He narrowed his gaze on her. 'Maybe,' he said. 'But if we're putting too heavy a load on you, I want you to tell me. I know you have to keep studying for your final exams, but don't forget, they're still months away. Don't overdo it.'

'Grant, really, I'm not. I love working here, and

though I hit the books every night, I'd rather keep on top of it than have to face those exams unprepared, or try to cram all the studying in during the last couple of months.'

'Good.' He set a black briefcase on her desk. 'Now, what I want you to do is take this to Cliff. It's very urgent and highly confidential, so you're to put it in his hands only. It'll be quicker and easier for you to take it than for me to try to get a courier company out there to his island hideaway.'

Lynne's head spun. Cliff? She had to take whatever was in that case to Cliff? See him? Talk to him? She'd thought she wanted to, longed to, but now, faced with the possibility, she was suddenly terrified.

'I thought he was on vacation,' she blurted.

Nita poked her head in the door. 'Pah!' she said derisively. 'He is, but the idiot refuses to take vacations seriously. You should have seen the stacks of stuff he took with him. The man's a workaholic. I wish he'd ease up on himself.' She grinned suddenly and gave Lynne a sweeping, speculative glance. 'Maybe he will, with you there.'

'But I won't be staying!' Lynne said in alarm.

'I'm afraid you'll have to spend the weekend,' Grant said. 'Cliff will need all that time to get the work done and will likely need an assistant. Nita booked a room in Kim's name at an inn close to the ferry terminal.' He glanced at his wife, who still hovered in the doorway. 'Can you give Lynne a map showing where Cliff's house is?'

Nita nodded and departed.

'You'll take this –' Grant went on as he patted the briefcase '– and hand it over to him. Whenever he doesn't need you, you're to spend time outdoors, do some exploring, have a little fun. Tell him I said he's to take you somewhere nice for dinner Saturday night. Expense account.'

Lynne couldn't see herself telling Cliff any such thing, but she nodded. Grant handed her an envelope. 'This will cover your ferry fare and incidental expenses. Keep the receipts and hand them in to Nita when you come back. Your room is already paid for on the company credit card.'

She bit her lip. 'But, I – '

Grant frowned again. 'Oh! I should have asked. You have plans, don't you? Joe Barnes? He'll understand, I'm sure. Or,' he added, tentatively, 'if you want, you could invite him along with you for the weekend. I don't know the state of your relationship, but . . . ' He shrugged.

Lynne knew she was blushing. 'We don't have that kind of relationship. I've gone out with him three times, Grant, and we're friends, that's all. And I have no plans for the weekend other than studying.'

Grant perched on the corner of her desk, making it creak ominously. 'Then what was the "but" all about?'

How could she tell him what had transpired between her and Cliff that night during the storm? How could she begin to explain that, as a result of it, Cliff wanted nothing more to do with her, wanted to keep her at more than arm's length?

117

She couldn't, of course.

'Nothing,' she said, shaking her head. 'It's all right.'

'Good,' he said. 'Then scoot now, get home and pack yourself a weekend bag. And Lynne,' he added, rising. 'I meant what I said about enjoying yourself. Don't let Cliff make you work all the time. Get some fresh air. There are lots of nice hikes on Galiano Island.'

She saluted. 'Yessir!'

With a grin, he left her to shut down her computer and clear her desk.

She shouldn't, Lynne knew, feel so eager to see Cliff again. He'd made his position clear, and that was something she'd have to live with. She'd play it cool when she arrived, hand him the papers, and offer her assistance, which she was certain he'd reject. Then she'd spend the weekend as Grant had ordered: getting some fresh air, enjoying herself, and taking some of those hikes. The information pamphlet she'd picked up on the ferry mentioned Montague Harbour, Bodega Ridge, and a spot high on a bluff from which a person could look down into a tree, in the top of which was the nest of a pair of bald eagles. It all sounded fascinating.

Cliff's house, thanks to Nita's map, was easy to find, and only a couple of miles from the inn near the ferry dock. After checking in, she drove there.

A teenager crouched at the edge of the driveway, lazily pulling weeds from flower beds created in pockets in the outcroppings of gray bedrock. He looked up as she came to a halt, unfolded his long legs and sauntered toward her. He wore shorts, no shoes, and no shirt. A baseball cap sat backwards on his head and tufts of blond hair stuck out between the plastic strap across his forehead and the cloth of the blue cap. The tips of his bony shoulders were pink and peeling.

'You Kim?' he asked. 'I'm Robbie. Mr Foreman said to show you around to the front of the house and tell you to make yourself at home. He'll be back around six. Went out with his boat to tow in a friend whose motor packed it in.'

'I'm not Kim. He couldn't make it. I guess I should just go back to the hotel and wait.'

The boy shrugged his skinny, sunburned shoulders. 'Suit yourself, but I think he wanted whoever came with the stuff he needs to stay. He told me to hang around until you arrived and let you in.' He looked at her curiously. 'You an accountant, too?'

She nodded.

'Then I guess you're what he wants.' The boy took the briefcase from her hand and walked up the drive. 'This way.'

She couldn't let him leave with that briefcase, however much she might want to run, so Lynne followed.

Reaching up to the top of a seven-foot high, solid wooden gate, he lifted down a key, unlocked the gate and pushed it open before setting the key back up on its high perch, out of sight. He handed her the briefcase. 'Just latch the gate on the inside,' he said, 'to keep wandering kids from drowning in the pool. Oh yeah, and Mr Foreman said to tell you – or Kim, I guess – to help yourself to the pool and whatever else you want. He left the patio doors unlocked so you can get into the house. Drinks and snacks in the fridge. I'm out of here now. So long.'

With that, he straddled a beat-up bike and pedaled away down the hill and around the curve in the road.

Lynne shoved the gate wider and stepped through, careful to latch it as the boy had said, 'to keep wandering kids from drowning.'

She followed a shrub-lined flagged path, almost like a tunnel with the bushes meeting overhead, cut back only far enough to create a passage, then stepped out into brilliant sunshine and baking heat rising from bare rock and a tiled patio and pool-deck. The area was completely screened from view, on the left by a large arbor, on the right by a massive stand of rustling bamboo. The only view was straight out over the water. Drawn by it, she skirted the bright turquoise pool and leaned on the granite block wall that formed a barrier at the very edge of a sheer drop-off.

A hundred or more feet below, at least fifty small boats fished between Galiano Island and Mayne Island, with a massive white ferry picking its way among them. Sailboats heeled and tacked, cabin cruisers made fanning washes that rocked the smaller craft before bashing up on the shores. Speedboats spurted rooster-tails of spume out behind them. Overhead, gulls and eagles wheeled, vying for airspace.

What a magical place!

Turning, she gazed at the house. Not large, it looked snug and welcoming. She set her briefcase and shoulder bag just inside the door, and sank back on to one of the four chairs deeply cushioned in bright tropical print fabric, surrounding the patio table with its huge umbrella. The cushions and matching umbrella surprised her. She would have thought a plain color, perhaps navy blue, more Cliff's style. The angle of the sun made the umbrella next to useless however she tilted it. Heat beat down on her. She considered going inside, but that, somehow, seemed too great an intrusion.

She rose and wandered to the shade of the arbor. Thick, lush grape vines grew over it, with clusters of half-ripe fruit hanging down.

Dragging a lounge chair from beside the pool, she set it under the arbor and sank on to it. The relief from the sun was wonderful, but she was still so overheated her cotton dress stuck to her, and her bra chafed uncomfortably.

She glanced at the pool. She glanced at her watch. She shook her head. Even if he wouldn't be back for two hours, even though he had said for Kim to make himself at home, he hadn't said *she* could. But oh, how tempting that water looked. A stack of large towels sat on a wicker table near the edge. He'd left them out for Kim, obviously. Would Kim have brought a swimsuit?

Only if Grant had suggested it to him, she was sure. And Grant had *not* suggested it to her.

Go skinny-dipping?

Why not? The gate, latched from the inside, couldn't be opened even with the key. Just a quick dip was all she needed, then she'd dry herself with one of those big towels, dress again, and go on waiting for Cliff.

Hardly had the thought formed than she was pulling off her dress. She draped it over the back of the lounge, kicked out of her shoes, slipped free of her underwear and took three running steps before diving in at the deep end.

It was heavenly! She swam several slow laps, then folded her hands behind her head and floated, reveling in the sensation of tiny wavelets rippling over her. The occasional flutter of her feet kept her from sinking, and her 'quick dip' lengthened into endless minutes of sybaritic pleasure.

Cliff recognized Lynne's car the moment he pulled his boat trailer in beside it. What in the hell was she doing here? A band of tension tightened around his forehead. His hands locked around the wheel, aching until he slowly, deliberately, relaxed his grip.

No. Wait. Don't jump to conclusions. Maybe she'd loaned her car to Kim. Cliff knew the other man's rattle-trap pick-up was less than reliable, and knew, too, how generous Lynne was.

Inside, the house was cool and quiet. He refrigerated the fish his friend had given him as thanks for the rescue, and noticed that the cans of beer and cola, and the bottle of wine he'd left for Kim to choose from, remained untouched, as did the block of cheese beside the drinks, and the box of crackers on the table.

'Kim?'

No answer. Must be outside. In the living room, he saw no indication that anyone had so much as entered the house in his absence. Maybe Kim had taken a walk, despite the heat.

Well, all he wanted now after his hours in the sun, salt and wind towing Barry's broken-down boat back to port, was a swim.

Unceremoniously, he stripped off his shorts and T-shirt, opened the door and padded across the patio. He took a couple of running steps and dove.

He heard a scream before his hands so much as touched the water, but then he was submerged and swimming strongly back to the surface.

A great froth of foam created by a pair of pink feet, kicking wildly, met his water-starred gaze. He blinked his eyes clear, shoved his hair off his forehead and stared.

'Go away!' Lynne said, still kicking up concealing foam. 'Please! You weren't supposed to come home so soon. I – oh, damn! This is so embarrassing!'

A few strokes brought him to her side where she sat on the bottom step at the shallow end, still flailing her legs energetically.

He couldn't help laughing. She blushed so nicely. Or was it sunburn?

'What,' he asked as evenly as he could manage with his breathing as ragged as that of a dying man, and his heart trying to run away with itself, 'are *you* doing here?'

'Swimming!' she wailed, still splashing. 'And I don't have anything *on*.' She wrapped her arms over her breasts.

'Neither,' he informed her, 'do I. So what are we going to do about it? Do you want to close your eyes while I get out and wrap a towel around me, or do you want me to close mine, while you emerge first?'

'I don't care,' she said, her eyes squeezed tight, her face half-averted.

'Or,' he suggested, 'we could just both continue to enjoy our swim. I mean, it's not exactly as though we're strangers to each other's bodies, is it?'

The splashes died down as her legs obviously gave out, and Cliff looked at her slim shape under the ripples on the water. They did nothing to hide her beauty. Her round breasts, under that concealing arm, floated just on the surface.

Her distress was evident as she turned to face him. 'I didn't *mean* for this to happen! Please believe me, Cliff. I don't want you to think I planned this in some kind of attempt to . . . to seduce you. I was just going to take a quick dip, then get dressed again and – Oh, God, you don't believe me, do you?' She released a sound so close to a sob he wanted to gather her into his arms. Hell, he wanted her in his arms, anyway.

'It's just like the night of the storm when I threw myself at you. I'm sorry. I'm so sorry, Cliff.'

He grasped her wrist and pulled her arm away. Her eyes popped open as she turned to meet his gaze.

'You seduce me without meaning to,' he said.

'You seduce me simply by the fact of your existence.' He slid one hand under her breasts, lifted them and bent to lick the drops of water off her nipples.

She made a small, soft sound deep in her throat and let her head fall back on to the top step where the water was only a few inches deep. Her hair floated out around her head like red-gold fronds of some exotic sea anemone. He cupped the back of her head, lifted it and kissed her mouth. 'Oh, God, Lynne,' he said moments later, 'how can I resist you?'

'I don't know,' she whispered. 'I can't seem to resist you, either.'

'Do you want to?'

Her lips trembled. 'No.'

'Is that why you came in Kim's place?'

For a moment, she looked indignant. 'I told you I didn't plan this. I came because Grant asked me to. Kim's mother is ill.'

'Is it wrong for me to be glad about that?' he asked, unable not to smile at her and touch her face, her neck, her shoulders, and her sweet, round breasts.

Lynne returned his smile. 'Probably,' she whispered as one of her nipples hardened and pressed against his palm. 'But I'm as guilty as you are.'

'No. You're sweet and innocent and I should be shot, but so help me, I can't go on like this. I've wanted you every hour, every minute, since the night of the storm. It's been eating away at me, a pain like I've never known.'

'Good,' she murmured, 'because that's how much I've wanted you.'

He kissed her deeply and then there was no turning back. Scooping her out of the water, Cliff carried her to the big lounge chair in the shade of the arbor, laid her on it and joined her, cradling her close while his hands and mouth explored her shape.

She quivered at his touch, gasped when he suckled on her breasts and cried out in stunned surprise when he parted her legs, and kissed her at the juncture of her thighs. Lifting half on to her elbows, she said, 'What are you *doing*?'

'Giving you pleasure,' he said. 'Do you want me to stop?' But he didn't, and before she could reply, before she could even decide if she liked what he was doing, she was caught up in a maelstrom of sensation that coiled from her core until she burned all over.

From a distance, she heard her own voice calling his name, then a whirlwind caught her, spinning her out of control, sending her flying into space and when she began to descend, he was there to hold her close, stroking her back, her face, her arms.

After a long time, she opened her eyes. They glowed. 'I guess we're not in Kansas, Toto.'

Cliff laughed, burying his face against her neck, drinking in her scent, the flavor of her skin. 'Are you likening me to a furry little dog?'

'No. I think you're more like the Wizard.'

He lifted his head to smile at her. 'Who was, as it turned out, just a little old bald-headed man with glasses.'

Her lips curved sweetly. 'You don't qualify. I mean, you're like the image of the Wizard Dorothy carried with her all through Oz.'

He went serious all of a sudden, lifting himself half away from her. But, as if it had a mind of its own, his hand stroked her hair back from her brow. 'I'm no wizard, Lynne. I'm just an ordinary man, with ordinary needs and more than ordinary faults. And I'm no good for you.'

Her eyes flooded with tears that undermined his intention of pulling away from her. 'Oh, Cliff,' she murmured, 'I don't know what to say to convince you you're wonderful for me. I don't know what to do. I want to give you as much pleasure as you gave me and maybe then you'll believe me.' She slid her mouth across his chest, down his abdomen, and he groaned, succumbing.

CHAPTER 8

'Well,' Grant said Monday morning when Lynne
arrived at work. 'You're looking great. The break
must have done you good. I take it Cliff didn't work
you too hard?'

To Lynne's disgust, she felt heat searing her face
and was grateful when Nita arrived to distract her
husband's attention from Lynne. 'Guess what?' she
said, her face a picture of astonishment. 'I just heard
from Cliff. He's taking off this morning for a drive
down the Oregon coast. He says he won't be back in
touch till his vacation's over. And,' she added, her
gray eyes forming disbelieving circles, 'he said he's
not taking any work with him!'

Grant whistled. 'Well! I guess you must have
done him some good, too, Lynne. I guess my
sending you over there to work with him for a
weekend was a smart move. He's very protective
of women. Maybe he's afraid if he hangs around I'll
send you over again.'

Lynne suspected Grant was absolutely right, but
not for the reason he assumed. She knew why Cliff
had gone. To escape her, to give her no chance at all

to go to him and make him feel guilty all over again for wanting her, for accepting what she wanted to give him.

Cliff had not worked her too hard, and she had learned far more about love than she had about accounting, and learned, too, how much greater importance the former had over the latter. That such depth of emotion was all on her side, she didn't doubt. Somehow, it seemed not to matter.

Loving Cliff was enough. Having him make love to her, hold her with exquisite tenderness, touch her with delicate care, seduce her with words and kisses and caresses, made up for his silence.

If he can't love me, maybe I can love enough for both of us . . .

Those words became her mantra, her hope, her dream, in the time remaining before he returned to work. Each night, she waited for him to call. He didn't.

When he did come back, he resumed treating her as a slightly annoying youngster for whom he felt reluctantly responsible, and seemed not at all put out to learn that Joe Barnes had escorted her to a concert in the park, and that they were planning to attend one of the weekend firework displays in Buchart Gardens.

Indeed, he seemed to be encouraging her friendship with Joe, slapping the other man on the back, commenting on his good taste in women, and not at all troubled by what the other staff expected to turn into an office romance.

★ ★ ★

'How does Taylor like your new boyfriend?' he asked as he caught up with her in the hall the Friday of the Labor Day weekend. They were the last two leaving the office, heading for the elevator together.

She glanced up at him, knowing perfectly well whom he meant. She feigned ignorance. 'Boyfriend?'

He gave her an impatient look. 'I know you and Joe have become an item. And that's good. He's just what you need.'

'Young, single, and looking for someone to have his babies?' she asked sharply. His assumptions annoyed her. What did he think she was, the kind of woman who flitted from man to man? Did he think she'd get over her feelings for him just like *that*, simply because he had none for her? Or didn't he believe she had feelings for him? She'd never told him in so many words, but surely he must know!

'I think you presume a lot, Cliff.'

'*I* don't think so,' he said. 'It appears quite obvious the two of you have something going.'

'And would it bother you if we did?'

'Of course not. I'd . . . be happy for you. I am happy for you.' His long, brown finger pressed the button for the elevator, then, moments later, pressed it again and held it.

' "Elevators come when elevators come," ' she said in a sing-song voice, quoting him. ' "You push the button once, and wait. Demanding their immediate presence is of little value." '

He had the grace to smile, albeit wryly.

Lynne took that as a softening in his mood. 'Joe and I merely keep each other company now and then,' she said. 'His girlfriend broke up with him a couple of months ago, and he's at a loose end. We're friends, Cliff. Nothing more. He hasn't met Tay and I seriously doubt he ever will. I have not been to bed with him, nor do I have any intention of doing so. He's aware of that and accepts it.'

'Oh.' The elevator doors slid open. They stepped in. 'I heard you telling Nita you were going home for the long weekend. I thought Joe would be going with you.'

'He's not.' Lynne pulled in a deep, steadying breath as the elevator stopped on the main floor and opened into an empty lobby. Impulsively, she put her hand on his arm. 'Would you like to?'

For a second, he closed his eyes. His teeth clenched. A muscle bunched in his jaw. 'Lynne . . .' His voice came out in a low, tortured groan. Then, opening his eyes again, he met her gaze, touched her cheek with the backs of his fingers, and his mouth moved in what she thought he meant to be a smile. 'No,' he said.

'But – '

He cut her off. 'Look, I know you don't understand the way I've been acting since . . . since that weekend at my place on Galiano. I'm sorry about that. But I'm trying to do what's best for you.'

'What makes you an authority on what's best for me?'

He swallowed. 'Maybe I'm not, but I know what's good for me, and an involvement with you would be wrong.'

131

'What we had – what we did – was wrong? I thought we were both consenting adults, Cliff.'

He merely grunted in reply. Lynne was not about to leave it at that.

'You're wrong,' she said. 'That weekend was wonderful. For me. For you, too, I think. I saw you for the first time as the man I think you really are deep inside. You were happy, relaxed. You laughed, you enjoyed yourself. When we hiked up to the top of the ridge and could see forever, it was as if you'd risen through some terrible, deep fog and come out into the sunshine. It showed in your face, in your voice, in your eyes.'

She had seen that same expression of deep joy on his face while they were making love, but that she didn't mention now. 'Why are you so convinced it's wrong for you? Don't you believe you deserve happiness?'

'I –' He clamped his mouth shut on whatever he'd been going to say. 'Go home, Lynne. Go to your brother and sister-in-law and their baby and remind yourself of all the things you need to make yourself happy, all the things you deserve out of life. And while you're doing it, remind yourself that those are things you can never have with me.

'You might have them with Barnes, you might have them with someone else. But never with me. Forget me, Lynne.'

Tears stung her eyes. She blinked them back, refusing to cry in front of him. 'I can't. You were the first – uh – well, the *first*.'

He snorted. 'Don't let sentimental nonsense get

in the way of practicality. Yes, I took your virginity. If I'd known, I'd never have done it.'

She flared, anger a powerful antidote to heartache. 'You *took* nothing! We *shared* something. Something beautiful. And not just once,' she reminded him. 'It was no accident, except maybe the night of the thunderstorm. There's no way you can blame heat-of-the-moment for the entire weekend at your place.'

'I know,' he replied softly, as the janitor came noisily up the stairs, clanking a bucket and a mop. He took her arm, steering her toward the double beveled doors at the entrance. 'But I can and do blame myself,' he said, shouldering one of them open for her to pass through.

'Don't worry,' she retorted, just as softly. 'I don't hold you responsible. I know the last thing you want is to feel any kind of responsibility toward anyone.'

Cliff thought she might have been hoping for a denial. He couldn't give her one. She turned away. 'Have a nice weekend, Cliff,' she said over her shoulder. 'Goodnight.'

The pain on her face sliced into him, increasing his own. She would never know how hard it was for him to stand and watch her walk out. He gripped the side of the door to keep himself from following her. He saw she'd driven her car to work that morning, saw her fling her purse into the passenger seat and slam the driver's door. There would still would have been time to go after her as she fastened her seatbelt, then backed out of her parking slot.

Traffic was heavy. She had to wait to enter the

street. He could catch her. He knew that. He closed his eyes and locked his knees to keep his legs from obeying his mind's dictates.

Moments later, as the light up the street turned red, she drove out into a break in traffic, leaving him there without another glance in his direction.

He did not have a good night. For the first time since that weekend he'd spent there with her, he returned to his cabin on Galiano, but the place echoed with Lynne's laughter. He saw her in every room, remembered the uninhibited way she'd strip off her clothes and dive into the pool; the hedonistic pleasure she took in a bathtub full of hot water and bubbles up to her chin, and how she'd tempted him to join her.

The tub had never been designed for two, and they'd created a happy mess, which they'd cleaned up together, with much kissing and touching and loving.

Loving . . . oh, God, *loving*? No! It had not been that. It had been sex, pure and simple. He laughed in self-derision. Simple? Right! As if sex was ever simple, especially with a woman like Lynne.

Being with her had been, well, fun. Talking, arguing, even creating meals together, though they didn't always agree over methods, had brought more laughter into his days than he could remember enjoying for many years.

Even working together on that big account had been a time of joy. He admired her eager mind, her quick, intuitive grasp of even unfamiliar concepts. With two of them on it, they had plenty of time left over for play, and he'd delighted in her delight at the places he showed her, the picnics she packed for them to eat on their hikes. He, who had willingly given up the dubious pleasures of eating outdoors when he'd walked away from construction work, discovered that picnics, in the right circumstances, could be positively festive.

He shouldn't have come back to the island, he decided early Saturday morning, and closed up the cabin. The next ferry off the island wasn't heading for Victoria, but for the mainland. Nevertheless, he took it. He didn't think about fate, didn't think about the subconscious working on his mind; he simply drove, drove to escape.

He stopped at a flea market and wandered, finding several matching antique doorknobs in excellent working condition. They'd need only a bit of brass-polish to make them look perfect. Before he realized he had no use for them, he'd paid for them and walked along swinging the paper bag containing them. Next, a beautiful, stained glass fanlight that would be a fine addition to any door in any house caught his eye. That, too, he bought and tucked awkwardly under his arm, sidling carefully through the crowds so as not to let it get broken.

Back in his car, he continued driving, until he saw a sign reading 'Ladner, 10.'

What the hell was he doing there?

He knew the answer before he consciously asked the question. If he went, would he be welcome? If he went, would Lynne take it amiss? He pulled off on to the verge and stopped the car, leaning his forehead on his hands on the steering wheel. If he went there, he knew she wouldn't take it amiss. She'd know exactly why he was there. She'd know it as well as he did. He'd be there because he couldn't stay away. He'd be there because she was, because he was drawn to her so strongly he wondered if there'd ever be an escape for him.

He clenched the wheel, lifted his head, and drove on.

The expression on her face made it all worth while. Her eyes lit up like candles in a dark room, filled with gladness at seeing him. Her smile paled the sun with its brightness. Her voice chimed like happy bells. 'Cliff! What in the world are you doing here?' she said over the sound of hammering from somewhere deep in the house.

He held out the bag and the fanlight. 'I brought these for Taylor,' he said, but they both knew it was a weak, poor excuse. They both knew why he was there.

'Thank you,' she whispered, taking the bag. She touched his face with her fingertips. 'Come on in.' Before he did, he slid a hand around the back of her neck and tilted her face up for a kiss.

Before he lifted his head, he heard a giggle from somewhere nearby. 'Smitten, I tell you, Lynnie. The man is smitten.'

As he reluctantly opened his eyes, he intercepted Lynne's glare, aimed straight at her sister-in-law, standing in the hall with the baby on her hip and a huge grin on her face.

★ ★ ★

If he was 'smitten', Cliff took great care not to let it show for the rest of the weekend. Though he agreed to stay in one of the spare rooms that had been finished and furnished since his first visit, Lynne knew without having to be told that he – and she – would both be sleeping alone Saturday and Sunday nights.

Taylor was delighted with both the gifts Cliff had brought, and equally pleased by the expert help he could provide. The fanlight, installed in the front door, sent great splashes of rainbow color across the deep shine of the hardwood floor in the foyer.

The two men spent the rest of the afternoon and even an hour after dinner hard at work, cutting, fitting, nailing, discussing, while Lynne and Ann did finishing work, sanding, painting, and even wallpapered one bathroom.

Despite the busy schedule, Lynne was not deprived of time with her niece who was now making her first, all-too-successful attempts at crawling, and was very proud of herself, not to mention very apt to get herself into trouble if not watched constantly.

As was Lynne – especially when Ann called a firm halt to all chores after the baby was down for the night.

'Get out of here, you two,' she said, shooing Lynne and Cliff toward the door. 'Go for a walk or something. You've both put in more hours than you should have. You need a break.'

Strolling along the riverbank with Cliff, her hand cradled in his, made Lynne ache for more than the kisses they shared once out of sight of the house. Leaving him later and going to her own room was torture, but it was torture she knew he shared. She still didn't know if his showing up indicated any kind of willingness on his part to take their abortive affair another step ahead, but she hoped so.

His kisses told her so, and his reluctance to leave her reinforced that belief. Still, he did leave her at her bedroom door, left her well-kissed and yearning. She suspected she could have overcome his resolve, but there was a delicious kind of agony in depriving herself, in proving to him that she could be as mature and as conscientious as he.

'I will not,' he whispered, 'abuse your brother's hospitality.'

She had to respect him for that, however much she wanted him to join her in her bed.

In the daytime, he was a model of circumspection, spending most of his time working on projects with Tay, leaving her to help Ann and play with Mandy.

Sunday night, it was even harder to part than it had been Saturday, and Lynne spent most of the hours awake, listening to the night sounds, wondering if Cliff was as restless as she. Hoping he was. Wondering what the next week would bring. Hoping it would see her dreams come true.

On Monday morning, it was nearly eleven when Lynne awoke. Shocked by the lateness of the hour, she finally had to agree with Ann, who insisted she was working and studying too hard. She did seem to require more sleep than ever before. She was bitterly disappointed to learn that Cliff had been up hours ago, and had left shortly after breakfast.

When she had finally to say goodbye to her family, Ann hugged her. 'See you next weekend?'

Taylor added, 'And bring Cliff with you. I can't tell you what a treat one more strong back is.'

'I'll . . . ask him.'

'We both did, too, but he was non-committal,' her brother said, 'so I leave it up to you to work on him. I get the impression there's not much he'd refuse you.'

'Maybe,' Ann put in with a grin, 'he doesn't like being just another strong back.'

And maybe, Lynne thought as she drove away, he was already regretting his impulse to accept her invitation to join her in Ladner for the holiday weekend. What, she wondered, would be the status of their relationship by the next one?

To her utter disappointment, it remained exactly as before. Despite the kisses they'd shared on their nightly rambles, despite the memories of the enchantment they could create together, in Victoria Cliff remained the junior partner in the firm with which she was articling. Just that, and nothing more.

Maybe, she told herself, if he went home with her again the following weekend, things would change.

The next weekend, though, Lynne had a stomach bug, picked up, she was sure, from the two little boys down the block, who had come to help her pick plums from the tree in her back yard. She remembered her mother complaining that the minute school was back in after the summer break, everyone in the household got every little bug that was making its rounds.

Lynne certainly had this one. She was so sick she couldn't even go to work on Friday. By noon, she felt a little better, ate some toast, and then spent the afternoon studying. By late evening, she knew she'd overdone it and should have stayed in bed. She was sick again.

And again the next day, and the next.

On Monday, she dragged herself out of bed and managed to get to work, but it wasn't easy.

'Good heavens, girl, go home,' Nita said when she arrived. 'You look ghastly.'

'I'm fine,' Lynne insisted. 'I just didn't feel like putting on make-up this morning.'

The following weekend, after a miserable five days at work, all Lynne wanted to do was sleep. That, to her relief, seemed to help. Obviously, frequent naps were the cure for this particularly nasty bug.

By Wednesday, though, it had returned with a vengeance, and when on Thursday she leapt out of bed, feet already flying as she dashed to the bathroom, she knew this was far more than an upset stomach.

Counting back, checking her schedule, realizing she had missed her period, she knew exactly what was wrong with her. Regretfully, she called in sick. She knew without going to a doctor, but made an appointment with the one she had seen for birth control immediately after she and Cliff had first made love, back when she had thought their affair might continue.

A quick test confirmed her suspicions; the pills she'd been taking had not done their job adequately before she went to Cliff's cabin in July. She learned about keeping dry soda crackers beside her bed to nibble on when she first woke up. Dr Lacey gave her pamphlets to study, gave her a prescription for pre-natal vitamins, and plenty of good advice along with a list of books she could find at the library.

But the one thing she didn't – couldn't – give Lynne was the courage to tell Cliff, who didn't want responsibilities, who didn't want babies, who didn't really want her – except when he couldn't control what she sensed he considered his base desires.

How could she tell him? What would she say? Leave it, Lynne told herself several times a week as September waned and the maples began to turn golden, the dogwoods and sumacs a deep wine-red. Her morning sickness abated as swiftly as it had arrived, and apart from a new tenderness in her breasts, she might not have been pregnant at all.

Leave it for a few more days, till you're feeling stronger, till you're more used to the idea yourself. Just focus on your baby, on this small, glorious miracle happening inside.

Nevertheless, he was its father, and she knew he had a right to be told.

Eventually.

She laughed, cupping one hand over the place where her baby lay curled, at the moment, hardly more than the size of her little finger, according to a book she'd gotten from the library. That wouldn't last, though, and soon there'd be no hiding it.

That thought brought her up short. What was she going to do? She knew without question that she could go back to Taylor and Ann, would be welcomed with loving embraces and no recriminations. But if she quit Simpkins, Foreman and Associates, there was that same old problem: she'd have to start from scratch elsewhere.

And how could she afford to do that when she had a baby to prepare for, and then to support?

'How are you and Lynne getting on?' Nita was nothing if not forthright.

'Fine,' Cliff said, aware that the sudden stiffness in his shoulders had translated itself to his voice. 'Why do you ask?'

'Because you work most closely with her. Because I know you've been to visit her family a few times and − '

'Once,' he interrupted. 'I've been there once, to take her brother some building supplies I found at a flea market on the Labor Day weekend.'

'Yes, and how did you know her brother would be able to use those building supplies you took him?'

'Why, I − uh − I guess Lynne must have mentioned it. She did. During Grant's and my first interview with her. She said he was renovating an old house out near Ladner. Then, the weekend Grant sent her to my place, we talked about it some more. Then, well, when I was in the neighborhood and found those things, I thought of her − er − *him*. Remember, I used

142

to be in the building trade. I know how hard it can be to find just the pieces to make an old house look exactly right, yet still be as sturdy as a new one. Sturdier, likely, because – '

He broke off abruptly. The smug expression on Nita's face told him he should have let it go and brushed her off. But while he'd been busy trying to justify his trip to Ladner, she'd plunked her bottom on to the chair on the other side of his desk and was giving him the kind of look he'd long since learned to distrust.

'But it hasn't just been once,' she said smoothly. 'First, there was the time you took her there to collect her belongings just after she joined the firm when we were away on vacation.'

He felt his jaw gape and quickly snapped his mouth shut.

Nita's eyes danced. 'Grant and I both hope word doesn't get around about how generous the company is toward new employees from out of town.'

Her grin made him scowl. Before he could ask how she'd found out about that, she continued, 'Lynne's a very well-bred young lady. She thanked Grant for the kindness shown her by Simpkins, Foreman and Associates in seeing to her moving expenses. Grant managed not to show his surprise and let her go on believing the firm actually had paid. So. I ask you again: how are you and Lynne getting on?'

'Perfectly well. She's a good worker, a quick learner, and has a strong desire to qualify by the end of her first year here.'

Nita crossed her legs, her cream silk slacks whispering, leaned forward and placed an elbow on the uppermost knee, resting her chin on her fist. Her brilliant, multi-colored blouse made his eyes hurt. 'Are you,' she inquired politely, 'being deliberately obtuse, or are you really so stupid you can't see that Lynne is desperately unhappy?'

'She can't be. She's always laughing and singing, and entertaining the gang at lunchtime.' He forced a laugh. 'I even suggested once that we should let her swap offices with Grant so she'd have more room for her luncheon parties. I've even seen you crowded into her cubby-hole with everyone else, so you must know she's the same bubbly girl who arrived here in June.'

'Oh, she's putting a good face on things, she's trying to act is if there's nothing wrong, but I know there is, though she won't talk to me about it. I'd hoped the two of you had grown . . . close enough, that she might have opened up to you.'

'Close enough?' To his shame, his voice cracked.

'Cliff . . .' Nita was patient. 'Anyone with half a brain can see that you're in love with the girl. And I, for one, have a complete brain, so don't try to put anything over on me, and don't try to deny it.'

He balled his fists on his things under his desk. 'Nita, leave it alone, please. I am not, repeat not, in love with Lynne Castle or anyone else, so just get that insane idea out of your head.'

Slowly, she shook her head. 'Sorry, can't do that. I love you like a brother. We've worked together for years. I saw the way you were after your divorce.'

144

'Annulment,' he corrected her.

'Whatever. What's the difference?'

The difference, he could have told her, was that in having their marriage annulled, because her religion didn't permit divorce, Julia, his former wife, had told the world that he hadn't measured up as a man. He hadn't even tried to fight it. It seemed only right that it be over. He didn't deserve to have had a wife, did he, if he couldn't give her what she'd most wanted: children?

'You grew hard after that, Cliff,' Nita went on. 'Then, in the three months Lynne has been with us, Grant and I both noticed that for a while, you softened somehow, became again the man we remember from before.' She paused. 'The kind of man who'd take it upon himself to see to the moving expenses of a brand new staff member.'

'She was sleeping on a leaky air mattress. She had no dishes, no furniture, nothing. I couldn't let her live that way.'

'Why not?' Nita's soft question might have sounded mild, but Cliff knew her iron will, and knew he wouldn't get away with just brushing off her concerns. 'Would you have done the same for a young man we'd just hired?'

He knew when he was caught, and knew there was no point in trying to convince Nita he'd have done what he did for anyone but Lynne. He closed his eyes, folded his hands behind his head and leaned far back in his chair. He swallowed hard, then brought himself upright and looked straight at her.

'Come on,' he said, 'do I look like the kind of man

to fall for a girl for whom I'd make a totally inappropriate mate?'

Nita tilted her head to one side, studying him. 'You look like the kind of man who has already fallen for a girl. And what would be so inappropriate about you and Lynne together?'

'Everything! I'm eleven years older than she is, Nita. I've been married before. She needs romance, good times, lots of fun out of life. I have nothing to offer her.'

'What makes you so sure of that?'

Briefly, he considered trying to explain how Lynne's face glowed when she held her baby niece, when she so much as spoke Amanda's name. And trying to explain to Nita that his inability to father children had cost him his marriage, so there was no way his feelings for Lynne could have a happy outcome. But not even to such a good friend could he make that kind of confession. It was too personal, too painful.

'Sure, Lynne's been working with me,' he said, 'but she's been *dating* Joe Barnes. Why aren't you on his case about it?'

Nita snorted. 'Because I know he has nothing to do with her unhappiness. Just a week ago, when he announced he was back with his girlfriend and that she'd agreed to marry him, Lynne flung her arms around him and danced him around in circles, pleased as punch for him.'

Cliff's heart constricted painfully for a moment. 'So there you have it. As you said, she puts a good face on things. If she's feeling miserable, it's be-

146

cause of Barnes.' He wanted, suddenly, and with terrible intensity, to do great physical harm to Barnes for having hurt Lynne.

'No. She's been unhappy since that weekend she spent working with you on Galiano. If not before that. Grant and I both noticed how forced her laughter was, how haunted she looked when she thought herself unobserved, ever since we came back from Alaska. Grant tried to talk to her about it, thinking maybe her workload was too great, with her studies on top of it. She denied it. And you're miserable too, Cliff.'

'I am not. I'm my normal self,' he protested.

'So,' she continued, as if he hadn't spoken, 'with Lynne creeping around looking more and more pale and peaked unless she forces some kind of animation for the benefit of others, and you acting as if you have a thorn in your foot, I figure it's past time you and Lynne dealt with whatever it is has come between the two of you.'

'There is nothing between us, Nita. There can never be anything between us.' Cliff stood. 'End of discussion.'

Nita remained seated for several seconds, then slowly rose, her gaze never leaving his face. He had a bad feeling that his thoughts and emotions were as open to her as if he were broadcasting them on all frequencies.

'Okay,' she said finally. 'Have it your way, Cliff, but remember, Grant and I both care about you a lot, and if you need us for anything, at any time, you've only to ask.'

He nodded, then, obeying an impulse that surprised him, he caught Nita in a hug and held her for a minute. As if she knew he was seeking solace, she put her arms around him and rubbed his back, then patted him, the way he thought she would one of her children or grandchildren.

It scared him how close he was to tears in that one brief instant, and how close he was to spilling his guts to Nita.

But he didn't give in to either impulse, of course. He couldn't, any more than he could give in to the aching desire to take Lynne, enfold her the way Nita had enfolded him, and tell her nothing would ever hurt her as long as he was alive.

The best – the only – way for him to protect Lynne against suffering was to remove himself from her life, because Nita was right and he knew it. Lynne was unhappy. She was unhappy because of him, because of things she didn't – couldn't possibly – understand.

Releasing Nita, he set her back from him and said, 'You and Grant are my friends. I think I can safely say, my only real friends. And I appreciate your caring about me. But . . .' He paused, drew a deep breath and let it out slowly, steadying himself, 'I think the time has come for me to move on. Let's get Grant in here. We need to talk.'

CHAPTER 9

Shock waves resounded through the office following the news that Cliff was leaving the company and joining up with a friend in Vancouver, an investment broker. It was an amicable dissolution of the partnership between him and Grant and Nita, and would change nothing in the basic structure of the firm. Grant assured Lynne that her arcticling year was not in jeopardy, and that they'd all help her through her exam preparations.

Though she couldn't say so, she didn't care about that. She could only nod, feeling numb, and wonder if Grant and Nita knew why Cliff had decided so suddenly he wanted out of the company. Nothing either of them said gave her reason to suspect that they knew, but that failed to ease her heartache. *She* knew, and that was what mattered. Did Cliff suspect she was pregnant? Was he running from that, too?

No. She was sure of it and felt guilty for the thought. He was too honorable to do that, and she had to tell him.

But it all happened so fast she didn't have a

chance to reach a decision about how to broach the subject. One day Cliff was there in the office across the hall, the next, he was gone. Nita still answered the phone by saying, 'Simpkins, Foreman and Associates,' his name remained on the company stationery, and the gold leaf lettering on the main doors was left unchanged.

There were, Lynne supposed, legalities to be taken care of, but once the decision had been made and announced to the staff, Cliff simply disappeared.

Joe Barnes and Donald Frayne moved in to share Cliff's former office, freeing up the slightly larger one Don had occupied, and Lynne moved there. This led to speculation that Grant didn't intend to take on another partner – or that maybe, just maybe, he hoped Cliff would change his mind and return.

Lynne knew better. She knew, too, that she could wait no longer to make her own announcement to him if she was going to make it at all.

She found his new address in Nita's Rolodex and quickly wrote it down when Nita was at lunch. The following Saturday, she drove on to the ferry and discovered he lived in a tall apartment building near downtown Vancouver.

If she gave her name, would he let her in?

Afraid to risk it, afraid of having to blurt out her news over an intercom, she rang his buzzer, prepared to claim she had a delivery for him, but to her surprise, he buzzed the door open without asking who was there.

'Lynne!' he said when he opened his tenth-floor

apartment door. 'I . . . I thought you were the pizza guy.'

He looked so stunned by her presence, she couldn't tell if he was happy or dismayed. After a moment's silence, though, he opened the door wide and said, 'Come in.

'What can I do for you?' he asked after seeing her seated comfortably on a leather sofa. He sounded, she thought, like one of her university professors who'd been disturbed in his office after hours; willing to do his duty toward a student, but slightly impatient with the intrusion. His jaw was tense, his eyes slightly narrowed, his mouth a straight line that looked like it had never softened to kiss her, never smiled at her, never moved over her breasts to bring her whole body alive.

He did not look like the man who had helped create her small, precious miracle and she knew in that moment that whatever faint hopes she might have been harboring had been for naught. So she, too, would do her duty. She squared her shoulders, straightened her spine, lifted her chin, linked her hands in her lap and said, 'Cliff, I'm going to have a baby.'

Cliff heard her words. He did not, could not, for several long seconds, make sense of them. He backed away, one step, two, encountered the seat of a chair and felt himself collapse into it with such force that the springs squeaked. He stared at her, at her wide, innocent, ocean-blue eyes. He watched her crooked attempt at a smile, and from a great, echoing distance, heard her say, 'I guess my birth control wasn't one hundred per cent. Of course I didn't use any that first time, but by the next time I was sure my pills would have protected me. I guess I wasn't on them long enough. The doctor says I conceived around the middle of July.'

Into his continuing silence, she rushed on. 'You don't have to marry me, of course. If . . . if you don't want to.' If her next sound was meant to be a laugh, it failed. 'Oh, what am I saying? Of course you don't. You've always made it perfectly clear that marriage has no place in your plans, but I thought you had a right to know what was happening.'

For several endless moments he remained unable to speak, his breath caught inside his chest under a vast log-jam of pain. Though he'd told her often enough to date other men, and had known of her relationship with Barnes, it hurt beyond his imagining to know she'd done a hell of a lot more than 'date' the younger man.

Finally, he rasped out, 'Why are you telling *me*?'

He saw his emphasis on the pronoun wasn't lost on her and she stared at him with an oh-so-puzzled silent question, one that had him incredibly close to believing her obvious lie. 'But who else would I tell? I thought you had a right to know. And before you suggest it, I have no intention of having an abortion. The idea is totally repugnant to me.'

Dimly, he recognized her quiet determination, an underlying strength he'd never before been fully aware of.

'I don't need anything from you if you don't want

to give it. I can manage on my own.'

He wanted, suddenly, ludicrously, to laugh at her. It was as if a Persian kitten were sitting there all fierce and determined, ready to take on the world with only its little claws for defense. 'And my brother will help me, I know, if there are things I can't handle alone. I just thought you should *know*.'

Maybe if she'd gone on meeting his eyes bravely, maybe if her voice hadn't cracked just that tiny bit, he would have been all right. But she stood abruptly, face half averted to hide, he was sure, tears, as she headed for the door, and he was lost.

He shot to his feet, gathered her into his arms, his own voice unsteady as he groaned, 'Lynne, oh, Lynnie, love, of course I want to marry you.'

'I told you he was in love with you, you simpleton,' Ann said with a smile when, the following morning, Cliff and Lynne arrived in Ladner. 'And I knew you were in just as bad a shape.'

'Do you think Taylor will mind?' Lynne asked, experiencing a certain trepidation despite her faith in her brother's equanimity.

'Mind?' Ann gaped at her, patting Amanda's back. The baby burped, was congratulated, then reached greedily for the bottle Ann had weaned her to. 'He's delighted.'

'I mean, mind that I'm pregnant before we get married.'

Ann grinned. 'Honey, if it hadn't taken me so long to catch, I could have been in exactly your place, and Taylor knows it. Sure, you're his pre-

153

cious baby sister, but he likes Cliff, admires him, and will admire him a lot more following this "confession". I'm sure Cliff is right now making with the normal, stiff kind of male apology, fully expecting a punch in the nose and willing to take it if that's what's needed to get Tay's approval.'

Lynne cringed inwardly. 'Do you think he'll get it? The punch, I mean. It was all my fault, you know. I – '

'Well, well, well. So my little sister's gonna be a mama!' Taylor came up behind and below Lynne, scooped her off the porch rail where she sat and lifted her down into the yard, holding her flat on his outspread arms as he spun her in a circle. 'You're planning to make me an uncle before I've hardly gotten used to being a daddy?' He set her feet on the ground, kissed her cheek loudly, and said, 'I'm really happy for you, Lynnie, and like I told Cliff, I don't think there's a better man in the world than he to take you on.'

'Take me on?' she protested, giddy from happiness and the spinning. 'You make me sound like a difficult project.'

He shrugged and shared a grin with Cliff. 'Some people renovate old houses . . .'

'So, when's it to be? And don't try to tell me "tomorrow" or anything like that,' Ann said half an hour later when a toast had been made and drunk – a tiny sip only for Lynne on her sister-in-law's firm insistence. 'I need a little time for preparation.'

'You have exactly one week from yesterday,' Lynne said, hopping back up on to the broad porch rail. Cliff slid an arm behind her as if to keep her from falling. 'If,' she added, 'you *must* make preparations at all. Neither of us wants a big wedding. Just us, you two, Nita and Grant, and a marriage commissioner to say the right words.'

Ann looked totally dismayed. 'But . . . if you don't have a big wedding and send out lots of invitations, you don't get all those piles and piles of lovely gifts.' Everyone but Ann laughed.

'Make fun of me if you want,' she said. 'But that's half the fun of having a wedding.'

Cliff tightened his arm around Lynne. 'I'm getting the only wedding gift I want.'

'I have to agree, two for the price of one is a bit of a bonus,' Taylor said. 'It took me three years to get the second half of what I wanted from my bride.'

Lynne thought she was the only one who noticed that Cliff failed to smile, that he slipped his arm from around her waist and took a chair a few feet away.

She knew he didn't see the baby as a bonus. She could only hope that, in time, he'd come to love their unborn child as much as she did.

If he did, he gave no indication of it. He seemed, instead, to ignore the entire situation. He was kind, loving, considerate, and concerned for her health and comfort. In bed, he was the lover she'd always dreamed of, and she tried hard to please him.

There, locked in an intimate embrace, making love with him, was the only time she truly believed in the love he professed every day. In him, she sensed a deep need she suspected she could never fill, a hint of desperation in his loving, as if each time might be the last. Was this a hold-over from his first marriage? Did the hurt he'd felt at its dissolution linger? Did he distrust her because Julia had left him and he expected no better from her? How could she ever hope to prove to him that her love was forever, except to be there for him, with him, forever? Or was it something from his childhood that still disturbed him? She knew virtually nothing of it except it had been unhappy.

Frequently, she tried to draw him out, but he evaded her questions, changed the subject, or laughed and said they had better things to focus on than his not-so-illustrious past. She had to let it go. He seemed to enjoy helping her furnish the nursery, and shook his head in disbelief at the sizes of clothing she selected for the baby's layette. 'No one can be that small,' he said as they unpacked following one such shopping spree.

'He won't be that small for long,' she agreed, 'but for the first couple of months, even some of these things —' she held up a pair of red-and-white striped terry-cloth sleepers – will be too big.'

'Why do you call your baby "he"? Don't you want a little girl just like Amanda?' Cliff and Mandy had become good friends over the past few months. On Christmas Eve, still a week short of eleven months, the little girl had flabbergasted her mother, father, and aunt by taking her first, stumbling steps from the side of a coffee table to Cliff's knee, where she clung, grinning triumphantly and looking terrified all at the same time.

'No,' Lynne said, taking his hand and sliding it over her rounded belly. 'I want a little boy just like you.'

For a moment, his face froze into hard lines and his eyes took on that closed look Lynne had come to dread, but it lasted only a second before he swung her up into his arms. 'I'm no little boy, chubby. Do you require proof?'

She smiled up at him, slid her arms around his neck and said, 'Why yes, I believe I do.'

He tried. Cliff knew he wasn't always convincing, but he did try. He thought he had convinced Lynne and her family that he was as thrilled about the baby as they all were, but it was himself he failed to convince. To his disgust, his abdominal troubles started up all over again and he was forced to go back on the medication that alleviated the symptoms. Whether it was the stress of commuting daily by ferry, the stress of his new partnership responsibilities, or the stress of knowing he was living a lie, he didn't know. He knew only that it grew harder and harder to pretend, to try to be the man Lynne needed.

There were times when he knew his reactions – or maybe his lack of them – disappointed her. Loving her as he did, he struggled with the demons inside himself.

You are not Logan Foreman, he'd tell himself when the fiends threatened to win. *You have none of his blood in your veins, so there is no reason for you to become a replica of the man. You can do this. You're strong and you love your wife more than anything else in this world.*

But what of the blood he *did* have in his veins? The question haunted him.

If his mother had been telling the truth, and he had little reason to think she might not have been – except his own unwillingness to believe her story – what kind of man might he resemble, not just in looks, but in personality?

Apart from his love for Lynne, it had been a gut reaction on his part to take responsibility, accept her big lie, never let on that he knew it was one, because, in doing so, he could think himself superior to the man whose blood he might carry.

Vincent Salazar, if I am your son, then I'm a better man than you are. He took refuge in that belief because it was the only consolation he could find as Lynne's due date grew closer and closer.

He wanted her to quit work. She wouldn't. 'I want to qualify. I'll take a couple of weeks off when the baby's born, of course, and Grant and Nita say there's no reason he can't be with me at work after that. My exams are important to me, Cliff.'

'Why?' he teased. 'Don't you think I can support you?' But there was an edge to his tone however much he tried not to let it show. The momentary pain in her eyes told him she'd heard it. But, as always, she excused him for it, maybe even pretended to herself it hadn't existed.

She smiled and nuzzled as close as her big tummy

permitted. 'I know you can support us. I know you will. But I still want to finish what I started. I don't ever want to be like my mom, Cliff. She had no training, no experience in the business world and twice she was left to try to fend for herself.'

'You'll never have to do that. I deeded this house to you the day before we married. I've also arranged for you to have an income for life. I'm not a poor man, Lynne. Most of my investments have paid off well over the years. I see no reason for them not to continue.'

'Cliff! You put this house in my name?'

'In your name and fully paid off. No mortgage. You'll always have a roof over your head and food on the table.'

'Thank you. Please, don't think for a minute I don't trust you to provide for us. But Mom made me promise I'd finish what I started, and I want to do that, to honor her memory, but for myself, as well. For my . . . self-respect.'

'I know,' he said, sliding his fingers through her hair. 'All right, then, work as long as you're comfortable and I'll tutor you in the evenings if you want.'

'No way. Evenings are for us. Especially with you commuting daily to Vancouver just so I can go on working here in Victoria. I'll get through my exams without extra tutoring.'

'All right,' he conceded. 'We'll do it your way, but once you get to put the initials "CA" after your name, I want you to think about staying home and just being a mother.'

Lynne smiled. 'Nope. Not unless you include the designation "wife" along with "mother".'

'Oh, I do that,' he said fervently. 'Do you feel like working on the "wife" aspect of your job-description right now?'

'Sure,' she said with a wide, innocent smile that warmed him, brought much-needed laughter rumbling from his chest. 'Would you like me to make you a sandwich or something?'

'I'll take "something",' he said. 'Especially considering that in another couple of weeks I'll have to settle for nothing.'

'Pooh!' she scoffed. 'My doctor says as long as I feel comfortable, we can do anything we want.'

'You feel about as comfortable as an over-stuffed sofa,' he said, then proved how much he liked such pieces of furniture.

Then, at last it was time. He forced himself to cover his fear by joking with her all the way to the hospital, telling her she wasn't doing it right. Weren't women supposed to go into labor in the middle of the night, rather than at a convenient seven o'clock in the morning, just before the workday started? 'This way,' he said, watching her fists clench in her lap as he waited for an interminably long red light to change to green, 'I can drop you off, catch the next ferry, get to the office on time and have a whole day's work done before I come back.'

Her blue eyes widened. 'You're going to *leave* me?'

He wrapped a hand around the back of her neck,

feeling the damp skin under her hair, feeling her muscles tense as another contraction hit. 'Never,' he vowed, as much to himself as to her. 'Never, my Lynne, my love. We're in this together, all the way.'

Except, would he ever be able to forget that *he* had not been in it from the very beginning?

Yes, he promised himself, only five hours later when Lynne, tired but triumphant, beamed up at him over her son's face. 'Oh, Cliff. He's so beautiful! Thank you, thank you, my darling.'

He had no voice with which to speak, could only bend and kiss her mouth. 'What's the baby's name?' the obstetrician inquired.

Again, Cliff said nothing. This was one more area where he had failed Lynne and knew it, where he had hurt her by his refusal to discuss names, telling her the decision was hers. 'Michael,' she said, finally, her glance consulting him, waiting for approval or disapproval. He could offer her neither; the baby was hers to name as she wished, but he stroked his fingertips over her hand in mute apology as she cradled the baby's head.

'Hello, Michael,' the doctor said, taking the baby away for a few minutes.

'He's going to grow up to be the same kind of wonderful, strong man his daddy is,' Lynne said propping herself higher on the pillows behind her, as if she couldn't bear to lose sight of her son. 'I think Michael even looks like him.'

Cliff clenched his jaw and stepped back to make room for a nurse.

He wondered exactly whose face Lynne might be

seeing in that amorphous assortment of crumpled, red features. All he knew for sure was that it was not his.

'Cliff, darling, what's wrong?' Lynne came upon him leaning against the window frame in his den, staring out into a moonlit night.

He turned and curled an arm around her, drawing her close to his side. She snuggled her face against his bare chest, breathing in the warm, comforting scent of his skin.

'Nothing's wrong,' he said, his cheek resting on top of her head.

'I don't buy that,' she argued. 'In the three weeks since Michael's birth, you've grown more and more distant. You're spending long hours at work, and scarcely sleeping. I know something's bothering you.'

'Lynne, truly, I'm fine. Yes, I've been working hard. I'm sorry if you're feeling neglected, but you're always busy with the baby.'

'Ah,' she said, leaning back against the curve of his arm and looking into his face as she recalled something Ann had warned her about. 'Are *you*, maybe, feeling a little bit neglected, Cliff?'

He snorted. 'Don't be silly.'

'I'm not being silly.' She stroked his bristly chin. 'Don't you know how much I love you? My love for Michael is simply an extension of that. It doesn't take away from it. Love's not like a pie that gets cut into smaller and smaller pieces to share among all those who need some of it. It just grows bigger and bigger with each new soul it has to feed. Please, darling, come back to bed and hold me.'

To her relief, he did, but she sensed he was as far from sleep as they lay together as he had been standing looking out into the night, thinking those dark, brooding thoughts of his, thoughts he would never share with her. She resolved to try harder to show him he had no reason to feel left out. She promised herself she'd give him all the love and understanding he required of her, and if that meant giving him space, she'd somehow do that, too, regardless of her own deep need of intimacy.

Yet, when, a week later, he threw a grenade into her secure little world, while her love remained steadfast, her understanding was as shattered as her life.

'Lynne,' he said, coming to a halt halfway across the living room, his hands behind his back, his face set into expressionless lines, skin white and taut, 'I can't go on this way. I have to tell you I know the truth. Maybe, from there, we can work something out, but this is killing me and hurting you, and it's time we confronted it.'

Michael's mouth slipped from her nipple as she sat erect in surprise. Automatically, she tilted him over her shoulder and rubbed his back.

'What are you talking about?'

'Him,' Cliff said, indicating the baby. 'I know he's not mine.'

Lynne couldn't help herself. She laughed. 'Are you crazy? Of course he's yours! Who else's could he be?'

163

'I don't know. Joe Barnes', maybe?'

'*What?*' Lynne shot to her feet so fast she scared the baby, who began to wail. Rocking him, she lowered herself back to her chair and put him to her other breast. He quieted at once. 'Cliff, if you're trying to be funny, go read a different joke book. That one doesn't qualify even remotely.'

Cliff sat on the edge of a nearby chair. 'I'm sterile, Lynne. There is no way I could have made you pregnant.'

'I beg to differ!' Her tone made the baby cry again, and she soothed him. 'There is no way anyone else could have done it, Cliff, since you are the first and only man I've ever made love with.'

He leaned forward, elbows on his knees, and buried his face in his hands.

'God, how I'd like to be able to believe that,' he said.

Lynne put Michael on the couch, set a pillow between him and the edge and crouched before Cliff, taking his wrists in her hands. 'Cliff, look at me. Please. Tell me why you believe such a thing. Please. I want to understand.'

'I believe it because it's true,' he said, and the pain in his voice brought tears to her eyes. 'I have proof, Lynne. Incontrovertible proof. My sterility is the reason Julia left me. She didn't divorce me. She had the marriage annulled. If it weren't for that proof, an annulment wouldn't have been possible.'

'But . . .' She blinked to clear her blurred vision. 'Cliff, tests can be wrong! For God's sake, you have to believe me! Have another test. If you love me, have it. Or we'll get blood tests, DNA, whatever it takes to convince you. Michael is your son!'

He stood and walked away from her. 'I did have another test, Lynne. Like you, I thought maybe the first ones had been wrong. Last week, I put myself through the same humiliation and had another one. The results came back today, conclusively. My sperm-count is too low to ever permit my impregnating any woman.'

She followed him and grabbed his arm, turning him around. 'Well, it wasn't ten months ago!'

An expression of ineffable sadness came over his face. 'It was, Lynne. Why don't you just admit it, tell me the truth, and as I said before, maybe we can take it from there? It's the lie I hate. I can't go on living with it. Please Lynne, you said if I loved you, I'd have another test. I did, because I love you so very much. If you love me, you'll tell me who fathered your son.'

'*You* fathered my son! *Our* son! How can I make it any clearer than that? You want the truth. That's what I'm giving you.'

He slipped a hand to the inside pocket of his suit coat and withdrew a long envelope, handed it to her, and said, 'Read it, Lynne.'

She read it and dropped to the couch beside Michael, who slept on. 'Cliff, it can't be. Please understand. It simply cannot be. There's a mistake. I want you and Michael to have blood tests.'

'A blood test won't prove anything except what we already know – that I cannot be your son's father.'

165

'DNA – '

He interrupted with a slicing motion of his hand. 'Why poke needles unnecessarily into an innocent little baby? Lynne, no test on this earth is going to prove what you'd like to have me believe.' He raked a hand through his hair. 'I don't understand you! Have you told yourself this lie so often you've actually come to believe it?'

Now, she buried her face in her hands, weeping wildly. 'It's not a lie, it's not a lie!'

He was silent for so long she thought he had left. When she raised her head, he stood before her.

'Counseling,' she said, hearing a terrible note of desperation in her voice. 'We can go for marriage counseling. Maybe with help we can work through this and – '

He shook his head. 'Lynne, I'm sorry. The only thing that has any kind of chance at saving our marriage is for you to tell me the truth.'

'But I did!' She was beyond tears now, aching so deeply inside she thought she might die from it. 'Why did you marry me, then, if you believe what you claim to?'

He looked at her sadly for a long moment. 'Because I love you. Because you bring out a tenderness in me, a protectiveness I've never experienced before. I couldn't leave you alone and pregnant.'

'But you can leave me alone and the mother of a newborn infant?'

'Don't make me leave, Lynne,' he pleaded. 'Just tell me the truth so we have a solid base to begin rebuilding.'

Now, she couldn't stop the tears that ran down her face, or the silent sobs that shook her shoulders. 'I have told you the truth.'

He shook his, head, turned, and walked out the door.

Lynne sat staring after him for a long time, waiting, hoping, sure he'd come back, tell her it was all some hideous kind of joke. He did not. Not that night, nor the next, nor the next week.

Somehow, she managed to return to work. Somehow, she managed to continue preparing for her exams. And somehow, mostly, she thought, because she had simply shut her mind down, she passed them, qualifying with outstanding marks.

But, as she was to learn in midsummer, fate wasn't done with her yet . . .

PART TWO

CHAPTER 10

Cliff's hand shook as, leafing through the mail his secretary had put on his desk, he saw the 'Personal' designation on the letter from a law firm he'd only heard of three weeks ago. For long moments, he held it, staring at it. He rose, locked the door, returned to his desk then slowly, reluctantly, slid his paper-knife under the envelope's flap. It was the third one he'd received in a month.

Exactly as the others had, it read, 'Ms Castle requests that you contact her either through these offices or at the above box number. Enclosed, please find a letter from same.'

Letter? The term was a joke. All the polite little missive said was 'Please get in touch with me, Cliff. It's past time for us to sort out our lives.'

It was signed, simply, '*Lynne*'.

Why, all these months after her disappearance, had Lynne suddenly decided to contact him? There could be only one answer, and it was not one he wanted to hear. 'Sort out our lives . . .' *lives* being the operative word. Plural. Separate. Negating the future he still hoped they could have, obliterating it. Her polite phrasing meant the expunging of their past and future the way his past had been negated, obliterated, and expunged not once, but twice before.

Could he bear to let it happen for a third time? And yet, when it came right down to it, since he was the one who had set in motion the destruction of his and Lynne's future, what right did he have to object now she wanted to make it official? The fact that she was contacting him through a law office more than suggested 'official'. He waited, daily, for the papers to be served, and wondered why she hadn't done so.

He slipped the lawyer's letter into its envelope, locked it in his private drawer, crumpled Lynne's note and tossed it in the trash. Then, after a moment, he retrieved it and smoothed it out before sliding it into his breast pocket.

Would he answer this one? No. If he didn't, he would never have to hear her say it. If he didn't have to hear her say it, maybe it wouldn't be true. He leaned back in his chair and closed his eyes, ignoring the rest of the mail on his desk, ignoring his secretary's repeated buzzing for his attention.

He couldn't ignore his partner's hammering on the door, his booming voice demanding to know what was going on.

'You look like hell,' Larry Cruikshank said when Cliff finally unlocked the door. 'Why don't you take a couple of months off?'

'I'm fine.'

'Bullshit,' the other man said. 'You haven't been

fine since you split up with your wife. You've been even less fine this past month or so. You're losing weight, losing your temper and, worst of all, losing this company clients and money. It's time to shape up or ship out, Cliff.'

Cliff shot to his feet, fists on his desk. 'Who the hell are you to talk to me that way?'

Larry took a similar position, nose to nose with Cliff. 'Your partner.'

'My *equal* partner,' Cliff said through clenched teeth. 'Not my boss, not my mother, not my god-damn keeper!'

'And soon to be ex-partner if things don't change pretty damned fast around here, buddy-boy. I'll take my option to fold.' Larry drew a deep breath as if waiting for Cliff to subside. When Cliff maintained his position, glaring right into the other man's eyes, Larry stood erect and nodded.

'Right. I hereby offer you the required two months' notice to collapse this corporation. You can buy me out at the end of that time – assuming we still have any assets left. I'll get it to you in writing by the end of the day.' He spun on the heel of one size twelve oxford and slammed out of Cliff's office.

An hour later, Cliff knocked on Larry's door and entered following a gruff, 'Yeah?'

'All right,' Cliff said. 'I'll take some time off.'

Two failed marriages, two failed business part-nerships? Not that his partnership in the accounting firm had failed exactly, but he had, by running away. What kind of loser did that make him, any-

173

way? Maybe he could at least try to save this relationship. Maybe he had to. Especially if, as Larry said, his inattention to business was costing them money and clients.

Larry's eyes narrowed. He ran a hand over his crisp, short-cut grey hair. 'When?'

'As soon as I get a few things in order. In the next couple of weeks.'

'Not good enough. Tomorrow.'

Cliff clenched his jaw and his fists in order to hold on to that temper Larry had accused him, rightly, of losing too often of late. 'All right, dammit. Tomorrow.'

'Two months.'

'*What*?'

'If you take two months, I'll withdraw my option to pull out. We'll renegotiate when you come back.'

Cliff snorted. 'Right. Two months. You'll be hollering for help before half that's up.' Larry had been the one, originally, when Cliff was still with Grant, to suggest the partnership, because the business had grown too big for one man.

'If I do holler for help, it won't be from you.' Larry leaned back in his chair, linking his hands behind his head. 'Don't you get it, Cliff? The state you're in, you're no help to anyone, but especially not yourself. Now get out of here, and come back whole.'

Cliff didn't answer, merely left.

He'd never be whole again.

Especially if he answered that short, terse note still tucked into his breast pocket.

Three days later, he braked to a stop in the driveway of his Galiano cabin and shot a sour look at a grimy station wagon parked on the side of the road, around which he'd had to manoeuvre to back his boat trailer in. He sat for a few minutes, tired, disheartened, leaning against the headrest, wondering why he'd bothered even getting up this morning, but then he shrugged. He'd gotten up because it was habit to get up. He'd gone fishing because that was what he did when he came here.

Alighting from the car, he unhitched the trailer, shoved it and boat into the garage, then reached into the back seat for a small ice chest. With that perched on one hip, he walked slowly up the steps and unlocked the door. He kicked it shut behind himself then leaned on it for a minute.

What the hell am I doing here? he asked himself, but of course there was no answer. For too long, there had been no answers.

The cabin was cool and quiet, so quiet that the lack of sound echoed hollowly in his ears. Apart from the past three days, he had avoided his summer cabin for more than a year, fearing exactly what he had found – memories and silence – and an absence of Lynne.

Entering the kitchen, he put the shiny salmon into the fridge. He shouldn't have caught it. It was too much fish for one. Especially one who had no appetite.

Emerging from the bathroom ten minutes later dressed in a clean pair of khaki shorts and a blue, short-sleeved shirt that he left unbuttoned, Cliff wandered into the cool living room to stare out over the pass where gleaming whitecaps raced along the expanse of crumpled blue.

He sighed, wishing for the courage to face the inevitable and then get on with his life. As he stood there, his gaze focused in nearer home, on to the patio, where the big chaise-longue normally sat by the pool. It wasn't there. Flipping the lock and sliding open the glass door, he stepped on to the patio, his heart racing, remembering another time he'd come home to find that lounge chair dragged into the grape arbor.

No! It was imagination. Wishful thinking and – '

He came to an abrupt halt. His breath left his lungs all at once. His heart slammed against his ribs and then stopped beating altogether.

'Lynne?' Unaware of the hoarse whisper that escaped him, he clenched his hands into fists. He swallowed convulsively. Had he conjured her up through pure wanting? Was this a hallucination?

Or could she be real?

Lynne, sound asleep as she waited for him to come home?

She was real. She lay asleep with her head on one bent arm, flat on her back except for her left leg, which was bent at the knee, causing her white eyelet skirt, soft cotton, as feminine as Lynne's clothing had always been, to slide back, revealing the satin skin of her inner thigh. He took two steps closer, paused again and watched the gentle breeze lift a soft curl from her temple and drape it over her right eye. In the sun, her red-gold hair shone like bright flames.

She shouldn't be sleeping, exposed like that; with her fair skin, she'd burn. She'd towed the lounge into the shade, but now the shadows lay only over her lower legs, the sun's low, angling rays catching in her lashes, producing a squint even as she slept.

Swallowing hard again, he strode on cat-like feet to her side and crouched, lifting a hand to gently brush away the hair from her face, and to shade her eyes with his cupped palm. His hand trembled. She was so beautiful! Slim now, as she had been when he first met her, delicately built, almost fragile.

That fragility was deceptive, he reminded himself quickly before he could forget again. Lynne was strong and determined, possibly even, in some ways, hard, though to look at her no one would ever guess. He believed it only because he'd known the strength it must have taken for her carry out her great deception.

His throat ached with the need to speak her name, to awaken her so he could look into her eyes and see if any love remained. Staring at her sleeping face, he kept silent, hardly daring to breathe. Her transparent skin showed the light dusting of freckles he'd always loved, darker across her nose and cheeks, fading to golden on her forehead, down her chest and on to the tops of her breasts. Her lashes, too, were gold at the tips, but of a darker shade nearer their roots. They lay now in soft arcs against the dark blue circles under her eyes.

An insect flew toward her, buzzed near her head. He shooed it away. He was not about to share this moment with her, this brief, precious time before she awoke and scrambled out of his reach, not even with a fly.

The breeze continued to toy with her short, curly hair, laying a strand into the shell of an ear. He smiled involuntarily as she turned in her sleep to rub that ear against her shoulder, then faced away from him, lowering her bent knee, wrapping her arms around herself.

The lights gusts of wind were chilling her. He saw goose bumps rise on her thighs and before he could stop himself he slipped on to the lounger beside her, edging closer inch by inch until their bare legs touched, until her back rested lightly against his chest and the bulk of his body shielded her from the breeze.

He feared the hard, erratic hammering of his heart might disturb her, but she slept on, even as he slipped an arm over her and laid it around her waist, tugging gently until she rolled back against him. His heart stopped again as she wiggled her bottom to fit herself more securely into the curve of his body, and then it resumed beating with a hard slam and a heavy, unsteady rhythm. Deep, glorious pain flooded his chest, much like the sensations he'd experienced the first time he'd lain with her, as mismatched as he'd known them to be.

He drew in a deep breath of her scent, his fingers skimming the softness of her hair. It couldn't hurt, could it, to caress her so lightly? It wouldn't wake her. And his need was so great, growing greater with each moment, to relearn the texture of her skin, memorize it for the long months and years ahead when he'd never be this close to her again.

If only he could do more than that, touch her, make love with her again before she told him that she intended to put a big 'cancelled' stamp on her account with him. Paid in full. Or, could there be something left, a small spark that he hadn't killed, that would make her willing to listen to him, willing to give them another chance together?

She made a sound, that soft, satisfied, contented little sound he remembered so well that said, *Hold me close*, that said, *I love you*, that said, *I'm glad to be with you*, and, even knowing it would at best be a subconscious memory to which she was responding, or at worst another lie, he wanted to believe it.

'Oh, Lynne,' he breathed, fighting the overpowering emotions that rocketed through him. For long moments he just held her, then even that was not enough. He turned her in his arms, tipped her face up and kissed her gently. Softly, so softly he was sure she'd never feel it, he let one hand cup a breast, curving his fingers around its softness, feeling its heat, then its weight, then its shape.

He gloried in the size of it: between the two extremes he remembered, small and hard when he'd first loved her, then full and rich in her pregnancy, and now, though different yet again, still absolutely right.

He felt her stir again. She rolled toward him, slipped her arm across him and ran her hand up and down his back inside his shirt. Her lips parted, warm and soft against the skin of his throat and he knew all at once that she was awake, awake and not running, not pushing him away, awake and holding him, aware it was he who held her.

He bent his head, one hand cupping her chin, looked into her sleepy eyes and smiled. 'Hi, Lynnie.'

Her blue eyes were filled, not with indifference as he'd feared, not with desire as he'd dreamed, but with sleepy questions, and she blinked several times then smiled that joyous, welcoming smile that he had seen every morning when he awoke, every night when he came home, every time she saw him – and every night in his dreams since they'd parted.

'Hi yourself,' she murmured, and a huge surge of relief shook his body. She hadn't come to ask for a divorce! That radiant smile said she still loved him!

'Lynne . . . oh, sweetheart,' he said, his voice thick and choked, then he took her lips with his own, parting them gently, kissing her with all the tenderness she had ever been able to arouse in him. *I love you so much!* He dared not speak the words aloud, but it didn't matter then, because her hands slid through his hair, pulling his head down to her, muffling his, 'I've missed you so badly . . .' with her kiss.

Finally, lifting his head, Cliff drew in a harsh breath, forcing it past the massive weight in his chest. He bent again and brushed her eyes closed with his lips, then took her mouth in another deep and potent kiss, reveling in her response, in the way her fingers clung to him, the way her legs scissored against his as she tried to move closer, closer, needing him as much as he needed her.

The sweet sounds of love she made deep in her throat sent exultation sweeping through him, and when she softened in his hold, letting him lead her on the wonderful dance they had shared with such passion before, he knew beyond any doubt that no matter what it took, he was not going to give her up.

Her hands splayed over his chest as her lips parted and then clung helplessly to his, returning his kiss with the same intense greed as he felt. The sounds arising from her throat became soft purrs and he stroked her back, knowing that she had longed for this moment as much as he had. It was a moment that he hoped would never end, and it stretched into minutes until time became a countless commodity, something that had ceased to matter, and immediacy became the only reality for two people who had loved, and lost, and now by some miracle loved again.

Lynne succumbed to Cliff's embrace, returned it, even when she was fully awake. She knew she should have fought harder against her own needs, should have pushed him away and told him no. She should have sat up, stood up, run from him, far and fast, before this ever began. But the feel of his body against her, the taste of his mouth on hers, the scent of him in her nostrils combined to create a heady rush of desire and she parted her lips for his kisses as they rapidly eroded her defenses, allaying her loneliness, filling her with yearning for more. He kissed her and held her as if starved for her touch, but gently, softly, with an infinite tenderness that made her ache deep inside where she thought all feeling had died.

She stroked one palm over his arm, reveling in the textures of the hard muscles under sleek, warm skin, and opened herself more fully to him, seeking his tongue, the roughness of it, the hardness, as he probed deeply and found, with agonizing slowness, the well of sweet moisture under her tongue.

Her nails raked lightly over his chest. Slowly, searchingly, she traced his muscles, around his sides, across his back, removing his shirt, grazing over terrain once known as intimately as she knew her own body. Her fingers traced down over his slim waist and inside the band at the top of his shorts and spread over the taut muscles of his buttocks. His sharp intake of breath, the convulsive tremors quivering through his body, told her of his need more surely than words. He fumbled with the buttons on her blouse and slid a hand within, fingertips brushing down inside her lacy bra. She answered his tremor in kind.

He murmured her name and the sound of his voice enchanted her. Her excitement rose at the feel of his hard arousal pressing against her thigh. The desire in his taut face as he lifted his head briefly and met her gaze moved her deeply and she stared into dark eyes. Sweat beaded his olive skin, and his voice shook as he said, 'Oh, love, to have you here, to feel you in my arms . . . I –' He broke off with a harsh groan. 'Oh, God, what am I doing?'

He rolled from her then and was gone.

'Cliff?' Half sitting, Lynne saw him striding away from her. 'Cliff!'

He didn't respond, only stood with his back to her, his head bent, his shoulders heaving as he gasped for breath.

She sat on the edge of the lounger, the patio tiles warm under her feet, the lowering sun hot on her back, a cold knot of sorrow chilling her from the inside out. '*Cliff*!'

He dove headlong into the pool, swimming toward the far end, most of the way underwater. He emerged for breath, continued on in a strong, rapid crawl, kicked off the bottom step and came back toward her. As if she didn't exist, as if what had happened – almost happened – between them didn't exist, he executed another kick turn and swam rapidly away.

Lynne stood, gathering herself and her clothing together, and went inside.

Cliff, she knew from past experience, would swim until exhausted. Then, he might listen.

Assuming she could figure out, in the light of her instinctive but unexpected and certainly unwelcome response to him, exactly what she should say.

Cliff heaved himself to the pool-deck and sat breathing heavily, muscles lax from his excessive workout.

What in the hell had he been thinking of? He huffed out a humorless laugh. Thinking? That, he had not been doing. That, he'd always found it difficult to do where Lynne was involved.

Now, he stood, his legs feeling feeble. The burning in his lungs had ebbed, though, as he towelled his back and chest dry and tugged on his shirt. He strode inside.

Lynne sat curled in a chair, staring at the floor. She looked up as he entered.

'Why did you come here, Lynne?' It wasn't what he'd meant to say. He didn't think it was. He didn't know what else it might have been, though, so he supposed it was as good a question as any.

He saw her throat work as she swallowed. She stood, as if somehow that might make it easier. For her, or for him?

'You know why, Cliff. I came to talk about our divorce.'

His laugh was hoarse and ragged. He felt as if it had been dragged from him. '*Divorce*?'

Though he'd known she'd come for that, known he'd have to face it, in the circumstances, the word sounded obscene and unbelievable coming from Lynne's kiss-swollen lips.

'Yes. I'm not asking for any child support, nor alimony,' she said. 'I'm not asking for anything except my freedom. If there are legal costs, I hope you will agree to pay them, because I all too often have a cash-flow problem. If you can't, or choose not to, then I'll find a way.'

She drew a deep breath. Before she began speaking again, he saw her lips tremble faintly. 'I'd also like it if you'd acknowledge Michael on his birthday and Christmas and things like that, just so he knows he has a father, later, when he's old enough for it to matter, but that's all I want.'

'God!' He stared at her in disbelief. 'Lynne. It's not all *I* want.'

She tossed her head, her eyes glittering like bright chips of blue ice. 'No? You've already made it clear, Cliff, that you don't want him – or me – and I seriously doubt anything's changed in that regard.'

Don't want you? he almost shouted. *Don't want air, don't want sustenance?* He clenched his teeth to hold back the words.

'I see.' His voice grated. He cleared his throat. 'I can't agree. Somehow, somewhere, we have to find another way.'

She stared at him, her eyes growing dark and stormy. 'What other way? I have a life to live, Cliff. I can't go on living it in limbo! Divorce is the only solution. You must have known that was why I wanted to see you.'

He strode to the patio doors, staring out at blue water, green leaves, bright flowers, yet seeing a monochrome world in shades of grey. 'You've met someone, of course. I knew that the minute I got your first letter asking for a meeting.'

He heard her swift intake of breath right behind him, felt the heat of her hand on his back. 'No!'

Relief made him sway, though he thought he detected pity in her swift, adamant denial. Turning quickly, he caught her and held her to him, a hand pressed against the back of her head, preventing her looking up at him. A man deserved some dignity.

'No other man?'

'No other man.'

He couldn't speak for several beats, then, when he had, wished he hadn't, his voice came out so ragged. 'Wanna hear a funny story?'

After a moment, she said, 'Sure, if you want to tell me.' From her tone, he doubted Lynne felt any more like laughing than he did. He wasn't even sure why he wanted to tell her. Maybe, he reasoned, it would help them both to understand what had happened out there on the patio.

'I've–I've lived celibate since, too, since I left you, Lynne.'

When several minutes had gone by without any response from her, he lifted her face and saw the tears he had felt against his chest.

'You were crying the last time I saw you. I never wanted to do that to you, Lynne. I never wanted to hurt you. I wish I could have been strong enough to – I wish I could have been the man you thought I was. Hell, I wish I could have been the man *I* thought I was, when I married you, knowing what I did.'

'You're the only man I've ever wanted.'

'Until now?' he asked. 'Is that why you're anxious to start divorce proceedings right now? You've met someone you'd like to start . . . seeing? Maybe, as the personal ads say, "Object matrimony"?'

Lynne stepped back from him. 'No! Dammit, Cliff, do you think I'd consider marrying someone else when I still feel the way I do about you?'

His lack of response was her answer. As always, Cliff believed what he wanted to believe, and nothing she could say would sway him.

186

Instead of trying to battle against his intransigence, she shrugged it off and took another tack as she returned to curl up in the chair.

'I don't like raising a son who screams in terror whenever a man comes near him because he sees so few of them,' she said. 'It's not fair to him and it's not fair to me because what you just said might well come true; maybe someday I will get over you and find someone else I can love. I know you said you'd never want to divorce me, but you must see that *I* have to divorce *you* whether I want to or not.

I can't go on the way I'm living now, in some kind of limbo – neither wife nor divorcee – just . . . alone. If I have to be alone, then I have to break free completely, make a life for myself. I hoped for a long time that you'd change your mind, that you'd accept the truth, accept your son, but I've waited long enough. Now, I need to be free.'

'Free? Do you think we can ever be free of each other?'

'Yes.' Determination replaced the doubt in her eyes. 'We must. I must.'

'I know,' he said heavily at last, without turning. 'I know, but I didn't want to hear you say it.' He laughed then, and it held mockery – for both of them – she thought. 'Do you have any idea how incongruous this is, your sitting there asking your husband, with whom you just nearly made love, for a divorce?'

'Do you have any idea how incongruous my whole life has been, these past fourteen months?' she retorted. 'Married to a man who has refused to

187

live with me and our child since Michael was one month old?'

Lynne saw the old familiar closed look come over his face and forced herself to go on without submitting to the temptation to renew the argument she knew she could never win.

'Why wouldn't you answer my letters, Cliff?'

His oblique response didn't answer her question. 'Did you know that I've been looking for you? That since last August – a year, Lynne, a full year – I haven't known where you were? Then, when I finally do hear from you, what address do you give me? A box number! A post office box number that I could write to, or a lawyer I could call, but no number where I could phone you, nor a street address I could visit, as if I couldn't be trusted not to molest you in some way!'

'I never worried about your molesting me.'

His laugh was short and bitter. He crossed the room and sat, despite his damp shorts, on a sofa at right angles to the chair where she'd sat. As he leaned forward, arms on his thighs, staring up at her from under his black brows, she resumed her seat.

'Looks like you should have worried about it, doesn't it?'

She sighed sharply in impatience and exasperation. 'Dammit, what just happened out there had nothing to do with molestation! All right, so our making love was a mistake – '

'That wasn't what *I'd* call making love. Foreplay, maybe, but – '

She went on as if he hadn't interrupted.

' – but it wasn't as if I didn't want it as much as you did *at the time*. I knew where I was, and with whom, within seconds of awakening, and there was plenty of opportunity for me to stop you, stop what we were doing. So don't worry. I won't be shouting attempted rape.'

She gave him a long, level look. 'And one more thing, if you'll recall: *you* walked away from *me*.' She didn't add 'again'. She didn't have to.

CHAPTER 11

Cliff ignored what he saw as a provocative statement geared to precipitate an argument. 'But what you got out there –' he gestured toward the patio '– wasn't what you came for.'

'No, it wasn't.' But oddly, his statement – and it had definitely been that; no hint of a question had colored his tone – instilled an element of doubt in her. Had she, on some subconscious level, harbored a hope that maybe, if she and Cliff were to see one another again, things might happen that would eventually lead them to an understanding? *Lead them back together*?

'No,' she repeated sharply, as much to reassure herself as in response to him. 'I came because I . . . because I had to.'

He nodded. 'You came because I forced you by not responding to your letters.'

'Yes. I thought at first it would be easier if we could do it all by mail, and through lawyers, not have to meet personally.' It was her turn to laugh sourly at the irony of what she'd said. Their meeting had certainly become personal. Their gazes met, clashed, held for a moment as they shared a smile that held more sadness then humor.

'Then I realized,' she continued, 'when you didn't write back, that it was the wrong way to go about dissolving things. I thought that was your way of telling me so. So I decided if we met at some . . . neutral place, it would be less painful.' The truth of the matter was, she didn't want him to see Michael. She didn't want to have to watch his face take on that hard, bitter cast she had seen too often when Cliff looked on their child.

'You said you'd been looking for me.' Why, she wondered, hadn't he gone to the most logical place to find her, the place he must have known she'd be?

'I just wanted to know that you were all right,' he said. 'At least at first. Then, I knew I wanted to see you for more reasons than that. I wanted to be with you again. I wanted to touch you, hear your voice, go to sleep with you beside me, wake up the same way. I wanted you. *Us*, again.'

Lynne's head spun. Was she still out there in the shade of the grape arbor, asleep and dreaming?

She wished she could believe that, but knew she could not. She wished she could believe in what Cliff was saying, and knew she dared not.

'Me?' she said, rising and putting most to the width of the room between them. 'Me . . . and Michael?'

'I'd . . . try.'

'Try?'

He said nothing and Lynne sighed as she looked

into the fathomless sorrow in his eyes, reading doubts, fears, the same old concerns that had torn them apart before.

'I see.' She had to blink her tears back. She wouldn't show him the depths of her emotions, not now, not when those emotions were so close to the surface, and yet running deeper than they had ever run before: sadness, grief, loss.

She had just shown him a different set of her emotions, with her voice, her arms, her lips, her body. She had offered him every ounce of her love. Yet even now he didn't realize that, for her, physical love wasn't enough.

She and Michael were a package deal, and she demanded deep, abiding love for them both. Commitment to their lives.

But . . . what if his willingness to try *could* lead to reconciliation?

She must have believed that, down deep somewhere, must never have given up entirely, because now it lay there, an infinitesimal ember that could nevertheless cause a massive conflagration if treated just right. It explained why, even after she'd come fully awake out there, and known she was really in his arms for the first time in over a year, not just dreaming of it, she hadn't pulled away. Because she had wanted him, too, all those months apart, and still did.

But Cliff was unable to treat that ember of their love the way it should be treated. He didn't know how to breathe on it with her, nurture it, keep it glowing until it flickered and then flared into the full life it deserved. The halfway relationship that was all he'd seemed capable of before, and probably wanted again, was not going to be.

While he might still want the fire of their love, he didn't want the responsibility of it.

Or the fruits.

He was still too ensnared by the erroneous belief that had stained what they had shared, and would continue to do so as long as he clung to it.

'You see?' she demanded. 'Nothing's changed! We –'

'No,' he said. Pain flared in his eyes as he strode to where she stood. 'Don't say it again. I don't want to hear it. If you hadn't been able to find me, I never would have had to, would I?'

'The fact remains, I did find you, Cliff. I did say what I needed to say, and I'm still waiting for your response.'

'My response?' he said, and dipped his head to take her mouth in another of those kisses she was powerless to withstand; and she clung to him, returning it measure for measure, until he lifted his mouth from hers and only looked at her, everything he felt outlined on his face, the desire, the fear and frustration. If this was saying goodbye, it was growing harder and harder to make it stick.

Especially following his next words. 'Dammit, Lynne, you don't want our marriage to end any more than I do.'

She wrenched herself out of his arms. 'I don't see any other options,' she said, her voice taut, strained. 'I told you, we can't go on this way.'

He made as if to reach for her, then stopped, but stared at her oddly for a long moment, deep lines in his face, lines of stress, and, she thought, of grim determination. He looked like a man resolved to risk swimming from his sinking ship toward a distant, inhospitable shore, because despite the dangers, there was no other way, no other hope. 'All right,' he said softly. 'We won't go on living this way.'

'Meaning?' she asked, chilled by a sudden sensation of something important about to happen, something she wouldn't be able to control, but whose outcome would affect the course of her life from this point onward.

Cliff wanted to form the words his heart had been speaking for months, but now that the moment had come, he didn't quite know how to tell her. But he did know that he'd made his decision and it was irrevocable. He didn't know where it was going to take him . . . them. He didn't even know if it was the right one or the wrong one. It was, however, the only one he could make. He drew a deep breath.

She looked at him, her eyes wary, and as if she were puzzled by the change that had come over him. 'Are you saying you won't contest my action?' Was that disappointment he detected in the tremor of her voice? Her next words negated the thought. 'I'll deed the house back to you,' she continued as if she had to keep on talking rapidly, to fill the void around them with speech so nothing terrible could come sneaking at them out of the silence. 'The money you put into my account is mostly still there. I used it only to pay taxes and utilities on the place. It's yours. All I want – '

'I know.' He pinched the bridge of his nose for a second. 'All you want is a divorce.' He met her gaze squarely. 'Well, you're not having one, Lynne. There will be no divorce.'

'What –?' she started, tried to move away, but he cut her off and held her before him. 'You can't stop me, Cliff. No court in the land would deny me a divorce from you.'

'If one of us petitions for prior counseling,' he said quickly, 'it will certainly cause a delay.'

'Counseling? But you – '

'I know. I wouldn't, before, when you wanted me to. I know it was my fault. I was the one who wouldn't try. But now I will. All I know is that I ca...'t let you go completely. We can do it, Lynne. We can find a way to be together. We have to.'

Before he could try to prevent it, she jerked away and stood several feet removed, glaring at him. 'What way?'

The question was curt and bitter, tone telling him more than words that she could see no way. 'What are you suggesting, Cliff, saying you can't let me go "completely"? That we see each other clandestinely, go to bed together now and then just to take the edge off?'

He frowned and barked, 'No!' too quickly.

Because, was that, he had to ask himself, entirely true? He wasn't sure, but maybe that had been what he was saying. Hearing her put it into words told him how tawdry it sounded, how insulting to her, and how impossible for them both.

'I – no,' he said again stubbornly. 'But I just know I can't let you go. I –' He gnawed his lower lip. 'I wish . . . My idea how we can work things out is still . . . sort of . . . nebulous. I need time to sort it out in my own mind.'

'If you've got some unique proposition about how to put broken eggs back together again, I'll be willing to hear it,' she said. 'But while you're waiting for your ideas to jell, I suggest we talk about what I came to discuss: terminating a marriage that's been over since probably before it ever began!'

He could only gaze at her, misery eating at his insides, indecision eating at his brain, stealing whatever sensible, logical arguments he might come up with. It was painful. Indecision was not a trait he would ever have characterized himself as having. Yet now, it seemed one of his foremost. 'I'm not ready to talk about that.'

'We have to talk about it.' Frustration and exhaustion filtered through her tone. Slowly, she sank back on to her chair, looking up at him, something, compassion, maybe pity, in her eyes.

'I think a divorce is something like a funeral,' she said. 'A closure. It's the turning of a page in a photo album, or the final locking of the door to a house you've sold. We might know what's on that turned page, but we've moved past it. We might remember fondly what's in that house, but it isn't ours any more. Our marriage has died. We can't resurrect it, so we have to end it, end our grieving and get on with the rest of our lives.

When my dad died, we all mourned him, but we came to learn that while things would never be the same again, maybe they would be just as good, in a different way. I know, since you have no family that you remember, no one you care about in your past, that what I'm saying might not make sense, but it's way of honoring what was good in your previous life to move forward and find something else to enjoy in the future, once you've accepted that there's no going back.'

'And that's what you want?' he asked. 'Something just as good, in a different way? Do you believe that you'll find something just as good? Or have you already found it?'

Lynne stared at him for several seconds, trying not to get angry, knowing it was his pain talking, not his rational self, and then shook her head. She stood. 'All right, Cliff. It's clear there's no point in my staying to discuss this with you. We have nothing more to say to each other. I will have my divorce. With your co-operation, or without it. Goodbye.'

'Dammit, just give me a little time! I told you I have an idea forming in the back of my mind. Let me have a few minutes to work on it.'

'Fine,' Lynne said briskly. 'Mind if I use your phone? I need to check on the kids.'

'*Kids*?' He fired the word at her like a bullet as he shot to his feet and grabbed her by the shoulders, dragging her up to stand before him. 'Kids, plural? Holy . . . hell! If you're going to lie, can't you learn to do it consistently? Didn't you tell me that there was no other man involved? And now you admit, if not to loving someone else, or living with someone else, that at least you've had another baby with him!

'Ah, God,' he said, thrusting her away as if he couldn't bear to breathe the same air as she did. 'Your lying sickens me! Go, Lynne. Just go. Just get out of my life and stay out! You can have your damned divorce!'

Lynne knew she should simply leave it like that, leave him believing whatever it took for him to accept her decision and let her go, but something in her rebelled at the thought of his believing just one more lie about her.

'There . . . is . . . no . . . other . . . man!' She emphasized her words with slaps on the back of the chair. 'There never was! I'll go, Cliff! I'll go just as soon as you tell me you believe that of me if nothing else! I am not a liar. I am not a cheat. And I do not, and never have, committed adultery! Look at me!'

She grabbed his arms and tried to shake him. It was like trying to move a stone wall. 'Dammit, look at me! Tell me you believe me!'

After a moment, she let out a sound that was a cross between a growl of fury and a sob of despair and turned from him. 'Oh, what's the use?' she said. 'Goodbye, Cliff. I'm sorry I came.'

'God almighty!' he said, catching her shoulder and spinning her back around to face him. 'Why did you wait so long before telling me? Didn't you want to marry the new baby's father before it was born? It is the new baby's father you want to marry, isn't it? Is he the same man who . . . is he Michael's father?'

Lynne stepped in close and slugged him in the jaw with everything she had to put behind her fist. Slapping was too tame a reaction for the fury that surged through her, robbing her of all control. She wished, in that moment, that she weighed a hundred pounds more and could flatten him with her blow. She wished there were some way to get through to this man, some language they had in common, but it seemed there was nothing. He didn't even give her the satisfaction of trying to ward off the second blow she aimed at him. All he did was recoil slightly, rub his jaw and stare at her while she nursed her sore fist with the other hand.

'You make me sick, Cliff Foreman!' she wept, hating him for reducing her to tears. 'There is no new baby. You are Michael's father, damn your lousy hide, and Amanda's father was my brother! Dear heaven! Did you think I'd just abandon her? I am her guardian and it's partly for her sake that I want to be rid of you, but mostly for my own, you rotten, ill-bred louse, you . . . you . . .'

Her voice cracked and broke completely as, shoulders shaking she wrenched away from him, turning her back, stumbling blindly for the door she knew lay somewhere in the direction she was heading.

She never got there.

'What did you say?' Cliff scooped her up off her feet, strode back to the couch and sat down beside her, his hands tight on her shoulders.

'Amanda? Your *niece*? What has she got to do with – '

He pulled her hands away from her face and stared at her as realisation began to dawn. 'Taylor? You said Taylor *was* her father?' Horror, disbelief, flooded through him. 'Is Taylor dead?'

She just stared at him, with contempt, he thought, true loathing, but it was nothing like the disgust he felt for himself. She'd said she was Amanda's guardian. That meant . . . 'Taylor *and* Ann?'

Her silence was all the reply he needed, that and her white face, her shattered expression. 'Why didn't you call me?' he ground out. 'Dammit, Lynne, why?'

He leaned his head back and groaned.

He knew why. Because he'd walked out on her. She hadn't called him for the same reason she hadn't lived in his house or accepted his financial support. 'Did you really hate me so much?' he asked, looking at her again. 'So much that you couldn't let me know?'

All the suffering she had felt was in her eyes, in her tone as she stared at him and asked in a raspy voice, 'Why didn't *you* call *me*? It was in all the papers, their being overdue, the search and finally . . . f-finding their bodies.'

She collapsed forward, as if bending in half would hold in her grief. 'Oh, God, Cliff, I've never felt more alone in my life!'

He lifted her against him, cradled her cheek in one trembling hand. 'I didn't know. Baby, believe me, I didn't know!'

He could see, though, that she was having difficulty believing him. Her eyes continued to overflow, and her face worked as she stared at him, shaking her head. He gathered her closer into his arms. She let him hold her, unresisting. 'Ah, sweetheart, what happened?' he asked.

It was several moments before she could tell him. 'Taylor and Ann were killed a year ago July in plane crash. It was on the news for days, the search for them. I thought–I thought you must have heard.'

And was hurt beyond measure that there wasn't a word of sympathy from you, a card, a note, a phone call. And no expression of grief from a man who had claimed to be very fond of his wife's brother and sister-in-law. He knew that's what she'd thought, how she'd felt, in the face of his silence.

'Oh, love . . .' He drew her head against his shoulder, holding her in a comforting embrace. 'Believe me, Lynnie. I didn't know,' he said again. 'I wasn't here. I was in Australia on business for six weeks last summer.' He'd gone hoping the pressure of business meetings, the consuming work, the taut negotiations would require all his concentration, help him to forget.

He shook his head. Of course he hadn't been able to forget. The trip had been a waste of time, a waste of money and no new business had arisen from it, most likely due to his personal lack of attention.

While he was away, Lynne had needed him and he hadn't been there.

He wanted to pound his fist through the wall to relieve his sense of frustration, of anger, of useless-

201

ness. Instead, he gentled his hold on her and murmured, 'Can you tell me about it, Lynne?'

She accepted his solace, and accepted just as easily that if he had been there and known, when it happened, he would have offered it then.

Somehow, being with Cliff made it easier to talk about it for the first time since it had happened. She'd never been able to share with anyone the agony of the long wait for news. Indeed, for the most part, she'd crowded the memory of it deep down into the bottom of her mind where the pain of it couldn't reach her, but it still surfaced at odd moments, tightening her throat, choking her with tears she had always shed alone.

Now, in Cliff's embrace, surrounded by his warmth, the protective circle of his arms, his caring, she was at last able to relate the story, to let the grief spill out.

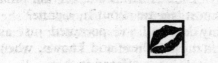

CHAPTER 12

'They'd been working so hard,' she said, 'and both of them knew they needed a break. I don't know if he ever mentioned it, but Taylor had a private pilot's license.' Her voice choked again. 'He'd wanted to be a commercial pilot since he was a little boy, but when Dad died – well, he never got beyond his private license. A friend offered them the use of his hunting camp up in the mountains, so Taylor rented a small float plane to fly into the lake the camp's on. Michael and I went up to stay with Amanda. We've . . . been there ever since.'

'And that's why you left our – *your* – house in Victoria.'

'Yes.'

'And why you didn't take the money I put in your account. Taylor left you . . . provided for? Is it enough, Lynne? You said you had a cash-flow problem sometimes. That money's yours! You must know I want you to have it.'

She sat erect, would have moved apart from him, but for the firmness of his hold. 'I don't want your money, Cliff. Taylor left Amanda's education provided for and the mortgage was life-insured. But she and Michael are my day-to-day responsibility. I can look after them and myself. I prefer it. I have a small accounting business going, working for a few little companies, and I take in boarders. I'm – we're – doing fine.'

'I see.'

Again, Cliff leaned his head back and stared up at the ceiling.

He *didn't* see. He didn't see why she would take in boarders in her brother's house in Ladner, when she had a perfectly good home of her own in Victoria. There would have been plenty of room there for Mandy, too. He didn't see why she wanted to be a part-time bookkeeper for a few small companies, when he'd been paying her enough to live on without her having to work.

Then suddenly, as clearly as if some booming voice from the sky had spoken, he knew that, no matter what else, 'seeing' was something he had to learn to do, if he was ever to have a real chance with Lynne.

At least he understood now why, in his search for Lynne, he had never been able to contact Taylor and Ann.

He couldn't remember their telephone number, and it wasn't in the book. He'd driven to their place once shortly before Christmas, hoping Taylor would tell him where Lynne had gone, even if he chose to beat him to a pulp first. He'd have taken that beating and more if it had meant finding Lynne.

There had been a pair of old ladies coming out the door of what had been Taylor's house, and one, a buxom, over-made-up old dolly, had smiled and asked if he was there to look at the vacant room.

'We could do with a nice young buck like you living here,' she'd said and her thin, frail companion had tittered nervously. 'Go on in and see Lou,' the large one had urged. 'She's in charge. Just tell her Bella sent you.'

'This is a rooming house?' he'd asked, not really expecting any answer but the one he'd got, and had left, believing that the reason for there not being a phone number for Taylor Morrison was that he'd packed up his family and moved on. And taken Lynne with him.

The truth had never once occurred to Cliff, and now that he knew, he knew, too that, despite her brave words, Lynne hadn't been doing fine. Any more than he had.

What he needed to do now was find a way to convince her of that. 'Sweetheart,' he said, bending to brush his lips over her temple. 'I am sorry. You know that, don't you?' His words made her break down again and she clung to him, weeping.

'I didn't even know that Taylor liked to hunt,' Cliff murmured, half to himself.

Somehow, that made it worse, he thought. He'd liked his brother-in-law, respected him, but clearly hadn't really known him. Now, he never would have that chance, just as Taylor and Ann would never have the chance for the dozen kids they'd laughingly, maybe jokingly planned to fill their big old house with, never knowing how it had pained Cliff to know that the one Lynne carried was the only one he'd ever be able to call his.

And if they had known, they would have cared, for his sake, just as knowing that Taylor's loving presence was there in the background for Lynne, that she had her brother to help her over the rough spots, had made much of their separation almost bearable for Cliff.

All this time, while he'd been consoling himself with the thought that Lynne wasn't as alone as he was, she had been. Just as alone. Maybe, because she'd always had family and he hadn't, more alone.

'It was summertime, not the hunting season. They went just to get away,' Lynne said. 'Ann had never been into the wilderness before, so it was a real treat for her. I remember how excited she was . . .

'She . . . they . . .' Her voice cracked and Cliff rocked her while she wept again.

'Don't, Lynne. Hush, now. You don't have to talk about it if you don't want to.' His own voice cracked and he swallowed quickly as he buried his face in her bright hair. He should have been there for her throughout that ordeal. That she'd had to go through it alone was something he'd never forgive himself.

She drew in a deep breath and let it out slowly. 'I do want to tell you. There's never been anyone else I could talk about it with.'

He held her tighter and she went on. 'They flew to the lake on a Friday afternoon. When they didn't return by Monday morning, a search began. It was obvious that they had made it in all right; they'd used the cabin and left a note of thanks for their friend to find the next time he went up. But they just didn't come back. The search went on for five days before they found the plane. They were both dead, of course, but Ann had lived long enough to leave a note for me, and one for Mandy.'

Lynne dropped her head to his shoulder again. Her voice came muffled. 'She was pregnant again. She miscarried and bled to death.'

'Christ!' Cliff's hissed word might have been a prayer, or a curse. His arms tightened on her.

'She named me Mandy's legal guardian,' Lynne went on, 'and asked me to adopt her, teach her to call me Mommy because every child deserves a living mother.'

She drew in a deep breath and went on. 'Mandy calls me that. She thinks of Michael as her baby brother. She's only two and a half now, and I think she's pretty well forgotten the life she lived before. We're her family, me, Michael, Louisa.

I am going to adopt Amanda,' she said, lifting her head from Cliff's shoulder and looking up at him again. 'But I can't do it as long as I'm married to you, not unless you want to adopt her, too, and I know you don't, not considering how you feel about what you consider "other people's children".'

'Lynne . . .' His voice was husky. 'Don't – '

'Don't what?' She sat up straight and pushed her hair off her forehead. 'Don't adopt Mandy?'

'Don't be . . . bitter towards me. I would have

come to you, if I'd known. Please believe that much of me, at least.'

She gazed at him with a deep surge of compassion. She cupped her hand around his jaw and said, 'I know that, Cliff.'

'But you didn't know it then.'

She shook her head. 'I was too . . . raw. Hurting too badly to think clearly. I just assumed that because the search was in all the papers, on TV, the radio, you must have heard. When you didn't call, I had to remind myself that what had been between us was over and there was no reason for you to . . . care.'

'I care now,' he said. 'I would have cared as much then.' Capturing her hand under his, he turned his face and kissed her palm.

'Yes.' She let him draw her face to his, and accepted his kiss, returning it slowly, softly, trying to tell him how much she cared for him, how little she liked hurting him, how deeply she wished that it could be different for them.

It was not meant to be a sexual kiss, but it was a totally sensual one, and before she knew it her tongue was parting his lips, inserting itself inside to find his wet heat, the taste of him, the feel of him, both rough and smooth at the same time, and deeply, incredibly thrilling.

He sucked gently on her tongue, then gave her his, and she returned the caress with sudden, trembling urgency, feeling the softness of his lips tighten and firm over hers as his lower body hardened against her.

'Cliff . . .' Her tremulous whisper of need seemed to inflame him, and his immediate response further inflamed her. His touch electrified her, his arms captured her, his kisses enraptured her. He dipped his head and nibbled at the tendons in her throat and she arched to his touch, her breath rapid, rising and falling in her chest as control slipped farther and farther from her grasp.

'Please . . .' Lynne gasped as his mouth closed over her breast, hot and wet through the thin cloth of her blouse and bra, his teeth scraping over the shape of her nipple until she cried out with need to feel him against her bare skin.

He slipped buttons free, stroked one finger around the lace edge of a cup and slid it down inside. The sensual touch was more than she could withstand and she reached up to unfasten the snap between her breasts, pulling the cloth away so that his moistness and heat were where she needed them.

He suckled and her head spun crazily with the pleasure of his mouth pulling at her flesh. He left that breast and licked slowly up the underside of the other, circling it with his tongue before drawing her hard, aching nipple into the depth of his mouth, sucking firmly, then softly, then widening his mouth to take in even more of her breast, his tongue laving her skin and flicking the hard bead at the tip until she gasped and pulled his head away, on the verge of explosion.

He met her seeking lips with another deep, hot kiss and she clung to him, shaking as wave after wave of sensation swept through her body. A hot wetness spread from her centre, tightening her abdomen and her leg muscles until she quivered, and she moaned with growing need as his hand found the hem of her skirt, pulled it up and bared her legs to his caresses. She gave an inarticulate cry when his seeking fingers slid past the narrow elastic at the top of one thigh and encountered the well of desire that had burst its banks and poured from her and, lifting, straining against him, she abandoned herself to the magic of his arousing strokes. The sun angling through the patio doors lay hot against her skin. His face was dark on her paleness as she lifted her head and watched him suckle her breast. The contrast was as exciting to see as his touch was to feel and she smiled when he glanced up and met her ardent gaze, not trying to hide her pleasure. She stroked him, her hands making forays around his neck and ears and mouth, her teeth nibbling, her tongue probing, but it wasn't enough. She shoved his shirt off over his shoulders, tore it from his arms and then moaned when his hard, bare chest with its thick mat of black curls abraded her nipples.

He laid her back on the couch, his heavy weight atop her, not holding back, and she locked her legs around him, her head flung back, hips moving in a rhythm that came from some place beyond her control, and slipped her hands from the sweat-slicked skin of his back into the elastic waist of his shorts, cupping his buttocks in her strong fingers, pressing, squeezing, nails raking soft tracks across his tender skin.

'Oh, Lynnie, love . . .' He panted as he spoke, and

cradled her face in his big hands, trembling thumbs closing her eyes as his mouth took hers again hard and desperately, then moved to her brows, her cheeks her chin and down her neck. She writhed under him, wanting his mouth on hers, wanting it on her breasts at the same time, wanting his touch everywhere, with every fibre of her being, needing him.

He lifted her, divested her of her panties, shucked his own shorts and entered her swiftly, both of them transported by the glory of this union.

'I love you. I love you. I love you.' Who had said the words? Maybe he had, maybe she had, maybe both of them, but it didn't matter. All that mattered was the deep, pulsating awareness flowing through them, more than physical, deep, rich emotion linking them, coiling and twisting from heart to heart, mind to mind, as their bodies twisted, seeking greater and greater closeness, closeness that could never be enough, could never make up for the months of deprivation they had both endured. She arched herself into a quivering bow that met his thrusts and complemented them, that took all he gave and gave all he sought, even when he demanded more than she'd ever thought she had to give.

She cried out again and again and then wept as completion came thunderously, dramatically, totally, sending her whirling away into a dark, hot place where she wanted to remain because it was a place that contained Cliff and herself in isolation and peace and love . . .

★　★　★

Cliff slowly became aware of a crick in his neck. Lifting his head from Lynne's shoulder, he gazed at her. Her lashes fluttered. Her mouth still trembled. Standing, he lifted her into his arms and carried her to the bedroom. Balancing her against one thigh, he stripped back the covers and laid her down, before sliding in beside her, drawing the sheet up over them. She smiled, never opening her eyes, and snuggled close to him. He stroked his hands down her back, sighing with pleasure at the feel of her nakedness against his own.

They lay silent, no words between them, yet tension built in great waves, washing over them both, until it translated itself to movements. At first, they were small motions; the curl of a pinkie against an arm; the flutter of lashes against a throat; a long, tremulously indrawn breath sliding nipple against chest. A flexing hand that elicited a bending knee, a shudder, a soft, delighted moan, a swift gasp and a parting of lips over heated flesh.

They rolled, joined, mated, soft cries and deep, from-the-inside-out shudders, muscles contracting and trembling, voices husky and ragged, breathing rough and hoarse, and always, bringing them closer and closer to the edge, those slow, strong and involuntary pulses of Lynne's inner core pulling at Cliff's flesh as he tried to lose himself in her.

'Cliff . . .' From far away Lynne heard her voice calling his name and felt his hands clasping her hips, her legs, as he drew her knees high so her thighs lay along his sides, and then he was clasping her waist as she convulsed inside and out, drawing him with her

212

into a maelstrom of color and light and buffeting forces that took an aeon to subside.

When Lynne awoke, it was dark, and she lay there wondering at the folly of what she had done. There had been a time, there must have been a time, when she could have stopped herself, stopped him. There should have been a moment for her to pull back, to reflect, to gather herself and her thoughts and recognize that making love with Cliff would do no good. To recognize the amount of harm it would do.

What had she been doing? Using him to assuage her grief? Or using him to celebrate life?

She breathed deeply of his scent, exhaled softly in a sigh, knowing that even if she had taken a moment to reconsider, if there had ever really been any thoughts in her mind that might have overcome the needs of her body, she wouldn't trade the past hours for anything.

But nor would she allow herself to repeat them.

Softly, so as not to disturb him, she kissed his cheek and slipped out of bed, going into the bathroom off the spare bedroom at the other end of the house. She was in the shower when he joined her, looking sleepy and sated and far too handsome for her peace of mind, all tousled dark hair, shuttered brown-black eyes and rough, five-o'clock-shadowed jaw.

Before she could even consider a protest, he encircled her with his arms; at that point, she could scarcely breathe, let alone protest.

Slowly, sensuously, he soaped her skin until

neither of them felt sleepy any more, or sated; then he lifted her so that her legs were around his waist and his hands linked under her thighs.

As he slid inside her, his mouth slid over hers, and they loved again with the deep, dark need of two people who didn't know what is going to happen in their lives, but did know that they couldn't stop loving each other.

Then they stood, just holding one another, until the water finally ran cold.

'What are we going to do?' Cliff asked as he followed Lynne into the living room.

Fully dressed, she turned to look at him. She carried her head and shoulders tautly, her stance belying the soft, pliant woman he'd held in his arms so recently. It was as if the cool water from the shower had frozen something in her. 'What can we do?' she asked. 'We go on as planned.'

'Whose plan?' He approached, but she side-stepped his seeking hand. He let it drop to his side.

'I wasn't aware that you had one,' she said, sliding her feet into her sandals.

'We can't go back,' he said. 'We can't erase the past few hours.'

'Maybe not, but nothing's changed because of them.'

He couldn't believe this. 'Everything's changed! You have to see that, Lynne!'

'What has?'

'Us. Or maybe what we have to accept is that we haven't changed.'

She met his gaze squarely. 'Yes. That's what I'm afraid of. So, with nothing having changed, I may as well go.'

'Go where? You've missed the last ferry.'

'I have a room in the hotel just down the road. I told Louisa I'd be there, so that's where I'd better be if she calls me.'

'We could have your calls transferred here. We could get something to eat. I caught a salmon. I'll –'

'No, Cliff.'

He couldn't let her leave. 'Who is Louisa, your baby-sitter?'

Lynne smiled, recognising a stalling ploy when she saw one. All right. She'd stay a few more minutes, try to make him understand why she had to cut herself free right now.

'Much more than a baby-sitter,' she said. 'She's my friend, my mother-substitute, and my housekeeper. And I don't think she'd understand if I spent the night anywhere other than where I told her I'd be.'

'Even if she knew you'd spent it with your husband?'

'Lou doesn't know I have a husband. She thinks I just have the kids. I'm Lynne Castle to her and the tenants. And how could I explain spending the night with you, even though you are my husband, when you very soon won't be, and we both know it?'

His eyes flared as high color stained his cheekbones. 'I told you, and I wasn't kidding. I want back into your life.' His voice softened. 'We have so much to give each other, love. We both have such a need for each other.'

She picked up her purse and dug in it for her keys. '*Our* needs aren't paramount here, Cliff. I have kids with greater need, so as far as I'm concerned there's nothing more to say. What we did this evening was a mistake. I know I shouldn't have let it happen, and I'll always regret that I did. But that's not something I can change, either, so like everything else I'll have to learn to accept it.

'We're human, both of us, and humans screw up on a regular basis. Goodnight, Cliff.'

He strode to put himself between her and the door. His jaw squared off stubbornly and in that instant he looked so much like Michael, she wanted to laugh almost as much as she wanted to weep. She did neither, only walked right up to him and waited for him to move.

He stood his ground. 'There's plenty more to say. At least on my part. I listened to you; now it's your turn to listen to me.'

She waited. He continued to stand there, glaring at her, his chest heaving. 'I'm listening,' she said.

'I'm thinking.'

'Think fast, Cliff. I need to leave.' She elbowed past him when he continued to hesitate.

'Lynne.'

Something desperate in his voice stopped her but did not turn.

'What?'

'Two months.'

She spun on one heel, searching gaze sweeping over his taut face. His eyes were bleak, his mouth tight, with a pale ring of tension around it.

'Two months, what?' she asked, despising herself for the blend of suspicion and indefatigable hope she heard in her tone.

'My partner claimed I was useless in the business and told me to take off for a couple of months. I have most of that left. So give me that time. Give me until the end of my vacation before we decide, once and for all.

'Come here. Bring the children. Let me get to know them. Then, after that time, we can talk again. Maybe we can live together successfully as a family, maybe we can't. But don't you think we owe it to ourselves to at least try?'

'No,' she said, angrier than she had been in a long time. 'No, I do not! In case it hasn't occurred to you, those children you so blithely mention are real, living human beings who, in that time, could easily learn to love you. Then what happens when you decide, after your vacation is over, that you don't want us any more? You want me to risk hurting my kids just for your . . . your . . . sexual gratification?'

'It's not like that!' he came back, suddenly just as angry because she wouldn't even make an effort to compromize with him. 'It could just as easily be the other way around, that I couldn't bear to let them go any more than I can bear to let you go, but you'll still insist on your divorce.'

'Oh, sure,' she said bitterly. 'I just bet you won't be able to let them go. At least Michael. I remember, Cliff! I remember the way you used to avoid looking at him. I remember how hard it was for you even to say his name. I remember that you never once touched him, nor held him nor showed any interest in him unless someone else shamed you into it by complimenting you on your wonderful baby boy. And even then, your responses didn't ring true, not to my ears.

Do you think I want to expose my son to that kind of animosity now that he's old enough to sense it? Forget it, Cliff. No more trying to convince anybody you feel something you don't feel. My kids are too important to me for that.'

'Your son is more important to you than your husband, that's what you're saying, right?' Cliff made no effort to hide his hurt.

Lynne's throat ached with the effort she made not to cry in front of him; her legs trembled as she forced herself not to run to him and comfort him in his pain, and her heart broke because she couldn't tell him that she didn't want to put the needs of her child over the needs of her husband – and herself. But she was a mother, and mothers, she knew, simply didn't have a choice when asked to make one between their own needs and the needs of their children. The children had to come first.

'If you want to put it that way, then yes. My son loves me unconditionally, you see. He trusts me. He believes in me. Which is a whole lot more than my husband does. Goodbye, Cliff. My lawyer will be in touch.'

CHAPTER 13

At the hotel, Lynne flew from the station wagon through the mercifully empty reception area, and up the stairs to her second floor room. As she'd driven, she'd been fully aware of the headlights sweeping along behind her, headlights that had caught up with her less than a minute after she had left Cliff's cabin. She locked the door and leaned against it, steeling herself for the knock she was sure would come.

After long minutes, when there had been no footsteps in the hall, no hammering on the door, she tiptoed to the window and pulled an inch of drapes aside, peering down into the parking lot. His car was there, pulled in beside hers. Cliff stood, leaning against the hood, as if too tired to do anything else.

Presently, he lifted his head, looked right at her window, stood erect and headed for the front doors. She dashed across the room to her door then froze, waiting, her body quivering, for his knock on the door. She didn't know how long she stood there, the silence profound except for the rush of blood behind her ears. Then, the sound of an engine starting sent her back to the window in time to see his tail-lights flickering red as he bounced out of the potholed parking lot and back on to the road.

When she emerged late in the morning after a night through which sleep eluded her until dawn, there was no sign of Cliff. Though she had dreaded his return, she swallowed hard, said another, and silent goodbye, then pulled out for the drive home to her family.

Cliff Foreman was no longer a part of her life.

'Mommy, Mommy!' Lynne bent and swung Amanda into her arms as the little girl ran toward her.

'Hi, darlin'. How's my girl?' She nuzzled her face into the warmth of the child's neck and blew noisily, rewarded by a spate of giggles.

'Mommy came home,' Amanda announced proudly to Louisa as the older woman emerged from the back door, wiping her hands on a tea towel.

'So I see. I told you she would, didn't I?' Louisa's often stern face relaxed into a loving smile at the sight of Mandy's delight.

Lynne's gaze flew to Louisa's. 'Rough time?'

Louisa nodded. 'For a while, last night, but we weathered it.'

'I'm sorry, Lou. I shouldn't have stuck you with that. I was afraid it might be hard.'

Amanda struggled to get down and Lynne set her on to her feet, watching her run off to the swing set where she flopped, belly down, on to the plastic seat and swung, head, arms and legs draped toward the ground.

'Nonsense,' Lou said. 'You need to get away occasionally. And Mandy's reaction was only to be expected.' Louisa took the keys from Lynne's hand and opened the trunk to pull out the suitcase her employer had taken with her. 'She'll learn to trust you in time.'

Lynne sighed, grabbing the suitcase from Louisa. 'It's terrible when a little child has to learn to trust the adults around her not to go away and die.' In her weariness, and her sorrow over the outcome of her visit with Cliff, she was vulnerable to self-pity. Her voice wobbled.

'Now, don't you get maudlin on me, young woman,' Louisa said briskly, leading the way into the house.

Lynne swallowed hard and then laughed. 'Was that what I was doing?'

'That's the way it sounded to me,' Louisa said, then added, tilting her head to one side, 'But now it sounds to me as if your son's awake. You go and get him and I'll get the rest of this dinner made. Got to cook extra tonight.' She took the lid off a huge pot of chilli and stirred, releasing a mouth-watering aroma into the room. 'Rented out Miss Larson's rooms at last.'

'Good,' said Lynne, and would have stayed to hear more about the new tenant, but Michael bellowed loudly and, well-trained mother that she was, she ran up the back stairs to where he waited for her, bouncing up and down in his crib, one sock off, T-shirt hiked up over his round belly, dimpled fists clinging to the top rail.

'Hi, bub,' she said, scooping him out of the crib and hugging him tightly. He smelled sweet and warm and familiar and she rocked him close for a long moment, telling herself that her children would be enough, she would make them enough; but even as she thought it, she ached with longing for this child's father, empty, useless longing that she would now have to learn to live with.

Just forget him, she told herself. *Clearly, he doesn't want the kind of life you want and need. So, forget the man.*

Yet how could she, when each time she held her son she ached to hold Cliff, as well? 'I wish it could have been different, little one,' she whispered against her baby's neck. 'I wish I could give you everything you're entitled to. But I can't so we'll just have to make the best of what we have. We'll get along, the three of us. We'll build a wonderful, happy life together.'

When she returned downstairs with Michael, Mrs Graham had come in from her part-time job as a dentist's receptionist, and sat at the table sipping tea. She bent and pulled Michael on to her lap. 'Mikey, Mikey, Mikey,' she said, walking her fingers up his fat tummy and tickling him under the chin. 'Was ums a dood boy today for Auntie Wou-Wou?' She glanced at Lynne. 'He howled half the night. We could hear him clear over in the other wing.'

Lynne gritted her teeth and apologized, letting

Mrs Graham's baby-talk go for once. Good tenants were hard to come by.

And speaking of which . . . 'Who rented Miss Larson's rooms, Lou?'

'Just what you ordered this time, honey,' said Louisa. 'I couldn't believe our good for – '

She broke off as a shrill cry came from the back yard and Lynne leapt toward the door. Michael, seeing her leaving so abruptly, added his howls to Amanda's, sure he was about to be abandoned again. She paused, grabbed him off Mrs Graham's lap and continued on her way out the door to where Amanda was sitting under the swing, her face covered with dust and tears, mouth open to reveal a punctured tongue that she'd bitten as she fell.

'Oh, sweetheart, come here,' crooned Lynne, crouching to pick Mandy up with her free arm. Standing, one child on each hip, she walked quickly back to the house where Louisa, ready as always, had an ice cube out of the freezer.

'There you go, sweetie,' the housekeeper said, giving Amanda the cube to suck on, tucking a washcloth under her chin for Lynne to hold. She plucked Michael off his mother's lap, strapped him into the high chair and gave him a piece of raw carrot to chew. Mrs Graham had disappeared, leaving her cup and saucer on the table. She liked the children as long as they were clean and dry and cheerful. Given the slightest hint of trouble, however, she slipped away to the solitude of her room in the other wing on the second floor.

'How was your friend?' Lou asked over her

shoulder, busy back at the sink again. Lynne gazed at her uncomprehending.

'Friend?'

'The one you went to see.'

'I . . . Oh! Fine. Just . . . fine.'

'Hmmm. I see. I thought she was sick.'

'Oh, yes. Yes, she was, but she got . . . better.' Lynne looked down, busied herself mopping Mandy's chin and felt guilty about having lied to Louisa.

'Uh-huh,' said Lou, vigorously shaking the container of salad dressing she was making. She tasted, added a sprinkle more of balsamic vinegar and poured the contents into a little glass cruet and set it into the refrigerator.

'You know,' she said conversationally, 'a lot of people think old maids are old maids because they never got asked to be anything else. They think that we don't understand about men and women and the needs they have when they're young. And not so young. Silly, isn't it?'

Lynne felt heat rising up in her face. 'I . . . uh, yes. I guess so.'

Chopping celery into small chunks, knife flashing rapidly, dangerously close to her fingertips, Louisa went on 'Any time you want a night out, young woman, I'm happy to stay with the kids. You don't have to invent a sick friend. And stop twisting your hair around your finger.'

'Lou!' Lynne had to laugh. There was no other choice. But even to her own ears, her laughter sounded slightly hysterical. 'I've suspected for months that you're some kind of witch. Now I know it. You weren't even looking at me. How did you know I was twisting my hair?' *And how did you know I didn't spend the night with a sick, female friend?*

'You've been doing it ever since you got out of that car, and judging by the little curl you have sticking straight out over your ear I'd say you twisted it all the way home. Who is he, Lynne? Why don't you bring him home to meet your family?' Louisa, Lynne knew, counted herself as one of the family.

'I . . .' She paused as Amanda squirmed to get down. She checked the child's tongue, found it had quit bleeding and let her go. Mandy ran out the door. In a moment, Lynne heard the bouncing of the miniature trampoline that Amanda adored.

'Why . . . Lynne! Are you crying?' Louisa's voice was quietly concerned. 'I'm sorry. I had no right to pry. I didn't mean to upset you.'

Lynne wiped her face on the washcloth she still held and lifted her head. 'It's okay, Lou. Must be PMS or something.'

Louisa, who of course wasn't prying, just stood and waited, a disbelieving look on her face. PMS, she had often said, was a crock.

Lynne sighed. 'All right, Lou. You didn't upset me, something else did, and I didn't feel that you were prying. I can't bring him home to meet my family because he doesn't want to be part of a family. I'm sorry I lied to you. And you were right. I didn't think you'd understand. I apologize for misjudging you. But I had to go and see him, one more time. To say goodbye, I guess. Only I had sort of a secret hope that maybe it wouldn't have to be like that. But it was. Nothing's changed.'

'Saying goodbye can be really hard, I know,' Louisa said. 'I've had to do it a couple of times myself. But I did learn one thing, and that's whether we're willing to admit it or not, there's always someone else just around the corner, waiting to say hello. Only you have to be willing to hear the word and say it back.'

'I do know that, Lou. My problem is, I don't want to say anything to anyone else. I don't want anyone else. And maybe I never will.'

'I doubt that. You're twenty-six years old, Lynne, dear. Things change. People change. Wants change. And if you're not willing to look around you and see what the world has to offer, I probably wasted a good lot of breath persuading your new tenant that he'd be more than comfortable here with four old ladies, one young one and two children as house-mates.'

'He?' Lynne didn't really care, though she had said once she thought they should rent to a nice elderly gent so that Michael would get used to men. Then, Louisa had been skeptical, saying that Florence Graham and Bella LeClaire had enough to squabble over without adding a rooster to their hen-house.

'He,' Lou said triumphantly. She must have decided that this one wouldn't become a bone of contention between the two tenants, who fought constantly.

'And he had to be persuaded? How come?'

' "Persuaded" may not be the right word.' Lou shrugged. 'He wanted to be here, all right, it was just that he needed a little convincing that you wouldn't have any objections.'

'Why would I object? Renting to some nice old fellow was my idea after all.'

'Um, well, he's nice all right, and a fella. But he's not . . . old.'

'Not old?' Lynne's gaze narrowed. 'Then that means he's young and –' Recognizing that look on Louisa's face, she jumped to her feet, hands of her hips, glaring. 'No matchmaking! I hate it when people do that and you know it.'

'Now, now, just take it easy. Nobody's going to force anything on you, but this one is a looker. Besides, he's an old friend of yours.' She waved toward the window over the sink. 'Take a gander and see for yourself. And Mandy likes him too.'

Lynne tossed the wet washcloth on to the counter and stood on tiptoe to see down to the end of the backyard.

She opened her mouth, tried to speak, closed it again and squeezed her eyes shut.

'Lou,' she managed to whisper. 'Oh, God, Lou, what have you done?'

Cliff stood patiently pushing Amanda, now seated upright on the swing and hanging on in white-knuckled terror mingled with glee, laughing as her red hair whipped back from her face, and then forward again.

'No,' Lynne whispered. 'My God, Louisa . . . You didn't! Damn him! Oh, damn him! How could he do this to me?' She raced out the door, slamming it hard behind her and caught Amanda as she swung toward her, lifted her off the swing and set her down on the ground.

'No, Mommy, me swingin'!' Mandy protested. 'Daddy push me high. Want to swing, Mommy. Me *rike* to go high!'

Daddy? The word slammed into Lynne's heart, tearing a huge hole. She reeled back, as if under a physical blow, and took several breaths, her damning gaze on Cliff's face, before she could make herself look down at the child. Then, with great effort, she calmed herself for Amanda's sake. No matter what, she had to protect her children from the turmoil that was swiftly engulfing her life. She had to keep them safe and secure, whatever kind of supreme effort it took.

'No, sweetheart,' she said with a sickly smile. 'Not right now. You can swing later. I'll push you high. I'll push you as high as the sky. But now, I want you to run inside and see Lou, okay? You can watch cartoons.'

With obvious reluctance, Amanda left, thumb in her mouth, and Lynne faced Cliff, hands on her hips, eyes blazing; face pale, lips taut.

'You . . . worm!' she spluttered when Amanda was out of range. 'You liar. You cheat! How dare you come weaseling your way in here, telling Mandy to call you Daddy!'

'Dammit, I didn't tell her to call me th – '

'Don't interrupt me!' Lynne interrupted. 'I told you I didn't want you having anything to do with my children! I told you you weren't going to be allowed to hurt them! Now get out, Cliff Foreman! Just get the hell out of my life and don't you ever come back! I can't stand the sight of your face! I – '

'Lynne!' He barked the word at her as he grasped her by the upper arms and gave her a shake. 'Cut it out! Give me a chance to explain.'

'You don't deserve a chance to explain anything, Cliff! The evidence is all against you! You had no right to come here, to invade my home! I told you I wasn't going to have an affair with you, that there could be only one relationship between us and if you don't want the legal one, the right one, the only one, then there won't be one at all and – '

'Stop it!' he snapped as he dragged her against his hard chest, nearly knocking the wind out of her. 'Stop it! Stop yelling at me!'

'I have every right to yell at you! This is my territory you've invaded. This is my home – '

He covered her lips with his own, hard, demanding, silencing her with a passion she couldn't resist. As it threatened to engulf her, to sweep her up in its fire, she tried to twist her head to the side, but he held one fist embedded in her hair. She grunted and pushed and struggled in his clasp, but he held her and when she lifted one knee to jab him cruelly, he was ready for her, slipping a thigh into her way. He lifted his mouth just long enough to say in a rough voice, 'Stop fighting me! Calm down.'

'Let me go! You're pulling my hair out by the roots, you bully!'

It wasn't true, his fist in her hair wasn't hurting

her, but she knew him well enough to know he'd hate the thought of doing so.

'Oh, baby, I'm sorry!' He eased his grip on her hair, smoothed it down over the back of her head and splayed his other hand flat on the small of her back. His tortured eyes gazed into hers.

'Lynne, listen to me. I can't let you go! If only I could! Don't you think I know it would be best for everyone if I could do that? But I can't, love. I just . . . can't.'

'Cliff, please. It has to be finished, what's between us. There can't be any more of this.' Suddenly, she was weeping, tears of exhaustion, of exasperation, of despair, her shoulders heaving as the sobs came tearing out of her very depths. 'You can't stay here. I'll . . . I'll want you too much if you're close.'

'Ah, love, do you think I don't know that? Do you think I want you any less than that? Don't cry, Lynne. Please, don't. I didn't come here to hurt you or to hurt your children. I came because I couldn't stay away from you, not after having seen you again, held you, kissed you . . . like this.'

His lips brushed over hers, gently, warmly, his breath fanning her cheek, eliciting a response she could not deny.

'Please, Lynne, let me explain.'

So soft had his voice become, so beguiling his seeking lips on hers that she parted them without thought, all her senses filled with him, her arms sliding around his neck, her fingers clinging to his thick, crisp curly black hair. When they broke their kiss and leaned their upper bodies apart, their lower halves remained pressed together, pulsing with arousal and need.

Her heart hammered hard, her breath came in quick, short gasps, and Lynne could only look at him, wishing she knew what was going to happen to them, wondering if she could withstand the agony of losing him again when it happened.

Hands linked behind her back, Cliff slowly bent and brushed his lips over her cheek. 'The minute we touch, we ignite each other. You can't deny that about us, can you?'

Wordlessly, she shook her head.

'Okay, then, Lynne? Will you give me a few minutes to talk?'

She sighed and stepped out of his embrace, sitting on the slanted board of the teeter-totter, knees drawn up, arms wrapped around them.

'Go ahead, Cliff. Talk.'

Cliff sat on a swing, the chains creaking ominously, and cast a wary eye upward at the steel bar from which they hung.

'The instructions said it was guaranteed for three hundred pounds,' Lynne said numbly, and then added with a small, broken laugh, 'I've often tried to visualize a three-hundred-pound child.'

He wanted to take her into his arms again, to hold her and protect her from the pain he knew she was trying to hide under light talk and brittle laughter. But he didn't. He only sat there on the squeaking swing and nodded solemnly. 'Or maybe three one-hundred pounders?'

'More likely they meant to make it safe for six fifty-pounders.' She sighed again and met his gaze with deeply troubled eyes. 'All right, Cliff. Go ahead. Explain. Why did you come?'

His hands gripped the chains as tightly as Amanda's had, leaving his knuckles white. 'When you left last night, I followed you to the hotel.'

She nodded. 'I know. I saw you. You . . . drove away.'

He wondered at the unconscious note of heartbreak he was certain he'd detected in her words. Had she wanted him not to drive away? 'I was going to come in,' he said, 'or, at least, ask to be let in. I wanted to, but I knew what would happen if I asked and you agreed.'

She knew, too, and they gazed at one another, both feeling the heat of that knowledge, both experiencing shafts of desire as they remembered the day before and yearned for what might have been all the night through, if he'd come to her door. 'I didn't think that was what you wanted, Lynne,' he said hoarsely.

She nodded. 'It . . . wasn't.' Her added thought, *But it soon would have been*, remained unspoken but nevertheless echoed between them.

'I know that won't help us solve this problem of ours,' he said.

She gave him a level look. 'We don't have a problem, Cliff. The way I see it, you have one. Your problem is that you can't believe the truth when it's sitting right before you.'

'And obviously, neither can you. Can two differ-

232

ent labs, at two different times, have been wrong, Lynne? Dammit . . .' He started to argue further, then made a sweeping gesture with his hand. 'Look, can we leave that aside for now? Can we agree simply not to discuss that part of it for the time being?'

Taking her silence for assent, he rushed on. 'First, I want to tell you that when I left the hotel last night, I was going to go to bed and forget the whole thing, forget you, put it all where I'd tried so hard to put it for the past year. But I discovered that I couldn't, no more than I ever had. Less, really, because you were so fresh in my mind, the scent of you was in my sheets. God, Lynne! I couldn't begin to sleep. I caught the first ferry off the island. There didn't seem to be any reason to wait, and I thought you'd be on it too. I knew I had to see you again, and I thought it would be better here, better for you if we met on your home ground, where you'd maybe feel safer, more secure, and might be more willing to listen to what I have to say. I never had any intention of taking those rooms your housekeeper offered me. That just sort of – well – it happened. And I still don't know how.

I told Louisa that I was an old friend, that I wanted to see you. I pretended to be surprised that you weren't here, though I knew you hadn't been on that same early ferry. I asked if I could wait and talk to you. Somehow, she got the idea that I needed a place to live and wanted to talk to you about that. She assured me that she was fully authorized to choose tenants and rushed me inside to see the rooms you were offering, and by the time your resident steam-roller got through with me, I was already inside and had paid a month's rent.'

Lynne had to smile. Resident steam-roller just about described Louisa, who had been hired, originally, only to help with the cleaning three days a week. Somehow, without Lynne knowing exactly how it had occurred, Louisa had become housekeeper, cook, confidante and mentor, five days a week, more if she thought it necessary. When Lynne had asked her to move in, it was really only a formality. Lou had been occupying the room behind the kitchen for two months by then.

'All right,' she conceded. 'So Lou bulldozed you into renting the rooms. I can understand how that happened. But you can't go around telling my children to call you Daddy!' She said that last even knowing that of course he hadn't, that Amanda used the word 'daddy' interchangeably with the word 'man'. Yet she wanted to rail at him, because if she didn't, she knew she was in grave danger of listening to his seductive voice and going along with whatever wild scheme he'd thought up that had brought him here.

'I didn't tell her to call me anything,' he said reasonably. 'Amanda started that all on her own. I said that my name was Cliff, not Daddy. That didn't seem to work. So I explained to her that since I wasn't her daddy she mustn't call me that, because other people might believe it and that would be a lie. She nodded and told me that her mommy said nice people don't tell lies.'

He frowned, leaned forward, placing his arms on his thighs, making the swing-set squeak again and added, 'It didn't seem to do any good. She persisted in calling me Daddy.' What he didn't say was that for some perverse reason, he hadn't really argued very hard with the little girl. Some part of him thought it was kind of nice to hear her call him that.

'Of course it didn't do any good to explain logically,' Lynne snorted. 'You can't reason with a two-year-old. They aren't reasonable people. What you have to do is correct her when she calls you that and if she persists, ignore her. Respond only when she calls you what you want her to call you. Not,' she added briskly, 'that it's going to be a problem you'll have to deal with for long. You really can't stay, of course. I'll give you back your month's rent on the rooms.'

'No,' he said. 'I'm staying, Lynnie.'

'Dammit, you are not!' She let her knees go, planting one foot on each side of the board, hands balled into fists she planted on her hips. 'Don't you see? This is exactly the same as what you proposed yesterday, except we'd all be living in my home instead of yours. And my objections are the same. I won't let you do that to us, infiltrate my life – our lives – only to have to stand and watch you walk away again when you discover that you were right all along, that you can't love my children, can't help me raise them. Forget it, Cliff. Just forget it.'

CHAPTER 14

Jumping to her feet, Lynne would have strode away, but his hand lashed out and caught her by the wrist, swinging her back to face him. 'Give me a chance,' he said quickly. 'I didn't finish explaining what I thought about last night before I decided to come here. No, not to live in your house, but to stay nearby for a while, to visit casually as any other man interested in you might, get to know your children in a relaxed, unceremonious way. I wondered if it might be possible for me to learn to love him – them – after all, the way you'd want any – uh – suitor of yours to do.'

'I don't have suitors!'

He looked at her as if he longed to believe that, but couldn't. Not quite. 'Lynne – why did you take your brother's child to raise?'

'Why? What kind of question is that? Because I love her.'

'If you hadn't? Say, if your brother had lived far away and you'd never met his daughter, never developed an affection for her. Would you then,

236

upon his death, have left her to the care of strangers? Or, I should say, other strangers, because if it had been like that, you'd have been a stranger to her, too.'

'Of course not. I loved my brother. Therefore I want to raise his daughter.'

'There. You see? I love you, Lynne. Why can't I want to raise your children because of that? With you, beside you, as part of their family.'

'Because you . . . because you don't really want to.' Her voice came out high and desperate, afraid. 'You didn't. You ignored Michael, Cliff. You –' She broke off, voice cracking. She tilted her chin up and faced him squarely. 'You hated him.'

'No!' His denial was swift and adamant. 'I never hated him. Yes, maybe I hated what he stood for, what he represented to me, but not him, Lynne.' He paused. 'Nor you.

'Let me stay,' he repeated. 'Give me this month. The past year I've grown, changed, come to terms with a lot of things. I'd like a chance to tell you about it. Maybe then you'll come to understand me a little better. Lynne, please. At least let us be friends.'

'Friends,' she murmured, skepticism in her tone.

Cliff ignored that. 'Maybe I've grown enough in this past year so I can look at things more objectively. Without seeing –' He broke off and shook his head again, distractedly, before continuing.

'All I'm asking is for us to be together as much as possible. Share a table at mealtimes, take walks together, play together, talk together . . .'

'Sleep together?' she put in bitterly.

'Lynne – dammit, I'm talking about the four of us!'

'No,' she said again, resolutely.

'I haven't finished what I need to say. Please, just hear me out before you decide. Sit down again?'

He said it so pleadingly that she complied, and he took his place again on the creaking swing, his eyes on the ground.

'I never told you about my childhood. I guess I should have.'

Startled, she stiffened. This was not what she'd expected. She wasn't at all certain she wanted to hear about it now. What if he simply planned to use a miserable beginning as a bid for sympathy? But no. She knew him better than that. Nobody who knew Cliff Foreman would ever offer him pity, not with impunity. 'I know it was unhappy, Cliff,' she said carefully.

He looked up at her then, and nodded. 'It was more than unhappy. It was . . . devastating. All the more, I suppose, because for the first few years of it I was like any normal kid being raised by parents with an upper-middle-class situation: happy, secure, certain that they both loved me.' He looked down again. 'I was wrong.'

Lynne frowned. 'Wrong . . . how?'

'Logan Foreman tried to be a good father to me,' Cliff said, and sighed unhappily, staring at the ground between his feet. 'Except,' he added with a quick, almost shamed glance up at her, 'he wasn't my father.'

Lynne started. 'Not . . .'

'That's right.' Now, he met her gaze steadily. 'Not my father. My mother's husband, yes, but to him, I was nothing. No . . . kin.'

Nothing . . . no kin. Exactly what he thinks Michael is to him, Lynne thought, her mind whirling. Why hadn't Cliff ever told her any of this before? As she was about to ask, he went on, looking down again. 'I know now how hard he must have tried, because he did love my mother.'

She stared at the top of his head. As hard as Cliff had tried, she wondered, with a child he believed to be no part of himself?

'But the older I got,' Cliff went on, glancing up again, 'the more time I spent outdoors, the darker my skin became. My hair grew blacker and curlier. By the time I started school, I knew my father hated my guts. But I didn't know why.'

Then, in a unexpected change of subject, he demanded, 'Have you ever heard of Vincent Salazar?'

Lynne blinked, thought for a minute, then nodded. 'Isn't he the one the papers call the Cannery Tsar?'

He was, she recalled, the son of Portuguese immigrants, a self-made man by all accounts, hard-living, hard-driven. That drive had catapulted him from a fish-cannery worker to the owner of several food-processing plants, including canneries, as well as a fleet of large seine boats and trawlers that plied the waters off the Pacific coast. He was reportedly so wealthy that even he didn't know his own worth.

He had also become almost a total recluse in the past twenty or so years, since his wife and daughter were murdered during a kidnapping attempt. He lived in supposed splendor somewhere up in the North Shore mountains in a well-guarded mansion, it was said, hidden by the forest, but with a view out over the ocean he had once loved. His rare public appearances always made the news, which was why Lynne knew of him.

'He's very rich, isn't he? And very reclusive?'

'That's right. That's him. Vincent Salazar.' He used the name as a bitter epithet and glared angrily at Lynne. 'The bastard who left my mother pregnant and alone. The man who screwed up my life and cost me the love of my family. My putative – I think that's the word they use – father.'

'Oh, Cliff!' She got up and went to him, but he didn't want her touch, her comfort. He snapped to his feet and strode away to the edge of the play area, reaching up to wrap his hands around the low branch of a cherry tree.

'That's right,' he said, his back to her, his voice a low growl. 'My father. Funny, isn't it? When I was a kid, even after Logan changed toward me, it never occurred to me that I didn't look like him, or like my mother, or my brother, that I must have got my olive complexion and dark, curly hair from somewhere other than my two fair-haired, light-skinned parents.

'Once I knew, it made sense. Vincent Salazar, donator of my Portuguese blood, reason for my Mediterranean coloring. All I got from my mother was a big dose of belated truth that stole from me everything I ever believed I was.'

He swung around to face her, his eyes burning into hers, his mouth taut, his hands clenched into fists at his side. 'I understand now why Logan started to hate me after my brother was born, after he knew what it was like to recognize his own son, his own flesh and blood. I've wondered how often he looked at me and saw instead the man who had really fathered me. I've wondered how many times he looked at my mother and wondered if she was making comparisons, yearning in secret for Vincent Salazar.'

'You're wrong, if you're saying – '

He cut her off. He knew what she was going to say. And he knew he would be no more able to believe it now than he had been fourteen months before – or two years.

'I didn't even know that Vincent Salazar existed, I never suspected, even for a minute, that Logan Foreman was anything but my own father. And I couldn't, of course, understand why he hated me so much. I reacted the way most kids do when they sense one of their parents is completely down on them. I acted like an utter jerk. It got a lot worse after my brother was born and I had to watch the man I called 'dad' dote on darling Darren. I hated Darren, too, and was so cruel to him I cringe in shame when I think about it.

'He detests me now, my brother. Half-brother. And I don't blame him.'

A muscle in his jaw jumped. 'That's why I told

you I had no family. They aren't dead, as I said. Well, Logan is, has been for four years; I read it in the paper, but I'm dead, too, to my mother and brother. Neither of them wants to have anything to do with me. For good reasons.'

He drew a deep, unsteady breath and released it in what might have been meant as a laugh. 'So there you have it, Lynne. You're married to a non-person. A man who doesn't really exist.' His smile was little more than a twisting of his lips. 'So how does that make you feel?'

'That's not the question, Cliff. How does it make *you* feel?'

'Like –' He told her in one, short, pithy word.

She nodded. 'I can understand that. But it's not true, Cliff. You're you. You're who you've always been, and always will be, and you're very, very important to me.'

He swung away.

This time, Lynne didn't let him turn from her. 'No. Look at me.' She took one of his hands and led him back to the play area, sitting on a bench and drawing him down beside her.

'The way you acted is understandable, you know. You were a child. You were striking out. You were being hurt and the automatic response is to hurt someone in return. How long is it since you've tried to see your mother?' Surely, she thought, his mother would have to understand, would be willing to forgive!

He shrugged. 'A few years.'

'How many?' she persisted.

242

'Ten,' he said heavily. 'I went to the house after . . . after the annulment. I went to see my mother. I hadn't seen her since I'd left.'

Lynne couldn't understand a family that would permit one of its members to be alone for ten years. Her heart ached for Cliff and the deep loneliness he must have endured and understood fully his need for his mother when he must have been in almost unendurable pain at the loss of his wife, especially given the reason for it.

'I don't know why I went,' he continued. 'It was an impulse, and a stupid one.'

'No!' Lynne couldn't accept that. 'Maybe you went to her because you felt very much alone? Lord knows you were entitled to feel that way. Maybe you were looking for contact with someone of your very own? I know that's what I'd have wanted, in the same circumstances.'

It had been what she'd wanted, when she'd lost her brother and sister-in-law. The terrible sense of isolation had been nearly impossible to bear. She had ached for someone to belong to, to belong with. She had wanted Cliff, she knew, but then, Cliff had not belonged to her. He still didn't, not the way she wanted him to. Cliff chose to belong to and with no one.

He shrugged. 'You mean I went to her looking for sympathy, or something? Could be. I . . .' He pulled a wry face and grunted a short, self-conscious laugh. 'Oh, hell, why don't I just be honest with you for once in my life? All right, yes. I was hurting and I went to my "mommy" because I wanted "a hug and

243

a kiss to make it better". I wanted her to tell me I wasn't the total failure I thought I was.'

Lynne blinked back tears she knew he wouldn't want to see, not if they were on his behalf. 'And did she?'

He snorted. 'Hell, no! She didn't even invite me in. But maybe that was my fault too. I didn't tell her that I'd been married for three years and that my wife had just had our marriage annulled because I was a washout as a husband, unable to produce the babies Julia so desperately wanted. I couldn't bring myself to tell her how I felt. I didn't tell her I needed her. When she asked me what I wanted, I just stood there on the doorstep and blurted out the first thing that came to my mind: Did I ever have a bad case of mumps as a kid?'

'Oh, Cliff. Surely, then, she wanted to know why you needed to know that?'

He shook his head. 'I guess it didn't matter to her. She was more concerned that Logan might come home and find me there. I could see how edgy she was. She kept looking past me to the street. My mother has always hated any kind of unpleasantness, and if Logan had come home while I was there, there'd have certainly been some of that. When he kicked me out, he said it was for good, and he meant it. My mother told me she didn't remember if I'd even had mumps, let alone a bad case, and if that was all, would I excuse her because she had a lot to do. Darren was bringing his fiancée home for dinner.

'She claimed Frieda was a wonderful young lady

from an excellent family. Very well-to-do. Like Darren, she was in pre-law. Her face glowed when she talked about them, so I congratulated her, thanked her for the information and left.'

He shrugged again, gave Lynne a crooked smile that didn't wipe away the bleakness in his eyes and said, 'That was that. As I told you when Michael was a few weeks old, I'm sterile, and don't know why, but do know that I cannot in any way, have made you pregnant with him any more than Logan made my mother pregnant with me.'

She tightened her fingers around his, bit her tongue so as not to beg him to go back to the doctor for another test. Circumstances changed, she knew, and with them, physical conditions, but the memory of the first time she'd suggested it remained too strong.

So no, this, she knew, was not the time for such a discussion, not the time to risk alienating him again, because at last he was opening up to her, giving her a glimpse of a terrible past at which she'd never even guessed. She'd suspected he'd been poor, believed him to be an orphan and, from odd little things he'd let drop, had guessed he'd lived on the streets at one time in his life.

Now, she knew more, but wanted the rest of it. Maybe then would come a better understanding, and if she had that, there might be a chance for them together.

'When did you learn about Vincent Salazar?' she asked gently. 'How old were you, Cliff?' The age of that learning could make a big difference, she knew.

'Sixteen,' he said with one of those who-gives-a-damn shrugs she was so used to.

Well, she, for one gave a damn. And sixteen, she knew, was a vulnerable age for anyone, but most of all a youth hovering between boyhood and manhood. It was as bad as she had expected it could be.

'I got thrown out of school,' Cliff went on. 'I was doing drugs, drinking, ditching, mouthing off, failing every class. They decided I was incorrigible. When that happened, Logan kicked me out of the house, too, and told me to get a job.'

He laughed shortly. 'That advice was the most fatherly thing he'd given me in years, and his turfing me out was the best thing that could have happened to me. While I was packing up a few things to take, my mom came into my room and told me that I had to try to forgive Logan, to try to understand him. She said it wasn't me he hated, but what I represented.

'That was when she told me about Vincent Salazar, about how much she had loved him, how she had wanted to marry him, how the two of them had sneaked around together, meeting secretly for months because her parents were wealthy and they couldn't permit her to date the son of a Portuguese immigrant.

Then, when she got pregnant, Salazar turned his back on her. He ran, because he didn't want to be saddled with a wife and kid. My mom was so scared, so ashamed, that when her family told her she'd have to marry someone, she chose Logan, because he'd wanted her for a long time and agreed to marry

246

her knowing she carried some other guy's baby.'

Lynne sat silently in thought, staring down at their linked hands, knowing that Cliff had done exactly what his stepfather had done – married a woman who carried, as far as he could believe, another man's child. Why? Because, like Logan Foreman, he loved the woman?

Cliff moved restlessly on the bench, freed his fingers from hers and stood, walked to the swing where he sat again, turning around and around as the chain wrapped together above his head. 'I've often wondered if my grandparents bought him for her. I never asked her that, but it would explain why he never trusted her or believed that she cared for him the way he did her. I remember plenty of times he accused her of cheating on him,' he said, while his back was to her, 'and always, she denied it. Once,' he continued, twirling to face her, 'once when I was fifteen he did that, I popped him a good one and nearly got kicked out then, but Mom managed to smooth things over.' His face twisted as he spun away again. 'Then, when I was leaving home, she not only told me about Salazar, but told me where – exactly where – to find him.

'How did she know that?' he demanded, the rotation of the swing bringing him back around to her, and he planted his feet firmly in the ground, holding himself still, fixing her with the same kind of accusing glare he might have his mother had she been available. Lynne watched his eyes flaming with anger. 'I was so stupid, so naïve, so sick with anger and fear at having to leave home, I never thought to ask, but if she knew the location of his secret hideaway estate, it could only have been because she'd gone there, maybe repeatedly, maybe all through my childhood, so Logan's accusations probably hadn't been so far off the mark!'

'Cliff, you don't know that. It's unfair to assume that she knew because she'd remained in contact with him. What if his family already owned that property when he and your mom were young people sneaking around together? What if he'd taken her there, showed her around, bragging a little maybe? Couldn't she have remembered how to get there and simply guessed that that was where he'd built his hideaway?'

He sighed. 'Maybe.' But she could see that he wasn't buying it.

'Did you go there? Lynne asked finally when he said nothing more. 'Was she right about where to find him?'

He sat still, the swing chains straight now. His dark gaze locked on hers. 'I don't know. I never went there, never tried to find out. I was too shocked, too numb, too hurt to think. I felt as if I had just had my guts torn into shreds. I hated him, because what if she had been seeing him all that time and he knew about me but never wanted to see me? And I hated my mother as much as I've ever hated anybody, for having lied to me all those years, for having told me I was somebody – something – I wasn't. Suddenly, I didn't have a past. I didn't even know who I was. All I knew was what I was not, who I was not. I was not Logan Foreman's son. Should I call myself Cliff Salazar? Did I have that right purely on my mother's say-so? Maybe Vincent Salazar's was a name she picked out of a hat that day I was packing, or out of the newspapers, having seen pictures of him and decided maybe I sort of had the same coloring or something and it was as good a story as anything.

'Maybe my real father was some itinerant brush salesman, or her family's gardener, or a guy she'd met at a dance. All I could think of was *Who am I? Where did I come from?* Was I really Cliff Foreman in spite of what she'd told me, or was I technically Cliff Anderson, illegitimate son of the unwed June Anderson?'

He spun the swing away again and sat again with his stiff back to her.

'A few months later, when I'd calmed down and had a little money ahead – I got a job as a laborer for a construction company – I sent for a copy of my birth certificate.' He turned back to her. 'Sure enough, legally my name was Foreman; Logan and my mother were married at the time of my birth and that's the name they registered me by. Also, I was used to it, all my papers bore that name, so I decided to keep it.'

His smile was unpleasant. 'Besides, it made me feel good, somehow, to use Logan's name, knowing how it must stick in his craw for me to have it.'

He was silent for a moment, looking at her broodingly before he added, low-voiced, 'It also served as a reminder to me of what a liar my mother

249

was. As long as I remembered every day what she had done, and how many people it had harmed, it was easy to go on hating her, not missing her.'

'You don't know that she did anything that any other girl might not have done,' Lynne said, 'fallen in love with the wrong man, a man who abandoned her when she was pregnant. You can't condemn her for that, Cliff. You mustn't. She's a human being. We make mistakes.'

'She didn't sound like somebody making any mistakes when she told me how to find Salazar, told me exactly what highway to take, exactly where to turn off on to the dirt road and exactly how many miles to drive to reach the log gate that closed off the driveway. No, Lynne, if she made a mistake, it was in having anything to do with a bastard like him in the first place.'

Lynne wanted to go and hold him tightly, ease his pain, but something forbidding in his pose kept her where she was. She thought maybe his low opinion of his mother would make it impossible for him ever to think well of any woman, even one he claimed to love. Maybe especially one he loved.

'Why do you think she wanted you to go to him?'

He looked at her long and hard. 'I don't know. His name had been in the paper a lot about that time. His wife and baby daughter had been kidnapped and murdered.' He shrugged. 'Maybe that's what made her come up with his name, or maybe she thought – if he really was my old man – he'd he'd be willing to latch on to me sort of a replacement. Hell, the man's as rich as an Arab oil sheikh;

could be she thought if he took me in there'd be something in it for her. Lynne, believe me, I've gone over and over this a thousand times until I thought I'd go crazy, but I just don't damned well know anything except what she told me and I'm not even sure if I can believe that. After all, the woman let me live a lie for sixteen years.'

There was nothing to say to that, no way she could alleviate things for him, no way to change the past. 'And Salazar?' she asked several moments later. 'Have you ever tried to see him?'

He shook his head. 'I thought about it for a few months, then decided that if Mom had been telling the truth about him getting her pregnant, since he clearly hadn't wanted me in the beginning, there was little chance of his wanting to know me now, and even less chance of my wanting to know somebody like him.'

'How do you know he didn't want you in the beginning, Cliff? Maybe he still doesn't know you even exist.'

He blinked. 'I . . . Well, obviously he didn't want me. I mean, if he really was my father. My mother claimed they were in love, but surely a real man would have taken her away and married her despite her parents' objections if he knew she was pregnant; but according to her, he didn't. He ran. She was obviously pregnant with me when she married Logan. My birth certificate compared with their wedding date showed that.'

'Cliff, none of that proves anything. Think about it. What if he truly did never know? What if, for reasons we can't understand, your mother never told him?'

He looked disbelieving. 'That's insane! Why wouldn't she have told him if he was the one? No, Lynne, maybe the one she didn't tell was Logan. I've given that some thought, too, you see. She could have convinced him I was premature or something. Maybe she was sleeping with both of them at the time I was conceived. Who knows?

Maybe, by accident, she chose the wrong guy to finger for the paternity. If Logan knew the truth, it obviously didn't bother him until my brother came along, looking so much like him that it made it more obvious how little I did. I was school-aged at the time and I remember the change in his attitude toward me.

Or . . . maybe he realized all along but pretended to himself as long as he could, until it got too heavy a load to bear, until he had a real son to love. But it's no wonder he hated me, no wonder he wouldn't let me near my brother. God! Darren was precious to Logan. And Logan had a right to feel that way. He's the only one in this whole mess I don't blame in the least.'

Lynne jumped up. 'Well, I blame him! None of it, Cliff, not any part of it, was your fault! You were an innocent victim, a little child responsible for nothing that your parents had done. He shouldn't have taken it out on you. If he could love when you were a little kid, why couldn't he continue loving you even after your brother came along, even if he hadn't realized until then that you weren't his child? The man had a screw loose!'

Cliff stood, leaving the swing moving behind him, and walked out into the bright sunshine. The light picked up blue glints in his black hair. 'Meaning I have one loose too? I know that. I've been – seeing someone – a counselor the past six months, a few times, trying to figure myself out, but I know, too, that Logan couldn't help what he felt then any more than I can what I feel now. I didn't realize it then, though, and I was too afraid of more rejection, so I never approached Salazar. Besides, I didn't need him. If I was going to have a family, I'd make one for myself.'

His voice cracked and he half turned from her. 'Or so I thought. Maybe that's why I married so young – I was just twenty-two-because I wanted to have a wife, children of my own, to make up in some way for my own lacking childhood, but it wasn't to be. Three years of marriage to Julia made that obvious. I guess if she hadn't walked out on me I might some day have considered adoption, but probably not. I'd have been too afraid I'd turn out like Logan, unable to love a child who wasn't really mine.'

Facing her fully, his steely gaze raked her face. 'That's why I left you when I did last year, Lynne, because I was so afraid of acting the way he did, or, worse, of hurting an innocent baby.'

CHAPTER 15

Lynne laughed derisively. It was the only way to keep from weeping. 'I don't think that was the only reason, Cliff, nor even the prime one. You wouldn't hurt a baby. You *couldn't*. But you left because your own hurt grew too big for you to bear. You left to protect yourself.'

She watched him swallow. 'All right. Maybe that's so. At least in part. But I knew I was hurting you by not being able to warm to him. I could only see it getting worse. I didn't want to put him through what I went through as he grew older and could sense my . . . resentment, or put you through what Logan made my mother suffer. It was because of me that they had a lousy marriage.'

'I doubt that. If they'd had a good marriage, they'd have found a way to get around Logan's feelings toward you.'

'You sound so sure.'

'I am.' She gazed at him questioningly for a moment. 'Was he very cruel to you? Logan, I mean? Did he beat you?'

He came back to her and took her hand, lowering them both to the garden bench, his face a tense mask, his hand gripping hers tightly. 'Of course not. Oh, he smacked my bottom when I was a little chopper and got out of line, the way any father would, but it's the other kind of hurting I was so afraid of doling out, the kind that started after Darren was born.

I swore I'd never put a child in the same position: second-best, unwanted, unloved. And when I looked at Michael at your breast, Lynne, I finally understood deep in my gut exactly where Logan had been coming from, and I knew the danger of my doing the same to your son was so great I had to get out before I damaged Michael as much as I'd been damaged myself. But now . . .'

She swallowed with difficulty, spoke in a hoarse voice. 'Now, Cliff?'

'Maybe because I'm forewarned – and you are too – we can guard against that happening. As I said, I've been . . . seeing someone, just to talk. A kind of therapist. He made me see I'm not a bad person, just a confused one. I feel less confused now, though, than I have in years. I want to try, love, to make that kind of good marriage with you that you said could overcome the difficulties. I want that so badly I can't begin to tell you how much. And when someone wants something that much, they're going to try harder than someone who's doing it for . . . other reasons.'

She tugged her hands free, got to her feet and walked away from him. She sat on the swing where he had sat, pushing herself in gentle arcs, thinking, wondering what the chances were, wondering if she dared to hope.

Poor Cliff. Poor little boy that had been. No wonder he had so little trust, so little faith in her, coming from a background like that. Should she take this chance to prove to him, once and for all, that she had never been unfaithful to him, that she never would be? And was there a hope at all of his believing her in the end and submitting himself to another test that might prove her right?

She knew, even if the hope was so slim as to be nearly non-existent, that she had to take it. Her entire future was in the balance. She stood up and turned back to where he sat, tense, waiting, his eyes never leaving her face.

'All right,' she said. 'You've paid the rent. You can stay. For one month. As a tenant. But that is all. You'll sleep in your bed. I'll sleep in mine. And my children will not call you daddy, Cliff. Is that perfectly clear? All of it?'

He smiled, stood, and came to her. 'Thank you.' He kissed her, meaning it to be a gentle kiss of gratitude, but it escalated into something much more and it wasn't until she gasped and pushed herself out of his arms that he even realized what had happened.

Then, he knew her edict was going to be impossible to live with. 'Lynne . . . you don't mean that. About the beds. You know it won't work that way. We can't be in the same household and not – '

'My terms or no terms, Cliff,' she cut in, her voice

curt, her gaze level, determined. He could see **that** she meant every word. 'You can stay as long as **you** don't touch me. At least like a . . . a . . .'

He met her hard stare bleakly. 'Like a lover,' he supplied for her and she shook her head.

'Like a husband,' she corrected him.

'All right,' he said reluctantly after a moment while he waited in vain for her to give in. 'Deal.' He took her hand and shook it solemnly. 'Friends.'

She closed her eyes, wanting with a terrible intensity to give him anything he wanted, to let him back into her life, not merely for a month on a trial basis, but to reach out and grasp any chance for the 'forever' she had planned with him.

As much to remind herself as him, she added, 'If you go up those stairs, enter that suite, it will be on those terms, or it will be to pack. Do you understand?'

He nodded. 'I understand, Lynne. If I stay, it won't be as your husband, or your lover. Our . . . personal relationship is still on hold.'

'Yes.'

He smiled. 'But on the other hand, I haven't gone up those stairs yet, have I? So no terms apply.'

'Cliff . . .' she knew she should protest harder, but she didn't. She let him tilt her face to his, and accepted his kiss, returning it slowly, softly, trying to convey without words just how deeply she loved him, how much she wanted their lives to be rejoined.

'Cliff . . .' Her tremulous whisper of need when he lifted his head to gaze at her seemed to inflame

257

him, and his immediate response was to gather her closer, tighter, half-lifting her off her feet.

Lynne wondered later if she had a guardian angel. With an enormous clap of thunder immediately overhead, and a flash of lightning that left her eyes dazzled, the skies opened up.

She broke free, stood staring at Cliff through the downpour, seeing his already soaked shirt, his dripping hair, and knowing she must look much the same. How the heck long had it been raining? Then, as lightning split the clouds, she bolted toward the back door. Whether Cliff followed to ascend the outside stairs leading directly to his suite, she didn't know, and told herself she didn't care.

All she cared about was that she get away from him before another moment went by – before she made more of a fool of herself than she already had.

'I shouldn't have let him have the rooms, huh?' Louisa asked, placing a large red hand on Lynne's shoulder, staying her flight as she would have escaped up to her room. 'I take it he's more than just "an old friend"?' She tossed Lynne a towel fresh from the dryer.

Lynne swallowed before she could speak. She met Louisa's concerned, loving eyes. She drew a deep breath and let it out in a rush. 'He's my husband. He's Michael's father. I wrote and told him I want a divorce.'

Rubbing her wet hair, she slumped down on the sofa in the playroom, noticing that both children were raptly intent on some fast-moving, noisy cartoon character.

Louisa sat beside her. 'This, I take it, is his answer?'

Lynne glanced out the window at Cliff, watched him walk, head down, toward the stairs. She heard his feet slow and heavy on the treads, heard a door close and then silence from above. Was he packing? Was he staring out at the rain, wondering, as she was, when the sky had clouded over, when the rain had begun?

'Who knows?' she said finally in answer to Louisa's question. 'I don't think even he knows, at this point, why he came here.'

After a beat, she added, 'You see, he believes he's sterile, that he can't be Michael's father.'

'Lordy!' Louisa's eyes widened. 'But aren't there tests?'

Lynne nodded. 'He won't have a blood test. He says – rightly – that it couldn't prove that he is Michael's father, only that he isn't, and since he already knows he isn't, there's no point in poking unnecessary needles in a baby.'

'I meant . . . tests to prove he is or isn't sterile.'

'He had one once. Twice, actually. He refuses to say much about it, but I know he felt humiliated by the whole process, and his first wife didn't make it easy at all. She had the marriage annulled on the strength of his sterility.'

'But . . . didn't he tell you that he was – thought he was? Before you got married?'

Lynne pulled her feet up rested her chin on her

knees. 'We weren't married when I got pregnant,' she admitted, wondering how Lou would react to that news. They were of two different generations. Standards had changed since Louisa's youth. 'I told him,' she added, 'and a week later, we were married.'

Lou leaned back, eyes cut sideways to Lynne, frowning, not in censure but in perplexity. 'He married you, then, believing that Michael wasn't his?'

'That's right.'

Lou was aghast. 'And you took him, knowing he believed you to be that kind of a cheat?'

'Oh, no. He didn't tell me then that he thought Michael wasn't his. He thought he could forget, pretend. He tried, Lou. I know that. He really, really tried, but in the end, after the baby was born, he simply couldn't handle it and he told me what he'd believed all along. Nothing I could say or do would change his mind. Then, or now.'

'So what does he want here?' Louisa asked angrily, then, before Lynne could answer, she heaved herself to her feet. 'Never you mind, hon. I'll get rid of him. The nerve, calling you a liar!' She headed for the back stairs.

'Lou.' Lynne stopped her. 'Leave it. He's paid his month's rent. I . . . told him he could stay. For that long.'

'Lordy!' Louisa said again. 'What for?'

'Because . . . what if there is a chance, however remote, that he could learn to accept Michael? Look at it this way: I took Amanda because I loved my brother, so why shouldn't he be able to take Michael because he loves me?'

'Does he love you?'

Lynne nodded. 'Yes. I believe that with all my heart.'

'And you him?'

She nodded again, lowering her head to hide the tears that blurred her vision. 'If he can learn to accept my children, to love them because he loves me, the way I love Amanda because I loved my brother, maybe we have a chance.'

'Well, I dunno, hon.' Louisa shook her gray head. 'Of course that's the way it should be. He loves you, therefore he should love your kids. But since it didn't work like that before, who's to say it's going to work like that now? I don't like it. I don't like it at all. Are you sure you really want a man who believes such a thing about you?'

Lynne hugged her friend. 'Lou, you're such a treasure. What makes you so certain I *didn't* lie to Cliff, that Michael isn't some other man's baby?'

Lou snorted disgustedly. 'Oh, come on, girl! I know you. You wouldn't foist another man's child on anyone, and especially not the man you love. And you didn't answer my question.'

Lynne thought for a minute before stepping away from Louisa. 'It's pretty simple, I guess. No matter what he might think of me, no matter how much he might have hurt me, I don't think I can ever get over wanting Cliff.'

* * *

Cliff's two rooms and a bath, which had once been Ann and Taylor's large suite plus nursery, gave him two choices of view from the L-shaped balcony. He stood now, gazing out over the front yard. The sudden storm had moved on, letting the sun flood the world again. It turned to sapphire his narrow glimpse of the river and highlighted a trellis splayed against a fence, up which grew a splash of orange and yellow and green: nasturtiums climbing for the sky.

He paced back along the balcony, turned the corner and leaned his back on the railing, looking at the curtains covering the sliding glass door to what had been Lynne's bedroom. Was it still?

The curtains were gossamer-sheer, pale blue, and the open door let a draft through, allowing the fabric to billow gently in and out. Was it only his imagination, or could he really pick up little wafts of her delicate perfume on that breeze?

His fingers curled around the rail. How could he bear to stay so near her – and not touch? Was she in her room now? Could she see him standing there? Did she ever come out and sit in that wicker chair near her door late at night when she couldn't sleep? And if she did, did she ever think of him?

His throat tightened as he contemplated slipping out his own door in the flower-scented darkness and finding her there, dressed in something flimsy, her soft hair tousled from her pillow, her skin warm and silken, her whispers muted and welcoming.

He would gather her up and sit down in the chair, cradling her slim body on his lap, in his arms. He would kiss her, slowly slide her nightie up over her thighs, down from her shoulders, kissing, touching, nibbling as he went, until she was as hot and wet and ready as his rigid hardness needed her to be, and then . . .

His body ached with reaction to the fantasy and he groaned softly as he forced himself to breathe evenly and think of something else. But how could he think of anything else when he could still smell her perfume on the breeze?

With a grimace, he paced back through the French doors into his own rooms and walked across the sitting room through the bedroom door beyond.

He showered, turning the water to cold, then dressed and flopped on to the bed, staring at the ceiling, visions of Lynne flitting through his mind.

A bell chimed, and he came to with a start, remembering that Louisa had told him the sound announced dinner. He rose, ran a hand over his hair, and tucked in his shirt. He squared his shoulders, feeling as if he were about to do battle, and went down the stairs and then hesitated outside the door leading to the dining room, reluctant to enter.

Because what if he looked at Lynne's son and could identify the man who had fathered him, the man whom he would always despise with every breath he took? Drawing in one of those breaths, and letting it out slowly, Cliff opened the door to the dining room and stepped in.

There were no children in the room.

With a shocking rush of relief he slumped against

the door-frame for a moment, pulling himself back together.

He was afforded little time for recovery, because his entry caught the attention of the woman seated at the table, and he blinked, trying valiantly not to gape at the blowsy one he'd met in the winter. Now, she smiled at him, her bright red lips bowed into a shape somewhat outside the path nature had intended, just as her high-arched brows were penciled in an inch and a half over where the originals had been shaved off. Her hair, no longer brassy blond, was now as blatantly red as her lips, and stacked into an elaborate upsweep that nevertheless looked slept in.

Indeed, the woman looked as if she had just got out of bed.

Wearing a wrapper of purple satin that barely covered her ample bosom, and purple satin mules with marabou feathers over her surprisingly slender insteps, she sat with her legs crossed, exposing one thigh for a long way up. She looked, he decided, like a member of the cast for *The Best Little Whorehouse in Texas*.

Maybe she was. Maybe, right after dinner, she was off to the theater for dress rehearsal. He could only hope it was so.

Her eyes, still shaded by impossible lashes, sparkled, though, and her smile, painted on though it was, held genuine welcome.

'Well!' she said, 'Well, well, *well*! I remember you. So you came back! Louisa didn't do you half the justice she could have. Oh, won't Edie be excited! She thought you were *sooo* cute.'

Cute? Cliff had been described in many ways, but not as 'cute' – at least not in the past thirty years, as far as he knew.

'Come in, come in,' the woman invited, patting the chair next to hers. 'Don't be shy, darling. Sit down and tell me all about yourself.'

Mesmerized, he complied. At least the sitting down part, but then a loud, 'Harrumph!' from the doorway made him jerk his gaze from that enormous bosom and its threat to spill from the front of the purple robe.

'Uh – good evening, ladies,' he said, snapping to his feet as a short, plump woman with gray hair came through the doorway, followed by the little frail one, somewhat younger, he realized now, than he'd thought last November, but still drab. She wore a gray dress buttoned high on her throat.

'Really, Bella,' said the plump one. 'With a gentleman in the house, couldn't you have dressed more . . . appropriately?'

'Is this inappropriate?' Bella asked, all innocence. 'I don't see why, Florence. After all, don't you come to breakfast in your robe?'

In high dudgeon Florence sniffed and tossed her head. 'This,' she said, 'happens to be dinner, and my robe is nothing like that!'

'For you, it's dinner. For me, it's breakfast. I just got up,' Bella explained to Cliff. 'Now, sit back down again and I'll introduce you. But first, you have to tell me your name.' She leaned toward him, gravity threatening both bosom and satin.

'Bella!' Florence hissed. 'For heaven's sake, woman, act your age.'

The little woman, also watching Bella's bosom, blushed right up under her wire-framed glasses, lifted a hand and appeared to be giggling behind it. Cliff winked at her. The throat-clearer, lips pursed, glared at him as though she might send him away to wash behind his ears.

Before the tension in the room could erupt into a battle, he said, 'I'm Cliff Foreman.'

Bella patted his hand. 'How wonderful. I do like a man with a strong name, don't you, Edie?' She beamed at the little gray-dressed woman, who nodded shyly and pinkened again. 'This is Edie York and Florence Graham –' she nodded toward the throat-clearer. 'I'm Bella LeClaire. Flo works for that dreadful old molar-cruncher, Dr Lefsky. Don't ever go to him, dear. Take my word for it.'

Mrs Graham snorted indignantly as she began to turn the same color as Miss Bella's robe, and probably would have spoken, but Bella swept on as if she hadn't insulted the other woman's employer.

'And my good friend Edie is head librarian in the children's division of the downtown branch, though I'm trying to persuade her she'd have much more fun if she joined me at my job.'

Again, Miss York giggled and blushed. Mrs Graham tsk-tsked disgustedly, and Bella ignored them both, concentrating on Cliff, a much more interesting subject.

'What do you do, Cliff, dear? Besides look good, I mean, and make female hearts go pitty-pitty-pat?'

she added with an outrageous wink of one set of her outrageous false eyelashes, and a tapping of those long nails against her bosom.

Cliff looked up in relief as if at a rescuer when Lynne came in, carrying a towel-wrapped basket of biscuits, and a wooden bowl filled with tossed salad. His heart stopped beating at the sight of her, her face flushed from the heat of the kitchen, her hair curled wispily from the steam, and her body shown off to perfection in a pale yellow jumpsuit that left her arms and shoulders bare. Her eyes seemed drawn to him like two blue magnets and he got up and took the basket from her, setting in on the table without even looking at where he was putting it.

Bella gave a gurgle of laughter that he scarcely heard as she guided the basket clear of the butter on to which he had nearly set it. He was too busy looking at Lynne, judging her reaction to him, reveling in the quickened breathing that lifted her breasts high, in the flush of color on her cheeks, in the flare of her eyes at the sight of him.

She couldn't hide that she loved having him here to the same extent that he loved being here.

Louisa, following with huge bowl of chilli, was forced to crowd past both Lynne and Cliff. 'Sit down, you two,' she said crisply. 'You can make cow eyes at each other later, out on the porch. I oiled the glider an hour ago so you wouldn't keep the rest of us awake.'

'I have never made cow-eyes at anyone in my entire life,' Lynne snapped, cursing the heat she felt in her cheeks. 'And as you know perfectly well, I have work to do tonight, so you wasted your time, Louisa. As well as your oil.'

And I also told you no matchmaking, she didn't say, but hoped her glare conveyed the message to Louisa.

She turned that glare on Miss Bella, who chuckled, and Edie, who giggled, then sat down, too aware of the speculative silence around the table, the gazes shifting from her, to Cliff, to Lou.

She was equally aware of Cliff, sitting just on her right, too aware of his knee so near her own, too aware that she wished with all her heart that she *could* permit herself to sit with him as the day ended, on the squeaky glider on the front porch, and spoon in the old-fashioned manner that Louisa had been envisioning.

'I hope you've all introduced yourselves,' she said jerkily. 'Please, go ahead. Help yourselves.'

The children, Cliff realized, were not to join them. And with that realization came an inexplicable surge of anger that completely wiped out his earlier relief. What was going on here, anyway? Was Lynne deliberately hiding her son from him? And if so, why? Did she think she could continue to do it for a full month?

He remembered how she had chased little Amanda into the house when he'd been pushing her on the swing. Did she mean to keep both the children away from him? It was crazy. It wouldn't work. Wasn't he there to get to know them?

'Where are the children, Lynne?' he asked.

'In bed.'

'Really? So soon?'

'They're both very little. They need to eat earlier than this.'

'That's too bad,' he said as Lynne put a scoop of chilli onto her plate. As Lou's chilli always was, it was rich and thick and aromatic. She took a bite. It tasted like ashes in her mouth. 'I was looking forward to meeting them,' Cliff said.

'You met Mandy,' she reminded him. He'd met Mandy, and Michael, too, and rejected the latter, though maybe he'd prefer to forget that now. It was not something she meant to forget. If he wanted to prove himself to her, he had a long way to go.

He smiled. 'Yes,' he said. 'She's a great little kid. She looks just like you. And Michael, does he look like you, too?'

Lynne gave him a hard stare. Mandy did not look like her. She looked like Taylor, and he knew it. He had commented on it often, in the past. And he knew just as well that Michael had the same dark hair as he did, the same curls, the same shaped eyes, just not as dark. Well, maybe he didn't know that, because Michael's hair had been little more than fuzz, and his eyes had still been baby-blue when Cliff left, but . . .

'No,' she said. 'Mandy looks like her father, remember?'

'Oh, yes.' His smile faded. 'And Michael? Does he resemble his father too?'

Suddenly, Lynne knew she couldn't sit here and take this double-edged conversation. She shoved

269

her chair back, shot to her feet. 'No!' she said in a taut, choked voice. 'Not in the least. Excuse me. I . . . I think I hear the baby crying.' She nodded to the diners. 'Please, go on without me.'

Lynne wheeled and made her way blindly out of the room, wishing she hadn't said Cliff could stay. This wasn't going to work, his being here! He would poke and prod and pick away at her, and he would never, not in a million years, believe the truth though it was staring right at him!

CHAPTER 16

'Nobody ever mentions little Michael's father,' Bella said into the thick silence that followed Lynne's departure. 'We think he must be dead.'

'I'm sorry,' Cliff said, then looked at Louisa. 'Truly sorry.'

'Not me you should apologize to,' she growled, but when he began to rise, to offer his apology where he knew it was needed, she barked at him to sit back down and eat. 'Leave the girl alone. You've done enough damage for one night.'

He shoved his food around his plate until Louisa took it from him and replaced it with a slice of lemon meringue pie that quivered from the force of her slamming it before him.

He took a bite. It tasted like glue in his mouth. He ate half of it before setting it aside and drinking the coffee the housekeeper poured.

Then, with the other tenants busy doing whatever old ladies did in the evening, he took himself away from the scene of his stupidity, and walked for hours re-exploring the neighborhood he had once ex-

271

plored with Lynne at his side. As he strode along, he remembered the happy times they had spent here with her brother and his wife, both before and after their marriage, remembered how it had been, feeling like a member of a family for the first time since his early childhood. Why couldn't the demons in his soul have simply shut up, stayed dormant, given him some peace, so he could have gone on enjoying the life he had created with Lynne's loving help?

Well, the demons hadn't left him, he thought, turning back toward Lynne's house. They had nagged at him, reminded him of her unfaithfulness all through her pregnancy, shouted and laughed at him each time he saw her child once the baby was born, and torn him limb from limb with the agony of having to face the result of her betrayal.

And again tonight he had let one of them have the upper hand, permitted it to lash out at her, hurt her. He was crazy to have come here. The right thing to do was leave. At once. He rattled his car keys in his pocket.

Why didn't he just get into the car and drive away? he wondered, turning into the sidewalk that led up past the wide driveway at the side of the big house. Louisa would be glad to send his things on to him. She'd be more than glad to see him go.

And Lynne. What would she feel when she woke up in the morning and saw that he was gone? Would she grieve, or would she be relieved?

He glanced up at the balcony that joined his room and hers. He could just make out Lynne's general shape and profile outlined against the light in her room as she sat in the chair outside her door, her head bent as if she were reading a book held on her lap, but he knew it was too dark for her to see properly. What was she doing? Thinking? Crying? Praying?

Then, as if sensing his gaze on her, she lifted her head and looked down at him while his heart thudded uncomfortably hard in his chest and his throat ached with words he wanted to say, but could not. She stood and for long moments they stared silently at each other, then, without a word, she turned and slid open her door, closing it with a thud audible even where he stood. He mounted the steps to the broad front porch, saw the glider Louisa had oiled for his and Lynne's personal use. He sat in it, swinging silently back and forth, feeling sick, feeling disheartened, feeling as if he had received a well-deserved slap. Did Lynne know how much he hated having a door closed in his face?

As he swung, he leaned his head back, thinking of Amanda on the back yard swing, remembering her red hair flying back from her face, then tumbling around it, thinking of her laughing blue eyes, her little, Cupid's bow mouth smiling at him. Lynne wanted to adopt her. She loved that little girl. She loved her, she said, for Amanda's own sake, as well as because she was part of her brother.

He knew that he, too, could easily learn to love Amanda for Amanda's sake. So why not Michael?

For several minutes he considered bypassing everyone else in the house and sneaking up the outside stairs that gave access to his second-floor

273

rooms. But that was the coward's way out.

Getting to his feet, he reached into his pocket for the front door key the housekeeper had given him, almost forced upon him when she was so eager for him to take the rooms upstairs. He stood for several moments, irresolute, bouncing it up and down in his hand. She had liked him then. She had thought, then, that he would be good for Lynne. His idiotic behavior tonight might have changed her mind, but he still had that key. And he could show her that her first impressions had been right, couldn't he?

He wouldn't let either Louisa or the demons inside force him to leave. Louisa might disapprove of him; she might even try, as the demons were doing, to keep him and Lynne apart as Lynne was trying to keep him and Michael apart. But he didn't have to let any of that happen, did he? He would fight them and he would fight for his marriage. And this time, dammit, he'd win.

'Did you have a nice walk around our pretty town?' asked Edie York as he entered the living room where she and Mrs Graham watched TV. There was no sign of the flamboyant Bella, and he remembered she'd said she worked nights. At what? He was almost afraid to wonder, and knew he'd never ask. He assured Edie, falsely, that he had enjoyed his walk.

'Where would I find Louisa?' he asked and, following the ladies' advice, knocked on the kitchen door.

'Come in,' she called, and as he entered, she swung her slippered feet to the floor in the sunken

TV-cum-playroom, and zapped the television off with the remote control. 'You don't have to knock,' she said gruffly, looking cross and still very much put out with him.

'I wasn't sure you'd still be up and I didn't want to disturb you if you were asleep,' he said, feeling edgy. Louisa sat erect in her upholstered chair, looking up at him as he stood on the kitchen level.

'I shut my door when I go to bed.' She gestured toward the room that Taylor and Ann had discovered when they ripped out the false wall to make the kitchen area larger. 'Nothing disturbs me once I'm asleep,' she said. 'You can come and go as you like in this kitchen. Everyone else does.'

So she wasn't going to kick him out, it seemed. Of the kitchen or the house.

'Well, come in, why don't you?' she went on. 'Can't abide people hovering in doorways. Sit down. Can I get you something?'

He stepped down the three carpeted stairs to the family room level and lowered himself to a matching chair opposite hers. He managed a small grin. 'How about a cup of hemlock?'

She snorted with laughter as she heaved herself to her feet. 'Sorry. Fresh out. Coffee do?'

He nodded and looked around the room as she went up the stairs and through the archway where he'd been 'hovering'. It was clearly the room where the children spent much of their time. There was an overflowing toy-box, a blackboard on an easel, a couple of shelves with books on them and a tiny plastic tricycle with a pink horse's head with handlebars sticking through its ears. A pair of the smallest Reeboks he'd ever seen sat on the arm of the chintz-covered sofa and Cliff stared at them, trying to picture the child who wore them, feeling the hurt and anger return as he thought of how Lynne was hiding her son from him.

'Where's Lynne?' he asked as Louisa came back with two mugs of coffee, pretending he hadn't seen his wife on the balcony, hadn't suffered her silent rebuke as she closed her door on him.

'In bed.'

'Did . . . did she eat anything at all?'

Louisa shook her head. 'She said she wasn't hungry. Lynne doesn't eat when she's upset.'

Cliff nodded miserably. 'Yeah. I know.'

He stared into his coffee mug in silence for a long time until Louisa spoke.

'And knowing that, knowing she was already upset, you still said what you did. And you meant to hurt her, didn't you?'

He looked at her miserably. 'I don't know. I guess I must have. Maybe unconsciously, but all right, yes, I suppose I intended to get at her. I just didn't expect it to hurt her that much. Her face . . .' He swallowed hard. 'I'll never forget her face when I said what I did.'

'Why did you?' Her tone showed only mild curiosity.

'She's keeping me from seeing him. Her baby. It hurt my feelings. It's as if she doesn't trust me.'

Louisa raised her brows. 'Maybe she doesn't. Why should she? What have you done to earn her trust?'

He took a sip of the hot coffee. 'Yeah, I see your point.'

She shrugged. 'I've never known Lynne to hold a grudge. Maybe things will be better tomorrow.'

And maybe not. 'Have you known Lynne for a long time?'

'Just since her brother died and she tried to take over this place on her own, and earn a living while raising two babies without any help.' Cliff didn't think it was just his guilty conscience that made him hear censure in Louisa's tone.

'Lynne hired me to take on some cooking and cleaning, part-time,' Louisa said. 'One thing led to another and I moved in because I didn't have anywhere else I wanted to be and this way I can rent out my house and have something to save for my old age.

'I spent my youth looking after elderly, sickly parents,' she went on. 'I was one of those unexpected babies, you see, that come along when their parents have given up hope of having any, so when I reached adulthood, they were getting on in years. My mother died when I was in my thirties, but my father hung on until I was well past fifty. Oh, don't get me wrong; I don't begrudge them the years I gave, any more than they ever begrudged me the years they spent raising me. But when they were both gone, I had no one, and not much chance of making a life for myself. So when Lynne needed me, I was more than willing to come here. She and those babies have become my family and I'm not going to let anybody hurt them.'

There was a distinct warning in those words.

'I don't want to hurt them,' said Cliff. 'I want to love them.'

'I got that impression,' she said. 'At least of the way you feel about her. That's why I was happy to rent you the rooms. Something told me you'd be right for Lynne. But . . .' Clearly, her seconds thoughts were a lot more potent than her first impressions had been.

'So?' she prompted when he said nothing. 'What are you going to do about the situation?'

He shook his head. 'I don't know. There are . . . problems. She says they're my problems, and I suppose that's true, only they've become her problems too, and because of that she's gone to bed hungry. I was thinking, as I walked, that maybe I should just leave. Maybe it would be easier on Lynne if I went.' Why was he telling Louisa that when he'd already decided not to go? Did he want her to beg him to stay?

If he did, he was disappointed. Lou looked at him expressionlessly. 'Are you going to?'

He gave her a level look. 'Not on your life. This is too important. Somehow, we're going to have to sort through this tangle and come up with something we can both live with.'

'All.'

'Pardon me?'

'All, not both. There are four of you to consider.'

He nodded. 'I know that. And I know it's not going to be easy. You see, I knew Lynne . . . before.'

She didn't so much as blink. Again he wondered how much Lynne had told Louisa. He didn't want to give anything away that she might want to keep private. 'When Michael was an infant,' he added by way of explanation. 'And before he was born. I wondered then who his father was. I . . . well, I wasn't very nice to her – or to her baby, I suppose. I cared about her and was jealous of the time she had to give him.'

He met her questioning gaze and went for broke. 'What worries me most is that there's no guarantee I'll feel differently about him now. It scares me. And I don't like feeling scared. It makes me do stupid things, say stupid things.'

Like I did tonight at dinner.

'What scares you about seeing Michael?'

'What if he looks like someone I know? What if I can identify the man who did that to Lynne, got her pregnant and then walked away? I'll want to slit his throat.'

'Tsk, tsk,' she chided mildly. 'Such violence. First suicide by hemlock, and now murder by slashing. You amaze me.' Her humorous twinkle told him that he also amused her.

Still, he felt he had to say, 'I wouldn't do either, of course. I'm not a violent man. At least, I don't think I am.' Though there was a time when he had been to protect himself when need be, and he knew if he had to he could kill to protect Lynne. There had also been that time he'd hit Logan to protect his mother's honor. But he hadn't been a man then. He'd been a boy, hot-headed and impetuous.

'I don't think you are either,' Louisa said, getting up and going to fetch the coffee pot, filling both their cups again. 'And I think what you said tonight did you as much damage as it did Lynne. Or, at least, her reaction to what you said.'

She gave him a penetrating look. 'You've been hurt a lot during your lifetime. And you don't like hurting others, probably because of that.'

He stared at her. 'Do I have it written in red across my forehead or something? *I was an emotionally battered child?*'

Louisa laughed comfortably. 'Didn't Lynne tell you? I'm a witch.'

'No. She just said that you are her friend and her mother-substitute.'

Louisa looked pleased and thoughtful at the same time. 'Mother-substitute, huh? Thank you. I didn't know that.'

He was glad he'd told her. 'Um . . .' He cut a glance sideways at her and said it again. 'Um . . . could you tell me about Michael? I mean, sort of describe him to me? So that if he does look like someone I know I have some kind of advance . . . warning?'

Louisa sighed heavily. Tenacity, she thought. If it's an inherited characteristic . . . She remembered a certain little boy who had taken plenty of tumbles before he learned how to back down off the sofa right here in this playroom, a little boy who had spent hours trying to master the art of getting one cup inside a bigger one.

She shook her head at Cliff ruefully. 'I'd have to

say that Lynne's wrong. The baby does, in many ways, take after his father.'

Cliff felt as if she'd just pole-axed him. Aware that his coffee was in danger of sloshing over the rim of his mug, he set it down jerkily. It slopped anyway. 'You . . . uh . . . you've met him, then? The baby's father?'

'Yup.'

'I . . . well, I sort of thought, like Bella, that maybe he was dead.' And hoped so, though till this minute, he hadn't realized the strength of that wish.

'Nope,' Louisa said. 'Or, only from the neck up.'

Cliff's head reeled. *Donald Frayne?* Could it have been? If so, it explained a lot. Dammit he'd warned her about Donald's vulnerability, told her the other man might misinterpret her kindness and compassion and – He stared at Louisa, seeking confirmation. 'Lynne's baby's father is paralyzed?'

'I said from the neck *up*, not down,' Louisa said. 'He's not crippled, just stupid.'

Astounded, Cliff said sharply, 'Oh!' He'd never have thought of Lynne's being interested in a brainless man. She enjoyed a good conversation too much, and rousing debates that could swing into hot arguments, even fights, which had always, between him and Lynne, led to making up and . . . Maybe all she'd wanted with the other guy was the making up? He felt like pounding his fist against a wall. Maybe he *was* a violent man, deep on some atavistic level.

'Could be he had other – uh, attributes, that

appealed to Lynne,' he said stiffly, a bitter taste in his mouth that had nothing to do with an excess of coffee.

Louisa shook her head again. 'Totally stupid.' She drained her cup and got to her feet. 'Well, I'm off to bed, so I'll wish you goodnight.' She opened a door at the far side of the playroom to reveal the end of a bed made with military precision. Pausing, she turned back to him. 'Tell me,' she said, 'what would it matter if Michael were green and had yellow stripes, as long as you love his mother?'

Because he had no answer for himself, he had none for her, and after a moment she added quietly, 'Lynne's very partial to lemon pie. And cold milk.'

She shut the door, leaving Cliff to his thoughts.

After several minutes, he rose, carrying their two cups to the sink. On the counter was a pie with only one piece out of it. He cut two more, found plates and forks and poured out two glass of icy milk. Setting it all on to a decorative tray he found behind the toaster, he lifted it and elbowed off the light switch.

'Okay, Lynnie-love,' he said as he mounted the spiral stairs. 'Ready or not, here I come.'

As he reached the second floor, he remembered that Louisa hadn't told him one solitary thing about what Michael looked like.

Okay, as always, he was on his own. He could take it. He would.

Cliff set the tray down on a pine chest and knocked lightly on Lynne's door. There was no answer. He tapped again, then softly, stealthily, feeling like a second-storey man, he tried the knob. Locked. Frowning, he picked up the tray and shouldered open the door to his own suite. Setting it down on a table in his sitting room, he stared at it, knowing he had no appetite.

The heat of the night was oppressive. He considered going back outside to pace the dark hours away, maybe find a whiff of breeze somewhere. He remembered how both sets of stairs, interior and exterior, had creaked under his feet as he ascended them and knew he could never get out of the house without waking everyone.

He peeled off his shirt, tossed it on to the sofa and paced his room, only there wasn't room enough to give him the long strides he needed. Picking up his shirt, he mopped his forehead then stepped out on to the balcony, remembering the way Lynne's curtains had billowed earlier in the day, and the way he'd imagined her scent wafting out of her room.

Now, her balcony door was closed tightly, in spite of the breathless heat of the air. She'd drawn her curtains over the glass, and tilted the slats of the blinds, leaving not even a tiny gap for him to peer through. The door was as securely locked as the one in the hall had been. Her light was out.

How long had it been since he'd seen her out here? Half an hour? Forty-five minutes? It was only shortly after eleven and she'd once been a regular night owl, reading herself to sleep, but often not until the small hours. How he'd grumbled about waking up to find her sound asleep, book on her pillow, light still on. Yet it had been loving grumbling and it hadn't hurt him to get out of bed, gently remove her book and turn out her light.

Maybe, with any kind of luck, she was lying there, as far from sleep as he was, but not daring to read lest he see her light and know.

'Lynne?' he said softly, his mouth close to the door. 'Lynne, please, I need to talk to you. I want to apologize. I brought you some pie. And some milk. Lynne?'

But there was no response, and the light remained off within her room. He clenched his jaw so hard his head ached, and sat down in the creaking wicker chair by her door, wishing he had a hammer to break the glass, or an ax to chop a hole in the wall, or a miracle to make Lynne believe in him again. He knew, though, that the only miracle to achieve that end would be the one of his finding a way to believe her preposterous protestations of innocence, to believe in an utter impossibility.

In time, he realized, he must have fallen asleep, because he wakened suddenly to the sound of a door sliding open and lifted his head, blinking, rubbing his eyes. Lynne was there, dressed in a long T-shirt with a stretched neck that hung down to expose one creamy-skinned shoulder.

'You fell asleep out here,' she accused. In the light now shining from her bedroom, he could see her eyes, wide and intensely blue, and her pink lips parted as she stood there looking at him. 'You should go to bed, Cliff.'

He stood and stepped closer, viscerally aware that

the heavy pounding of his heart echoed the rapid pulse beating in her throat. Slowly, unable to hold himself back, he reached out and touched that point with a fingertip. She drew in a sharp and tremulous breath as she jerked her head away and he let his hand fall back to his side.

'I thought you were asleep,' he said.

'I . . . almost was.' Her voice was breathless. 'But then I heard you at my door. That woke me up. I listened to you go into your own room, then come out here.'

She nearly smiled, but he saw her catch herself. 'My chair squeaks when anybody sits in it. As I said, I waited to hear you go back in, but when I didn't. I thought I should come out and check on you.'

'I'm sorry,' he said, feeling like an intruder. He stepped back. Her chair; not 'the' chair. And if she wanted to share this balcony with a tenant, there would be two chairs. 'This really is your private place, isn't it?'

She shrugged. 'I guess I've come to think of it that way. Miss Larson, the previous tenant, never used it. She was afraid of heights. It's often where I come to unwind at night before I can get to sleep.'

'And now I've woken you. Do you want me to go so you can sit here and unwind?'

She met his gaze for a long moment and then shook her head, reaching out a hand toward him. 'No,' she said, her voice little more than a whisper, and he knew that she wasn't only talking about his leaving her alone to unwind. 'No, Cliff, I don't want you to go.' Again, he lifted his hand to her throat, and this time she didn't jerk back. His touch stroked up her neck into her hair, and he felt the silken curls coil around his fingers as if trying to capture him.

Didn't they know he had been captured long ago and would remain that way until he drew his last breath?

Under his palm, he felt the curve of her skull, the warmth of her skin, and again that surge of emotion that was more than desire swept through him.

He stepped close and tugged until her cheek rested on his bare chest, his hand pressing her head to hold it there though she was making no attempt at escape. But neither did she reach out to him.

She simply stood leaning lightly on him, accepting his caress.

He wondered if she was as accepting of his words. 'Lynne . . . please, forgive me? For baiting you at dinner. I'm sorry.'

She nodded but refused to meet his gaze, resisted his efforts to turn her face up. 'Sure. It's okay.' She tried to push herself away but he held her.

'Ah, baby, I love you so much,' he said. 'And I hurt you tonight. I used to tell myself that if by some miracle I ever found you again, I'd spend my life making up for the damage I'd already done, and would never hurt you a second time. And yet I did. And I think maybe I did it on purpose.'

After a moment, she lifted her head and looked up at him. 'Yes,' she said, putting her hands on his chest so that he couldn't pull her any closer. 'I think you did too. You were angry because I put Michael to bed without your having seen him.'

He let her go and leaned his hands on the rail, head hanging, shoulders hunched. 'I shouldn't have been, should I? I mean, you have a right to protect your children. And you're still afraid that I'll hurt them.'

'I'm afraid of a lot more than that, Cliff.'

'I know.'

He half-turned, facing Lynne again, one hand gripping the railing. 'I know you're afraid, love. And so am I. We're both afraid that I won't take to Michael. Both afraid that if that's the way it is, it'll mean an end to us. But how can we find out if you never let me see him?'

'I'll let you see him. Of course I will. But you know something I've been thinking, Cliff? That even though we were married for eight months, we know very little about each other. Or, I know little about you. Maybe we should think about that as well.'

Lynne suppressed a shiver of pleasure as he took her shoulders in his hands. 'I'm thinking about that constantly.' His voice was husky, his hands on her felt very hot, especially the one that caressed the skin where her T-shirt neck had stretched enough to droop down. 'And we've been married two years, Lynne, not the eight months we lived as husband and wife after the magic words were said over us.' There was bitterness in his use of the phrase 'magic words', but still the same old magic in his touch.

She shrugged free of him, her heart running wild inside her chest. She saw his gaze on the jutting nipples her nightshirt couldn't hide. 'Don't!' she said sharply, crossing her arms over her chest. 'That's not what I meant about not knowing each other. We have an agreement. You don't need to prove anything to me. I already know we're sexually compatible. That's not our problem, is it?'

'I want you, Lynne,' he said huskily, 'and I think you want me just as much. And all that wanting, all those unresolved sexual feelings between us are going to cause tension. How can we expect to have your kids like me if you leap out of your skin each time I touch you?'

'Then don't . . . touch me,' she whispered jerkily, sitting in the chair and drawing her knees up to her chest, wrapping her arms around them, her defensive posture making Cliff feel like a black-belt louse.

Dammit, he didn't want her defensive. He didn't want her jumping away from him. He didn't want her to look like that at him, eyes full of misery, mouth taut, and shoulders hunched as if to ward off blows.

He knelt before her and grasped her ankles, pulling her bare feet down to rest on his thighs. He could feel their warm soles right through his jeans and he rubbed them gently with his hands.

'I have to touch you sometimes, Lynne. I have to. I can't be near you and resist the lure of your skin, the scent of you, the memories of you in my arms any more now than I could at the cabin yesterday.'

'But don't you understand?' she said, her mouth tremulous, her voice unsteady, her eyes narrowed as if in pain. 'If you do, then I won't be able to say no.

You're right. I want you, too, just as much as you want me, but if we become lovers, we'll let that become the most important feature of our relationship and the problems we need to solve will get swept aside, overlooked, forgotten, while we concentrate on making love.

'Today, when I said *you* had problems, I was simply mad, and being bitchy. You were right. Those problems belong to both of us and it will take both of us to solve them. We won't deal with the real issues, Cliff, unless we deal with them first, and if we don't, if we let ourselves get involved sexually again without sorting through the mess our lives are in, those problems will be there, waiting for us, like snags under the smooth surface of the river out there, waiting to grab us and tear us apart when we least expect it.'

'Hell, Lynne . . .' He swallowed hard and sat back on his heels, looking up at her. A moth fluttered around the bright flame of her hair.

'Dammit –' He had to laugh. 'It frosts me when you confound me with logic. Of course, you're right. But I . . . oh, hell, go to bed.'

He got to his feet and turned from her.

'Seems to me I heard someone offering me pie and milk a while ago,' she said softly behind him.

He couldn't help himself. He turned back to her, and met her smile with one of his own, sorrowful, wry, but loving nevertheless. 'Little pig,' he said. 'You always did have weird tastes in midnight snacks.'

'And in men,' she said. 'And in men.'

He laughed as he followed her into his sitting room where the milk and pie still occupied the tray. The milk was no longer ice-cold, and she took a sip, then wrinkled her nose.

'I'll pour fresh,' she said, and tiptoed out of his room carrying the two glasses. He listened, but heard nothing as she went down the stairs. Lynne, it seemed, knew where all the squeaky treads were.

CHAPTER 17

Lynne swallowed the last bite of her pie – or possibly Cliff's, since she'd eaten both pieces – and leaned back on the sofa, her stomach full, her eyes heavy with sleep. She knew she should get up and go to bed, but it was too nice, sitting here with Cliff close beside her. She breathed in the scent of his skin, felt the warmth of his body beside hers, looked far into the depths of his eyes – and loved him, yearned for a lifetime of having him at her side.

In only a few hours the kids would both be awake again. Her busy day would begin and there would be no time for . . . them. And she knew they needed time, time to talk, to get to know one another properly.

Time for her and Cliff. Would the month she had promised him be enough?

Would a lifetime?

Lynne gave Cliff a sleepy smile and said, 'This is going to sound kind of dumb, coming from someone you've been married to for a couple of years, but how did you get from construction to accounting, and how come I never asked that kind of question before?'

Cliff shifted an inch closer, aware of the warmth of her shoulder nearly touching his. He found her hand tucked under her thigh and pulled it free, linking her fingers with his. 'Maybe because I never opened myself to questions,' he said, answering the last one first. He lifted her hand and brushed the back of it with his lips before cradling it on his lap.

Lynne's insides turned over slowly, but she let her hand lie there, forcing herself not let her fingers curl over the hardness of his thigh, to test the muscles encased in smooth, faded denim, to slide higher . . .

'And maybe because I was too inexperienced and too stupid to realize that we didn't have a real relationship when we knew so little about one another, that even after we married, when we weren't making love, we only ever talked about unimportant things like our jobs or my family and the renovations going on here. We concentrated more on other people than on ourselves and each other.'

'Again, my doing,' he said, 'because I didn't want to discuss your pregnancy. I wanted to pretend it wasn't even there.'

She smiled and shook her head. 'Fat chance, huh?'

'Yeah.'

'Our not talking wasn't all your fault, Cliff. Don't ever think that,' she said.

Her eyes were big and dark blue as she met his gaze, and he ached to bend forward those few necessary inches and kiss her. 'You were never stupid,' he said, 'and I knew how inexperienced you were. If the relationship didn't work, it *was* my fault, love, and I know it. I don't mind admitting it. Once we'd got married, there were many things I should have told you, among them that I could never father children.'

His lips quirked in a wry smile. 'Of course, there are those who'd say I should have told you that long before we ever got to the point of marriage.'

'Except,' she said, 'we didn't have that kind of relationship.'

'No, we didn't.'

'Do you . . . did you think that I got pregnant to trap you, Cliff?'

He lifted his free hand and laid his fingers across her lips to hush her.

'No,' he said. 'And I didn't put that into the conversation to start an argument or to find fault. All I'm saying is that if I'd been honest with you from the beginning, neither of us would have suffered as we did. So I intend to be as honest with you now as I wasn't then. Whatever you want to know about me, ask. To you, I'm an open book. I want you to be one to me too.'

She looked at him sadly for a long moment, then, with a soft sigh, she shrugged. 'Okay, then start at the beginning. How did you get out of construction and into accounting?'

He smiled crookedly. He had just hurt her again,

hadn't he? She continued to want him to believe that she already was an open book to him.

God help him, why couldn't he could force himself to tell her the big lie she wanted to hear – that he believed *her* big lie? If he could do that, then their problems would be solved. At least outwardly.

He thought for a moment about what she'd said regarding snags under the smooth surface of a river, and knew she was right.

He had to come to terms with the results of her lie, not only the lie itself, before they could go ahead with this relationship, and giving her another lie in turn was not the way, so he couldn't pretend suddenly to believe her. Instead, he answered the question she had asked.

'The "how" was simply long, hard hours of study at night school, lunch hours and vacations, and maybe "hard" is the wrong word, at that. Numbers have always been my thing. They're concrete, solid, they always tell the truth and they're never open to interpretation, not when used correctly. As an accountant yourself, you know that. They simply . . . are. Absolutes, pure and clean.

The "why", though, was a whole lot more complex. I liked being part of a construction gang. I liked the outdoor work, learning how to do things . . . practical things, like pounding nails and taping dry wall and grouting tiles. I enjoyed mixing cement for sidewalks and foundations and patio decks. I loved the scent of raw wood and damp earth. But it burned me knowing the only people who made any real money at it in the end were the bosses, the contractors. Hourly laborers got their pay checks and that was it. The real profits went to the owners.'

He fell silent, ruminative, and at last she nudged him verbally. 'That doesn't explain why you got out of it and went into accounting. Unless you figured you could make enough that way to become an owner?'

He shook his head, smiling. 'You know yourself how long it would have taken a junior accountant to save enough to invest in the construction business. I'd have had as much chance, maybe more, trying to do it as a laborer. I also had to face it, I'm not a builder. I was a good worker, but I'd never have made a good boss. I don't know enough about building, and didn't want to bother learning it.'

He shifted, turned sideways and hitched one knee up. It pressed against Lynne's thigh, warm and solid and masculine. He laid an arm along the back of the couch and fluffed the short hair at the back of her neck with his fingertips. She shivered, felt goose-bumps rise on her arms, felt her nipples pucker and tighten and was glad he was gazing into her eyes as he talked. She wanted so much more than this, but knew she had to content herself with talking, listening, learning about this enigma to whom she was married. It was what they needed most right now.

'I never figured to be anything more than that, either,' Cliff continued, as if completely unaware of the effect he was having on her. 'I was eighteen when I started, I went where I was told, did the job

I was assigned, and I think I did it well even if, after a while, it stopped being a challenge. It never really occurred to me during those years that I could be wasting my mind along with wasting what I earned. After I paid my rent and bought a bit of grub, I spent the remainder in the bar, or gambling, or going to ball games with my buddies.'

He paused, thoughtful, and she knew he was considering whether he should add women to the list. He didn't.

'Then,' he said, 'one day I woke up and realized I was twenty-two years old and still doing exactly what I had done when I was eighteen. I hadn't grown. I hadn't changed. And I was living from pay-day to pay-day like a kid, only I wasn't a kid any longer.'

'Most people do that,' she said, moving her head, turning so that he couldn't keep teasing her with that gentle touch on her nape. 'At least most single guys. They don't settle down and start saving until after they're married. And some,' she added, 'according to things I've heard and read, don't even do it then.'

'That's right, but I was on the verge of getting married. I knew I had to change, but I didn't know how, didn't know what I wanted to do with my life, except that staying on as a construction laborer wasn't it.'

He looked uncomfortable. 'Well, Julia thought it wasn't it. She kept telling me I could do better than I was. That bothered me because I wanted her approval. She was a couple of years older than me, a college graduate and making good money working for a computer software development company.

Then, one day I fell off a scaffolding and broke my leg.' He tapped his right femoral area. 'It was a bad break, literally and figuratively, coming just before my wedding.'

She spread her hand over his thigh, caressing, and though he knew it was an involuntary motion, his pulse raced. 'Oh, Cliff!' she said, those big eyes wide as she looked at him in concern as if he'd just broken it yesterday. His thigh burned and he caught her hand, lifted it to his chest where it wouldn't do so much damage. He hoped.

He put his feet out on to the coffee table and slid his arm around Lynne, drawing her half across his lap, so her legs stretched out on the couch and her head rested on his chest. She stiffened.

'Now, wait a min –' she started, but he interrupted, laying his fingers over her mouth again, his eyes smiling down into hers.

'Hush,' he said. 'We'll both be more comfortable this way.' After a tense moment, she softened and snuggled a bit closer and he wrapped his other arm over her, stroking her cheek with his thumb, aching with a deep longing for her.

'While I was laid up,' he went on, 'I nearly went nuts, looking for something to do. It was April and some of the guys brought me their income tax stuff to look over. They knew I was pretty good with numbers; the pay office never made a mistake on my check that I didn't catch. When one of them said,

"Thanks, buddy, you just saved me fifty bucks,"
Julia accused me of giving away what other people
charged for, and it got me to thinking.'

'And so you went to night school?' She spoke
through a yawn. 'And worked during the day?'

'That's right,' he said, smoothing his thumb over
her eyelids. She let them remain closed. 'It was
three years of pretty intensive study combined with
long hours on the job, with little time left over for
play. Maybe that was part of what went wrong with
my marriage to Julia.

But it was what she wanted me to do, what she
pushed me toward. Oh, don't get me wrong. I
wanted to do it, too, but she was the driving force
behind my ambition. I made my first investments
through the company she worked for, and they
turned out pretty well. They led to some others
and, well, you know the way it goes. You sometimes
hit it lucky. In a year, I had enough behind me to
quit work and go to school full-time. That put a lot
of stress on me, and on her, I guess, but it speeded
things up, education-wise.'

But long before that, while I was still in night-
school, still working full-time in construction, and
trying to be a good husband, the stress made me
develop a chronic condition called something im-
pressive but which in effect was a bad belly-ache.'
He shrugged. 'At least it gave me a lot of pain in my
abdomen and interfered with my . . . well, my
bowels. Luckily, there was medication to take care
of that.'

'I remember.' Her gaze fixed on his. 'You had to

go back on that same medication during our marriage.' She yawned. 'So I caused you the same kind of stress as she did.'

'No!' His answer was swift and adamant. 'The stress I was under when we were together was not your doing. Don't forget, I had just bought into a new business, too, and was working hard to help develop it. My marriage to you was nothing like mine to Julia.'

Of course, knowing why Lynne had married him – why he'd married her – watching her baby grow inside her, change her slim figure day by day, had added greatly to that stress. But it was not her fault. He wanted her to understand that, once and for all. He didn't blame her. He hadn't been forced to marry her. He had chosen to, of his own free will. That he hadn't been able to cut it when it came right down to it was also not her fault.

'You made me happy, Lynne. You made me laugh and enjoy life, despite all the tension I was under. I'd probably have been in a lot worse shape without you than with you.' *Especially if you hadn't been pregnant*, he didn't say. 'With Julia, the happiness was short-lived. I never felt I measured up to her expectations. Which, of course, was the case. She – '

Realizing Lynne hadn't made a sound for several minutes, he asked, 'Does it bother you, my talking about my marriage to her?'

Her only reply was a soft sigh, and he smiled, looked down and wondered how long she'd been asleep. He cradled her closer, and held her for another fifteen minutes, before sliding one hand under her knees and coming carefully to his feet, still holding her.

'My bed or yours?' he whispered, looking into her sleeping face. He knew whose bed he wanted to put her into, but knew just as well that if he did it, it might be the last time. It might ruin any chance he had of making headway with Lynne.

Reluctantly, he carried her back out along the balcony and into her own room.

The room smelled of Lynne, and was as dainty and as feminine as he'd known it would be, done in shades of cream, pale blue and navy, with bright splashes of turquoise and orange – a bunch of dried flowers against a palm fan on one wall, a cushion in an overstuffed chair, a frilly-skirted flamenco dancer standing on her dresser, admiring herself in the big mirror.

Through a door, he saw a small bathroom, and thought of her lying naked in that tub, mounds of bubbles over her. Quickly, he moved toward her bed, and as he laid her on it, drawing the covers up over her, she smiled in her sleep. It was all he could do not to lie down beside her and gather her close again.

But with strength of character he found surprising, he backed away and went to his own room, where he lay on his back, hands under his head, and stared for a long, long time at the changing shadows on his ceiling. How long could a month be, after all?

A lifetime, that was all.

* * *

A muffled cry, a thud and then a high-pitched wail brought Cliff fully awake. 'Mommy!' the voice cried again.

He heard Lynne open her door, heard her feet on the floor of the hallway and then the sound of her voice, but not her words, and then lost even that as she closed whatever door she'd opened. Which child had cried out in the night? He thought it must have been Amanda. It hadn't sounded like a baby's cry, but then, what did he know about the way a fifteen-month-old baby might sound? He only knew it would be different from the way a one-month-old baby had sounded. The boy would have changed a lot since he'd seen him. If he had found a way to stay with Lynne, would seeing the child grow and change and learn have helped him overcome his feelings of bitter resentment, or would he have been like Logan, his animosity growing daily until it overcame everything else?

It was too late to think of things like that now. This was the present and if he meant to make the future work, he had to forget the past, so maybe he'd better go to Lynne and see if he could help. That it was most likely Amanda she was with, not Michael was a thought he didn't dwell on.

Because of course had it been the other child, he'd have been just as willing to help. Truly.

He pulled on his jeans then hesitated. What did he think he could do? Lynne did this all the time. And he'd only get in her way if he tried to help. But wouldn't he try to help if he were, indeed, the father of her children? Wouldn't it be expected of him?

301

Still hesitating, he had his decision made for him when another cry, this one quite different from the first, rang out. It was an inarticulate sound that nevertheless conveyed distress and how could Lynne, busy with one child, possibly respond to a second?

Quickly, before he could change his mind, he swung the door open and stepped through.

Lynne heard Mandy's door open and glanced up, surprised that Lou had heard and decided to investigate, then even more surprised to see Cliff standing there, his curly hair tumbling around his forehead and his jeans only half-zipped, scratching at his hairy chest with one hand, blinking in the light.

'What's wrong?' he asked, coming to crouch beside her, looking at Amanda's contorted face. 'Is she sick?'

'I don't think so. She sometimes has bad dreams.' With a gentle hand, she felt Amanda's forehead. 'She feels a bit warm, but it's such a hot night and . . . I just don't know. I'm out of fever strips.'

'Do you want me to take her? I heard . . . Michael cry too.'

Hearing the hesitation in his words before he could manage to articulate her son's name hardened all Lynne's soft, grateful feelings toward him. 'No,' she said quickly. 'Go back to bed. Tenants aren't expected to provide childcare.'

'But I'm no ordinary – '

'Yes, you are. Goodnight,' she said firmly.

'Michael's fine. He's asleep again. Mandy's crying must have disturbed him. And Mandy will go to sleep again, too, in a minute. Won't you, sweetheart?'

Mandy cried fretfully and Cliff half turned to the door, but just then, Michael howled again, louder, more insistently. Lynne groaned. 'It's going to be one of those nights,' she said, and tried to put Amanda back down in her bed.

'Mommy . . .'

Lynne sighed, her gaze flying to Cliff's face as she gave him a speculative look. *Could he be trusted to look after Amanda adequately?*

As if he'd plucked the question right out of her mind, he nodded in answer and took the little girl from her arms, sitting on the bed with her. Mandy seemed not to care who held her. She burrowed against him and made soft, sorrowful sounds. His hands looked big and awkward as he tried to soothe her.

Just as Lynne opened the door to the bathroom that joined the children's rooms, Mandy shot upright in Cliff's arms and threw up halfway across the floor.

'Oh, no!' Lynne cried, whirling back, but at the same instant, there came another sharp cry from next door and the unmistakable sounds of Michael vomiting too. With another doubtful glance at Cliff, Lynne ran.

For the next few hours, Cliff had a crash course in one of the more difficult aspects of parenting. He sponged the carpet on Mandy's floor, changed her bed, changed her clothes, sprayed deodorizer and held a basin as needed. He ran loads of laundry down to the basement, and learned to work an unfamiliar brand of washer and dryer, sometimes meeting Lynne in the hall, or on the stairs, or when she came through the bathroom between the kids' rooms to see how he and Mandy were doing.

And when it was over, he sat by the little girl's bed, slowly stroking her hair back from her face. She was sleeping peacefully, her skin cool, a soft smile on her pretty little mouth, a hand wrapped in a death-grip around one of his fingers. He sighed and bent to kiss her cheek.

'How's she doing?' Lynne opened the door quietly and stepped in.

He looked up at her, noticing for the first time that she'd put on a long housecoat over her T-shirt nightie. It had a zipper down the front, a zipper that she'd done right up to the base of her throat, as if she wanted to look as sexless as Edie York. He smiled at her, wondering if she thought she'd succeeded, and asked, 'Would it bother you to know that I've fallen in love with another redhead?'

She shook her head, a tired smile playing over her lips. 'Not if Mandy's the one you mean. Is she okay now?'

'You're asking me? I'm the apprentice here, remember?'

Coming closer, Lynne sat down and brushed a hand over Amanda's face, stroking the back of Cliff's hand as she did so. He thought her touch lingered on him, but when he shot a glance at her face, she appeared to be concentrating fully on the child.

'Nice and cool,' she said, pulling the cover up over Mandy's shoulder. 'Mike's fine now too.'

'Does this happen often?' he asked, smoothing his thumb over Amanda's hand as it gripped his finger, his eyes on Lynne's face. He wished he could smooth out the small frown between her eyebrows. Her skin, he knew, was as velvety as Amanda's.

'No. Not really.'

'What would you have done if they'd both got sick and I wasn't here?'

'Woken Lou up, I guess. I'm glad I didn't have to.' She looked down for a moment, then lifted her gaze to his. 'They don't usually get sick both at the same time.' She gave him a wry smile and added, 'As a rule, they manage to string it out a bit better, one keeping me up all one night, the other, the next. Or one throwing up all day, the other all night. I hear it gets even worse when it's chicken pox. Supposedly a family of four kids can make that last for a good six months. Luckily, I have only two.'

He swallowed, thinking that it was indeed lucky that she had two, but that if they did manage to work things out and get back together, she'd never have more than two and he could only hope they'd be enough for her. Did she want to be kept up at night with chicken pox for six months?

'Was it something they ate?' he asked, only to

keep her there talking for a few minutes longer.

'I doubt it,' she shrugged. 'Little kids just pick up stomach viruses the way dogs pick up fleas.'

He disengaged his finger from Amanda's hand and turned off the small light by her bed.

In the corridor she said, 'I hope you don't catch whatever bug they had.'

He grinned. 'Would you rock me and sing to me if I did?'

She gave him a steady look. 'Goodnight.' She turned toward the door of her own room then hesitated and looked back at him as if she couldn't quite force herself to leave. 'Thank you for helping me with them.'

'With Amanda,' he corrected her carefully.

She frowned, glanced at him sharply, knowing his choice of word had been deliberate. 'Do you know,' he asked, 'how careful you were to keep me from going into Michael's room tonight?'

She met his gaze squarely. 'Do you,' she countered, 'know how careful you were to make sure there was never any need for you to do so?'

He gnawed on his lower lip and then nodded. 'Yeah. All right. Maybe that's true. But he was sick. And you said he's afraid of men. I sure didn't want to upset him more when he was sick.'

'Okay,' she said. 'That makes sense.'

Her agreement pleased him. 'It does, doesn't it?' Then honesty overcame him and he added ruefully, 'Too bad it had very little to do with my not going into his room.'

Lynne had to laugh. If nothing else, Cliff was

brutally truthful. Especially about his own short-comings.

As if her laugh had drawn him, he crossed the hall and put his hands on her shoulders. Bending, he kissed her very briefly.

'Look,' he said, sounding surprised, and turned her to face the window at the end of the hall. Dawn light streamed in. Outside, birds sang. A cat pussy-footed across the lawn, leaving a silver track in the dewy grass, walked up the teeter-totter board, hesitated just plus of center, took a couple of cautious steps and waited for the high end to drop, whereupon it walked down the slope and off into the wet grass again. A crow swiped a cherry from near the top of the tree and flew away.

Lynne patted a yawn with the tips of her fingers and at once Cliff was contrite for having kept her up even these few extra minutes. 'Are you going to be able to get any more sleep?'

She flicked a glance at him. 'Some,' she said. 'A couple of hours, I guess.' Then, as she opened her door, she smiled at him, a genuine smile this time, with a light in her eyes that filled him with a sudden rush of emotions that nearly made him reach for her again.

'You get some sleep too.'

Forcing himself to stand where he was, he nodded, then waited until she had gone into her room before entering his own.

He went outside to the balcony, noticed she'd dropped her blinds again and drawn her drapes, then turned and leaned against the rail, looking out over the lawn, across the fence and to the river visible through a gap in the trees. Mist rose from it in silver wisps. A couple of fishing boats ran for the open water, leaving long, V-shaped wakes behind them. How many of them were owned by Vincent Salazar?

Salazar. Dammit, why had his name popped up like that? He normally went days, months, could even be years, he supposed, without consciously remembering the man's name. But, with having talked about him to Lynne yesterday, the man's foggy image refused to leave his mind. Did he know he had a son – if, indeed, he did? Would he care? If Cliff had gone to him when he first heard the man's name, would he now be skippering a fishboat for a living? He wondered if Julia would even have spoken to him if he'd smelled of fish, rather than fresh lumber?

Funny, he realized now, he'd never mentioned Salazar to her or tried to use the possibility that he had a wealthy father to hold her. Which it would have, he believed. She'd have put up with a lot more than his sterility if he'd been rich enough.

Since the break-up of his first marriage, he'd considered at times going to see Salazar, but always, at the last minute, he'd backed away. Why?

Because, he admitted now, he'd been afraid of receiving from him exactly what he had received from Logan Foreman, and what he'd given to Lynne's son.

His old nemesis. Rejection.

CHAPTER 18

'Where's Lynne?' Cliff asked, having followed the aroma of freshly brewed coffee to the kitchen where he found Louisa alone, up to the elbows in flour as she kneaded bread dough.

'Gone to the park,' she said, taking the tray from him and glancing at the two empty glasses and the lemon-smeared plates. 'Had a little midnight picnic, did you?' Louisa set the dough into a bowl, covered it with a towel and rubbed the floury dough off her hands and arms.

'Not me,' said Cliff with a grin, as Louisa washed under the tap. 'Lynne. She ate both pieces. Good thing, too, because she needed her strength. Did she tell you that the kids were sick all night?'

'She told me,' Louisa said with a dry smile as she set a cup of coffee in front of him and then tested the waffle iron with a bead of water. It danced high and she poured batter. Cliff sat back and listened to the sizzle, his mouth watering. He couldn't remember the last time he'd had home-made waffles. 'She also told me you were up most of the night with her.

Being a father's not much fun, is it?'

'I wouldn't know,' he said, 'never having been one, but seeing Mandy through a night of illness made me feel . . . I don't know, useful, I guess.'

Louisa nodded but said nothing. Cliff sipped his coffee and watched steam escape from the waffle-iron. Presently, Louisa flipped out the first waffle on to a plate and set it before him. He buttered it liberally and added syrup. 'Delicious,' he said around the first, hot bite.

She smiled.

'That,' he said, twenty minutes later, 'was the best breakfast I have had in about thirty years. Where did you say Lynne had gone?'

'She took the kids to the park. There's some kind of entertainment there every summer morning from ten to twelve. Arts, crafts, music, you know, the stuff that appeals to little kids.'

He didn't know. 'Oh! Uh, how are they?' he asked, feeling guilty that he hadn't asked that first thing. Louisa shot him a glance full of silent censure and he realized that his belated question showed that he had forgotten all about the kids while he packed in syrup-sweetened waffles and gallons of great coffee. A real father would have shown more concern, he knew.

Well, he'd have to try harder. He'd show Lynne. He'd show this disapproving old woman. And he'd show himself.

'I should have asked sooner,' he said contritely. 'But when Lynne and I finally went to bed, they seemed okay.'

'They are,' Louisa said. Her expression told him she might disapprove of him but she was willing to forgive when he screwed up. She seemed to realize that he had very few clues to go on, no guidelines to steer by. 'Why don't you go and see for yourself?'

He felt as if a hammer had hit his chest. 'Go the park?'

'Yes. It's only a few blocks away.'

'Right,' he said, getting to his feet. 'Sure. Go to the park. See . . . the kids.' He swallowed hard, shoved his hands into his hip pockets and nodded. 'Yeah.'

'Turn right when you get to the end of the street.' Louisa's voice floated to him as he went out the back door. It took all his energy not to get into his car and drive away as fast as he could. Instead, he continued to walk, and obediently turned right when he got to the end of the street. He could do it. He could go to the park. He could go and find Lynne, Amanda . . . and Michael.

Cliff heard the noise emanating from the park long before he saw what caused it, and when he got there, he encountered a large circle of mostly women and children, some standing, some sitting, all clapping and singing, surrounding a one-man band who played energetically and loudly if not well. He searched for Lynne's bright hair in the crowd, but couldn't see it. Walking around the outside of the circle, he peered at people seated at the far side, always searching, and spotted, not Lynne, but Amanda sitting on the grass.

Crowding through, he managed to get to her side

311

and sit down between her and a large blue stroller with the hood pulled up shielding its occupant from the sun, and from his view.

'Hi, pretty girl,' he said to Amanda, putting an arm around her. 'Where's your mommy?'

'Right here,' said a strange and harsh voice behind him. Startled, he looked up at the big woman who stood there glaring at him. She took a step toward him and he pulled his arm away from Mandy. He might need both of them to defend himself, he thought, not that he wanted to pit his six-foot, two-hundred-pound frame against her six-foot, two-hundred pound frame. She looked as if she could take him apart without even setting down the baby she held on one beefy arm.

'You're not her mother,' he said. 'Where's . . .?'

'Hush, Daddy. We singin'.' Amanda's words sent the big woman back to her place with a startled look on her face.

'Sorry,' she said. 'I didn't know you were their father. Lynne didn't say. She's gone to the rest-room.'

'Sing, Daddy,' said Amanda, but he shook his head. She didn't know what she was asking. When he sang, everyone else left. He sounded like an maladjusted foghorn with no mute button. 'Sing,' she insisted, so he compromised by humming, which seemed to satisfy her. She gave him a bright blue-eyed, sunny smile, and sang merrily about ants marching six by six, hurrah, hurrah, though everyone else was singing something about a little rabbit that apparently beat up on field mice by bopping them on the head. And he'd been reading that learning about violent behavior encouraged it in children.

Looking straight ahead, Cliff stared hard at the one-man band, who was wearing a bright yellow shirt, green pants, a red hat with a tall bobbing feather on it, and blue shoes. He played a set of drums and cymbals with a pedal attached to one foot, and held a baton in one hand, with which he clanged the notes on a glockenspiel. In the other hand he held a French horn that he tootled now and then alternately with a harmonica. The noise he made was surprisingly melodic at times, and the children and their mothers – a few fathers as well, he noticed – all seemed to know the words to the tunes he played. At least they all sang enthusiastically.

As he watched, and as he hummed along as best he could, the baby-stroller at his side grew larger and larger in his imagination. As long as he looked straight ahead at the entertainer, he could avoid seeing the stroller's hidden occupant. But if he were to lean forward six inches, he knew, he could see the child's face.

He leaned back, feeling unreasoning panic wash through him. Lynne was going to come back. She was going to see him. She was going to take the baby out of that stroller and possibly hold him up for Cliff to see and he was scared spitless at the idea.

Dammit! Shame made his skin feel hot all over. He tugged at the neck of his T-shirt. He loathed such cowardice in himself.

He had to look at the baby before Lynne came

back. He had to be prepared to face her with a calmness he might not be feeling. He had to be capable of meeting her eyes, his own hiding whatever turmoil he might be undergoing and smile, and smile, and smile.

Carefully, slowly, he leaned forward. He could see that same little pair of tiny Reeboks he had seen in the family room, and the cuffs of a pair of blue overalls. But he couldn't see the baby. With one unsteady hand, he reached out and grasped the fender of the stroller and rolled it back a foot and a half, then looked sideways at the child it contained, feeling himself go light-headed, hearing a dull roaring in his ears before everything, even the singing, was silenced by the lurching of his mind into another realm.

The owner of those little shoes was black. In only seconds he recovered. Part-way. Of course that baby wasn't Michael. He had seen Michael when he was an infant. So he knew. This wasn't Lynne's baby. The baby grinned at Cliff and banged his fat fists on the little tray at the front of the stroller. Drool ran down two of his chins. Cliff grinned back at him and the mother of that curly-haired tot gave him a strange look as he smiled weakly up at her. Then, pointedly, she rolled the stroller forward again, out of his reach.

Quickly, he picked Mandy up and held her between his bent knees, bouncing her in time to the music so that it wouldn't be so obvious that he was shaking all over.

'Well, this is a nice surprise,' said a breathless

voice behind him and turned to catch that brilliant, joyous smile on Lynne's face, the brilliant, glowing sun gleaming in her red hair like a shining halo. She wasn't carrying a baby. Relief washed over him again and he patted the grass beside him.

'Hush, Mommy,' he said solemnly. 'We singin'.'

She grinned at him. 'Pardon me.' She turned and reached for the baby the children's bodyguard was holding and sat down beside Cliff, her gaze on his face, grave now, waiting, it seemed for his assessment of her child, his approval, perhaps. Or the opposite.

Cliff looked at the baby. Curly brown hair, faint brown eyebrows. Startlingly thick and curled lashes, as black as his own, and light, nondescript blue-gray eyes, different from the vacant, vague blue he'd recalled from Michael's infancy. The little boy looked like no one he had ever seen before, but that was not what surprised him. What did was that he felt – nothing. Not one solitary emotion. He felt no different about the baby from the way he had when the big woman was holding him. He wanted to laugh at himself for all the fears that had churned through him. He wanted to cheer because he'd met the biggest hurdle, and cleared it without pause. He wanted to meet Lynne's eyes and reassure her but he couldn't tear his gaze from the face of her little boy.

Michael, however, didn't feel quite so sanguine about the situation. Here was a man, not two feet away, and he was looking at him. Michael responded as Michael always did to men.

He opened his mouth and howled.

Quickly, Lynne turned him away, hiding his face against her shoulder, and Cliff felt sick as he watched his small, bare feet dig into her midriff as he tried to escape from the danger by climbing her frame.

When he had forgotten that Cliff was there, the howls ended, but then he looked back and started all over.

'Hell, Lynnie, this isn't going to work,' said Cliff, putting Amanda down and preparing to get to his feet. 'I can't torture the poor kid like this.'

'Sit down,' she said quietly. 'We've started it now. We have to see it through. He'll get used to you, Cliff.'

He sat, feeling tortured himself. Climbing back between his legs, Amanda said, 'Sing, Daddy.'

'Cliff,' corrected Lynne.

'Sing, Cliff.'

He shrugged. 'Okay, kiddo, you asked for it.' And then he sang, his voice rising far above the lighter voices of the women and children as he belted out a chorus of 'Johnny Appleseed'.

Lynne looked at him in astonishment. Amanda turned and stared up into his face, her hands on his knees, her knees on his feet. He grinned down at her and kept on singing. The one-man band, realizing he was in danger of being drowned out, played louder. The children clapped harder, most eyes turned to the extremely loud man now providing most of the entertainment. And Michael stopped bellowing.

He turned in his mother's arms and looked quizzically at the source of the horrendous noise. Then, flopping sideways like a limp piece of string, he caught a fistful of Amanda's T-shirt, pulled himself off Lynne's lap and half on to Cliff's.

Cliff froze and, to everyone's intense relief, stopped singing. Michael opened his mouth, stared at his father and then howled again, too frightened even to scramble back to the safety of his mother's lap. She pulled him away from Cliff and said, 'I guess you're going to have to sing again,' in the manner of a woman making a great sacrifice for the sake of her child.

Once more, as Cliff bellowed, Michael did not. He stared, fascinated, getting as close as he could, standing on Cliff's legs, hands on his shoulders, looking into his mouth.

Suddenly, Lynne laughed. 'I've got it,' she said.

'What?' asked Cliff, turning to look at her – and at Michael.

'No, no. Keep singing,' she urged. 'He likes the way your fillings flash in the sun. Keep it up and you'll have him eating out of your hand in no time at all.'

Fillings? thought Cliff. All the kid can find to like about me is my dental work?

After a week and a half spending his mornings in the park and his afternoons oiling hinges, weeding vegetable gardens and other make-work projects he found for himself, Cliff was ready for a change. Change? He was ready to climb out of

317

his skin! Dammit, he was bored! He glanced over at Lynne. Boredom was no problem for her. She sat on a blanket with Michael, trying to keeping him from wandering too far, getting up and chasing him when he did, both of them giggling and enjoying themselves.

Cliff had a book with him, but he wanted something, anything, different from this. He wanted to go back to work. He wanted to talk to some men. He wanted to wish both Michael and Amanda on to another planet and take Lynne out to Galiano Island and make love to her for six days straight until neither of them could walk or talk or think.

He did not want to be a friendly stranger who lived in rooms in her house, ate at her table, conversed in the evenings with three old ladies in the lounge, or Louisa in the kitchen, or Lynne on the occasions when he could drag her away from her computer and her accounting business, persuade her to take a walk with him as the evening cooled. In spite of Louisa's having oiled it, that damned glider on the front porch remained unused – at least the way she'd intended. If he even had that, what had Louisa called it? – spooning – in the evenings, he might stay halfway sane, but this was plain, damn ridiculous. No man could live this way.

'Both down for naps?'

Cliff's voice startled Lynne. She'd thought he was lying in the hammock he'd strung two weeks ago between a couple of shade trees in the front yard.

She looked out from under her wide-brimmed sombrero and dropped a handful of weeds into the basket she'd been pushing along the row of beets she was weeding. He got down on his knees in the next row and plucked out the things she'd previously showed him didn't belong in the vegetable garden.

'Both the kids, and Louisa too,' she said, 'though I wasn't sure Mandy would go down. She's going through one of those "you love Michael more than you love me" stages. I know it's because he takes up more of my time than she'd like, but if this is the sibling rivalry I've read so much about, I never knew how difficult it would be not to feel guilty over it.'

'I wish I knew how to help,' he said.

'You do help by giving Mandy the attention she needs.' She grinned. 'Yesterday in the park it looked like the two of you were having a ball, painting each other's faces instead of the mural you were supposed to be painting.' She'd sat, leaning against a tree, feeding Michael a bottle of juice, and wished she could join the other two.

'But it would have been better if I could have taken Michael and given him his bottle,' Cliff said. 'Then Mandy could have had what she really wanted and needed: your undivided attention for a few minutes.'

He looked into her eyes and reminded her, 'You told Mandy that I didn't want to feed Michael. That wasn't quite true, Lynnie. I would have, if I'd thought it wouldn't have upset him or scared him or whatever it is makes him bellow when I get too close.'

She nodded. 'I know, Cliff. I've seen how you've . . . changed. Grown.'

But not enough, Cliff thought. Not as much as I'd like to. Not as much as I know I need to. He didn't know if his inability to do that one thing he feared so deeply would affect the problems he shared with Lynne, but he did know it was a step he needed to take for the sake of his own personal development, and wondered if he'd ever find the courage to take it.

His heart pounded heavily and his mouth grew dry as he thought about it. All he'd need to do was get into his car and drive northwest from here. He knew the road to turn on to. His mother had told him. He knew the number of miles his odometer would show when he'd reached the right gate. He knew he had to do it. Some day.

But not today.

Because maybe the answers he'd find when he got there wouldn't be of any help at all, and right now, his need to settle things with Lynne had to take precedence.

He and Lynne weeded together for several minutes in not-quite-companionable silence, but at least with nothing outwardly uncomfortable between them.

'Do you feel anything for him?'

Jolted, he sat back on his heels. What the hell was she doing, reading his mind now? 'How do I know if I feel anything for him? I've never met the man!'

She stared at him, hands still. 'I meant Michael, Cliff. You were thinking of Salazar?'

Relief flooded him. 'Michael. Oh. Oh, well, he's

. . . cute. He has the neatest little ears I've ever seen, and his almost non-existent eyebrows along with those wide eyes give him a constantly startled look. Whenever I see him, I want to smile. I do smile, and every so often, he actually smiles back. So yes, I guess I feel something for him. I feel . . . pleased that he doesn't scream the house down the way he did the first few days. I wish he'd come to me because he's your child and I love you. I will learn to love Michael just as I've learned to love Amanda. With her, it just happened, I guess because she's so much like you and she accepts me. It was as if she and I had an instantaneous affinity for each other. We . . . well, we clicked.'

'You did that long ago. Remember, you were the one she took her first steps to? I knew then you'd be as wonderful a father as I'd always hoped.'

'But I'm not, am I? I'm sorry it hasn't happened like that between me and Michael. I know it hurts you, but don't forget, it's only been a couple of weeks.'

She sighed. 'You're right, of course. It's just that I had such high hopes. I mean, that first day in the park, when you sat there staring at him as if you'd never seen him before, I thought maybe there was some tiny glimmer of . . . of . . . Oh, I don't know what, recognition, maybe. A sense of . . . of kinship?' she added with a hint of unconscious hopefulness in her tone.

Aloud he said gently, 'Lynne, love, don't rush this, okay? Give us, both Michael and me, time. After all, isn't that what we agreed it would take?'

She nodded and got to her feet, brushed off the knees of her jeans and pulled off her gardening gloves, slapping them on her thigh. The wind caught her hat and tumbled it away into his row. 'Sure. But . . .' Careful not to come too close to him, not to risk touching him, she stepped over the row of lacy carrot tops into the one he occupied and reached for the hat.

He got to it first and held it, wiped one hand on the seat of his jeans, then smoothed her hair back from her forehead before setting the hat back onto her head. Gently, he curved his hand around her jaw, holding it there. She stiffened at his touch and her eyes went wide and dark as, for a moment, her gaze clung to his. Then, with a small, pained sound, she jerked away from him.

'But, what, Lynne?'

'But . . . there is . . . *that*. You . . . touch me and . . .'

He groaned softly and took her upper arms in his hands, not pulling her against him, but still holding her close enough that he could feel the warmth emanating from her body.

'And?' His voice was a low growl and she felt it in her bones as much as heard it. She wanted to draw away from him, but could not. 'I touch you and . . .?'

'I . . . I think I'll go in now. I've had enough sun.'

'No!' He'd had enough equivocation, enough putting things off, enough of *her* putting *him* off. 'I want to know what you were going to say. Remember, Lynne? This was supposed to be a

322

time for us to get to know each other better, too; it wasn't just for me and Michael. So talk, dammit. Say what's in your heart.'

She only looked at him, her face pale under the shadow of her hat. 'You know what's in my heart. I don't need to say it,' she whispered finally.

'Maybe I need to hear it.'

He could see her trembling even as she struggled to be firm and steady, could hear her breath rasping in and out erratically, and the darkness of her eyes told him more of her inner turmoil than she would have guessed. She shivered in the heat and whispered, 'I can't go on like this.'

'And neither can I, sweetheart.' He lifted one hand, stroked the back of her neck under the brim of the hat, feeling the muscles under her warm, damp skin quiver at his touch, and slowly, all the days and nights of rigid control began to unravel in both of them. As Lynne's breathing changed, becoming even more agitated, need overcame Cliff and he knew that nothing short of a nuclear attack would stop him now.

That, or Lynne's telling him she didn't want him any more.

'The future, Lynne. It's ours. Together, love. We have to take it.'

She slid her hand up his chest and made a soft, explosive sound that he couldn't begin to interpret.

Her thin bra couldn't disguise the distension his touch had caused in her nipples. As Cliff skimmed his hand higher, he stroked his palm across the peak of one breast and heard that soft sound come from her throat again. Gently, he squeezed the nub between finger and thumb, rotating it, rolling it back and forth. Her eyes grew so dark that they appeared nearly indigo. Her lips parted, moist, yearning . . .

There was something wildly erotic in touching her this way, in broad daylight, in the middle of a vegetable garden, with the sound of neighbors' voices coming from the far side of the fence, and in knowing that for once she wasn't jerking away, wasn't telling him to stop. She needed him equally as much as he needed her.

He slid his hand down finally, to the waist of her cutoffs and undid the snap. He drew the zipper down and inserted his hand into the V he created, feeling another spasmodic tremor of Lynne's muscles, hearing her soft sound that was half-gasp, half-moan. With his hand flat against the satin of her belly, his fingers slid inside the low elastic of her panties, just above the mat of tangled curls, and slowly probed with gentle insistence into the moist, shallow groove he found there.

With an inarticulate cry, Lynne swayed, sagging heavily against him. He turned her face up and, without opening her eyes, she licked her lips. Their lush moistness was more than he could resist. He bent forward and placed his mouth on hers. It opened at the first thrust of his tongue against her lips and then clung as they shared what both had been longing for since the day he arrived.

'Lynne . . .' he groaned, discovering that they had collapsed to the sawdust path between vegetable beds. Her hat lay crushed under his shoulder, the straw of it prickling his bare skin. He didn't know where his shirt had gone.

'Get up, sweetheart. Let's go inside. I'm damned if I'm going to make love you in the dirt.'

He pulled her to her feet and, arms wrapped around each other, they tried to leave the garden, but it was no use. He had to kiss her again, had to hold her body fully against his. He was shaking so hard he could barely move, but he knew this couldn't go on.

He was ready to explode and he had to have Lynne . . . now.

With arms so weak he wondered if he could do it, he lifted her and carried her, not toward the house, but farther into the garden. On a strip of thick grass behind the tall, lush bean plants, between a dense row of broccoli and another of cauliflower, he laid her down.

There, under a blue, blue sky, with the sound of bird-song all around, and a gentle breeze wafting the scent of carnations over them, they made love with the roughly tender urgency of people driven, compelled to come together, bodies, minds and souls entwined until there was no telling where one ended and another began.

Mutual need gave rise to barely controlled violence. It was aching emotion overflowing two hearts, straining muscles, yearning flesh that demanded more than seemed possible, and short, hoarse cries of frustration that it wasn't fast enough and hard enough and big enough and deep enough to convey all the love they ached to give each other, but in the end it transcended anything either of them had ever experienced and Cliff held Lynne, feeling her silent tears slick both their faces as they kissed and smoothed and healed the bruises inflicted in their haste and all-encompassing need.

'Did I hurt you, love?' he asked presently.

'No,' she said, though she knew she would ache in every muscle by tomorrow. They were aches she would cherish, would feel she had won as the result of a long, worthwhile battle. How could she have ever let herself believe there was no future for them? No matter what, they had this, and it was an important ingredient in their marriage. With the love they shared, somehow they would make the other details fit together as well as the two of them did. She smoothed the bite-mark her teeth had left on his shoulder. 'Oh, Cliff. Look what I did to you. I'm sorry.'

He looked, then kissed the fingertips that continued to rub back and forth over the fading mark. 'If it hurt,' he said with a husky chuckle, 'either it hurt good or I didn't notice.'

He cradled her close, his hand sliding slowly from her thigh to her shoulder, back down again, then up, riding the curve of her hip, dipping into the hollow of her waist, long, smooth stroking that would have lulled her to sleep had not voices sounded just on the other side of the board fence that separated her garden from her neighbors'.

'Lynne!'

There was a sharp note in his whisper and she

rose up on her elbow to look down at him. 'What?' She ran a languid hand through his hair, around his jaw, feeling the beginning of an afternoon bristle. One thumb stroked his bottom lip. It was soft and warm and pliant until he spoke again.

'We just made love in the garden!' he hissed.

'Yes. I noticed.' She reached out a hand and stroked the leaf of a tall broccoli plant. 'I bet they'll grow better now.'

He shushed her. 'Listen! There are people next door. They must have heard us.'

She laughed and shook her head. 'I doubt it. They're both elderly and deaf as posts. They yell at each other and neither one ever hears right. They have some interesting, if totally off-the-wall, conversations.' She hooked one knee over his legs and ran a hand into the hair on his chest. 'You're like a bearskin rug,' she murmured, and found one of his nipples hidden in the mat. She rubbed it and felt it harden. 'My bearskin rug.'

'Stop that,' he said, flattening his hand over hers. 'Or we'll be starting all over again.'

'Good,' she said with the old, impudent grin he'd fallen in love with at the beginning of time. 'Once more, for the sake of the cauliflower.'

CHAPTER 19

Cliff laughed, an easy, rolling, relaxed laugh that filled her heart with its goodness, making tears well up in her eyes again and run down into her ears as she flopped on to her back. 'You're such a pagan,' he said, sitting up. 'Hey, would you quit that?' He caught a tear as it escaped from the corner of her eye.

'I love you so much,' she said with a watery smile. 'And I thought for such a long time that I would never hear you laugh again.'

'Come back to me, Lynne,' he said, pulling her up to cradle her against his body. 'Be my wife again, in every way. I need you, too, your laughter, your love, your presence in my life to help me make sense of it all.'

Slowly, she nodded. 'Yes. I was wrong, Cliff, in trying to keep us apart while you and Michael get used to each other. I know you won't deliberately hurt any of us. And I know that if you're given a chance you'll learn to love him, and he you.'

'Thank you.' Their kiss was one of solemn

reaffirmation, a restatement of vows made nearly two years before. Only this time, he was promising more than to love, honor and cherish her; he was promising to take her children unto himself, to love them and protect them and cherish them, too, and the knowledge filled her with unprecedented joy.

'Ah, Lynnie,' he said when they broke apart, 'your trust means more to me than I can tell you. I love you so much.'

He got to his feet and held her naked body in his arms, gently moving her back and forth across his chest, reveling in the feel of her breasts against him. 'And if we don't get out of the garden, we're going to be teaching the rhubarb stuff it's probably never even guessed at.'

When they had dressed, he plopped her hat back on to her head and then tilted the brim to peer under at her shining eyes, her flushed cheeks, her joyous smile.

'How long does nap-time usually last?'

She laughed softly and glanced at her watch. 'Another hour or so.'

'Oh, hell,' he groaned. 'Not nearly long enough for what I have in mind, but I suppose parents have to take whatever time they can get.'

'Either that or weed carrots.'

The carrots got weeded another day.

'Horsey ride, prease, Daddy.'

Cliff obediently crossed his legs and Amanda straddled his foot, holding his hands as he 'galloped' for her, making her hair fly and her giggles rise up to fill the room. 'More!' she said when his leg gave out and he let her slide off on to the floor.

'You're just like your mother,' he said, sliding a glance over his wife's face. 'Greedy.'

Lynne grinned and said, 'Complaining?'

'Not on your life, but when I'm too tired, I'm too tired.'

'Don't you believe it, Amanda,' murmured Lynne.

But Cliff was firm. 'No, Mandy, honey. You wouldn't want my leg to fall off, would you? Let Daddy rest for a few minutes, okay?'

'Okay,' she said obligingly, and ran out through the kitchen, into the backyard where Louisa was picking raspberries for tonight's dessert. Through the big window of the playroom, Lynne and Cliff watched as she helped Louisa pick, one for the berry basket, three for her own smeared mouth.

Cliff leaned back and crossed his legs again. 'I'm happy,' he said, looking over at Lynne. 'I never thought that there could be this much happiness in the world. These past weeks, since we've been together – really together – again, have been the happiest in my life.' He looked at Michael, who toddled around the room, pushed Amanda's tricycle for a few feet before he tipped it over then went on to something else. The baby had relaxed, easily accepting of Cliff's presence now, although he had yet to come to him.

Lynne smiled and nodded, rubbing her right thumb over the wedding band she now wore again. She loved to see it there. 'I know. Me too.

I'm going to hate it when you go back to work.'

'Oh?' He smiled and slid a hand around the back of her head, kissing her long and hard. 'Afraid naptime will be lonely?'

'I know it will,' she said, sliding her arms around his neck. They were deep in a dreamy kiss that made delicious promises when the door opened and Mrs Graham cleared her throat. Reluctantly, Lynne broke away from her husband.

'Excuse me,' Mrs Graham said. 'So sorry to interrupt.' Her expression said otherwise. 'Louisa didn't change my towels today. I wanted to speak to her about it.'

'Mrs Graham, Lou's been busy preserving everything she can get her hands on these past couple of weeks. All the fruit and vegetables seem to be ready at the same moment. Please feel free to help yourself to fresh towels whenever you want. I believe we've mentioned that before. This isn't a hotel, and you can't expect daily maid service.'

Mrs Graham huffed and marched out.

'That's something else I've been thinking about,' Cliff said. 'We don't need the revenue your tenants bring in, and I'd like us to have a home of our own, just us, our family, with no one interrupting when I'm kissing my wife.'

Lynne laughed. 'The kids interrupt more than the tenants.' But she knew he was right. They did need a home just for them. She stared around, at the familiar playroom, the big kitchen beyond, at Lou and Amanda so happy together outside, at Michael, sitting by the side of the big, built-in toy-box, happily playing with a musical ball. She thought about her three old ladies and what would happen to them if she closed up the house, maybe sold it, or put in a manager who'd be less sympathetic to their peculiarities.

It would be a wrench, leaving this place, but it would be wonderful for us to have a real home together. 'Yes,' she agreed. 'We need a home just for us.'

He bent and kissed her, his tongue sliding along the seam of her lips, parting them, flicking in and out, then plunging deeply, eliciting a groan of pleasure from her as her breasts hardened and pressed into his chest. His hands encircled her head, holding her as he made hot little tracks all over her face, her neck, her shoulder, and then moved back to her mouth.

'Lynne . . .' he breathed. 'Oh, lord, woman, you turn me on! Come upst – '

'Ide!' said a commanding voice, interrupting Cliff's impassioned plea. 'Ide, Dad-dad!'

He and Lynne broke apart and stared down at the small boy sitting astride Cliff's foot, his fists clinging to his father's pants. He gave an experimental bounce and said again, 'Ide.'

Carefully, slowly, Cliff reached his hands down and unhooked the tiny fingers from his jeans. They wrapped around his forefingers tightly and Cliff crossed his legs, lifted his foot, and bounced the baby as he held him securely by both hands, and he and Lynne gazed at each other, stunned.

Lynne could barely see through the spurt of tears

that flooded down her face, but she wanted to see this, she had to see it, so she wiped her eyes dry with the palms of her hands and watched father and son together in their first spontaneous communion, saw Cliff, foot still moving gently up and down with Michael astride it, saw his tense, tough struggle to control his emotions by squeezing his eyes closed, clenching his teeth and swallowing again and again, spasmodically as a muscle quivered in his jaw.

Let go, she wanted to say. If you have to cry, then cry.

But he didn't, of course. Cliff Foreman did not permit himself to cry. Instead, he opened his eyes and looked first at Michael, then at Lynne.

Cliff saw the love in her glowing face, the tender compassion in her eyes, and knew she understood everything he felt at this moment – possibly even better than he did himself. Slowly, sweetly, they shared a smile.

Michael simply enjoyed the ride and Mandy might have been very jealous if she'd seen how long it took before Cliff's leg gave out.

Leaning back again, Lynne's head on his shoulder, Michael clambering from one lap to the other as if they were both the same to him, Cliff said in a hushed voice, 'You remember what I was saying about being happy?'

She nodded.

'I was wrong. There was greater happiness just around the corner and now I've got it. But I know now, love, it can never, ever get better.'

Lynne hugged him tightly and closed her eyes.

She was glad his happiness was complete.

'Lynne?'

'Hmm?'

'For you, too, love? Is it good, this life?'

'It's perfect, hon,' she assured him, drawing her hand lovingly along his jaw. 'Of course it couldn't be better.'

But it could, she knew in her secret heart, if only Cliff would look in a mirror some day and see that a baby with curly brown hair and blue-gray eyes looked suspiciously like the image he saw of a man with curly black hair and dark brown eyes. But he wouldn't, she knew. He would only see a fair complexion as opposed to a swarthy one, and remember the humiliation of knowing someone else had done what he was certain he couldn't do.

She sighed and snuggled close to him, refusing to let it eat at her. This was her life, too, and it would be what she made of it – what they made of it, together – and she was going to make certain it was the best one any family had ever lived.

Maybe in time Cliff would believe in himself enough to believe in her.

As if a dam had been broken, Michael, from that day onward, was all over Cliff, fighting Mandy for time with him, jealous of any attention he paid the little girl, demanding with rapidly increasing vocabulary his turn, his ride, his daddy. And when the day came that Cliff had to go back to work, his son wandered around the house all day, disconsolate. He was still awake when Cliff arrived home and shook the bars of his crib almost to pieces until he had received the hugs and kisses and attention he felt were his due.

After a week of this, they began a serious search for the perfect home for themselves.

'Lou, will you come with us when we move?' she asked one evening when the two of them were discussing it together. They hadn't told the ladies yet, unsure of exactly what they'd be telling them.

'No,' said Louisa. 'You and Cliff need to be on your own in your own home, raising your children without any interference.'

'You wouldn't interfere,' said Lynne. 'You never have.'

'You need to be on your own,' Louisa reiterated firmly. 'And what would happen to the ladies if I left?'

Lynne frowned. 'I've been thinking along the lines of selling this place and investing the proceeds for Mandy's future, but I am worried about what would happen to the tenants. Do you mean you'd like to stay here and look after them?'

'And what else would I do?' Louisa asked, offended. 'You sell this place and I'll be out there with them, looking for a new home. *My* tenants have just renewed a year's lease.'

'You nearly finished, sweetheart?' Cliff poked his head in the door of Lynne's office one Saturday evening.

Turning from her keyboard, she gave him a smile and held out her arm. Hugging him close, she leaned her face against his middle, and nodded.

'Another ten minutes or so,' she said, looking up. They'd spent most of the day house-hunting so she was playing catch-up with her clients' accounts.

He glanced at the spreadsheet on the computer screen. 'Projections?'

'Mmm-hmm. One of my clients is applying for a bank loan. By the look of this, if their projected profits materialize, they really will need to expand or the tax bite will be horrendous.'

'Think they'll get their loan?'

'Oh, sure. Now scram, and I'll finish up so we can get to bed.'

She hurried through the rest of her tasks. She had a date with her husband she didn't want to miss.

Lynne entered their room to find Cliff lying on the bed, hands behind his head, his eyes closed, a strange expression on his face. Standing in the doorway, she watched him for several moments then stepped softly to the foot of the bed, giving it a little shake.

'Hey, super-stud, you fall asleep on me?'

Opening his eyes and his arms, he sat up and she went to him. 'No,' he said. 'I've been lying here thinking.'

'That,' she said, 'Can become a dangerous habit in a man.'

He pulled her down to lie with him, holding her close. 'Hey, I'm serious.'

'So was I.'

He chuckled. She ran her hand through the thick mat of hair on his chest and said, 'I hope they were good thoughts.'

'Yeah,' he said. 'They were.' His breath ruffled her hair she turned her face to look at him. 'I've suddenly realized that I'm not the slightest bit jealous of Michael any longer.'

Lynne laughed. 'I know that, silly.' Then, sobering, she regarded him seriously. 'I have to admit, though, that sometimes I feel a hint of that emotion myself when you seem more interested in the kids than you do in me, after you've been at work all day and come home, heading straight for wherever they are, sort of bypassing me in the process often with nothing more than a kiss on the side of my ear. But it's supposed to be that way,' she added, smiling again. 'And it's exactly the way I want it.'

Cliff didn't return her smile. Sitting up, he pulled her up against the padded headboard with him. 'I was jealous of him, even when I denied it. It made me ashamed of myself. I was afraid that if things went on the way they were, with you holding yourself apart from me, I'd end up hating him again the way I did when he was first born.'

She disengaged herself from him, turned and sat cross-legged, gazing at him, her eyes wide and pain-filled, and he nodded. 'Yes,' he said hoarsely, 'yes, you were right. I did. I'm ashamed of that, too, but it's true. Then, I didn't know who I was most jealous over, Michael or his father, but – '

His words took her supreme joy and smashed it like fine crystal. 'Dammit!' she cried, leaping off the bed, 'you are his father!'

Her voice cracked. Her eyes filled with tears she refused to shed, blinking rapidly to hold them back.

'Cliff, what have these past few weeks meant to you? Hasn't there been any building of trust? Hasn't there been any growth of your confidence in me? Hasn't – ?'

'Lynne, sweetheart!' He rolled off the bed and strode to where she stood, clamped his hands on her shoulders, gazing down into her eyes, his expression full of love and tenderness – and not a little stubbornness. 'I'm telling you you don't have to pretend any longer, love,' he said. 'Can't you see that? Haven't I been as open with you this past while as I never was before? Can't you do the same for me?'

'I have been!' she cried, snatching herself free of his hold and turning from him, her fists clenched in the drapes as if she would rip them from their rod and fling them in his face. 'I've always told you the truth!'

'Lynnie, please, listen to me! Listen to what I'm saying.' He stroked her tense shoulders, rubbed the back of her neck. 'The fact is, darling, it doesn't matter! It makes absolutely no difference now who planted the seed. It's totally irrelevant. You are Mike's mother. I am you husband. Therefore, that boy is mine.'

Couldn't she hear the conviction in his voice? It felt to him as if it were clanging so loudly in his heart that the whole world must know. It had taken him so long to recognize it and now he found that amazing. How could such a revelation have remained half-hidden in his heart the way it had, nothing more than a sensation, a nebulous feeling that couldn't quite be nailed down? It wasn't nebulous any more. Now, it filled him to overflowing with assurance such as he'd never known.

He had been so completely stunned by the knowledge as it swept over him while he lay there, it was no wonder he'd been inarticulate about it, so overwhelmed had he been by his self-discovery. Now, all he had to do was convey the same sense of gladness, of freedom, of certainty to her.

'Lynne, turn around and look at me.' When she did not, he took her shoulders, and gently turned her to face him. 'Listen to me,' he said again, surprised at the tremor in his voice. He smiled, felt a joyous laugh trying to force its way out. With difficulty, he controlled it. It was so important that he make her understand what he finally now understood on every level of his being.

'It's like some kind of miracle has occurred in me,' he said. 'I suddenly realized that I'm not another Logan Foreman. I don't have to share those emotions that turned him against me. Oh, God help me!' he groaned when she continued to stare up at him without comprehension. 'Lynne, I'm trying to make you understand what I'm feeling! It's as if I've spent my life teetering on the edge of an abyss, but it doesn't matter because I've suddenly learned that I know how to fly! I was not, and never have been, Logan Foreman's son.

I've been tearing myself apart all this time over nothing. What's important now is that I, Cliff Foreman, or whoever the hell I am, intend to fill the role of Michael and Amanda's father to the very best of my abilities, even if those abilities are pretty scant just now. They'll grow. I'll grow. And my love for both of our children will do the same.'

He hugged her tightly and spun her around and around, high on elation. 'Oh, love, I feel as if the sun has just come out after months of hiding! I feel as if my soul is free to reach out and encompass everything good in the world and you are the very center of that!'

Lynne stared at him as he set her back on her feet. Was she hearing what she wanted to hear, or was she misinterpreting altogether? Her voice shook as she pulled free of his embrace and faced him. 'What are you saying? That you believe me now? That you know there must have been a mistake made all those years ago? Do you believe, finally, that you are Michael's father in every way possible?'

He moistened his lips, let out a long breath and said, 'What I'm saying, Lynnie, about Michael's . . . parentage, is that we don't need to discuss it ever again. I'm saying that I've finally realized it doesn't matter any longer.'

Lynne shook her head, staring at him with growing horror as she stepped back from him, one pace, another. 'What do you mean, *it doesn't matter?* Dammit, Cliff, it matters to me! It matters so much! I've been telling you the truth all along, and you just won't believe me. I don't want your magnanimous . . . forgiveness . . . for something I never did!'

In despair, she turned away. There was no hope for their relationship, no matter what he said. It had been an exercise in futility from the very beginning.

Turning back to him, she said in a quiet voice. 'Please, Cliff. If you care about me as much as you claim, just . . . leave. You can spend the night, of course, but in the morning, go. Please. I don't think I can ever bear to see you again.'

'Lynne . . . no,' he said, but he was speaking to her back as she walked out of the room and closed the door quietly behind her.

CHAPTER 20

Cliff was far up the Coquihalla Highway before he realized it, driving with no destination in mind, just . . . driving. When he knew he could go no farther because fatigue blurred his vision, he pulled over and sat, head on the wheel, thinking, wondering where it had all gone wrong, what he'd done to screw things up again.

If only he could tell Lynne the lie she so longed to hear. If only he could make himself believe that somehow, some kind of miracle had occurred and what she insisted was true was true. But . . . he could not.

Presently, he turned his car and headed back toward the city of Vancouver. Hours later, as dawn broke, he was surprised to find himself parked outside the house where he had spent his first sixteen years. The drapes were drawn, the lawn neatly mowed, and a pickup truck was parked in the car-port with a ten-speed bike chained to a bolt in the wall beside the front steps. A basketball hoop hung high on the garage.

A kid on a bike, broad strap of newspaper bag across his forehead came by then, stopped behind Cliff's car and plucked a rolled paper from his tote. He didn't toss it, as Cliff had tossed papers when he'd had a delivery route, but sauntered up the walk and shoved the paper between the screen door and the main one.

Cliff stepped from the car. 'Hi,' he said. 'You had this route long?'

The kid nodded, looking wary, and got astride his bike again. 'Coupla years. Why?'

'I once delivered papers in this neighborhood, too, and I . . . uh . . . grew up in this house. I was sort of wondering who lived here now and how long they'd been here.'

The boy looked less leery. 'Mrs Foreman, the lady who lived here before, got married a few months ago and her new husband has a condo someplace so she moved in with him.'

The boy frowned. 'She tipped good, too, specially at Christmas.' He shrugged. 'These people, I dunno.'

Cliff nodded in sympathy, took a twenty from his wallet and handed it to the boy. 'Well, just in case they don't,' he said with a grin at the boy's startled smile. 'Thanks, buddy.'

It occurred to him as he drove away that he didn't even know his mother's name now.

He snorted in disgust. 'What the hell, I don't even know my own name!' he muttered. He pulled into an all-night convenience store, bought a large cup of coffee and sipped it as he drove on aimlessly, not

343

knowing where he was going, where he should go, where he could go.

His apartment, of course, was an option. The cabin on Galiano, or even the office. But he didn't want to see anyone there any more than he wanted to be alone.

Dammit, being alone was no longer normal.

Lynne and the children, Lou and the ladies had spoiled him for that. He wanted to be . . . somewhere. With someone. With them.

Pain struck. For just a moment, he'd forgotten that they were no longer his, not even through love, because Lynne had made him leave.

As he drove, the question continued to plague him.

Who was he? What was he? Where had he come from?

As if from some deep inner well he'd never known existed within him came the conviction that he must, if he was to survive, find that answer once and for all. He couldn't put it off any longer.

He checked the next street sign he saw, identified his location and made his decision, heading toward the Second Narrows Bridge and North Vancouver.

It was as if his mother's speaking them had imprinted the words on his brain that day shortly after his sixteenth birthday. Otherwise, why would he have such an exact memory twenty years later? But it was there, and he knew it was time.

He didn't know if there'd be any answers even if he were to meet Vincent Salazar, but maybe he wouldn't feel so terribly alone, so much that he had, through his own reprehensible actions, been thrown out again, rejected, told he didn't belong because he had no right to belong.

He carefully counted off the miles on the odometer until the right one clicked by and there, on the left, was a turn-off on to a narrow road. He continued at not more than ten miles per hour between tall, thick cedars and firs. Now and then, small openings held glades of ferns and in one spot, where the mountainside came close, a sparkling waterfall.

If there was a mansion concealed in this forest fastness, it was well hidden, but as he rounded a bend, suddenly there was a gate, high, strong, wrought-iron, with a pair of leaping porpoises in the center. They looked, he thought, happy, laughing, as if unaware that they were welded into iron bars, trapped, frozen in time.

A man stepped out of a small hut into the road on the far side of the gate, rifle at port arms, while another stood in the door of the gate-house, leveling a serious-looking black revolver at Cliff's head. The man with the rifle opened the gate and beckoned Cliff through. He gave Cliff an almost cordial nod as he leaned forward gingerly and opened the car door.

'Out,' he said, stepping back into position before the car. 'Very, very slowly. Keeping your hands in sight at all times. Then stand still.'

Cliff complied, leaning against the side of his car, one ankle crossed over the other, arms folded.

'You don't,' he said pleasantly to the man with the revolver, 'have to point that thing at me. I'm unarmed.'

'*You* don't' the guard said, 'look like the oilman.' He swept the barrel of his gun down the length of Cliff's car. 'And that,' he added, 'doesn't bear any resemblance to an oil delivery truck.'

'You're observant,' said Cliff. 'In case you're interested, I'm looking for Vincent Salazar.'

'Why?' The man now leveled the revolver on Cliff's his chest, a larger target, Cliff knew, than a head. This guy didn't mess around.

He shrugged one shoulder. 'That's personal.'

The guard's eyes narrowed. 'Uh-uh. You don't decide what's personal. You tell me, I tell the boss and he decides if it's personal, then maybe Frank up there steps aside and lets you drive on. Maybe. If it's true you're unarmed.'

He paused, gave Cliff time to speak and when he didn't, continued, 'Well? What's so personal? Believe me, I'm in the boss's confidence. Totally.'

Cliff shook his head. 'Not in this you're not.'

The gate-house guard frowned, pinned a searching gaze on Cliff's face, then asked suspiciously, abruptly, 'You ever meet the boss?'

'No.'

'Then how do you know this is Salazar's place?'

'So it is, then.' Cliff smiled. Until that moment, he hadn't been completely sure.

The guard's mouth tightened. He didn't like being bested, even so slightly.

Cliff relented. 'Somebody who once knew him, and came here, told me where to find it. It was a long time ago, but today I decided I wanted to find it.'

346

'Uh-huh. But I still need to know what kind of business you think you have with a man you've never met.'

Cliff smiled and shook his head. 'Like I said, it's personal, and I don't let other people, especially those with guns, make my decisions for me. Maybe Salazar would prefer to decide this one himself. Why don't you call him on that phone beside you? Isn't that what it's there for?'

The guard's stare narrowed as he continued to look Cliff up and down. 'You might be right on that one.'

He lifted the phone, never taking his eyes or his gun off Cliff. 'Boss, there's a guy out here who says he has personal business with you. Um, I . . . well, I think maybe you should see him. No, I don't know what he wants, I just have an – instinct of some sort telling me to send him in to you. You'll see for yourself what I'm getting at. I think. Yeah. Okay. Will do.'

He covered the mouthpiece by pressing it against his shoulder and looked Cliff over carefully again. 'Who shall I tell him is here?'

Cliff drew a deep breath and said, 'Cliff –' Then shook his head. What was he going to say? Cliff Foreman?

That wasn't who he was. That much, at least, he knew.

Cliff Salazar? Again, it wasn't a name to which he was entitled.

June Anderson's bastard son? He bet that would grab the old man's attention. But, if it did, what would it matter? Would it make any difference in Cliff's shattered life? Would it help put it back together?

He shrugged again and turned from the man with the gun, getting into his car.

'Forget it,' he said. 'I've changed my mind.'

Carefully, slowly, he backed the car through the gates and turned around. Then, without looking back, drove away.

He didn't need to see Vincent Salazar to know what he was. He knew it without anybody telling him.

He was Cliff. Just Cliff. A coward and a loser.

And that, he decided, was something he was simply going to have to learn to live with.

'He's gone,' Lynne said to Lou when the housekeeper asked her at breakfast where Cliff was. 'I asked him to leave.'

Lou raised her brows. 'Well, his month was more than up. I guess we'd better advertise those rooms, huh?'

Lynne burst into tears and ran upstairs.

'Where's Daddy?' Amanda asked nightly, and, just as when Mandy had once asked for her original parents, Lynne had no answer. All she could do was hold the little girl and try to provide what small comfort there was in one pair of parental arms.

Michael kicked the slats out of a supposedly indestructible crib.

Louisa cooked too much dinner three nights in a row, then grumbled at the waste of food. 'Rent out those rooms, for heaven's sake,' she snapped. 'You didn't want the man, so quit moping and get on with your life.'

'I did want him,' Lynne wept into her pillow. 'I do want him. And I don't care about anything else.'

It was four o'clock on a Friday morning when she awoke Louisa, fully dressed, car keys in her hand and said, 'Look after the kids. I have to go away for a day or two.'

Lou sat up, her gray hair frizzed out around her face. She grinned. 'Sick friend, huh?'

Lynne shook her head. 'Sick marriage. Needs immediate attention.'

'Damn right,' Lou said. 'Either that, or we rent out those rooms.'

Cliff stood under the shower, feeling the cold needles of spray sluice the soap from his skin. It should have been waking him up, making him alert, giving him a jump-start on the day ahead, but after another sleepless night it had little effect. He stepped out, toweled himself more or less dry and, hearing the doorbell, stopped to get his wallet from the top of the dresser.

'All right, all right,' he grumbled, flipping through bills as he stumbled down the hall of his apartment toward the front door.

How the hell much did he pay the paper boy, anyway? Was he known as as good a tipper as his mother had been? Hell, he was trained as an accountant, for Pete's sake, handled vast sums of other people's money daily in his business, and he couldn't even remember what the paper cost each month?

All he could remember was a pair of big blue eyes filled with anguish and tears that didn't fall, and a small, weary voice saying, 'It matters to me, Cliff. It matters to me . . .'

He jerked open the door and looked down into those same blue eyes, saw the same anguish in them and heard her voice, not small, not weary, but sure and determined, say, 'Come home, Cliff. Please, darling. We need you.'

For once, Cliff by passed the children – what he did, Lynne realized, was sneak past them so they didn't attack him – and bent to kiss the side of her ear and then, deeply, her mouth. She sat immersed in her task of sewing a button on a pair of small red overalls, and hadn't heard him tiptoe across the kitchen floor. She wriggled to her feet and wound her arms around him.

'You're home nice and early,' she said when she had control of her lips again. 'What's the occasion?'

'The occasion is that I want to take my wife out to a fancy place for dinner for a change, so go get fancy, wife.'

'How fancy?' she asked. 'I mean, where are we going?'

He named the best seafood house in the area and she nodded. 'That'll take at least forty-five minutes of fancy. Why don't you go play with the kids while I shower?'

He played with the kids for ten minutes, and

caught her just as she was ready to step out of the shower. She got fancy, but it took a little longer.

'That,' Lynne said, 'was the best dinner I've had in a long time. And exactly what I needed. A night out. I didn't know they had a dance-floor here.'

'What I need,' he said softly, 'is to take you home and peel you out of that dress.'

She licked her lips. 'Slowly?'

Swallowing the last of his coffee, he said, 'Very, very slowly. Dancing with you has been some kind of torture for which you have to be paid back.'

With a tantalizing smile, she said, 'All in good time. I'd like some more coffee first, please.'

'You're a witch,' Cliff told her, but he signaled the waiter and then sat back admiring Lynne while she took her time over her second cup of coffee, knowing the wait would be well worth it. She was especially beautiful tonight, he thought, with her hair brushed to a shiny halo that captured ambient light. She wore a blue silk sheath that enhanced the color of her eyes and showed her luscious figure to advantage. The scooped neck at the front of the dress, and the back, cut almost indecently low, showed plenty of creamy skin. He knew, and every other man who looked at her knew, that she was not wearing a bra. Nor, he knew, since he'd watched her dress, was she wearing panties. Just that shimmery silk dress.

He'd seen the lascivious glances she got as they walked to their table, and even after they'd sat down. One man in particular had continued to show his interest, his eyes on them as they danced between courses, and after. Throughout the evening, Cliff had been peripherally aware of the same pair of eyes gazing their way with a strange intensity. It was too dark in the corner where the other man sat alone for Cliff to get a good look at him, but for a painful moment he had felt himself wondering – *is he the one?* – before he brought his thoughts up short. No. He was not going to think of that again. Ever.

The man was staring simply because he appreciated the sight of a beautiful woman, and was maybe permitting himself to indulge in a little harmless fantasy.

'I could use a good long walk,' Lynne said as they stepped out into the now cool night air. 'After a huge meal like that, I couldn't stand sitting in the car.' She'd consumed an almost indecent amount of fresh, steamed clams, followed by a main course of rock cod on a bed of spinach nested on a plateful of rice, served with a wonderful teriyaki sauce.

'The car is three blocks from here, remember?' Cliff said, his voice tight, and she smiled, taking his hand. She knew he wanted to get home as quickly as possible, and knew why, but ever since he'd watched her slide her dress on over her nude body, she'd been bent on teasing him. 'We have to walk to get there,' he added.

'Oh, but that's not nearly far enough,' she said.

'You think not?' He halted under a streetlamp and stared down at her. 'If I were to do to you now what I want to do, I'd get arrested.'

'Gee, then I guess I would, too. Think they'd put us in the same cell?'

'No,' he growled. 'It doesn't work that w –' He broke off, as he sensed someone coming up beside her and turned protectively, keeping himself between the other man and Lynne, but not before she caught sight of the stranger's face.

'Oh, hello,' she said, and gave the man a quick nod and smile as he came abreast of them and cast a glance sideways at their faces.

The man nodded just as briefly and strode onward without speaking, not pausing for a second, though he was the one, Cliff was certain, who'd been staring at Lynne all evening.

'Who's that?' he demanded, gripping her arm with unintentional firmness.

She smacked his fingers. 'That hurts!' With a murmured apology he smoothed the place he'd squeezed. 'I don't really know who he is,' she said. 'Just a neighbor, I guess. A new one, I think. I've seen him a few times around the neighborhood when I've been out walking with the kids and occasionally he waves as he drives by.'

She laughed. 'Dammit Cliff, if you're jealous of an nice, grandfatherly old man, then I'm really going to have to do something about you.'

He grinned, relaxing. 'Such as?'

'Such as convincing you that you're the only man who could ever interest me.'

'And how do you plan to do that?'

'Well,' she said, 'first we'll take a nice, long walk together, holding hands, say, along the waterfront, breathing in the smell of the salt and seaweed and beach, and then we'll take a nice long, leisurely drive home, and then I'll . . . I'll give you a backrub.'

'Lynne!' he groaned in protest, only half joking as he grabbed her and dragged her arm through his, heading for the car at a rapid pace.

'Oh, are you tired? We can go home right now, if you need sleep.' She rubbed her cheek against his shoulder like a kitten.

He took a deep breath and steered her in the direction of the oceanside park, chuckling softly. 'I need to get home and into bed,' he said, his voice a raspy growl, 'but sleep is the last thing on my mind. I want you woman, wet and warm and willing.'

Stopping where a big maple tree shaded them from the overhead lights, he kissed her, rubbing his hands over her bottom, making her feel as if the silk of her dress wasn't even there. There was, she admitted privately, an erotic thrill in knowing that he knew she wore no underwear.

'Let's go home,' she gasped when he released her mouth.

'Oh, no,' he laughed. 'We're having a nice long walk, remember?'

And, arms around each other, deliberately prolonging the delicious agony of waiting, they walked farther along the waterfront, stopping now and then in the shadows to heighten their desire with deep, potent kisses and soft, thrilling caresses.

They had turned and were nearly back to where they had left the car when Lynne, seeing something in the shadows of the trees off to the left, said, 'What's that?'

'I don't know.' Cliff stopped, staring in the direction she pointed.

'Look. It moved. It's a man, Cliff, lying on the ground. Maybe he's hurt.'

'And maybe he's a drunk. You go get in the car.' He gave her the keys and pushed her in the direction of their parking spot before striding to where the man lay. He bent down, checked him and then stood quickly, returning to the car at a lope.

'He's all right, just passed out. Give me the keys and let's get out of here.'

She clutched the keys in her fist. There was no way he could get them from her without hurting her. 'No,' she said. 'We can't just leave him.'

'I'll go to the nearest phone and call the cops to take care of him.'

'No!' she said again. 'They'll just heave him in the drunk-tank. He needs help, Cliff, not abuse. Please. Bella will know what to do about him. Let's take him to her.'

'Bella?' he said, staring at her. 'What can she do?'

'She works in a mission just over the bridge. They help people like this man. Please, Cliff. We can't leave him here. The police might not get around to him for hours. He'll be pretty low on their priority list, you know that!' Her eyes were big and injured as she looked at him. 'It's starting to rain. He'll die of exposure.'

'Lynne, it's late August, not mid-January. He won't die of exposure.'

'You can't be sure of that.'

Cliff stared at her, knowing her determination but equally determined not to give into it. 'No. I'm not putting a drunk into the same car with you.'

'He's not going to hurt me. He's unconscious, or close to it. Besides, you know perfectly well that if I weren't in the car you'd take him to the mission yourself,' she insisted, seeming not to realize that if she hadn't told him about the mission, he wouldn't have knowing it existed.

He shook his head. Bella? Working in a rehab center? And all this time he'd had a sneaking hunch her 'working nights' indicated a much less honorable profession.

'We can't just abandon him, Cliff. He's a human being!'

He sighed again and shook his head. She was right, dammit. Alone, he wouldn't hesitate to take care of the guy. Then, she added the capper she'd been holding in reserve. 'Besides, think how much quicker we'll get home to bed if we stop arguing and act now.'

With a slow, rueful shake of his head, he said, 'Okay, okay, but I warn you, he doesn't smell pretty.'

Lynne had to agree about the semi-conscious man's odor, but the trip to the mission was short, and made with the windows open. The damp fresh breeze blowing in the windows must have revived the man somewhat, because he managed to keep his legs under him while Cliff got him into the mission, but once in the entry, he collapsed again, leaning on his benefactor, his grimy clothing leaving traces of muck on Cliff's perfectly pressed suit.

Lynne winced in sympathy with her husband as Cliff lowered the man to a bench. She rang the bell on the desk and Bella, a white lab coat over her garish clothing, appeared.

'Why, Lynne! What are you doing here?'

'We found a client for you,' she said with a gesture at Cliff, still propping the fellow on the bench.

'Oh, Jerry,' Bella said sorrowfully. 'Not again.'

'Obviously, yes, again,' Cliff said. 'Where do you want me to take him, Bella? He's getting heavier and heavier.'

'Oh! Oh, here, let me have him.'

She talked to the old man, patted his cheeks, spoke sharply to him and called him by name, getting him to his feet through what appeared to be the sheer force of her will.

With Cliff's muscle providing motive power, Bella helped the man into a room at the back. They flopped him on to a bed, where Bella turned him on his side and propped him that way with pillows.

They had scarcely finished when the bell out front tinkled sharply.

'It's going to be one of those nights,' Bella said, leading the way back to the front.

Cliff smiled at Lynne, leaned down kissed her quickly before taking her hand and following.

'What was that for?'

'Because I'm a lucky man. Because I love you. Because you are the kind of person who helps me be the kind of person I really want to be.'

'And what kind of person is that?'

'One with the compassion to lend a hand to someone who's down and out. I like caring about people, Lynne, and if it weren't for you, I might have gone on for the rest of my life, all closed in on myself, never seeing the world around me. I think . . . I think I'd forgotten how to care, until you showed me. For the second time.'

She didn't know what to say, so she kissed him again.

Behind them, Bella spoke.

'Excuse me, Cliff. There's a man out there who wants to talk to you.'

'To me? But . . . How would anybody know I was here?'

Bella shook her head, staring at him strangely. 'He didn't give me his name. He simply said he had to see the man who'd carried in the drunk and . . .' She gave him a searching look. 'I think you'd better see him.'

Cliff stepped out into the foyer and looked at the stranger who stood there, a perplexed frown on his seamed face, his fists clenched at his sides, his nearly black eyes all but lost beneath heavy dark brows with tufts of white bristling from them.

It was the man who had stared at them all evening, the man Lynne had greeted on the street, yet a man he'd never seen before in his life until tonight.

'Yes?' he said. 'You wanted to see me?'

The man drew in a deep breath and let it out in a

long, audible sigh. 'I . . . yes. I did. I'm sorry. I know this is an intrusion. But . . . please, tell me, what is your name?'

There was a tremor in the man's voice, and a tension that transmitted itself clear across the room, alerting something primitive in Cliff. The hair on the back of his neck, on his forearms came erect, tingling.

He bridled, took a step closer and said 'Cliff . . . Foreman. Who are you and why do you want to know?'

He felt Lynne's icy hand grip his as he heard her sharp intake of breath. Dragging his gaze from the face of the stranger, he half turned and looked at his wife. Her eyes were wide, her face pale, her lips parted. She looked not at him, but at his visitor.

'What is it?' he asked her. 'Lynne, what's wrong?'

She only stared at the man on the other side of the entry and said softly, 'Oh, dear heaven! It's you!'

'Who the hell are you?' Cliff demanded, shaking free of Lynne's convulsive grip and stepping forward, putting himself between her and the intruder.

'Vincent Salazar.'

The name came from the man's lips, and, Cliff realized, from Lynne's simultaneously. He gaped at the man, then back at Lynne. She was still staring at the newcomer, but slowly, her gaze lifted to his.

'Vincent Salazar,' she said again. 'I don't know why I didn't see it before, but until I saw the two of you together, it never occurred to me. Cliff, it's so obvious. This man is your father.'

CHAPTER 21

Vincent Salazar's eyes – and suddenly Cliff had no doubt that this was who the man was – darted to Lynne's face as she stepped forward, her fingers clinging tightly to Cliff's.

'What did you say, girl?' he demanded in a rasping voice. Tension emanated from him; it was in his hunched stance, in his tight face, in his dark eyes under his thick brows. It paled his brown face, making his eyes seem even blacker. 'What did you say?' he asked again in a voice hardly more than a rough whisper. Lynne didn't reply. She knew perfectly well the man had heard what she said.

'How can you know that?' Salazar barked abruptly, not moving an inch except to straighten, squaring his big shoulders, but suddenly seeming to fill the room with a menacing presence. Cliff stepped protectively in front of Lynne again, staring the man down.

Lynne, refusing to let Cliff face this alone, slipped around him and lifted her chin as she said, 'I know because, in seeing you, I see what my husband will be in another thirty years.'

The man nodded and suddenly, as his shoulders drooped, the menace left his stance. 'Yes,' he said. 'Oh, yes. That's what I saw, but I was looking at it backwards. When I saw him back there in the restaurant, I thought I was seeing a ghost. I thought for a moment I was seeing my father as he looked when I was a child. But . . .'

He frowned at Lynne, looking more like Cliff than ever. 'How did you know my name?'

'I know your name because I know Cliff's father is Vincent Salazar.'

Salazar moved then, stepping closer. He paused, his fists still clenched at his sides, but there was nothing threatening in his posture now. He seemed, instead, almost to be pleading. 'How do you know that? How *can* you know it? And who . . .?' He swallowed, transferred his gaze to Cliff, looked pained and asked softly, 'Who is your mother?'

Cliff seemed to come to life. He completely ignored Salazar's question to him. 'She knows it because I told her my father's name,' he said in a voice as harsh and as hoarse as Salazar's, and much louder, filled with accusation and loathing. 'And I know it because my mother told me when I was sixteen years old that you had made her pregnant and left her on her own, hero!'

'No! Never! I – '

Cliff raised his dark brows. 'Never? Don't bet on it, Salazar. Here I am.' He rapped his chest with his knuckles. 'Living, breathing proof. You suspected it

361

because your guard saw the resemblance and told you, didn't he? I suppose he wrote down my license number and you had me traced. You followed my wife and children around our neighborhood – for what, I'd like to know? You – '

'I followed no one. I found you lived there. I wanted to see you, wanted to see this resemblance Andrew mentioned, wanted to see the man who somehow knew where I lived, demanded to see me on personal business then left as suddenly as he'd come. I never managed to see you until tonight when you were getting into your car. I saw this lady, yes, and her children, but I didn't connect them with you until tonight. I did not know who you were, what you were to me, why you had come to see me that day and then left. I thought maybe . . . a distant cousin, from the old country, something, but tonight, when I saw you . . . ah, yes.

Ah yes, then I knew. Only . . . I don't understand how . . .'

'You're damned right you knew! You knew it or you wouldn't have followed me from the restaurant. You wanted your suspicions confirmed. Well, they have been, so now you can leave.'

'No. No. Please. I must talk to you. There are things I do not understand, I tell you. Things I – '

Cliff didn't know where his rage came from, knew only that it had bubbled up from the very source of his soul and was threatening to consume him. 'I don't care about that,' he grated, his throat tight. 'I don't care about you! What you don't understand is none of my concern. You are none of my concern. I came to that very firm decision on your oh-so-private road leading to your oh-so-private estate, where you have goons with guns stopping people who want to see you. Do you think I want to be associated with that kind of man? A man so much a coward he hides away from the world? You know, as I drove away from your fortress, Salazar, I realized that yes, you must truly be my father, because I, too, am a coward, so much a coward that I couldn't bring myself to meet you. So you wasted your time, following me because I don't want to see you.'

'No, please, you must – '

'Look, haul ass, old man.' Cliff took a step toward Vincent Salazar. 'Move it. Get out of here. I don't want to see your face. That's all you need to understand. You did what you chose to do thirty-seven years ago. Now, I'm doing what I choose to do. I don't want to know you. I don't need to know you. You are nothing to me and I am nothing to you.'

'Nothing to me?' Salazar said, his swarthy skin paling even more, taking on an unhealthy sheen. 'If this is true, and I believe it is, though I don't see how it could have happened without my knowing, you are my son! My only child. My only living relative. That is . . . everything . . . to me. My wife, my baby daughter – my beautiful little Maria, an angel only six months old – dead all these years and I had a son, you . . .'

'Tough,' said Cliff, all the years of pain and rejection and anger toward Logan, toward his mother, toward this man, crowding out whatever sense of compassion he might have felt hearing the plea in Vincent Salazar's voice, the protesting murmur of Lynne's soft cry at his side. 'It doesn't mean a thing to me. I have a wife. I have two children. You, I have no use for. Now, get out of my way.'

With Lynne's hand gripped tightly, he shouldered past the man and strode out the door, oblivious to her plea that he stop, that he wait. Behind them, Bella gave a sharp, startled cry, but he didn't turn even at that.

Shoving Lynne in the driver's side of his Buick, he pushed in beside her, sliding her under the wheel and past it. His hand shook as he tried to put the key in the ignition and he still hadn't succeeded when Bella pounded on the car window then yanked open the door.

'He's collapsed!' she panted, her face red, her elaborate hairdo beginning to fall in lank strings onto her neck. 'Please, you have to help me! I can't handle this alone.'

'No. I can't help you,' said Cliff, his face a mask of pain. 'I can't help him. Call an ambulance or something, Bella, but keep me out of this!'

With an inarticulate sound of fury, Bella wheeled and went back into her mission. Lynne flung open the door on her side and leaped out, running back inside. She paused at the entrance to the building, looking over her shoulder at Cliff, who sat hunched behind the wheel, his head down, his shoulders rigid as if he were holding them tightly so they wouldn't shake with the sobs he was fighting.

She ran back to him. 'Cliff, listen to me,' she said urgently. 'You didn't abandon a pregnant woman, even believing the baby wasn't yours. You didn't abandon an unknown drunk. You had the compassion to give him the help he needed. How can you abandon your own father, now that he needs you?'

He looked up at her, his face tortured. 'He did the same to me, didn't he? To my mother!'

'I don't think so. I believe him, Cliff. He didn't know you existed until tonight. Darling, please, for both your sakes, come back inside. Face him. Deal with him. Don't turn away from him. Cliff, this is important!'

For what seemed like forever, he sat there, looking at her and through her and far into a past over which he had no more control now than he had as an infant. Then, with a shudder, he slid out of the car and returned to the mission.

Bella looked up from where she crouched by the fallen man, her face full of anxiety. 'The ambulance is coming.'

Cliff nodded and took the blanket Bella had brought. Carefully, he wrapped Vincent Salazar, pulling the covering up to his chin, tucking it around him warmly.

Vincent Salazar's eyes opened and he looked at his son.

'Two children?' he said.

Cliff nodded, conscious of Lynne crouching on the other side of the patient, beside Bella. He let his glance rise to hers for a second before looking back at his father. 'That's right. A girl and a boy.'

Vincent smiled, a faint crooking of his lips, but Cliff knew it was meant to congratulate him. 'That's good. I will live to see them.' He said it almost as a promise to himself as his eyes eased closed.

His breathing became labored, stertorous. After a moment, he opened his eyes again, alarm showing in their depths. 'I will see them? You will let me?'

Cliff's face froze and his mouth went hard. Quickly, Lynne touched his hand where it lay on Vincent's chest.

He frowned, then nodded reluctantly. 'Sure. You can see them.'

'Good. That's . . . good. My own blood.'

Cliff's broad shoulders hunched as if he were warding off a blow, but he said, as the sound of a siren began to grow in the distance. 'That's right, Vincent. Your own blood.'

He and Lynne exchanged a long, silent stare before they looked back again at Vincent who lay on the floor, his eyes closed, his face pasty, but still breathing, if shallowly.

In Cliff's mind echoed the determined words: *I will live.* Was Vincent Salazar's strength of will the source from which his had now sprung? It was a strange, and disturbing notion.

'He'll live,' said the doctor an hour later. 'He's stabilized enough so we can move him to Vancouver General for better cardiac care than we offer him here. Will you be going with your father, Mr Salazar?'

'No,' said Cliff, just as Lynne said, 'Of course.'

'He's asking for you,' the doctor said. 'Would you like to see him, Mr Sal – '

'My name not Salazar! It is Cliff . . . uh, Cliff.'

'Oh. Excuse me. The patient said you were his son so I assumed . . . Foolish of me.'

'Never mind. Sorry I barked. Yes. I'll see him, but just for a moment. Then, I'd like to get my wife home. We have two small children and she needs her sleep.'

'I understand. This way, if you will.'

Ten minutes later, Cliff was still sitting beside Vincent's bed, to his eternal amazement, not in any great hurry to leave, to take his gaze from the sleeping man, as if by his mere presence he could help strengthen the hold Vincent had on life.

It felt . . . good, he decided, looking at the relaxed face that Lynne had said his would resemble in thirty years. It gave him a sense of, well, almost of belonging, a connection, not only with the past, but with the future. Could she be right? His father's dark hair had only a few threads of gray in it. His craggy face showed very few signs of aging. A sag here, a line there. It was nice to think that he, himself, could maybe expect to wear as well.

A nurse came in, handed him a note. He took it, read it and shook his head. Lynne. His wonderful, wise Lynne. She had taken the car, she wrote, and gone home. She'd drive into to Vancouver tomorrow and get him. His father needed him now, and, she said, she believed that he needed his father.

Cliff folded the note and tucked it into his pocket, then rested in the high-backed, soft recliner the hospital provided for the comfort of relatives who spent the night at the beside of a patient. As usual, Lynne's instincts were right. There was much, so very much, he wanted to learn from this man. So, in that way, he did need Vincent Salazar.

And maybe in other ways, too, he thought, though as he recognized the need, something hard rose in him, fear, denial, maybe even hunger to believe that none of this was true, that the man lying on the bed, the man who wore a face so very familiar, so similar in shape and coloring to his, was not really his father, that he did not truly owe his very existence to this man any more than he had ever owed it to Logan Foreman.

What should it matter now? He was thirty-six years old, far from childhood, far from the pain of the rejection dealt him by Logan. So where was all this pain coming from, to tighten his throat, make his shoulders ache, his chest hurt? Why the terrible, deep desire to crawl away somewhere to a secret place like a wounded animal and howl out the agony that filled him?

If this man, who had lain on the cold tile floor of a mission for down-and-outers and looked up at him with eyes that pleaded for understanding, for acceptance, if this was really his father, why was he being such a bastard and trying so hard to reject all that could come of this relationship?

Tension grew in him, part sweet, part bitter, as he stared down at Vincent Salazar. Tentatively, he reached out a hand toward the one that lay so dark and still on the pale green coverlet, then pulled back, staring at his own hand. Slowly, quietly, so as not to disturb the sleeping man, he laid his hand beside Vincent's.

The skin tone was nearly the same, his slightly lighter because he spent more time indoors, most likely, the fingers the same length, the same small twist to the pinkie, the same blunt, thick thumbs, with spatulate nails on all. To the bristles of black hair on the first joint of each finger, those two right hands could have been poured in the same mold.

He stared at them for a long time and realized, when a weak voice said, 'Pretty much identical, wouldn't you say, son?' that tears burned unshed in his eyes and that Vincent was staring at him.

Ashamed of those tears, he lowered his face to the side of the bed, hiding, and felt that wonderful warmth he had missed for so long, a father's hand on his head.

As he sat there, there came over him a final sense of finding, of being found, of coming home. Harshly, with great difficulty, Cliff wept.

'He was a Catholic. He spoke with an accent. He filleted fish for a living.' Cliff sat in the hospital cafeteria, his hands wrapped around a mug of hot chocolate, his eyes meeting Lynne's broodingly. 'He wasn't a fit suitor for June Anderson, daughter of one of the chief industrialists of the Pacific region. He loved her, Lynne.'

Cliff paused, took a sip from his mug then went on. 'And he believed, until she married Logan, that she loved him.

'I don't know why I find it so much easier to believe what Vincent says than I do what my mother told me. But I know he's telling the truth when he says that if he'd known she carried his child he would have moved heaven and earth to get to her, to take her away where her family couldn't influence her.'

'He has no reason to lie to you, Cliff.'

He nodded in agreement. 'He didn't abandon her, like she said. He didn't abandon me. He says maybe she was right, in what she did, that she wouldn't have been happy with a poor, struggling man who couldn't give her everything she wanted, and of course she couldn't know he was destined to become far richer than anybody ever dreamed.'

He looked down for a minute, toyed with a spoon, then glanced at Lynne, shame in his eyes, shame for his mother. 'The way I read it, she wanted the excitement, the adventure, of being with someone her parents would find abhorrent, and when she got caught, she panicked and grabbed Logan, who had wanted her since they were schoolkids.

Vince says she used to go to country club dances and things with Logan, and he used to rage inside that she didn't see him as fit to accompany her there. She blamed it all on her parents, of course, but he wanted her to stand up to them, tell them she loved him. She wouldn't. Claimed she couldn't.'

'I don't suppose she was trying to hurt anybody, darling. She was just a girl, maybe in love with Vincent, maybe merely infatuated, but under her parents' thumb. Things were different then, don't forget. And when things went too far, maybe she didn't know what to do. She'd have been a scared, pregnant girl who did what she thought would be best for herself in the long run. She couldn't possibly have foreseen what the outcome would be.'

'You're as generous toward her as Vince is.'

He gulped down half the contents of his cup and bit into a sandwich Lynne had insisted he eat. He went on. 'And maybe you're both right. Judging by her later actions, I'd have to say that she did learn to love Logan in the end. At least, she sent me away so she could make peace with him. Maybe that was the only way she could prove to him once and for all that what she had once felt for Vincent was in the past.

You were right, you know, in what you said about her knowing where his country place was. They'd gone there for most of their secret meetings, to a little cabin his father had built beside a lake, where he could go fishing. Land was important to Vincent's fath – to my grandfather.'

As he spoke the word, a small smile curved his mouth. Lynne covered his hand with hers, gave it a squeeze. He turned his and linked their fingers.

'Grandfather Salazar bought a good-sized chunk of it up there when it was dirt-cheap. Selling off pieces of it is what gave Vince his start.'

He smiled. 'I'm kind of proud to come from stock like that, you know, people who worked hard to get where they did. My grandparents came from Portugal with little more than the clothes they wore and half a dozen white lace tablecloths Vincent's mother had made. One by one, they sold them as they needed money to get started. Vincent has one left. He . . . he wants you to have it.'

Lynne looked at his weary face with compassion. It amazed her how, over the past five days, getting to know Vincent Salazar had revealed a different Cliff, one more open, more sensitive, more willing to explore his own and other people's reasons for acting the way they did.

She wondered if now was the right time to suggest, once more, that he have the blood test done that would show him that he was – or could be – Michael's father, or even perhaps the other test, the one that had left him feeling so humiliated and unmanned.

'I'd be thrilled to have your grandmother's lace cloth,' she said quietly.

Cliff swallowed hard, his hands gripping his mug, his gaze suddenly wary as it met hers then slid away. He cleared his throat. 'He, uh, he also wants me to have his name.'

He heard Lynne's smile in her voice. 'If you take it, I'd be proud to share it with you, darling.'

Cliff closed his eyes for a moment, as if in prayer, then looked at her again. 'He'll be released next week,' he went on, then hesitated, biting his lip.

'I was wondering how you'd feel about our making a quick purchase of that house we were considering so we could move in and he could come home to us.' He cleared his throat. 'Just for a little while. The doctors want him to be closer to a large medical facility for a couple of weeks, and that house is plenty big. He and his nurse could have the

372

rooms at the back, where it's quieter. That is, if you wouldn't mind.'

'Of course I don't mind,' she assured him. 'If you don't think the kids would be too much for him.'

Cliff smiled and lifted her hand, rubbing his lips over her knuckles. 'I think the kids will be the best medicine he can possibly get.'

He opened his mouth as if to say something, then shut it, leaned across the small cafeteria table and kissed her quickly.

'Then it's settled,' he said, standing and pulling her up into the circle of his arm. 'Thank you, Lynnie. Thank you for being there for me, for loving me, for your understanding.' He smiled down into her eyes. 'From here on in, everything is going to work out just the way we both hope it will.'

And the funny thing, Lynne thought a few weeks later, thinking back on that day, after Vincent had gone back to his mountain retreat, healthy now, busily making plans for his grandchildren's futures, for their first visit to him, his further visits to them, was that she had believed Cliff without reservation. Of course things were going to work out perfectly. They had love. They had each other. They had the children. They had a lifetime of happiness ahead of them.

They also had a very tiny problem that she knew would grow bigger and bigger as the days and months slipped by.

CHAPTER 22

'Mrs Salazar, are you all right?' Dr Baker put her hand on Lynne's shoulder.

'What?' Lynne pulled herself back from wherever it was her whirling mind had taken her and said, 'Oh, oh, yes. I'm . . . fine.' She was still having difficulty answering to the name Mrs Salazar, but this . . . Lord, this was even more difficult.

The doctor settled back in her chair, frowning slightly. 'That's good.' She looked down at Lynne's chart, fiddled with a pen and said, 'I see here that you have two very young children. You know, don't you, that the medical profession recognizes that there are times in a woman's life when a pregnancy is all wrong, and that arrangements can be made? It's safe and effective and quite simple at an early stage like this.'

'No!' Lynne's voice was sharp and one hand curved protectively around her lower abdomen. 'Oh, no. Thank you, but no.'

As Lynne got behind the wheel of the car, she wondered dimly if she should even be driving, the

374

condition her mind was in, but she got home safely, paid the baby-sitter and then curled into a corner of the couch, staring at the wall.

How had she let this happen? The funny thing was that not once had she considered doing something so that it couldn't. Had she thought, on some level, that Cliff was right in his firm belief about his sterility? How *was* she going to tell Cliff?

Don't tell him, whispered a little, panicked voice inside her. 'Yeah, sure,' she muttered. 'Don't tell him. He won't notice a thing.'

She laughed, contemplating ways to hide her pregnancy from her husband, and heard the note of hysteria underlying the threads of laughter. Abruptly, she got to her feet, forcing herself not to cry, not to let terror or panic undermine her self-control.

She knew what she had to do and that she had to do it right now. There could be no hesitation, no waiting around to decide if this were the right move or the wrong move. For the sake of her children, it was the only move, and she had to make it immediately before she lost her nerve. She had to leave, be gone before Cliff came home from work, because one look at her face would tell him that disaster beyond description had befallen them.

When the kids were up from their naps, she was ready. 'Where we goin', Mommy?' Amanda wanted to know.

'To visit Lou for a while, sweetie. Won't that be fun?'

'Daddy comin'?'

'No, darling. Daddy won't be coming.'

'Grandpa?'

'No. Not Grandpa, either. Remember, Grandpa went back to his own house.'

'We gonna visit Grandpa, too, Mommy?'

Lynne fought down a choking sense of panic in her throat again. How many people were going to be hurt by this? So many! Her children, who would lose their father, Cliff, who would lose everything he'd come to believe in – only he'd never believed in her, had he? If he had, she wouldn't be running like this. She couldn't even begin to contemplate how much she would be hurt by it all. Somehow, because she must – again, she put her hand around her lower abdomen – she would survive.

'We'll see,' she said to Amanda, wondering how Cliff would explain to Vincent, *if* Cliff would explain to Vincent. Their tacit agreement, never since discussed, made that night on the mission floor to let Vincent believe the children were 'his blood' had never been changed.

'Here, don't forget your baby,' she said, as she stiffened her spine, handed Amanda her ragged little doll and led her out to the car where Michael was already strapped into his seat. Then, without letting herself look back, she quickly drove away.

Cliff stood holding her note in his hand, watching it tremble. It was a piece of pale green paper. He almost smiled, remembering aspen leaves in the spring. They, too, trembled. Why was this pale green paper shaking so? Oh, yes. He remembered and tried to focus on it, but could not. It didn't matter. He had no need to read the words. He'd already done that. What he was doing now was trying to make sense out of them. She hadn't left. She hadn't taken the kids and gone. It was some kind of strange game and any minute now they'd all leap up and say, 'Surprise!'

To his eternal shame, he leaned his hands on the high back of the sofa and peeked over it, expecting to find the three of them there, laughing silently, ready to leap up and say 'Boo!' Of course they were not. He groaned and slumped down to bury his face in his hands.

No! Dammit, no! He was not going to let this happen! They were his family! They couldn't do this to him!

The urge to jump into his car and go tearing off after them was great, but he forced it down. Something in Lynne's note needed more thinking about. If he could make sense of that, then maybe he could figure out where he'd gone wrong, what he'd done to screw things up so badly that she'd felt she simply couldn't stay.

Smoothing it out over his knee, he read it again.

I was right in what I said when you followed me home that day. We should have stayed apart until we sorted out our differences. Remember, I talked about a snag that could lie in wait for us and reach out when we least expected it?

It's happened, Cliff. There was a snag under

*the smooth surface of what we'd built together
and it's torn the bottom out of things for me –
for us. So it's over. Really over, this time. I've
gone home, but I'll be in touch. Please, don't
come after me . . .*

There was more, but he didn't need to read it. The
important message was in those first few para-
graphs. A snag. What snag?

Dammit, what snag was she talking about? He
leaned back, feeling the heat of tears stinging in his
eyes but blinked, forcing them back. There was no
time for that. What in hell did she mean?

All right. Let's take this one step at a time. What
was the big hang-up, or snag, of our relationship?
Michael. Or, not so much Michael, as his father.

Cliff sat up abruptly. Lord! Had she met up with
Michael's father again?

He rejected that notion almost as quickly as it
came. Of course she hadn't been seeing another man
apart from the fact that she had been with either
him, or the kids, or Vincent twenty-four hours a day
since July, she wouldn't, even if she had the opportunity.

This, to him, was simply a given. Lynne didn't
cheat. Lynne, he knew, didn't have it in her to cheat.
She had too much integrity.

For a long time, he sat thinking those words over
and over, letting them run through his mind, feeling
the truth of them, admitting the full force of them to
his depths. And the corollary: Lynne was incapable
of cheating, ergo, Lynne had never been capable of

it. Only, if that were the case – *and it was* – then something else he had taken as a given also had to be in error.

Lynne didn't get up from the porch glider when she saw Cliff coming. She'd been expecting him, though she'd told him not to come. She felt sick at the thought of having to tell him about her pregnancy, but knew she'd been a coward to run without having done so. Of course he had a right to the truth.

Even if he wouldn't believe it.

He sat down beside her, not touching, and leaned back, his long legs outstretched, hands behind his neck. Rolling his head sideways, he glanced at her.

'All over, huh?' He sounded, she thought, as if he didn't care.

'Yes.' Her voice was little more than a whisper.

'Okay,' he said easily. 'If you say so. But what do we do about custody of the kids?'

She jerked forward as if on a string and stared at him. 'What do you mean? We do nothing about custody! The children are mine.'

He unlinked his hands and sat forward, too, forcing her to lean back. He was too close. 'Not exactly, Lynne,' he said. 'Not entirely yours. Two of them are mine. And, as Vincent would have done if he'd known about me, I'll fight you in court if necessary for custody. We Salazars take great pride in the family line. Of course, I'd rather have all three of them, and you, home with me without a fight, but if you make me, I'll fight you all the way.'

Lynne gaped at him. 'Three . . .?' she asked hollowly.

'Three. Amanda, Michael and little whatsit, in there.' He slid a hand across her abdomen and felt her shudder. Slowly, he drew her into his arms, across his lap and kissed her wet face for a long time before speaking again.

'I'm not going to ask why you didn't tell me, love. I know why. Would it help if I told you I'm sorry for all the hell I've put you through because I believed what I now know clearly has to have been a mistake? Today, when I realized that being pregnant was the only thing that would scare you bad enough to make you run, I knew that there could be no doubt who the father of your child was.'

She gazed up at him and asked, 'Are you saying you went and got tested?'

He shook his head. 'Nope. I figure I've been tested, sweetheart.' A slow grin spread over his face. 'And it looks like I got one hundred per cent.'

Lynne stared at him, not quite willing to believe what she was hearing, what she saw in his eyes.

'Didn't you wonder whose it was?' she asked bitterly, sitting up and walking jerkily away from him, to the porch railing where she hitched herself up, hands by her thighs, and looked at him in the dim light cast by the silver of moon low on the horizon.

He got up and came to stand before her. 'Yes,' he said honestly. 'For just an instant, I did wonder, but then I started thinking, really thinking about you, for the first time in my life. I analyzed you as I would an investment possibility, and realized I didn't have to do that because I already knew you, Lynne. I know you don't lie. I know you don't cheat. I know the depths of your honor. Therefore, I knew that if you were pregnant, it was with my child.'

Her breath caught in her throat, nearly choking her. 'Do . . . do you mind?'

He stared at her. 'Lynne! Did you have to ask that? Don't you know? Don't you . . .?'

'I had to ask. I had to be sure. And for the very last time, I have to say this, Cliff: Michael is your son.'

He shook his head rapidly. 'I know that. Of course I do! What do you think this is all about?' He reached out and touched her face, drawing his finger tip down the curve of her jaw. 'Vince says that Michael looks like me. I wonder if he'll think this one does too?'

She reached up and curled her fingers around his neck. 'But you said . . . when you first got here . . . that two of the children are yours and – '

He snatched her close, crowding between her knees, hands pressing on the small of her back to bring her even closer. 'You thought I meant Amanda and the new one? Darling, did it occur to you that, legally, technically, Amanda is neither yours nor mine and won't be until we adopt her formally?'

She tilted her head back and laughed softly. 'No. No, in fact, for the moment, I'd forgotten everything but that you and I had made another miracle together.'

'Good,' he said. 'Let's keep it that way.'

For the next several minutes, both forgot even where they were. Then, lifting his head and gazing down into her shining eyes, he found her welcoming smile on her face.

'Where are we sleeping tonight, love? Wherever it is, I think we'd better get there fast,' he said in a shaken voice.

She looked stricken. 'I was going to sleep on a cot in Lou's room. The kids are on the pull-out sofa in the playroom. All the other rooms are rented out.'

'Never mind,' he said picking her up and draping her over his shoulder. 'There's always the carrot patch.'

'Cliff!' she laughed, trying to be quiet. 'Put me down! I am not going to spend the night in the garden.'

'Why not,' he said. 'Adam and Eve did it.' But he deposited her on the front seat of his car, not into the carrots. Looking up, he saw a curtain part and gave Louisa a cheerful wave. She waved back and the curtains closed.

'Yeah,' Lynne said, as he slid under the wheel, 'and look what happened to Adam and Eve.'

He pulled her close as he reversed out of the driveway. 'So? Look what happened to us.' He spread his hand over her lower belly. 'This is so incredibly wonderful! Sensational! Stupendous! I didn't know a man could feel like this.'

As he pulled into the front of a motel with a 'Vacancies' sign, she lifted her head from his shoulder, and smiled. 'We've never spent the night in a motel together. I feel positively wicked.'

'Me too. Especially since we don't have any luggage.'

'Do you care what the desk clerk thinks of us?'

He dragged her with him out of the car. 'Not in the least.'

'Do you have any idea of how happy I am?' she asked, several minutes later, leaning her full weight on him as he leaned back on the door of their room, looking down at her with all his love in his eyes.

Clasping her face between his hands, he smiled tenderly and nodded his head.

'Remember after we'd got back together, and I said I didn't think I could be happier?' he asked. 'And then I discovered, when Michael finally accepted me, that I could be? And when I accepted Vincent as my father, discovered how much he needs me – us – I believed nothing could top what I had then. Lynne –' His voice cracked and he cleared his throat, looking sheepish and half-amused at himself. 'If my heart gets any fuller, it's damned well going to blow up from the pressure. If you're anywhere near that happy, then I guess I know how you feel.'

'Yes,' she said, reaching around him to turn off the overhead light, leaving the room lit only by a small lamp near the big bed. 'Oh, yes, that's exactly how happy I am.'

'Good,' he said. 'Now show me.'

And she did.

EPILOGUE

'Cliff, you'd better go wake your dad up and tell him we're leaving.'

'Huh? What? Leaving? Where are we going?' Cliff came instantly awake, if not instantly intelligent.

'To the hospital, silly. Dr Baker said, when the contractions were five minutes apart, to call her and then to come in. I've called her and she'll be there waiting for us.'

He sat up in bed staring at her, stark terror on his face. 'Lynne, now wait a minute. I don't think I can . . . I don't know if I . . . Oh, my God! Now? Right now?'

Lynne nodded and sat on the edge of the bed, rocking back and forth for several long seconds while Cliff held her shoulders and prayed. Hard.

'Go and wake up your dad,' she said when she could breathe evenly again. 'So he knows he has to listen for the kids and make them breakfast and stuff.' Vincent had insisted on spending the last three weeks of Lynne's pregnancy with them for just that reason.

When Cliff came back with a tall, straight and immediately alert Vincent in tow, Lynne wondered just who should drive her to the hospital, but it was Cliff's privilege, even if he wasn't much use at the time.

He'd calmed down considerably by the time she'd been examined and the two of them walked up and down their birthing room, his arm supporting her, his strength holding her when a contraction struck, and could talk more or less coherently to Dr Baker when she asked, smiling, 'Well, Cliff, have you forgiven medical science yet?'

He laughed and held Lynne through another contraction. 'You get us through this, Ellen,' he said, 'and I'll forgive medical science for anything.'

She referred, he knew, to his initial fury and disbelief that the medication he'd been on for his stress-related condition during his marriage to Julia had caused a low sperm count in some men, some times. No one, then, had known of that particular side-effect; even now, it was just becoming a well-known fact to physicians. He was far past the anger, so caught up in the glory of what he and Lynne shared that what might have been no longer mattered. What was, was what counted.

Having stopped the medication long before he met Lynne, his sperm-count had gone right back to normal. Then, during her first pregnancy and his stress over that, he'd required treatment again. Naturally, then, his second test had also come back showing a low count. Medical science hadn't been giving him the wrong answer, merely an incomplete one.

And it had nearly ruined his life.

But no longer! He held Lynne's hands as she squeezed his so tightly that he thought his bones might crush.

Before this day was out, they'd share yet another miracle, he and his beautiful Lynne. Knowing that made all that had gone on in the past worthwhile, because it had brought him to this moment, this pinnacle of joy.

It was mid-morning when he phoned his father and said, 'Dad, get over here right now, and bring the kids. There's someone I want you to meet.'

When Vincent came into the room, a child's hand in each of his, looking tentative and alarmed, he shot a swift glance between a beaming Cliff and a softly smiling Lynne. 'In my day fathers and grandfathers and brothers and sisters didn't get to come into the mother's room and see the baby. Are you sure this is safe?'

Cliff tossed him a yellow gown and said, 'Sure. Put this on,' then, moments later took the small bundle from his wife's arms and passed it to his father.

'Vincent,' he said formally, 'I wish to present your youngest granddaughter, Ann Maria Salazar.'

Vincent looked down at the small, puckered face, the down of dark hair and the wide, vacant blue-gray eyes. 'Hello, Ann Maria,' he said, then drawing a solemn Amanda close, he said, crouching before her. 'See? Just what you wanted. A baby sister.'

Michael crowded in close. 'Gampa?'

'Yes, Mike?'

Michael reached out with a small hand to touch **his grandfather's** face and asked, 'Big boys c'y?'

Cliff scooped Michael up and held him high over his head, laughing as tears ran down his own face. 'Sometimes, son,' he said. 'Sometimes big boys do.'

THE EXCITING NEW NAME IN WOMEN'S FICTION!

PLEASE HELP ME TO HELP YOU!

Dear *Scarlet* Reader,

As Editor of *Scarlet* Books I want to make sure that the books I offer you every month are up to the high standards *Scarlet* readers expect. And to do that I need to know a little more about you and your reading likes and dislikes. So please spare a few minutes to fill in the short questionnaire on the following pages and send it to me.

   Looking forward to hearing from you,

Sally Cooper

Editor-in-Chief, *Scarlet*

QUESTIONNAIRE

Please tick the appropriate boxes to indicate your answers

1 Where did you get this Scarlet title?
Bought in supermarket ☐
Bought at my local bookstore ☐ Bought at chain bookstore ☐
Bought at book exchange or used bookstore ☐
Borrowed from a friend ☐
Other (please indicate) _____

2 Did you enjoy reading it?
A lot ☐   A little ☐   Not at all ☐

3 What did you particularly like about this book?
Believable characters ☐   Easy to read ☐
Good value for money ☐   Enjoyable locations ☐
Interesting story ☐   Modern setting ☐
Other _____

4 What did you particularly dislike about this book?
_____

5 Would you buy another Scarlet book?
Yes ☐   No ☐

6 What other kinds of book do you enjoy reading?
Horror ☐   Puzzle books ☐   Historical fiction ☐
General fiction ☐   Crime/Detective ☐   Cookery ☐
Other (please indicate) _____

7 Which magazines do you enjoy reading?
1. _____
2. _____
3. _____

And now a little about you –
8 How old are you?
Under 25 ☐   25–34 ☐   35–44 ☐
45–54 ☐   55–64 ☐   over 65 ☐

cont.

9 What is your marital status?

Single ☐ Married/living with partner ☐

Widowed ☐ Separated/divorced ☐

10 What is your current occupation?

Employed full-time ☐ Employed part-time ☐

Student ☐ Housewife full-time ☐

Unemployed ☐ Retired ☐

11 Do you have children? If so, how many and how old are they?

_____

_____

12 What is your annual household income?

under $15,000	☐	or £10,000	☐
$15–25,000	☐	or £10–20,000	☐
$25–35,000	☐	or £20–30,000	☐
$35–50,000	☐	or £30–40,000	☐
over $50,000	☐	or £40,000	☐

Miss/Mrs/Ms _____

Address _____

_____

_____

Thank you for completing this questionnaire. Now tear it out – put it in an envelope and send it, before 31 August 1998, to:

Sally Cooper, Editor-in-Chief

USA/Can. address	*UK address/No stamp required*
SCARLET c/o London Bridge	SCARLET
85 River Rock Drive	FREEPOST LON 3335
Suite 202	LONDON W8 4BR
Buffalo	*Please use block capitals for*
NY 14207	*address*
USA	

HIEMB/3/98

Forthcoming *Scarlet* titles:

NO SWEETER CONFLICT Megan Paul
When she's sent to interview her 'cousin' Jacob Trevelyn,
Florence tries to act with journalistic detachment, and at
first succeeds. Until the fact that there's no blood tie
between them – *and* her memories of their shared past –
start getting in the way!

DANCE UNTIL MORNING Jan McDaniel
Claire Woolrich is used to a wealthy lifestyle . . . drop-out
Wheeler Scully isn't at all impressed! They are forced to
spend the night together, but surely Claire doesn't need to
worry about making a lasting impression on this unsuitable
man?

DARK DESIRE Maxine Barry
Dedicated to building up her career, Electra Stapleton has
no time for romance. She is particularly wary of handsome
stranger Haldane Fox. But Haldane is on a mission which
will have an everlasting effect on Electra . . .

LOVERS DON'T LIE Chrissie Loveday
Simon Andrews might be very different from the student
she originally fell in love with, but Jenna finds him even
more irresistible second-time-around. Trouble is, Simon's
now married with a child – isn't he? And with a secret in her
past she *must* hide, Jenna *can't* give in to her desires.

JOIN THE CLUB!

Why not join the *Scarlet* Reader's Club – you can have four exciting new reads delivered to your door every month for only £9.99, plus TWO FREE BOOKS WITH YOUR FIRST MONTH'S ORDER!

Fill in the form below and tick your two free books from those listed:

1. *Never Say Never* by Tina Leonard ☐
2. *The Sins of Sarah* by Anne Styles ☐
3. *Wicked in Silk* by Andrea Young ☐
4. *Wild Lady* by Liz Fielding ☐
5. *Starstruck* by Lianne Conway ☐
6. *This Time Forever* by Vickie Moore ☐
7. *It Takes Two* by Tina Leonard ☐
8. *The Mistress* by Angela Drake ☐
9. *Come Home Forever* by Jan McDaniel ☐
10. *Deception* by Sophie Weston ☐
11. *Fire and Ice* by Maxine Barry ☐
12. *Caribbean Flame* by Maxine Barry ☐

ORDER FORM

SEND NO MONEY NOW. Just complete and send to SCARLET READERS' CLUB, FREEPOST, LON 3335, Salisbury SP5 5YW

Yes, I want to join the **SCARLET READERS' CLUB*** and have the convenience of 4 exciting new novels delivered directly to my door every month! Please send me my first shipment now for the unbelievable price of £9.99, plus my TWO special offer books absolutely free. I understand that I will be invoiced for this shipment and FOUR further *Scarlet* titles at £9.99 (including postage and packing) every month unless I cancel my order in writing. I am over 18.

Signed ....

Name (IN BLOCK CAPITALS) ....

Address (IN BLOCK CAPITALS) ....

....

Town .... **Post Code** ....

As a result of this offer your name and address may be passed on to other carefully selected companies. If you do not wish this, please tick this box☐.

*Please note this offer applies to UK only.